Lifelong romance addi... Zealand. Writing feeds ... happy endings and the ... You can follow her at j... com/jcharroway, Instag... Twitter.com/jcharroway.

Ever since **Lisa Childs** read her first romance novel—a Harlequin story, of course—at age eleven, all she wanted was to be a romance writer. Now, with over forty novels published, Lisa is living her dream. She is an award-winning, bestselling romance author. Lisa loves to hear from readers, who can contact her on Facebook; through her website, lisachilds.com; or her snail-mail address, PO Box 139, Marne, MI 49435.

If you liked
Bad Reputation and *Dating the Billionaire*
why not try

Tempt Me by Caitlin Crews
Pure Attraction by Rebecca Hunter

Also by JC Harroway

The Pleasure Pact

Bad Business

Billionaire Bachelors

Forbidden to Want
Forbidden to Taste
Forbidden to Touch

Also by Lisa Childs

Legal Lovers

Legal Seduction
Legal Attraction
Legal Passion
Legal Desire

Discover more at millsandboon.co.uk

BAD REPUTATION

JC HARROWAY

DATING THE BILLIONAIRE

LISA CHILDS

MILLS & BOON

First Published in Great Britain 2020
by Mills & Boon, an imprint of HarperCollins*Publishers*
1 London Bridge Street, London, SE1 9GF

Bad Reputation © 2020 JC Harroway

Dating the Billionaire © 2020 Lisa Childs

ISBN: 978-0-263-27762-3

MIX
Paper from
responsible sources
FSC **FSC™ C007454**

This book is produced from independently certified FSC™ paper
to ensure responsible forest management.
For more information visit www.harpercollins.co.uk/green.

Printed and bound in Great Britain
by CPI Group (UK) Ltd, Croydon, CR0 4YY

BAD REPUTATION

JC HARROWAY

MILLS & BOON

To love in all its forms.

CHAPTER ONE

Neve

THE RED BIKINI seemed to cover more in the shop but, as statements go, it screams *notice me*. But will it work on my best friend? Simply craving such a risky thing makes me want to abandon him here in the Maldives and catch the first flight back to London.

I slide my finger under the edge of the bikini bottoms and retrieve the shrinking triangle of fabric from between the cheeks of my backside. The elastic pings with a snap. I should never have taken my tall, athletic sister bikini-shopping. This would look way better on her svelte frame.

Panic squeezes my abdomen. Oliver might notice me all right, but for all the wrong reasons—like a catastrophic wardrobe malfunction when I dive into the pool…

'Careful what you wish for,' I mutter as I strike a sideways pose in the mirror, observing from a different angle how the teeny tiny scraps of fabric barely seem to cover my nipples. What the hell happened between my last-minute shopping spree—when despite my winter-white flesh, I'd convinced myself this bikini made me invincible—and now, when even an entire bottle of fake tan and twenty-four hours under the Maldivian sun couldn't stop me feeling almost as exposed as being naked?

My best friend Olly happened, that's what.

Oliver Coterill and his bedroom eyes, damn him.

Of course, those smouldering, come-hither looks aren't intended for me. Not today, not ever. I've witnessed them being flashed at countless women over the nine years we've been friends. But a girl can dream, and my imagination sparks with what-ifs every time he flashes his gorgeous, slightly lop-sided smile.

I sigh and tug the two triangles of the bikini top closer together to cover my cleavage. How would it feel, just once, to be visible to him in a sexual way? To be the recipient of that dazzling, bone-melting attention I've watched hordes of lucky women receive over the years? To step out of the friend zone and have him see me as a flesh-and-blood woman…?

'Pathetic,' I say to my reflection with an accusatory point of my index finger. Unrequited lust sucks.

I slap a smile on my sun-blushed face, stick out my chest to its best advantage and snap a selfie, firing it off to Olly on the message app we use to keep in daily contact.

I'll be out in a second...

He replies straight away.

Chop, chop, Never. I'm stuck with an investment banker wanker friend of my cousin. It's snorkel time.

So impatient. So easily bored. So fucking hot...

Ignoring his use of the nickname he'd christened me with the first day we met in a uni bar—he'd asked me to spell my name and I'd said, 'It's like never without the r'—I sidle up to the window and squint through the mosquito net for a clandestine glimpse of him semi-naked. I catch sight of his damp, dark-blond hair. He's chatting to some guy while draped over a sun lounger wearing only a pair of board shorts, which are wet and cling to his thick, muscular thighs as if they want intimate knowledge of what he's packing underneath.

Lucky board shorts. Of course they want intimate knowledge. The whole world wants intimate knowledge and, if I had my way, I'd be first in the queue.

Familiar longing fizzes in my pelvis.

Why are you doing this? Don't torture yourself. Whatever you do, do not look at his crotch.

Too late.

I press my thighs together and allow my mouth to hang open while my greedy, glutton-for-punishment stare traces the over-achieving bulge between his

legs. It meanders with blissful agony up the ladder
of his abs, touching on the scattered ink decorating his torso, then idles over his buff pecs, which
are sprinkled with manly dark chest hair. His single
nipple-piercing glints in the sun.

I swallow my drool. How will I survive the rest of
this holiday as his plus-one for his cousin's wedding
and ignore my constant state of lust? How will I get
through the toughest friend mission to date without
confessing the depth of my un-platonic feelings…?

The shrill cackle of feminine laughter drags me
from my perv-a-thon. Two women from the wedding party loiter near the edge of the pool, their
leggy, lithe and toned bodies presented for his in-
spection and their eyes flicking in his direction with
nauseating eagerness.

I step back but can't look away. The constant
female attention he attracts is the only downside
of our friendship. That and the fact I want to shag
him, of course…

Unlike me, these two are exactly his type—
exquisite, body-confident women who probably
achieve multiple orgasms during tantric sex… I
force myself to watch the impending train-wreck,
as if in slow motion, seconds before impact.

Thanks to Oliver's workplace stance on 'healthy
body, healthy mind', he's always at the gym he in-
stalled for his employees. But even with a flabby
dad-bod he'd turn heads. It's his arresting eyes—too

blue to look natural. Plus the cheeky, wonky smile and the God-given confidence he wears almost as well as his bespoke suits.

I massage my temple, breathing through the bout of testiness, which shunts my hormones into the danger zone. Why doesn't he put on some bloody clothes? It's only a matter of time before he gets bored of waiting for me to freak out over my shrinking bikini and approaches his admirers. Then I'll have to spend the rest of the holiday being the third wheel. Again.

At least his deluxe bungalow is at the opposite end of the resort from my single room. Despite his cajoling, I insisted on paying for it myself so I won't have to hear the sex noises coming from his bedroom.

Ignoring the women, Olly picks up his phone, reads the screen and frowns. He looks straight at my window from across the pool, as if he's staring right at me. I catch my breath and, even though I'm hidden behind the gauzy curtain, jump back for cover. Don't want to come across as pathetic and needy by being caught mooning at him and his female groupies.

I fire off a second message.

On my way.

My heart thumps my ribs with excitement and dread. How will I survive day two of his barely

clothed company with nowhere to hide in this min-
iscule excuse for a bikini? I retie the bottom ties to
give my nerves time to settle. But I can't go out there
in this state—flustered, turned on, distracted. I dither
in front of the mirror, my gaze flitting longingly to
the contents of my partially unpacked suitcase.

I tap my teeth with a fingernail. Do I have time?
The vicious throb of my nipples against my bikini
top demands that I *make* time.

Oliver's already bored of waiting. He's probably flashing his bedroom eyes at the blondes as
we speak. His reputation for stunning dates is renowned, although the chosen ones never last beyond
a couple of weeks. In all the years I've known him
he's never invited a woman to a family or work-re-
lated function. He says that's my role. We argued
about it once, back in the beginning, when I accused
him of wanting to have his cake and eat it. He'd
stated reasonably that he preferred my company and
didn't want to give his casual hook-ups the wrong
impression. When he was ready to commit to a relationship, he'd introduce a woman to his family.

Prickles dance over my skin, the constant longing
turning into a fire I have no hope of extinguishing if
I'm spending the day with the man who presses all
my sexual buttons. Unknowingly, of course.

Why not take the edge off?

Better to present myself for snorkelling some-
what satiated than in a sexually charged frenzy of

frustration. That way I won't be tempted to take up the challenge issued in a margarita-fuelled pact by my girlfriends, Brooke and Grace, and hurl myself at him lips first.

No. I can't think about the promise I made to them to use this trip to finally confront my feelings for Oliver. Not in my current state.

Instead, I rummage in the bottom of my case for the bag buried under my clothes. I am going to need every single toy I possess to survive this beach holiday with my sex-on-a-stick friend. Why, oh, why couldn't his cousin's wedding have been held in Siberia or Alaska?

I select my favourite vibrator from my single woman's survival kit —the trusty Rabbit— then I toss the bag onto the bed and stamp off to the bathroom. If forced to watch Olly's semi-naked, wet body all day, I need to take care of myself first.

I slam the bathroom door closed, switching the vibrator on and off to test the batteries.

How would it feel to have him notice me, just once? To look at me with those ready-to-fuck eyes he usually bestows on other women? To see me as more than his reliable friend—a woman who would literally drop everything to be at his beck and call?

No. I know what happens to those women. They come, they go. Always temporary. Oliver isn't relationship material, and having him the way I want him could make me temporary too.

It's not worth the risk. I made my decision years ago—better to be his friend than to pass through his life in a brilliant flash of burning metal for a few heady seconds and then fizz out to nothing.

But, oh, how I'd love for once to feel that incandescent heat…

Brooke and Grace were right. I need to stop this unhealthy and long-standing obsession with Oliver. He didn't notice me at nineteen and he certainly never would now at twenty-nine. I've been single for eight months. Time to keep my vow, to open up that dating app and give some other guy a chance.

Right after I come…

Before the mood completely deserts me, I swish back the shower curtain and plonk my butt on the edge of the bath. I fire up the Rabbit once more, slide my bikini bottoms down my thighs and close my eyes, summoning my favourite fantasy.

The first shocking touch forces a gasp from my throat. I drop my head back and imagine Oliver striding across the tiles around the stunning infinity pool outside, making a beeline for my room, his handsome face taut with single-minded determination. I ease the vibrator inside as fool-proof, Oliver-themed images flash behind my scrunched-up eyelids. Imaginary Oliver throws back the curtains at the French windows, calls my name in his husky, nipple-tingling voice and slams open the bathroom door…

I want you, Neve. I've always wanted you…

I bite my lip, adjust the angle of the toy and spread my thighs wider, the fantasy fuelling my exhausted libido. He's here, his eyes on fire and glued to the action between my legs. But dream Oliver is no shrinking violet. He strides into the bathroom, takes my face in his hands and kisses me the way I fantasised the first night we met. Bold. Unapologetic. Frantic. As if he'd die without the connection of our lips…

Chasing the pleasure, I focus on his dreamy eyes, the sinfully thick black lashes and the mischief glinting in his penetrating blue irises. Mischief I love, even if it does put me squarely in the category of friend.

I press the Rabbit's head to my clit with a gasp, recalling how fantastic he smelled last night on the dance floor—clean, spicy top notes, exotic mid notes and uniquely Oliver base notes.

I'd tried to pay attention to his hilarious, implausible tales about his extended family, whom he'd flown here in his company jet—did I mention kind and generous?—but I'd momentarily lapsed into what it would be like to bury my face in the open neck of his shirt and suck on his skin until he growled my name with arousal… The sexy scruff on his chin scraped against my face as he'd pulled me in close for a slow dance. The smell of his shampoo from his slightly long, unruly, dirty-blond hair.

His broad, hard chest grazing my nipples awake as we'd swayed together on the dance floor...

My head falls back, one foot braced on the edge of the bath, as the Rabbit and I find the sublime rhythm I need.

I gasp. Make-believe Oliver grips my wrist, withdraws the vibrator and unbuckles his jeans. His mouth opens to speak. Perhaps a throaty, *'Let me help you with that,'* or a husky, *'Why not have the real thing?'* I can always rely on my Oliver fantasies to get me there.

So close... Just a few more seconds...

A harsh rap sounds on the bathroom door.

'Come the fuck on, Neve,' Oliver calls. 'You're taking for ever in there.'

I yank the Rabbit from between my thighs and slam my legs closed, as if he can see what I'm up to through the closed door. My face burns, my clumsy hands fumbling with the vibrator's off switch as it hums with the force of a million mosquitos. At last I silence the device and shove it into the back of the cupboard under the sink, behind the spare toilet rolls. Breath gusts out of me in a panic. Did he hear me? Does he know what I was up to? Did I say his name aloud?

I jerk my bikini bottoms up and run water to hide the thunderous sound of my erratic heartbeat.

'I'm coming.' I wince at the irony, splashing cold water onto my face to extinguish the scalding heat.

Perhaps I should blast the showerhead between my legs to douse my lady-boner.

Bloody Oliver…

I dry my face with a fluffy hotel towel and force my breathing to slow while I stare down my flushed reflection.

Keep it together. Act like nothing happened. Pretend, same as always.

When I emerge gingerly from the *en suite*, Oliver is collapsed on my bed, his arms spread-eagle and his stare trained on the fan spinning lazily overhead. His board shorts are dry and he swings his feet over the edge of the bed, because he's not very good at keeping still.

My clit throbs in retribution. I want to climb onto him and…

'How can it take you half an hour to clean your teeth?' he says without looking up. 'You'll have no enamel left at this rate.'

I shuffle over to a chair near the window, pretending to hunt for my prescription sunglasses while I boil inside—one, because I'm always simmering when Olly is around, and two, because my primed clit didn't get the memo that fun time is over.

'I should never have given you a key to my room,' I snap, venting frustration. 'Why can't you just be by yourself for five minutes?'

He looks up, props his elbows under him and stares, as if seeing me for the first time—his piercing eyes narrowed a fraction and his big, manly body still for once.

I freeze, unease dancing over my exposed skin. Why did I wish for that focus to be turned on me? Its intensity makes me want to run back to the bathroom and hide in the shower.

'I can be alone,' he says. 'The investment banker started asking me about work and, aside from the Japanese telecommunications deal, I don't want to think about business. I'm on holiday, and I thought we were going snorkelling.' His voice, as deep and magnetic as always, and tinged with a transatlantic twang from his dual nationality, carries that 'lost little boy' edge that keeps me enslaved. I can't help it. I have a terrible case of saviour complex where Oliver is concerned. I always have. I see something in him from which he needs rescuing. Although, clearly *I'm* the one in desperate need…

'Sorry,' I say, sighing. 'I didn't mean it.' I perch my sunglasses on top of my head and turn my back on him to push my feet into my flip-flops. 'I didn't sleep well last night. I'm testy.'

Oliver is quiet, so rare an occurrence I'm terrified to look down in case I still have my Rabbit in my hand or I forgot to re-don my bikini bottoms. I tense, my back aflame with the thought of his eyes on me, exactly the scenario I wanted when I purchased this teeny tiny excuse for a bikini.

I spin in a tentative arc to face him.

He's still laid out on my bed like a sacrificial lamb, still propped up on his elbows like some male pin-up, only now he's looking at me with a puzzled expression. Only Oliver could pull off that face and still look entirely fuckable.

'What?' I demand, in no mood for the usual teasing banter we share.

'Nothing,' he says, his jaw slack. 'It's just…'

His eyes stay on mine, but I look down anyway in case one nipple has made a bid for freedom. But no, I'm good.

'Why are you staring?' Perhaps the sexual frustration is pasted all over my hot face.

'I'm not. I mean…it's nothing. It's just that…you look good in red, that's all.'

That's all? I deflate. I want to cry and laugh in the same breath. I want him to scour every inch of my body with his sexy stare. I want him helpless to look away. Helpless against the transformation into my daydream Oliver, who would have stripped me naked and been rattling the headboard by now.

I snort. Move towards the mirror, where I pretend to tweak my messy hair that's caught up in a topknot, while my body tingles with awareness that I'm scantily clad, alone in a room with the object of my every adult desire.

'Thanks,' I say in my best unruffled tone, forcing my muscles to relax. My head spins and I talk my overactive imagination back from the ledge. Olly—

despite his infamous reputation with women—is a gentleman. He's always complimenting me when I dress up, or cheering me on when I crack a tricky case at work. Just as I listen to his work woes about his tech company, even though I don't understand a word. But that's what *friends* do. Support one another. He doesn't mean anything by his comment. Certainly not what I'd like him to mean.

'Are you wearing sunscreen?' I ask to cover my full-body meltdown because, where I turn lobster-pink before returning to pasty, Oliver tans to a deep bronze almost overnight. So not fair.

'Yes, Mum.' He grins.

I toss my tube of factor fifty at him, sighing when he sits up and catches it in one hand with lightning reflexes. See? Good at everything…

'Ha ha,' I quip. 'You can do my back.'

No! Fuck…why did I ask him to do that? His hands on me…touching…with my aroused state heightened and my orgasm interrupted. Not a good idea.

'I will.' He drops the tube onto the bed and leans back on his hands, arms straight. 'First tell me why you're testy. You're on holiday too. You're supposed to be relaxing.'

How can I relax when I'm on high alert for any sign he might've noticed me in a sexual way, or when I'm just waiting for him to hook up with one of the wedding guests right in front of me? It's happened before. He wasn't a dick about it, giving said woman enough breadcrumbs to keep her keen while also attending to me, the friend he brought along as his plus one. But the next morning the smug look on his face told me she'd miraculously found her way to his room once we'd said goodnight.

'I am relaxed,' I say, grimacing past my clenched jaw.

'You don't seem relaxed.' Amusement tinges his tone. 'You've put lip gloss on three times. Without wearing your glasses.'

Sometimes it sucks that friends know you so well... I cast him a glare, something so rare it seems to shock both of us.

'I'm fine,' I bite out, desperately trying to blank out the pact I made with Brooke and Grace—to orchestrate a holiday fling with Oliver. I should just embrace a bloody dating app. At least then I could vet prospective boyfriends from the comfort of my pyjamas. Instead I'm standing here dithering over the merits of actually confessing my feelings of lust to Oliver versus spending the rest of my life always wondering.

At my lame assurance, Oliver flops back down onto the bed in disgust. I ignore him. Continue with my rant, because it's *his* fault I'm in this state.

'I just...needed a few minutes to myself,' I say, huffing. 'I told you I'd meet you by the pool. Plus my bikini seems to have shrunk since I tried it on in the shop, and I wanted to make sure I didn't have any tan lines showing.' I pace to my suitcase and find my sarong, then knot it around my waist. Makeshift body armour.

'It's all right for you guys,' I continue. 'You can just throw on a pair of shorts and parade around in all your manly, hairy glory, attracting stares of appreciation from the opposite sex…'

He's fidgeting, another of his annoying habits I find attractive. Damn, everything he does appeals to my libido, but now I've started it's as if my sexual frustration has discovered an oral pressure valve.

'But us women, we have to wax shit and plump stuff and squeeze our bodies into ridiculous, minute fashion statements…' I grab my mascara and slick a layer over my stubby upper lashes. I locate my glasses, push them on and check my mascara. I'm happy with me. Mostly. I'm an attractive, smart, bordering on a proud nerd with my own forensic-accounting business.

But I'm not done venting.

'And you know how challenging it is running your own company,' I say, wiping a smudge of black from my cheek. 'I've had a very stressful week, with three new clients and meeting deadlines in order to have this week off. So forgive me if I can't simply switch on the party girl just to keep *you* entertained.'

I can sense without turning around for confirmation that he's stopped listening. But, instead of riling me further, his inattention deflates me. I'm being unfair. I'm not really angry with him. I'm frustrated with myself, at my continued inertia where he's concerned, because maybe Brooke and Grace are right. Maybe I should have told him I fancied him the night we met. Maybe it's time to tell him how I've felt about him all these years… At least then we could laugh about it, clear the air and move on.

My blood runs cold at the very idea. No. A swim in the ocean is what I need. Douse my hormones and reboot my mind-set to fun, holiday Neve.

'Neve…? What's this?' he asks, with the rustle of a plastic bag.

'Hmm?' I mumble as I tackle my lower lashes with the mascara wand, a feat that requires a bizarre facial contortion while my glasses are perched on the end of my nose.

'I said, what's this?' His voice has dropped several octaves to that smoky quality of all my filthiest fantasies.

But there's no time to enjoy the sound.

I freeze.

The mascara wand hovers near my eyeball, ready to blind me with one false move.

No, no, no… Please, no.

I turn, horror a tight ball cramping my stomach.

Dangling from Oliver's long, elegant and tanned index finger is my bag of sex toys.

CHAPTER TWO

Oliver

THE PLASTIC HANDLE digs into my fingertip, so monumentally weighted are the surprising contents. I swallow past my dry throat, my body heat rising as if I've sat too long in the sun. The minute I peeked inside the bag, Neve became a living, breathing sexual being in my mind. I've spent nine years avoiding thoughts of her that way. Thinking about sex and my best friend in the same head space...

Nope.

I'm not a masochist and that would have rendered our entire long relationship hellish. It's bad enough that she's amazing—kind, smart, funny. Plus, she just gets me. Hence, best friend.

The knock of my excited heart against my ribs mocks the boundaries I've used to keep our friendship intact. It's too late to un-see the sex toys. Too late to switch off the torrent of erotic images featuring my astounding Neve and her gorgeous body.

I grit my teeth and keep my eyes away from the tiny red bikini I want to rip off so I can complete the Neve jigsaw. The triangles of fabric concealing her best bits remind me I'm not supposed to wonder what she looks like naked. But my imagination is intent on torturing me.

I focus on her pretty, familiar face as the silence pulses around the room. She's panting, flushed, realisation dawning. I stare into her eyes, because that bikini fried my brain the minute she stepped from the bathroom and I can't think of a single nonsexual thing to say to my friend. At least this red offering is better—and by that I mean worse—than yesterday's white one, which was hard enough to ignore. Or maybe she's actually growing sexier day by day...

Of course, a gentleman would have ignored the bag on her bed. Even a degenerate would have discreetly closed it on discovering its contents. But I've been labelled worse—womaniser, lothario, playboy—my reputation is renowned. Just like my father's.

More seconds, more silence.

Part of me wants her to deny that this bag of dildos and vibrators belongs to her, to say that she found them in the wardrobe, anything that might stop me imagining her using them. The very idea sets me on fire, balls first.

At last, she lifts her cute, slightly upturned nose

in defiance. 'It's a bag.' She crosses her arms under her breasts, pushing them up and accentuating her cleavage, all seen with my highly evolved peripheral vision. Because I've perfected looking indirectly at Neve's forbidden zones.

I release a curse in my head for the thousandth time today and it's only ten in the morning. I've seen her in a bikini before. What's changed? Why am I struggling with the line, a heavily policed line I put in place nine years ago when I realised she was different and some smart corner of my primitive, immature brain decided to keep her as a friend? My first instinct was to shag her of course—she was striking, beautiful in that girl-next-door way, nerdy just like me and with a sense of humour dry and dark enough to make me forget all my troubles. Upon meeting her, my day went from shitty to 'it's going to be okay'. No mean feat, considering I'd just been through my one and only heartbreak and learned some valuable life and love lessons from my asshole father.

But despite fancying her I instantly knew she was too good for me—a messed up, commitment-phobic charmer with a bad reputation and an embarrassing family. I'd selfishly wanted her in my life, the act of keeping my hands off my proudest moment.

Of course, I'd tarnished my mature conduct by sleeping with Neve's then-roommate that night, but I *am* the son of a rock-and-roll has-been.

'Did you look inside?' she says at last, her cheeks darkening while she waits for my answer.

'I might have looked inside,' I say, fighting the urge to smile, because this is serious. How will I spend the rest of the week, with her in those barely-there bikinis, knowing the intriguing and highly informative contents of this bag? Knowing the girl I made asexual in my head, to keep me sane, is all grown up and likes to play?

Damn, could she be any hotter?

I shift my hips, trying to get comfortable while my shorts garrotte my dick.

'Okay, I lied,' I say, giving free rein to my smile. 'I definitely looked inside.' I don't know what I'm doing, but I know the lid to Pandora's box has flown off with this discovery.

The idea of my beautiful, funny, sweet Neve using sex toys does strange and wonderful things to me. Dangerous things, because now I just want to get my hands, mouth and dick on her.

Will I ever be able to contain my desire for her again?

This is the first time I've seen her this naked while she's been single. Since she dumped her latest serious, hoity-fucking-toity boyfriend who wasn't good enough for her. What was his name... Liam? Yes, that's it. I christened him Limp Liam.

Not that I'm good enough for her either. The opposite, in fact. Otherwise I wouldn't be snooping in her bag of dildos more turned on than I've ever been in my life. For a woman who's always been there for me, always believed in me, even when I didn't value myself.

Finally snapping into action, Neve stamps closer. 'Don't mess around—you have no personal boundaries.' She snatches the bag from my hand.

I grab the bottom of the bag in an immature game of tug-of-war, my fist curling around a phallic object inside.

'You've always known I'm an arsehole—it's genetics,' I say, waggling my eyebrows. 'Tell me, do you always travel with such an extensive toy collection?' I don't want to tease her, but it comes out dripping with playful challenge. Because that's the way I've always skirted my attraction to her. But something inside me, the part seeing Neve in a whole new and sexy light, doesn't want to play games. I want to know more about her sexual side.

And I always get what I want.

My blood thrills, hot and laced with adrenaline. She's so close I can see the delicious flush of her neck and the tiny teardrop-shaped imperfection of her right pupil with which she was born with and that makes her uniquely Neve.

'I'm not ashamed of my needs,' she says, lifting her chin. It's an adorable display of grit that's at odds with her petite stature and freckled nose... and the fact that I know her so well I'm certain

JC HARROWAY   29

she'll forgive me for this indiscretion. Damn, she's
so sweet. I fight a smile at the fact she's wearing
two pairs of glasses—her regular pair and her sunglasses perched on her head.

'Quite bloody right.' But now I'm incandescent
with curiosity. Does she use them all? Every day?
In the shower?

Bile hits the back of my throat—did she use
them with Liam? Or with the dick-wad boyfriend
before Liam—Tristan? Or, as I liked to call him,
Tris Tosser? The one who disliked her girlfriends,
Brooke and Grace, and suggested she try a carb-free
diet… He'd been heading for a rendezvous with my
fist, right before Neve dumped him.

Then it hits me, my lusty sluggish brain fitting
the pieces together. The noise coming from the bathroom when I came in. It wasn't an electric tooth-
brush.

My cock surges against the fabric of my shorts.
If she happened to look down she'd see how inap-
propriately perverted I am. Lusting after my only
true friend. The only person who knows the real
me and all my fucked-up family bullshit. The only
person to unconditionally, unselfishly care about
me—not for my famous father or because I can get
free tickets for his reunion tour.

My precious Neve.

But I can't resist. I have to know.

'Were you just using one of these? When I

knocked on the door?' I tilt my head towards the bathroom, my eyes burning with the effort of steering clear of her delicious body.

She flushes a deeper shade of puce. 'I might have been—your timing sucks, by the way.' She snatches the bag free of my grasp and tosses it into her open suitcase. 'I've been single for way too long.' She braces one hand on the curve of her hip. 'In fact, I've finally downloaded that dating app Brooke recommends. After eight months, it's time to get back out there.'

She over-talks when she's nervous. But this little nugget of information is like a slap in the head. Neve's past boyfriends have all graduated from the school of Serious Boring Fuckers—or the SBF Club, as I like to call it—but at least she met them in person, got to know them, dated them for a while before making it official. Not that any of them had particularly taken to me, of course, even though I was no threat—I've never laid one finger on her in a sexual way. A few of her exes even tried to break up our friendship or insinuate themselves into it by throwing a sister or cousin at me in the hopes the four of us could double date.

'What…?' I drop my voice from the squeaky pleading that tries to escape. 'Dating apps aren't the way to go. I know. I've used them.' As far as I'm aware, she's not into one-night stands. She'll be eaten alive in the shark tank of the dating app scene. She's way too kind and sweet.

'Why not?' She holds eye contact, waiting for my explanation, but my brain is still mush from the knowledge that I interrupted my sexy goddess friend taking care of business with a battery-operated phallus.

My flesh-and-blood phallus throbs.

'Because…' Comprehension kicks in. She's back on the market. Actively seeking the next wanker who'll probably wind up hurting or disappointing her. I was certain the last one would have the balls to pop the question, but I'd known almost instantly he wasn't man enough for Neve…

But the next one might be. And then what? A husband won't have the tolerance that a boyfriend might for me in her life. We're close and I don't want that to change. But, as this current little pantomime proves, I'm selfish, inappropriate and lack boundaries. She'd choose, and I'd lose. Lose my Neve.

I swallow hard, the razor blades slashing through the lust gripping my throat.

'Do you have a better suggestion?' She offers a nervous laugh and looks down at her pretty painted toes in that way that tells me she's feeling vulnerable. 'Any dishy single friends who want to date a woman who works ten hours a day running her own business and prefers a night in with her cat watching baking shows to an evening out on the town?'

My thoughts turn murderous at the idea of any of my single friends with Neve. I want to rush to the bathroom, scoop up as many towels as I can find and cover all her gorgeousness from view in case any other single wedding guest gets any ideas.

'Don't put yourself down,' I say. 'Any guy would be lucky to have you—you're intimidatingly intelligent and have a wicked sense of humour.' The Neve I first met used to compare herself unfavourably to her younger sister, who's a professional swimmer, although I've never understood why; Amber bores me to tears.

Neve sighs, shoving a beach towel into her bag. 'Look, I know it's not the best way to meet someone, but beggars can't be choosers, and I'm heading towards my thirties—'

'In a year,' I scoff.

She shrugs and flashes her playful smile at me, the one that kicks me in the gut every time. 'Yes, but my toy habit is pretty expensive—time to find a real live substitute with enough staying power that I don't need a truckload of double As.'

Of course my accountant friend would balk at the cost of her sex-toy addiction. She has a spreadsheet for every occasion, including her grocery list. 'Wait, are you saying Limp Liam…?'

'Don't call him that.' Her eyes flash with censure.

I ignore her outrage. 'Are you saying he was lacking in the bedroom?' I bite down on my glee that the patronising, toffee-nosed Liam with his old Etonian judge father was somehow flawed, even while my chest clenches with sympathy for my wonderful Neve, who deserves all the good things, including well-hung, attentive boyfriends with extreme stamina.

I think I'm going to puke.

She shrugs. 'Not so much lacking… I guess it was largely down to me. Why are we talking about this? Let's go snorkelling.' Neve develops a sudden fascination with her outfit: a shift of a bikini strap here and retightening of her sarong knot there.

What the hell…?

'Nuh-uh, no way.' I shake my head and lean back on my hands to show her I mean business. At least these latest revelations—that she's joined a dating app and that her relationship with Limp Liam wasn't all roses and screaming orgasms—douses the heat in my shorts, shrinking my hard-on quicker than a cattle prod to the arse.

'What was down to you?' I can't let this go, torn between arousal and jealousy of the exes who saw a side of her I can only dream of.

She looks down, thinks better of it and slams her eyes back to mine. She's ballsy and brave even if we've never skated this close to deeply personal— read sexual—details before. At least, not *her* sexual details. Mine tend to make it into the celebrity gossip headlines thanks to my reckless teens and the example set by my ageing-rocker father. Stories which feature me apparently out-debauching him with beautiful women seem to sell twice as many newspapers and magazines.

'I'm saying that amazing sex, mutual, perfectly timed orgasms—angels singing, stars bursting and unicorns prancing—don't happen for everyone.' She sighs. 'Not that you'd know anything about that with the amount of practice you've had.' Her eyes roll with derision.

My shoulders hunch with tension. I knew it. Those *are* the sex toys she used with Limp Liam… I'm going to have to bleach my brain once this conversation ends.

'Hey,' I say, holding up my hands in supplication. 'I have no beef with however your ex got the job done.' I just don't want those images in my head. Images of Neve pleasuring herself, on the other hand, I can surely keep for later personal use.

'In fact,' I add, 'I'm quite impressed he was man enough to buy you sex toys.' I nod in the direction of the bag, which might as well be filled with snakes. Green snakes. Their venom fuelling my envy. 'He didn't seem the type.'

Neve huffs. Collapses into a chair and narrows her eyes behind her glasses. 'I bought them myself. And I didn't use them with him.' She nibbles her lip and examines a fingernail. 'He was a bit insecure in that department, to be honest.' She flushes, as if she can't quite believe she's telling me all of this.

I'm a little gobsmacked myself, truth be told, my body veering wildly between excitement and sick, twisted fascination.

'So what do you mean it was down to you?' Creepy-crawly legs skitter up my spine. Part of me dreads her answer in case it fundamentally changes something between us, although haven't things already changed? Like me allowing myself to look at her in a way I've spent years shying away from? My inexplicable jealousy over the dating app? The idea that she might have been short-changed by the men in her past...?

'Well...you know. I...' She covers her mouth with her hand, as if holding in some terrible secret, and then blurts it out. 'I never had an orgasm with him.'

'What the hell?' I clench my jaw when I realise I've actually said this aloud. But I'm livid enough to crack my own teeth. I hold up my hand. 'I'm not judging you. It's his fault, not yours. If he didn't know his way around a woman's body, and he was insecure about using toys, that's on him.'

I fume inside; I knew he was a dick-wad.

Instead of nodding in agreement or telling me to shut up, like she usually would, she turns pale, her vulnerable stare cutting me to ribbons. 'Thanks for being so loyal, but it can't be him, because it's happened before.'

I curl my fingers into fists to stop myself pulling her into a hug and holding her until that look fades from her eyes. We've hugged a thousand times—brief, platonic hugs, preferably where her breasts don't come into contact with my chest and my boner doesn't show—but this time I wouldn't stop. I'd kiss her. Taste those soft lips she habitually nibbles when she's pretending she's not upset. Kiss that ticklish spot on her neck. Stare into her mismatched eyes until we both feel better.

'So you've had a couple of dud boyfriends.' I shrug, torn between utter horror for my friend and a gleeful delight that the intimidating, serious number-nerd arseholes she's dated in the past were lacking in the most crucial department. The urge to kiss her builds, a furnace in my chest. There's no way I'm introducing her to any of my single friends now.

She's special. She needs a special guy, one who'll worship her the way she deserves, treat her right and rock her world.

No. Don't think about your friend orgasming. That's shit you'll never erase from your brain...

Then again, none of those exes of Neve's dragged her into the gutter by splashing her picture all over the tabloids in some salacious story like *Latest Squeeze of Layabout Son of Rock Royalty!* or *On Again, Off Again Girlfriend of Serial Philanderer Oliver Coterill!* The consequence of our friendship.

Guilt makes my skin crawl.

'It happened with *all* of them, Oliver. All.' She stares, her green eyes huge and mesmerising. 'I've never once had an orgasm with another person.' She stands now, as if she can't contain the tension her confession has produced and needs to move. I, on the other hand, am shocked to stillness, gaping like a stunned mullet.

She pulls on a T-shirt as if she wants to hide. My horny and flabbergasted brain recalls how we're supposed to be going snorkelling. She's supposed to be taking clothes off, not putting them on.

My entire body is aflame now, my eager dick twitching in my shorts. Neurones fire. One single coherent thought emerges: I could give her what others failed to do, now I'm a man. I'm not a teen-ager with no control over his poor decisions or his dick, like I was the day we met.

What the hell? No, no, no, no...

'So it must be me,' she says with a sad little laugh. 'Perhaps there's something wrong with me...' She looks away, her lip taking a thrashing from her teeth as she fiddles self-consciously with the hem of the T-shirt.

'There's nothing fucking wrong with you—I can assure you.' Her back is to me so I indulge in a quick perv of her arse, a cute heart-shape that does things to my pulse. Even though it's covered by a sarong, I can picture the way the bikini bottoms disappear between her cheeks, exposing her glorious globes in an adorable, lopsided way. I want to lick and suck…

'How do you know?' she hurls over her shoulder.

My ire rises, drowning out testosterone and propelling me from my slouch on the bed so we're standing face to face. 'Tell me, do they work?' I point at the open suitcase and the bag of toys, praying my hands aren't shaking with the adrenaline pouring through my blood. I want to touch her so bad. Just once.

She splutters, her mouth opening and closing, making me notice her perfect little kissable Cupid's bow. 'What?'

'Do they work? Can you make yourself come with your bag of tricks?'

Stop talking. Walk away.

'Yes, but—'

'Well, then,' I say, my hands on my hips. 'There's nothing wrong with you.' My fists clench, my heart jackhammers in my throat and lust boils in my belly at the very idea of Neve making herself come with a dildo.

For the first time in the nine years I've known her, I free myself to look at her the way I want, my stare travelling her body.

From her green eyes, gawping at me as if I've lost the plot, to her lush lips, parted so her breath can gust in outrage. Down the slope of her neck to her freckled shoulder, which has escaped from the wide opening of her T-shirt. The swell of her generous breasts straining against the fabric, with her laboured breathing and curvaceous hips screaming 'woman', right down to her pretty toes painted with purple nail polish.

The release, the euphoria, the freedom fills me in a rush so deep-seated I want to groan aloud and fall to my knees.

I feel the vacuum created by her indrawn breath.

Force myself to look up.

Our eyes meet.

This is hallowed ground. Forbidden territory. A no-going-back moment. I watch her lips, which seem to tremble, waiting to hear her thoughts.

But now I know her secret, know the rough deal she's had with the SBF Club, there's no way I'm allowing her to meet some jerk from some app who wants nothing more than to get his rocks off.

I stare at her lips. If she asked me to kiss her now, I would.

But, oh, the price of that kiss. Just one foot over that line could ruin everything...

But didn't I already ruin her long ago—her reputation, at least—by simple association? Hasn't she already paid the price for being my friend? Not that she ever complains, so steadfast is her loyalty—which I don't deserve.

'This conversation is getting weird,' she says in a breathy voice, ignoring the fact I've just ogled her, with lust, from head to toe. Her gaze flicks to the door, to escape, but it's back before I can draw breath.

'I think we bypassed weird a long time ago,' I manage to say past my constricted throat. 'I'd say we're well and truly in outlandish territory. I'm not happy, Neve.'

Her eyes widen, her plump lips pressed together in a line. 'Why not? It's my situation. I don't see how it's your problem.'

Her point is valid on every level except for one rather crucial and burning logic.

I take a calming breath, fully decided on my course of action. Exhale. Stare deep into that unique pupil so she senses the import of this moment.

'What if I want it to be my problem?' I say.

CHAPTER THREE

Neve

COULD HE MEAN what my addled brain thinks he means?

As far as my libido is concerned, there's only one interpretation…

But no… Of course not. The excited fluttering in my belly peters out. I'm nothing like his usual women—glamorous, immaculate, sexual beings only looking for a brief, casual fling. There's no way I want to become one of those temporary women. Never once in all these years I've known him has he had a relationship that lasts longer than a week. Emboldened by alcohol after a few too many drinks, I once asked him about his relationship avoidance, and he said that he only had to look at his father— who's been married six times—to know that he hadn't inherited the commitment gene.

'What? Do you want to have a crack at it?' I

snort, trying to make light of a situation that makes me feel like I've waded into the sea up to my neck.

'I could. Why not?' he says, regarding me intently, as if with new-found fascination, until I burn with exquisite temptation.

I finally look away from his handsome, deadly serious face. 'Very funny, Olly.' *Oh...yes, please.* 'No, thanks—I'll stick to the dating app.'

He rolls his shoulders back, a move that pushes his buff chest closer to my peaked nipples. 'Why? So you can have a string of depressing dates with a string of selfish guys who can't keep a girlfriend— because otherwise they wouldn't be on the dating app in the first place? No way am I watching you put yourself through that, not after what you've just told me.'

'Then close your eyes,' I snap. He's crossing the line here, and part of me is enthralled and part of me equally appalled.

He carries on as if I didn't speak. 'You deserve so much better than that after your experiences with your exes, who I assumed were at least satisfying *your* needs, despite acting like superior wankers towards me. All of your needs.'

My eyes burn with incredulity just looking at him; he's seriously not joking…

'Most men our age use dating apps for hook-ups,' he ploughs on. 'Do you think those types are going to be any more attentive to your needs than Limp Liam or Tris Tosser?'

I fist my hands on my hips, ignoring his nicknames for guys who'd disliked him in return, their animosity a source of many an argument during our respective relationships.

'You've had your fair share of hook-ups,' I say, 'So I bow to your superior knowledge. But it's not your place to determine what I deserve.' I aim my index finger at the centre of his sternum. 'And don't you dare feel sorry for me.' If I'd wanted to feel second rate again, I'd simply have watched him crack on with the blondes outside. There's always a queue for Oliver's attention.

He leans closer, eyes sparking with gravity, until my finger brushes his chest. He tenses his pectoral muscles, the tip of my finger almost swallowed in the deep valley formed.

I drop my hand, retreating from the physical stand-off.

'You're my best friend,' he says, his seductive voice almost unrecognisably un-friend-like. 'I care about you being hurt or disappointed again.'

His words wash over me, wonderful and irritating at the same time. Because I want to be more than his friend. A part of me always has. 'You're hardly qualified to speak about relationships—you've never had one in your life.' Something that, for me, helped maintain the boundaries of our friendship. I might not have been the chosen one in his bed, but for sheer staying power in his life I had all those other women beat.

He grits his teeth. 'I may not want a relationship, but I'm damned well good at fucking, which is all that's on offer here. I could make you come until you screamed your throat raw. I promise you that.' He steps closer, so close his tall frame and broad chest eclipse my vision, so he's all I see.

I sway on my feet, weak with lust just from the ecstasy of his words. But I'm used to ignoring my libido where Oliver is concerned. Used to lecturing myself on protecting a good thing—our friendship—from something as underwhelming as sex, which has been my experience.

Although, I know with him it would be far from underwhelming. In fact the English dictionary boffins would need to come up with a new adjective—perhaps ultra-whelming. Still, can't tell that to Mr Cocky.

'Oh, I believe you.' I say. 'I've seen and heard enough of your conquests over the years to know that's no idle threat.' I close my eyes and drop my head back in mock ecstasy. *'Fuck me harder, Olly. OMG, Olly. Olly, I'm coming!'* I mimic the sex cries of Oliver's past lovers, who hadn't been able to contain their delight during that brief and hellish-for-me month when he'd lived with me in our early twenties.

When I open my eyes there's amusement in his intense stare, his lips twitching with barely concealed mirth. I want to kiss the smirk right off the self-satisfied prick's face.

He leans in, his manly scent washing over me until I'm weak from the head rush.

'Jealous…?' he says, his voice low and enticing enough to vibrate the air around my nipples through two layers of clothing. But no amount of armour can protect me from the effect he has on my needy body. Because I've always been jealous, part of me desperate to be on the receiving end of some Oliver loving just one time…

And isn't this that chance? A once-in-a-lifetime offer?

I huff, brace my hands on my hips and stick out my chest. 'I am perfectly capable of taking care of myself, as you can see.' I wave my hand towards my bag of delights. 'I don't need you or anyone else.'

But how would it feel to cast off the exhausting battle of denial just for a few minutes? To throw myself into his bulging arms and say, *Yes, I am jealous, show me what I've been missing!* To surrender to every desire I've kept at bay all these years and allow my rampant libido loose on Oliver Coterill?

Would I survive? Would he?

The day I met him in a student pub, he was so charming, but with a sadness in his eyes that seemed to fuel his behaviour and a cynicism too profound for someone of our age. We'd clicked immediately. My attraction was instant, and for a few heady hours—laughing over stupid jokes and being competitive over game after game of pool—the insecure younger woman I was back then had hoped that maybe, just once, I might score the sexy, funny, charming and best-looking guy in the bar.

Then, green with longing and furious with myself for daring to dream I'd be his type, I watched him slope off with my room-mate of the time. Back in our tiny student flat with paper-thin walls, the sounds of Oliver's sexual prowess kept me awake most of the night. Fortunately for my ears and my sanity, their relationship ended after a couple of days—she didn't get his dry sense of humour and she hated pool. When he spent more time talking to me than he did fucking her, she turned on both of us. I tried not to take sides, but as soon as she realised that nothing would put her back in Oliver's bed she called me his pathetic puppy dog and moved out, leaving us to our budding friendship and me to cover all of the rent.

'I know you don't need me, or anyone else,' he says, his beautiful eyes temptation enough. 'But I'm not talking about disappointing dates or relationships or second-rate, battery-operated orgasms.'

Simply hearing him say the word 'orgasms' aloud in his sexy baritone sends shockwaves of delirium down my thighs, almost triggering a mini-climax.

'I'm talking about sex,' he says. 'Full-blown multiple orgasms that will make your extensive, and I might add impressive, toy collection redundant.'

I can barely stand, my lower limbs like rubber, even though I know he's teasing. But he's sown seeds of 'if only' in my brain, and it's like a greenhouse in there, shoots sprouting all over the place, each possibility more graphic than the last until I'm a turned-on mess. I want to beg him—*please stop for the sake of my hearing...*

But he's still talking, his sinful mouth crafting wonderful, dangerous words. 'You should at least experience that once, so when you do date the next serious, condescending arsehole you'll have expectations beyond discovering his career aspirations, whether he's allergic to your cat and if he's prepared to watch those baking shows you love.'

A gasp slips out through my slack mouth at his expression. 'You're *actually* serious?' It's finally computing in my head that this isn't some elaborate, bored Oliver practical joke at my expense, although he's not usually cruel.

I grow lightheaded with need, my imagination running at warp speed. Oliver and me. Sex. Orgasms.

'Deadly,' he says, no hint of amusement now. 'Why not? Apart from today's shocking revelation, we know everything there is to know about each other.'

I have to bite the inside of my cheek to stop myself wincing. Oh, Oliver, if only you knew how long I've lusted… How many fantasies, how many orgasms, you've already aided unbeknown…

'I'd never hurt you,' he continues. 'And, as you said, I'm an expert at casual and I deliver. Blokes on dating apps lie—they'll claim to be the best lover in the world and send you some Photoshopped picture of their enormous dick…which begs the question why they can't find dates in the first place.'

The room starts to spin, so oxygen-deprived is my brain.

'So how will that go?' I lash out, because he's made me hornier than ever before with the way he's looking at me and with all his talk of orgasms. But I'm not a toy. He can't take me out of the friend box, play with me and then put me back. Red rage boils behind my eyes. 'Would I be some sort of altruistic pity-fuck?'

My question falls into the tense silence.

I've only seen Oliver truly angry once—with some pap who stuck a camera in my face outside a swanky restaurant he'd taken me to for my birthday a few years ago. It's not a thing I ever wish to revisit, especially if said anger is directed my way, but there's no escaping his furious stare and the strain radiating from his rigid body.

I hold my breath, my heart leaping through my T-shirt like that of a cartoon character.

'Don't.' His single-word reprimand is little more than a throaty whisper with the effect of a blow, given the sincerity in his eyes and the harsh set of his jaw. 'Don't you dare demean my respect for you. You're more precious to me than the sum of everyone else in my life.'

I shudder, confused by his words, but ready to swoon at his feet. Like this, all sexy, commanding and self-assured, he's ten times as hot as when he's just laughing, friend Olly.

We're so close, I feel his heat. When my head starts to swim because I've forgotten to breathe, I inhale his air.

'I want you. And I'm a selfish bastard. An orgasm for you means an orgasm for me.' He clicks his tongue, a hint of that roguish smile of his. 'Come on, Neve. You're a feminist—you know the way equality works.'

He wants me the way I want him? I open my mouth to speak, to tell him to stop teasing because it's not funny, to argue that there are willing blondes more his type out by the pool, but he silences me, a finger resting on my lips with infinitesimal pressure.

I try not to pant my excitement onto that solitary fingertip, because then he'll know all the longing and conflict bubbling inside me.

'If I have to watch you parade around in these sexy bikinis for the rest of the week, fighting my hard-on for you, we might as well both get our money's worth, don't you agree?' He lets the last question hang for a beat or two, his mouth kicking up once more, although his eyes stay banked with heat. 'You know how much you enjoy being frugal.'

Two compliments in a row from Oliver scrambles my disbelieving brain, especially when one of them contains the words *sexy* and *hard-on*. He thinks I'm sexy. Has a hard-on for *me*.

Go red bikini!

But, no, I can't. There may as well be a neon line painted on the timber flooring between his toes and mine. Even the tip of a toe over that boundary changes everything. If only we could somehow forget that line for a while.

His finger slides down my chin and falls away. I groan in my head because his touch, flirtatious bordering on seductive, may as well have delved into my soul to massage my wildly beating heart. I want him to touch every part of me in that way until I'm so full of sensation, there's no room for reason, doubt or fear.

And it seems I can have what I want.

'But…' Why am I stalling? This is what I secretly craved when I agreed to Brooke's silly pact, back in London. That he'd suddenly wake up and notice me. Why am I not laving my tongue over his pierced nipple, over every inch of him as if he's a giant lollipop, and then ripping off those shorts with my teeth?

'It's a stupid idea,' I say, 'because it will change things between us.'

I'm not naive. Oliver is Oliver. He's not going to miraculously morph into boyfriend material overnight. He doesn't do relationships, just sexfests. We'll sleep together, and it will be great, but then what? Will we be friends with benefits every time we're both single and feeling horny? Will our friendship end as soon as the shagging ends, Oliver reverting back to type, growing bored and moving on? The roll of butterflies reminds me of his value in my life. And to risk it all... For sex. Probably one-sided sex, like all my other experiences. No—it's not worth the price.

But, couldn't I have a little taste of what I've always craved? Just one time?

'It'll only change things between us if we let it,' he says with a shrug. 'It's just fucking. You'll tell me what feels good,' he says, his stare tracing my mouth. 'And we'll get you over this hurdle, no big deal.' He's still the voice of reason, and if I didn't know better I'd think he'd waited all these years just for this chance. And he makes it sound so easy. So neat and compartmentalised.

'Don't you want to know what your body is capable of?' His voice brims full of delicious promise. 'I want to be the one to show you.'

At my continued hesitation he holds up his hands, palms out, and moves back a fraction. 'I don't want to pressure you. It's your decision. And if I'm being inappropriate here I'll apologise and we'll never mention this conversation again.'

Panic flares in me. I grip his forearm, stalling. 'Hold on a second. I'm thinking.' Could I keep my distance emotionally and just enjoy the sex? Take the orgasm on offer, learn from the master and keep feelings and expectations out of it? Would I be any worse off? And at least I'd know one way or another if there's truly something wrong with me. If I can't come with Oliver, no other man stands a chance. And he's right. I shouldn't dive back into dating with such depressingly low expectations.

As long as he keeps his word that it won't change our friendship, this is my best shot at a safe space of sexual exploration…

He stands stock-still, his stare glued to mine while my pulse flies.

I narrow my eyes to what he calls my 'mum look'. 'Let's say for argument's sake we're the first couple in the history of the world to make friends with benefits work… We'd need to have a defined set of ground rules.'

His lips twitch. 'Of course. A person with an analytical, spreadsheet-wielding mind like yours could rattle those off in seconds.' He crosses his arms and lifts his chin, playfulness deepening the creases around his eyes. 'Hit me with it.'

My voice is too breathy, because the longer we talk about this the hornier I grow. And the more of an actual possibility it seems, not just talk. But there's a riot going on inside my stomach as I ponder the practicalities, nerves beading perspiration on my top lip. Still, he's right. Rules and numbers don't lie.

'You've already stated rule number one,' I say. 'That it won't affect our friendship.'

He nods. 'Done.'

'Rule number two,' I say, ignoring the way he finds this amusing, warming to my theme. 'What happens on the island, stays on the island.' As long as I keep the rules coming, I can delay the moment when I have to make an actual, life-changing decision. But is there really any question? Am I really going to turn him down when a part of me has never had platonic thoughts where he's concerned?

'Yes, of course...' He's growing impatient. Bored.

I roll back my shoulders. If we're doing this, I'm putting in the safeguards. I won't let him railroad me. 'Rule number three—we *never* speak about this with each other after today. Ever.' Perhaps that way we'll both forget it happened and therefore protect our friendship.

He gestures a mock salute. 'Roger that.'

'And four—no kissing and telling.' Heat boils up my neck at the hypocrisy of this last point, because if Oliver lays one finger on me in lust there's no way in hell I'll be able to keep it from Brooke and Grace. I'll be spilling my guts in our group chat before he can say 'take off your clothes'.

My heart thuds.

'As if I'd do that. And I've already agreed that we keep it a secret. You're repeating yourself now,' he says with an indulgent smile. Oliver slowly reaches for the sunglasses I'd forgotten were still perched on my head, folds them and tosses them onto the chair.

Of course I'm babbling—I'm a bundle of nerves.

'Let's shake on it,' he says, his deep voice more dark and dangerous than I've ever heard before. With eyes locked on mine, he holds out his hand palm-up. His big, sexy Oliver shaped hand is so familiar. But the gesture, us shaking on a deal to step over the friend boundary together, is so alien that the scant inches between us may as well be miles. My own arm feels leaden, hanging at my side with paralysing inertia.

My fingers twitch. Burn for his touch.

My eyes burn with longing, trapped by his vivid blue stare.

My throat burns, all the reasons and arguments and conditions dried up.

I lift my hand so it's hovering over his.

Before I can vacillate further, Oliver closes the gap and slides his palm against mine in a strong grip. I suck in a gasp and then flush, because there's no way he missed the sound. We're not hand hold-ers, Olly and I. Despite the hundreds of sexless touches that have passed between us, this touch is breath-stealing, scorching.

But, if I'm gasping at hand-to-hand contact, what happens when there's some breast action going on? I'll probably self-combust.

My thighs quiver at the very idea.

This is the longest handshake in history. I try to pull my hand free, but Oliver holds firm, using the momentum of my recoil to propel me closer, my breasts now only millimetres from his hard chest. I look up from his mouth, the breath panting from my lungs.

'Olly,' I plead, my body almost touching his in all the places that matter.

'Rule number five…' he says, his stare blatantly tracing my parted lips with the hunger I've longed to see a million times—the bedroom eyes.

'No more Olly.' His deep voice is full of unfa-miliar command. 'Only Oliver.'

I nod my agreement, my knees too weak to keep the tremble from my legs.

Olly is my friend. Oliver will be my lover.

Temporarily.

'Say yes,' he says, tempting me.

I feel my pulse to the tips of my toes.

'Yes,' I say, on a heavenly wave of surrender.

CHAPTER FOUR

Neve

HIS NOSTRILS FLARE, as if he's sucking in a silent gasp, but he's outwardly calm and so controlled. My friend has a sexy alpha side... My entire body feels stiff enough to snap. Not that I want to escape but, now this moment is here, the actual realisation of all my hopes and dreams, I'm a physical and mental wreck. So high on longing and the thick thud of desire, I can almost imagine the orgasm he claims to be able to deliver.

'Fact one about orgasms,' Oliver says huskily, his full, sensual lips only inches from mine. 'They start in your mind.'

I look up from his mouth and the expectation of his kiss, my stare clinging to his for fear I'll pass out before we even get to the good stuff. Because bedroom Oliver is even more confident than when he's running his multi-billion-pound company. I went to a tech conference with him once in Silicon Valley, where he'd been invited as a speaker. His intelligence and authority was so hot, I'd had to leave before the end of his talk to rub one out on the bathroom.

'Close your eyes,' he says, voice low and seductive as he woos my body to his will. 'Let me paint you a picture.'

I obey his hypnotic words, although I don't want to miss one second of the look of lust on his face. I'd walk over hot coals for him on any given day, so on *this* day, where I'm so close to the fulfilment of my deepest fantasy, I'm his to command. One hundred per cent.

When he speaks again, I'm so attuned to every nuance of his voice—as if I'm hearing it for the first time, so heightened are my senses—that every word is audible over the sound of my own ragged breathing.

'It's hell watching you walk around in these sexy bikinis,' he says, his breath warm on my cheek. 'I don't know what's happened, because I've seen you in a bikini too many times to count, but I haven't been able to keep my eyes off you, off your gorgeous body, since we arrived.'

My neck collapses, my head falling back, a gasp of ecstasy floating past my parted lips at his arousing confession. I'm petite, curvaceous. Why have I

never known that he thinks my body is gorgeous?
His poker face must be a good as mine.

He lifts my glasses from my face and I fight the
urge to open my eyes. 'I want to see what's underneath these tiny triangles,' he says, his dark voice
vibrating the air between us.

Moisture gushes between my legs. I want to show
him. How can he do this to me with his voice alone?
With his ordinary words? But to me, they're not
ordinary.

'I want to taste the sweet little nipples I see pok-
ing through the fabric,' he says, his warm breath
now feathering over my neck, my collarbone, as if
he's about to take off my T-shirt and bikini top to
do exactly that.

'I want to know if you're wet while I stand here
speaking my dirty thoughts aloud.'

I am, oh God, I really am.

I grip his fingers more tightly because I feel faint
with desire.

He hums a sexy noise in his throat. 'I want to
drop to my knees right now and suck on all that
heat and sweetness. And I will. Soon.'

My pants grow frantic, as if I'm a vixen in heat.
I want to open my eyes, to see the lust I hear in his
smoky voice. I've never been this turned on before,
and he hasn't really touched me yet, but I don't want
to break the spell. I'm high on the promise in his
voice, which I've waited so long to hear.

Wave after wave of delicious spasms clutch at my core muscles. I might actually come standing here. With him touching nothing more than my hand and my mind with his aphrodisiac words. How can he do this to me? And why did I wait all these years to be this brave?

'But more than any of that,' he whispers, worming his way deeper into my mind, 'I want this.' The heat of his breath registers on my lips a split second before his firm kiss lands, and I go into meltdown. With an impatient grunt, he drops my hand to grip both sides of my face and holds me still, captive, enraptured, while his firm, thrilling kiss directs my pliant lips apart. His tongue delves inside my mouth at the same time his leg slides between my legs, my sarong parting so the only thing between my very wet crotch and fizzing clit and his muscular thigh is two thin layers of fabric.

My pulse whooshes in my head; I'm kissing Oliver.

As if my brain is jolted with electricity, I snap out of the seductive trance he put me in the minute he touched my hand. My eyes snap open to see his swimming before me, out of focus but bold with triumph and challenge. I could die happy right now, because I've taken that giant leap, I've made something happen.

His strong arm scoops around my waist, hauling my body up and mashing my tingling breasts to his hard chest, so I feel the bar through his nipple. I'm desperate to discover if it's sensitive for him. My tongue pushes against his, a mewl forcing its way from the back of my throat as I claim the kiss I've only dreamed of for nine years. It's everything I imagined and more. A first, but somehow familiar, because he's no stranger. I know him inside out. And I want him with terrifying ferocity.

My hands tangle in his hair, fighting to bring me closer to the source of such wrecking pleasure as Oliver Coterill's kiss.

I want it never to end. I want to rush it along. I want so many things, I'm practically levitating, only the tips of my toes grounding me to the timber floor.

Then my analytical mind starts a placard-waving demonstration. I scrunch my eyes closed in the hope of silencing the protests. I don't want to see sense. I don't want to think of all the reasons that this shagging my best friend dooms me to a lifetime of heartache. I just want him. Just one time before I abandon my futile crush for good and give up my fantasy.

Because there's been a secret, shameful part of me convinced I've held something back from past boyfriends, as if waiting for this moment. For my shot with Oliver. Perhaps I even sabotaged my own past relationships, holding out for this long-coveted eventuality. Perhaps that's the reason my exes were jealous of our friendship; they saw what I tried to conceal.

And Oliver's right. I want to experience the amazing sex everyone talks about. That it might be with him, is too perfect to contemplate.

Without breaking the kiss, Oliver releases my face to work on the knot of my sarong. My lips cling to his like limpets, my arms so tight around his neck, I might inadvertently strangle him. But if I let go he might change his mind. I might change mine. That he wants me, that he's actually fumbling to get me naked and it's not just a figment of my rampant libido and overactive imagination, already makes this the best sexual encounter of my experience.

His mouth tears from mine, his head bent closer while he struggles with the knotted fabric.

'Let me,' I say, swatting at his fingers. 'Take off your shorts.' I'm almost too afraid to see him naked—the experience will likely be life-threatening. And he'll see me—uncharted territory.

He abandons the knot in the sarong and steps back. 'Oh, no. There's no way we're rushing this.' He lifts the hem of my T-shirt at the same moment I free the knot around my waist. With a whoosh of falling fabric, and a tantalising glide of his knuckles over my waist and ribs as he divests me of the T-shirt, I'm back to just my tiny red bikini—my lucky charm. For all the heat in his stare as he eyes me up and down, I might as well be naked.

My knees knock. *I'm going to let Oliver see me naked.*

'We'll get to the good stuff,' he says with a hint of his teasing smile. He grips my face once more and slides his mouth over mine. 'But first you need warming up.'

I thought men couldn't multi-task, but Oliver is a pro. His lips never leave mine as he manoeuvres me, inching me back to the bed. My thighs hit the mattress and I collapse backward, clinging to his waist to pull him down on top of me.

It's a 'sprawl of limbs, clash of teeth and grunt of laughter' moment, but then his arm scoops my waist and he rolls me on top of him, my body in contact with his hardness from breasts to thighs.

I drag my mouth from his, every inch of me on fire. 'I'm warm, trust me.'

'Good,' he says, his hands gripping my buttocks.

Laid under me, his hair desecrated by my hands and his eyes dark with desire, he doesn't look like my Oliver. But he's never looked hotter. And, considering he rocks business suits like a Hollywood heartthrob, wears jeans and a T-shirt well enough to make designers weep and struts his board shorts like he's modelling surf wear, that's no mean feat.

I push up onto my haunches, kneeling astride his thighs for a better view of his sculpted chest and abdomen. That's when I see the thick rod of his erection for the first time I actually whimper behind the hand pressed to my mouth.

'Oh...' My words dry up as I salivate, blatantly staring at the object of so many of my fantasies. A taboo object, which until now has been as shrouded in mystery as the Bermuda Triangle.

His sensual mouth, slightly swollen from our kisses, stretches. 'It's showing off—ignore it.'

That he talks about his penis in the third person makes me want to laugh, make jokes, start some of our usual banter, but I want him too much for levity. The fact that he's here with me with that snake in his shorts, and that he's mine to touch and kiss as I please, starts a series of body-racking trembles.

Desperation makes me a little fractious. 'I thought the whole point of this was that, for once, I didn't have to ignore it. In fact, I thought I could lavish all my attention on it.' I deliberately lick and then bite my bottom lip.

His pupils dilate, his breath coming faster. 'You've had to ignore it in the past?' The look of mild incredulity on his face confirms my excellent acting skills.

I shrug. 'I'm a woman, you're a guy... Not that I've ever seen it showing off before, of course.'

He smiles, a hint of his friend smile hidden behind the lust transforming his features into those of a man I don't recognise. 'Well, you can lavish all the attention you like on it,' he says. 'Just not yet.'

My sulk evaporates when he reaches up and unties the bikini strap at the nape of my neck. 'The first thirty minutes are all about you.' He peels down the triangles and my breasts spill free, just like that, my nipples peeking out, as if they don't know we're supposed to be just friends.

'Thirty minutes…?' I croak. Won't it all be over after ten? We'll probably be snorkelling in thirty minutes…him satiated and me still wondering if there's something wrong with me…

No. I trust that he's good at this. He's had enough practice. All I have to do is surrender to his plan.

'Mmm-hmm. Lean forward,' he says.

I brace my arms on either side of his head on the bed, my freed breasts dangling. I have a fleeting thought that it's not the most flattering angle, but then Oliver does two things that blank my mind. One, he cups my aching breasts in his warm hands and, two, he jerks his hips up from the bed, as if he can't keep still, the thick ridge of his erection bumping my clit and making my eyes roll back.

'Argh…' I love this plan. Best plan ever.

'Tell me.' His thumbs rub my nipples in small circles, his big hands cupping and caressing. 'Are you feeling turned on?' Another tilt of his pelvis. Another nudge of my clit.

Turned on? I'm molten. He'll feel my heat, my soaking bikini crotch. He'll know it's for him… But we crossed the line where I hide my raging attraction to him long ago.

'Yes.' I open my eyes to see him studying me with fascination. 'I was turned on before you walked in here.'

His nod is lazy, his eyes hooded as if he expected that answer and is picturing what he interrupted in the bathroom.

'What do you think about when you use those toys you love?' he asks. 'And don't you dare say nothing, because I won't believe you.'

I flush—I feel the heat spreading across my skin like a tidal wave. This is Oliver... He rolls each nipple between his thumbs and forefingers, the bite of pressure enough to make me forget everything but how good he's making me feel. I'm so aroused by what he's doing and the way he's looking at me, as if he can't wait to put that magnificent penis inside me, that my mind forges ahead with blatant honesty.

'You.' I realise my mistake immediately and bite down on my lip to engage some filters. 'I imagine you making all your women come hard enough to release those screams I've heard through the walls.'

'And?' he says, his fingers stroking and pinching at my nipples in perfect synchronicity so that I'm gasping.

I want to hide from being this vulnerable with him, but I don't want him to stop what he's doing. I look deep into his eyes. 'And I imagine it's me you make scream. Me you make come.'

Fire rages through me, scalding, scorching. But there's no room for shame or awkwardness because his pupils flare, his stare burning hot. 'I will. More than once.'

I close my eyes. I love this confident side of Oliver. That his commanding conviction extends beyond business to the bedroom fills me with trickles of hope and excitement that, this time, I might just make it over the finish line.

My hand makes a dive for his erection, but he intercepts, gripping my wrist. 'Twenty-seven minutes until you get anywhere near the contents of my shorts,' he says, his voice gruff, body strung taut beneath me. He abandons my breast and grips my hips in his hands, grinding me over his hard length, meeting the helpless undulations of my hips with small thrusts. Teasing. Tempting.

I release a frustrated yelp and slide my lips down his neck to his nipple piercing, which I flick with my tongue until his fingers dig into my skin.

Oliver tugs the side ties on my bikini bottoms and peels fabric away from my backside, his hands grasping and massaging the bare cheeks of my arse. Then he pulls the front of the bikini until I push up onto my knees a fraction, the whole garment sliding between my legs with a scrape of fabric over my most sensitive parts.

He tosses the bottoms and releases the final tie on the top at my back, throwing it after its partner, so I'm now completely naked astride him. At the mercy of his fierce stare and exploring hands.

'This isn't fair,' I choke out as he roams my nakedness freely with eyes and hands. I want to see all of him too.

'Who said it had to be fair?' Giving my hips one final grind onto his erection, he jack-knifes up into a sitting position with a crunch of his sexy abs so that we're nose to nose. 'Kiss me,' he says in his husky voice.

No second time of asking required. I forget I'm stark-naked astride my friend's lap, drape my arms over his broad shoulders, tangle my fingers in his hair and go to town on his mouth, my heart thumping that I'm allowed to kiss him, touch him. Will I ever be able to stop? To go back just to watching his mouth move when he talks and recall how it tastes?

No. No time travelling. Enjoy the moment.

We kiss for what feels like an hour, me naked and writhing in his lap and him displaying a degree of restraint and patience I hadn't believed possible from my highly sexed friend.

If he wasn't intermittently grunting and moaning, his cock rock-hard between my legs, I might have thought he was bored. I've never known a guy to turn down dick action. For thirty minutes!

'Oliver...' I moan, need building in me like steam.

'Tell me how it feels.' His familiar face is almost unrecognisable, slack with desire, his lips swollen and eyes hooded but penetrating.

I can't keep still, my hips jerking on his lap. 'I'm burning up. I need you.' My mind clears from the lust fog and I realise I'm actually close. Amazingly, unbelievable close. As if a stroke or two of my clit could carry me over the edge. But surely not? It can't be that easy.

But I've been here before, the high elusive, my orgasm building only to fade away again.

But he hasn't even touched me there yet, only my breasts. And his kisses.

He must hear my thoughts, because he slides one hand between my legs, his other a vice around my back, as if he doesn't want me to get away.

But why would I go anywhere? I'm exactly where I want to be. He's still wearing his shorts—there's been zero penetration—but already it's the best sex I've ever had.

He stares at my face while his fingertips slide over my mons, my skin sensitive thanks to the full Brazilian wax I had for the holiday. I grip his shoulders, fingernails digging into his skin, anticipation coiling in my belly. And I can't look away from his eye contact, even though I'm burning alive at the unchartered intimacy.

He grazes my clit with his fingertip, bolts of electrical current zapping along my thighs. 'Tell me what you like.'

I nod, so desperate now to know if his skills, his boasts, are justified. 'Touch me again. Like that,' I say, beyond caring that my voice is a breathy pant and I'm barking sexual orders at my best friend.

Another glide of his fingertips, and then another. Delicate circles growing in pressure until it's too much to bear and I throw my head back on a desperate cry.

He pushes a finger inside me, then a second, his thumb still circling my clit, and then his facial scruff scrapes the skin of my breast, his mouth devours my nipple and I clench in a violent spasm around his fingers.

'Yes… Oliver…'

This is happening. It's really happening… I'm so close, and not a battery in sight.

He sucks down hard, pressing my nipple flat between his tongue and the roof of his mouth before releasing it to the rapid lap of the tip of his tongue. I look down, watch his mouth on my breast, feel his hand doing incredible things between my legs, and the tension builds.

'Harder,' I say. 'Suck me harder.' And he nips at my nipple with the barest scrape of his teeth.

Fire races along my nerves, thick, languid heat pooling in my pelvis, a desperate empty feeling deep inside.

'I want you inside me,' I manage huskily.

'Not yet.' His tone is final.

'Suck harder, then!' I gasp, my hips joining the rhythm of his pumping fingers. He obeys, his mouth clamped down on my nipple, pushing a third finger inside me and pressing his thumb down on my clit.

And then he looks up, his eyes searing into mine while his mouth is at work, the contact bold and intimate, and the final catalyst igniting my pleasure.

'Oliver...' His name is all I can utter before I fall. The waves of sensation batter my weak body, spasm after miraculous spasm wracking my internal muscles.

I buck and jerk in his lap, both seeking and avoiding the heavenly pleasure, but his grip around my waist shackles me, so I'm his puppet until the last wave smacks my spent body and I slump forward with a strangled plea.

'Enough...enough!' I'm limp in his arms, collapsed against his broad chest, his scruff scraping my shoulder and neck as he nuzzles his mouth over my skin.

'I'd say that's one orgasm down, one point to us, wouldn't you?' I feel his heart thudding against mine, feel his smile against my neck. I can see it in my mind's eye—smug, playful, those grooves bracketing his beautiful mouth.

I want to call his bluff, to pretend I faked it, to wipe away the arrogance I'm certain is on his face.

But, even if I hadn't all but snapped off his fingers with the force of my orgasmic spasms, I'm too wrecked to do more than offer a lame huff of protest.

I have nothing to say. My mind's blessedly blank. I can't believe what just happened. With Oliver, of all people.

But then another thought occurs to me, sending my heart leaping into my throat. Because before this one time is over I have a few more demands. I straighten and look him straight in the eyes—although he's a little blurry because I'm not wearing my glasses—and test out my croaky voice.

'Now I get to touch your penis.'

CHAPTER FIVE

Oliver

'OH, NO, NO…NO.' I check my watch behind her back. 'You still have sixteen minutes of your time left.' I hold her to my chest and turn my face into her mussed hair to inhale the scent of her shampoo. My brain battles the frantic rage of testosterone in my blood to make some coherent thoughts. What the hell has happened to my Neve? Was she always this hot, this sensual, provocative and demanding? I've been walking around with my eyes closed. For self-preservation. But how can I have missed so much for so long? Been so idiotically stupid?

Because she's my friend and I was terrified I'd fuck it up. Because, unlike Neve, I've only had one relationship. As a teenager. Jane was a lot like Neve, except that she broke my heart. Then my father's cynical take on women and love—and my own reckless behaviour—taught me to shut myself down to that kind of risk.

But I can do this—keep my friendship with Neve separate, sacrosanct, and enjoy the sex. Fuck, I gave her her first shared orgasm… And I still have sixteen minutes to touch and lick every gorgeous inch of her until she's imprinted on my mind. I want to get up close and personal. I want to taste her and force her back into orgasm number two, now I know she's had a rough deal from her exes. If I can reset the sexual imbalance she's tolerated for way too long, the risk is worth taking.

I slide her languorous body from my lap and she collapses onto the bed, her face buried as she gifts me a vision of her sexy backside. My dick throbs, pushing at the front of my shorts in revenge for having to wait. But I'd walk around with blue balls for a week in order to show Neve the good time she's missed out on.

I can't resist touching her, though. My fingers trace her ribs and the tattoo of an infinity symbol she got for her twenty-first birthday. I'd held her hand, jealous as fuck of the dude inking her skin just to the side of one full, beautiful breast. Not that I'd fully seen them then. But, now I have, the delicious images will be scored on my memory for evermore. Although, somehow, I'll have to try and forget the details once we return to being just friends…

Neve stirs, rolling onto her side and propping herself up on one elbow.

'How did you do that?' she asks, her flushed face full of genuine awe.

Pride builds in my chest. I may be related to a man-whore who sucks at commitment, but I've given her something those other supercilious dick boyfriends of hers couldn't. I shrug, stroking her hip with my thumb. 'Sex is easy. You just have to be honest about what works.'

I lie on the bed facing her, my head on my bent arm, and caress her buttock, filling my hand with her pale rounded cheek. 'Tell me. What was the best part of what just happened?'

She huffs, rolling onto her stomach again to hide from my question. 'You don't need your head to grow any bigger.'

'Come on, I'm serious. Tell me. There's a reward for the best answer.' We've always been playful with each other, shared a similar sense of humour. That I get to combine one of my favourite parts of our relationship with one of my favourite activities— sex—makes me feel more alive than ever, and I haven't even come yet.

Then an idea occurs. 'You think about your answer.' I rise from the bed and march to her suitcase, retrieving a toy from the bag—a bright-pink dildo—while she buries her face in the pillow and grumbles about being so candid. But I need to know. I have plans.

I place the toy on the bed, out of her line of vision,

kneel astride one of her legs and brace myself over her back. While she mumbles excuses into the pillow, I push her hair out of the way and kiss her freckled shoulders and the valley between her shoulder blades.

'If you want to replicate an outcome,' I say, my voice thick with lust, 'you must analyse how you arrived there. Consider it an audit, if you like.' All the while my mouth is occupied with her satiny skin and my questions, my throbbing dick is distracted.

'Mmm,' she moans, her breath catching. 'It was all good.'

I can see she's going to need a little encouragement. If she's allowed herself to be short-changed by her exes, talking dirty probably doesn't come naturally. 'Was I too rough with your nipples?' I slide my mouth down the bumps of her spine, learning new things about her, like her sensitive, ticklish spots.

'God, no.' She groans. 'That was good. Perfect. I liked the nibbling and tweaking.'

'See, that wasn't so hard—this is what I want to hear.'

I press kisses in the small of her back and then kiss each cheek before pressing my teeth there with the barest hint of pressure. 'And the biting? Too much?' Oh, how I'd love to mark her, give her a hickey so she remembers this in the days to come every time she looks in the mirror.

'Um...no!' she squeaks, bucking her pelvis. 'That was good too.'

I grip her hips and encourage her to roll over onto her back.

I look down at the woman I know so well, pride building in me that she trusts me enough to gift me this incredible privilege. Flushed and panting, looking at me as if I'm the only man on earth.

Not a womaniser with bad genes.

Need roars through my head. Why have I denied myself this possibility for so long, and how can I take full advantage of my luck before Neve wakes up to my true nature? Because not all my decisions have been as awesome as this one.

When I met her I was a monumental fuck-up, more like my father than I care to admit, and she was amazing, someone I knew I wanted in my life despite being out of her league. But I'm older now. More mature. I have no intention of losing her or allowing her to regret this.

But the clock is ticking.

'So the nipple play was good.' I scoot down the bed and lift one leg, bend her knee and press her ankle up to my lips. 'What about the kissing?'

Her mouth hangs open, her breasts rising on every laboured breath. 'That was fine. Oliver, do we have to talk?'

I swirl my tongue around her anklebone. 'Oh, yes, I'd say the talking is essential for orgasm number two. I'm not sure I'm happy with just fine.' My tongue laves up the curve of her calf to a sensitive spot behind her knee. 'Mmm... I'll have to try harder with the kissing.'

She's panting now. 'Okay. Good. The kissing was good. It definitely helped. But I don't think I'll be able to come again...'

I slide onto my stomach, shouldering her thighs open until I'm positioned exactly where I want to be. I press a kiss beneath her belly button, smiling up at her outraged but aroused expression. 'Don't make this even more exciting by issuing a challenge.'

Slowly, deliberately, I look down between her legs. Lust robs my breath. She's completely bare, all that gorgeous pink pussy on display for me.

Neve whimpers and covers her face with her hand. 'Oh...'

'Don't you hide from me,' I say, tracing kisses and licks up her smooth inner thighs, while my stare jumps from her face to my new favourite view.

She lifts her head and glares. 'Oliver...' But the reprimand lacks conviction, her voice so strangled and needy.

'Tell me,' I say, sucking in the scent of her arousal until my dick starts to weep, 'was two fingers enough? Is three too ambitious?' I trace her opening with one feather-light fingertip.

She shakes her head, her bottom lip trapped under her teeth, her eyes wide, pleading. Her lips actually tremble.

Damn, she's incredible.

'No?' I press a kiss to her mons, swirl my tongue there, avoiding her most sensitive areas until I'm certain she's ready to beg…or demand.

'I loved everything you did to me.' She's panting with need now, desperation hovering in her eyes. 'Couldn't you feel how hard I came?' she whispers.

I grin; my Neve is warming up. 'I could. Let's see if you're ready for another.'

Panic flares in her beautiful eyes, but there's desire too. 'I…I can't.'

I grin, blow a stream of air over her exposed lips. 'I think you can,' I say and lower my mouth to her, sucking and tonguing her sweet flesh like I'm French-kissing her pussy.

She cries out, her thighs jerking and her head falling back between her shoulders. I part her with my thumbs and find her swollen clit, plump and ready.

'Oliver…' She says my name on a gasp that makes my blood pump harder because there's reverence in her voice that makes me feel invincible somehow. Right now, I'm so much more than the sum of my parts. More than her commitment-phobic friend. More than a casual fuck. More than a man.

I'm everything she deserves in this single moment.

'Why don't you watch what I'm doing and direct proceedings?' I suggest, my pulse hammering hard enough to deafen me. 'That way, I'll know what you like.'

Her huge eyes are round as she stares at me between her legs and then watches my mouth lave kiss after kiss to her pouty clit.

She's addictive. Her scent is so arousing I'm worried I might come in my shorts. I ease my hips back to dampen the friction and flatten my tongue over the taut bundle of nerves that all my verbal preparation has swollen to a tight bud.

'Yes...' Neve hisses, grasping my head with both hands so she can rock her pelvis against my mouth.

I keep up the suction, searching the bed for the dildo with one hand. I see the moment she notices the toy, excitement flaring in her eyes. I look down, lining it up at her slick entrance, and then search her face for permission. Her nod and whimper is the green light I need. I ease the thick toy inside her, my dick throbbing as we both watch the shocking-pink shaft disappear between her lips.

'Oliver,' she pants, her thighs trembling at the invasion. 'Suck me.'

I want to beat my chest in triumph at how perfect she is. Sweet, shy Neve has left the building. This Neve is greedy for orgasm number two. And I'll give her anything. Do anything to make her happy. To watch her come again.

I obey, my mouth finding her once more, alternating sucks and flicks of my tongue with plunges of the dildo inside her, knowing all the while she's watching.

This time her orgasm builds slowly. Her cries, her chanting my name over and over, and the jerks of her thighs, are all clues of the impending climax. Number two looks and sounds as good as the first. Neve's pleasure is one of the best sights I've ever seen, as she shatters and collapses back onto the bed, spent.

Testosterone roars through me, my abstinence equally depleted. 'Do you have any condoms?' I toss away the toy and race out of my clinging shorts, which feel two sizes too small. Have I ever been this turned on? This hot for a woman? Is it just because I know it's a one-time deal? A novelty? Forbidden? Or is it wonderful Neve and her addictive abandon?

Neve waves her hand in the direction of her wash bag on the nightstand and I rummage, my shaking fingers quickly locating my prize. I sheath myself and climb on top of her still spent body. She welcomes me, her kisses fast and frantic and her hands grabby, tugging on my shoulders and buttocks as I line myself up.

Part of me can't believe I'm actually doing this—about to penetrate my beautiful Neve, a woman I've forced myself to ignore sexually for so long. But, just as her pleasure is precious to me, so is she. I'll pay the price, make everything all right between us, if I can just have this one time.

With teeth gritted against the impending ecstasy, I sink forward into her tight warmth, my mind blank from all the reasons this is a terrible idea and I plunge home, thrust after thrust. Her cries and kisses urge me on. Sweat breaks out, stinging my eyes. But I don't want it to be over so soon, even as animalistic instincts take hold of my hips. I brace my arms either side of her head, my thrusts rocking the bed into the wall. She feels amazing. She is amazing. Perfection.

'Touch yourself. Your nipples. Your clit,' I bite out, and she nods, whimpers and obeys, one hand delving between our hips and the other plucking at one red, swollen nub.

Her pale skin is marked from my mouth and my facial hair, the sign of possession I craved.

My climax builds at the base of my spine, fire boiling in my belly. But still I want her with me, coming around my cock the way she milked the toy and my fingers. I want everything she has now I've stepped across the line. I want her corrupted. Ruined for mediocre sex for ever. Not my sweet friend, but this sexy woman who's ripped apart everything I thought I knew about her.

'Are you close?' I grit out, hips slamming into hers.

Miraculously she nods, her head thrown back as she wails, and we come together, angels singing, stars bursting and unicorns prancing.

CHAPTER SIX

Neve

I GRIP OLIVER'S waist and rest my cheek against his
sun-warmed back, hiding from the worst of the sea
spray as he spins the jet-ski in a tight arc. Adrenaline forces a squeal from me. I grip the seat with
my thighs and cling to him for dear life. My heart
thumps so hard, I'm sure he must feel it against
his back.

After the astounding and miraculous orgasm
medley this morning, we took the jet-ski and snorkel gear and headed out for the afternoon, exploring the pristine lagoon and teeming reefs of the
Maldives. A good thing, because if we'd been anywhere near our rooms at the resort I'd be dragging
Oliver back to bed.

I close my eyes and rest my forehead between his
shoulder blades. How can I know him so well but
still feel like I don't know him at all? The sex was

everything I imagined and more, no fantasy able to compare with Oliver's sexual talents and my body's wondrous release. I'm still unsure how he managed to drag not just one but three orgasms from me in quick succession. Perhaps it was his bedroom eyes, or the bossiness, or the dirty talk… Or a winning combination.

But, while I'm still celebrating the miracle, a part of me hasn't been able to shake the doubts since.

Because we can never take back what happened.

I was blind to the shoal of tropical fish decorating the reef while we snorkelled, my mind occupied with how I'd had the most incredible sex of my life, but that it couldn't happen again, because it was with my best friend. A man with no interest in forming anything long term. And that's good, right? Because one time is recoverable, but more than that could become habit and therefore dangerous.

Over the years I've watched Oliver perfect the several-nights stand, which never turns into a relationship. And while right now, with my body still singing hallelujahs, several nights of Oliver's brand of sex sounds like the best plan ever, I cannot get carried away. There's a real risk if we did it again and again and again…

I suck in the scent of his skin, my body aching. How will I survive the next few days if it doesn't happen again? How can I go back to pretending that I don't crave his touch, his kisses, his body? I'll need to learn to lie all over again.

And is he still my best friend? Is it possible to return to what we were after such an incredible but disastrous side-step over the line?

Oliver swings the jet-ski in a figure-of-eight through the warm Indian ocean, as if it's business as usual. True to his word and the strict rules we'd set out, we haven't discussed it since, even though the memories are fresh enough. If I close my eyes while I suck in the scent of his warm skin, I can recreate a thrilling, involuntary clench of my internal muscles.

I sit up straight, mentally shaking myself. Olly and I are good enough friends, mature enough adults, to make a one-time holiday hook-up work. Our relationship is too important to spoil because we had sex… Even the kind of sex that surely sets off seismic activity on the ocean bed…at least for me. Perhaps it's always that way for him.

And there it is, the core at the centre of my doubts—that I'm an anomaly for him. Not his usual type. He's had a lot of partners, but he always manages to find women who want the same things—a casual good time.

One of the major reasons my last few relationships ended was because I'd grown a little more committed than my exes. I seem to have a knack for choosing men who aren't quite as invested in the relationship, and no one wants to feel like a stop-gap until someone better comes along. And then, of course, there was the bad sex…

But I can learn from my experience with Oliver. Now that we've proved there's nothing wrong with me, that I've just been sleeping with the wrong partners—selfish partners uninterested in my pleasure—we can go on as if it never happened.

Right?

But, oh…it *did* happen, and I'd do it again in a heartbeat. My heart thuds against his back, excitement building at the idea that, if I'm disciplined with myself, I can have more of him…perhaps until we have to go home…?

No—if Oliver can stick to the rules we laid out at the start, I sure as hell can. And there's no way I want to be the friend he hooks up with every now and then. A sexual placeholder in between his other women.

'Let's get a drink,' he yells over the sound of the engine. I give him a thumbs-up and he slows the jet-ski and heads for shore. In the shallows we dismount and tug the craft up onto the sand, handing our life jackets back to the waiting resort staff.

There's a bar on the beach, tables and chairs spilling from the deck onto the sand. We head for the sun-loungers underneath palm-thatched umbrellas that face the endless blue sea and give our order to a nearby waiter.

'That was so much fun,' I say, flopping down onto a lounger and relaxing back against the pillows as if I'm not sneaking looks at Oliver's wet, ripped body from behind my dark glasses.

'Mmm...' he mumbles, settling beside me.

We sit in silence, punctuated only by the arrival of our drinks, a cocktail for me and a beer for him. The warm breeze raises goose bumps over my skin, each excruciating second stretched indefinitely.

What now? This was exactly the kind of awkwardness I feared.

Both of us take a generous swallow, as if we're avoiding the moment when we'll be forced to have a normal friendly conversation. A conversation that has nothing to do with nipples, erections or orgasms.

Why is this so hard? He's still Olly. Still my friend.

I take a second gulp of the delicious drink and then place it on the table between Oliver's lounger and mine, presenting a calm, unaffected exterior while my heart thumps against my ribs and my stomach sinks.

I can't think of a single thing to say to a man with whom conversation has always flowed easily. My mind snags on the image of Oliver's face as he'd come inside me this morning. You should never know what your best friend's sex face looks like. I can't un-see that. I can't go back to thinking of him *just* as my friend, because he's more now. Can I even pretend he's a friend when the lust incapacitating me makes the previous nine years of lusting seem inconsequential?

Do I even want to go back to being friends now that I know how devastating sex with him is? But I've already written off being his lover, the potential heartache too risky.

Ugh—I'm going around in circles. I grab my drink once more, an occupation for my fidgety hands. We've ruined what we had and there's no future outside friendship in which we can both be happy.

'Okay,' he says, shaking me from my brain freak-out so that I literally jump, spilling a splash of sticky cocktail on my belly. 'I know we promised we wouldn't talk about it, but let's talk about it.'

I wipe at the spill with a napkin, delaying the moment when I have to look at him. 'Is that a good idea?' I mumble, settling my eyes on the view while the renegade neurones in my brain fire silent question after silent question.

Is our friendship irreparably damaged?

How was it for you?

And, most pressing, can we do it again?

'We said we wouldn't talk about it. Ever,' I remind him. I just need to prepare for the return of abstinence.

'I know.' He shoots me that look, the one he issued earlier when he said those magical words *I could make you come until you scream your throat raw.* 'But that was before you started to freak out.' His voice is way too calm for my liking, as if for him what we shared this morning is no big deal. It's a big deal for me. Gargantuan. It was spectacular and my body wants a repeat I know I can't have. I'd say that's worthy of a decent freak-out.

'I'm not freaking out,' I say, chasing full-blown denial. 'We agreed the subject was closed. You're breaking the rules.'

Thank goodness he raised it—I was close to cracking myself.

I'm still avoiding looking his way, but I feel the smile in his voice. 'Ah, come on, Never, you've always known I'm a bad influence,' he says. I've previously secretly adored my nickname, because it was just between us, like a secret handshake. Only now its use douses me with chills.

Neve was his lover. Never is definitely his friend.

'Can't a guy gloat when he's having the best day of his life?' he says, and my head whips around. He's having the best day of his life? I narrow my eyes. Is he teasing?

As if he's perfectly content with his revealing statement and my shell-shocked reaction, he stretches out his long body on the lounger.

Then he looks at me, playful once more, his voice

low. 'Oliver and Neve, three,' he says about my orgasm tally. 'SBF Club, zero.'

He grins, and I want to kiss him so badly, to sit astride him out here on the beach and take his magnificent penis into my mouth until it's all he can do to lie helpless and turned on under me—the way I behaved earlier. He's far too smug for my state of mind, which veers from wildly aroused to cranky and confused.

Bloody Oliver…

'SBF Club?' I ask, fully aware I'm skirting a forbidden conversation and indulging Oliver's ego. Part of me dreads knowing what he means by the initials.

'It stands for Serious Boring Fuckers,' he says, looking faintly annoyed. 'Your lazy exes.'

I gasp, casting a frown in his direction. 'You had a club name for them?' I knew there was little love lost between Oliver and the men of my past, especially after I split with them, but this is the first time he's ever admitted it aloud. But why, unless he was… No, he couldn't be… Jealous?

Trickles of sick delight run through my veins, knowing that misery loves company and that he might too have suffered frustration over the years. Until today, he's never given one indication that he sees me in a sexual light—probably the reason I'm reeling about what this morning's deviation means. And his jealousy could just be possessiveness over our friendship, nothing more.

He nods, resting his head back on his hands so all his delicious bronzed chest is on display and his arm muscles flex, distracting me from mounting sufficient outrage. 'To think I used to feel intimidated by them. If only I'd known they weren't taking care of you properly.'

'What are you talking about?' I vent my frustration. He's making me all kinds of hot and bothered. Turned on, then annoyed and then overjoyed… We're not supposed to be discussing this morning. It's hard enough to forget when he's stretched out semi-naked, calling to me like a feast catered to my specific needs. When I can still smell his scent on my skin, can still recall the taste of those lips and the commanding scrape of his sexy voice.

I scoff. 'You design outrageously clever software for a living that I don't even try to understand. Your tech company is worth billions, and no doubt the current negotiations with one of the world's largest telecommunications giants will make you insufferably wealthy. Why would you be intimidated by anyone?'

I stare into his beautiful eyes, see the doubt that lurks there whenever Oliver talks about his father, whom he's christened the world's crappiest role model. Kids, even teenagers, shouldn't have to drive their parent to rehab or attend their string of celebrity weddings. It's a miracle—one Oliver often incorrectly attributes to me—that he isn't an alcoholic junkie himself, although he's often wondered if he's something of a sex addict.

But I can guess the answer. His success is due to how hard he pushes himself, almost as if he's outrunning both the reputation of the Oliver I first met and the reputation of his outlandish, rock-and-roll father as well as the frequent comparisons made by those who don't know the real him, especially the media.

One of the hardest things to do during the early days of our friendship, while our competitive natures bonded over pool tournaments and university maths club, was to watch him sabotage himself time after time with bad decisions—partying, skipping lectures and frequent one-night stands—which only seemed to increase the hollow look in his eyes.

'The Kimoto deal has reached a delicate stage,' he says about the Japanese telecommunications corporation, displaying an uncharacteristic flash of vulnerability that I haven't seen in a long time. This business deal means a lot to him.

I soften my tone, probing. 'This is the artificial intelligence software you launched?' I ask, in no way pretending to know what he does for a living. His company has so many irons in the fire, it's hard to keep up. If it's cutting edge, Oliver and the geniuses he recruits to his company are all over it.

'Yes. Kimoto is passionate about robotics. They want my AI software, but they're haggling over the small print.' He takes a swig of beer. 'Anyway, I'm not intimidated by your exes anymore. Although a couple of them did their best to remind me how my family skeletons and past reputation made me unworthy of your friendship.' He looks away, focussed on the horizon. 'And, while they may not have taken care of you between the sheets, at least they didn't taint you, expose you to their embarrassing, media whore of a father and all the baggage he attracts.'

My heart clenches for him. He's referring to articles written about his misspent youth, painting him as the philandering, layabout son of rock royalty, a chip off the old block, which I know he despises. Try as he might, despite his self-made billionaire status or his business success, he feels he can't shake his past. Or comparisons with his father.

'I've never met your father,' I say, my voice tentative, because I know this is his weak spot, the only part of his life where he seems to doubt himself and his intuitive instincts.

As a teenager, growing up on two continents, shipped back and forth between his acrimoniously divorced parents—his father in LA and his mother in London—he struggled with his identity, which was defined by celebrity gossip mongers before he had a chance to develop his own sense of worth. In the shadow of an extroverted, outrageous and perpetually adolescent father, and an embittered mother who'd been passed on for numerous younger models over the years, it's no wonder the Oliver I first met had hang-ups of massive proportions.

'Too right, and you're the better for it, trust me. He'd probably try to marry you or something. No wonder Kimoto Corp are cautious about doing business with me.' He snorts, but there's no humour in the sound. There's a tension in his body, one that regularly accompanies any mention of his father.

'He's already married,' I say about his famous father, a larger-than-life character who grew up in South London before hitting the big time as part of an eighties rock band. 'And I'm sure the business community sees what you've achieved, not who you're related to.'

Of course, he could simply have embraced the role of LA layabout, living off his trust fund, but he had too much pride and integrity for that, determination he'd channelled into a global success. Just as numbers and balancing accounting records keeps me grounded, nerdy tech-wizardry fuels Oliver's sense of worth. Despite him looking like the archetypal beach bum layabout the press would have the world believe.

'Anyway, I thought we were discussing this morning,' I say as a distraction.

'We are, but being friends with me isn't easy,' he says. 'You were accosted by some journo sniffing out a story at that Christmas gala last year. And I've lost track of how many times you've had your picture splashed over the gossip rags in some speculative bullshit story about us every time you're single. It's as if they can't believe I could attract a friend of your calibre.'

He's agitated. I want to comfort him, as I normally would on this subject, but touching him more than absolutely necessary could overwhelm my already strung out body.

'I can't imagine what it was like for you to grow up in the public eye. To have everything you do scrutinised and gossiped over.' No wonder his sense of privacy is fierce—he's the exact opposite of his father, who seems to court the attention, good and bad.

'I'm grateful to your exes, actually,' he says, his mouth a grim line. 'At least they protected you from the stories that tried to paint you as pitiful and in love with me, something I failed to do.'

My heart stops beating. Because, while I too hate the mocking tone of those stories, I fear the world will see that they carry a grain of truth; part of me was, is, a little bit in love with him.

As his plus-one, I'm the woman most often and consistently photographed with him, often dubbed the desperate off-again, on-again girlfriend. Exactly the thing I'm anxious to avoid, now we've crossed the line of physical intimacy.

'I don't care about the gossip sites. We know what we are to each other—just friends.'

Or at least we were, before today. Have I become what the world sees? A woman clearly besotted, content to wait in the wings for my chance with him while he takes his time deciding if he's ready to commit?

Have I subconsciously followed him around for the nine years it took him to notice me? Yes, I chose friendship over a relationship, but was part of me too scared back then to force his hand and make him choose, knowing he wasn't ready for a relationship?

'Have we ruined it? Us?' I ask, my voice barely a terrified whisper. I don't want him to choose any more than I want to make that decision. I want us to have both, just a while longer. Because I crossed the line with my eyes wide open, knowing that, one way or another, things would be different.

But I need to know.

Oliver jack-knifes into a sitting position, swinging his legs over the edge of the lounger to face me. 'No. Don't say that. We're fine.' The same panic gripping me seems to flash in his eyes. 'You know your friendship is the only good thing in my life beside my work—I'd never jeopardise that. Ever. I know I broke the "talking about it" rule, but I'd never break the first rule.'

I warm at his words of reassurance then break out in shivers. 'But—'

'No. There is no but.' He scoots to the edge of the lounger so he can reach across and grab my hand. 'I need you. You know all my family bullshit. You understand me like no one else—see things in me no one else sees. You've never once made me feel like I have to be something I'm not or prove myself. You've got my back and I've got yours.'

I shiver at the vulnerability of his pleading expression, struck dumb by my outpouring of feelings for this man.

'Perhaps I was just jealous of your exes,' he says. 'Jealous that they could give you something I can't. Anonymity, normality and protection.'

His fingers squeeze mine so hard I press my lips together to hide a wince.

'Well, there's no need to envy them.' I point out. 'I dumped them for a reason.'

He shrugs. 'It just didn't work out. Now I know about the sex, I'm not surprised.'

I hedge, reluctant to continue down the heavy turn this conversation has taken. 'But the predominant reason for me was the disparity in our investment in the relationship. A woman likes to feel adored. To never have to doubt that she's the number one priority, not just convenient.'

He stares, silent, his eyes burning my skin. Why am I telling him this? He's not interested in relationships. He doesn't need the pointers. He has as much success with the ladies as he wants.

'Promise me again,' he says, throwing me off my guard. 'Promise me that you won't let what happened this morning change anything.' He punctuates his words with tiny tugs on my hand. 'Because I'm not sorry it happened, but I'll always need you in my life. You'll always be my best friend.'

The words stick in my narrowed throat, because our relationship has already changed. Almost beyond recognition. Yesterday morning I wanted him in an abstract, imaginative way. Today I want him with a fire hot enough to turn the sand under us to glass, even though I should be sated, satisfied and heeding the warning signs flashing before my face.

'I promise,' I whisper.

What else can I do? We crossed the line. I had my orgasms. It's time to be mature and remember everything else we've meant to each other all this time. Support, laughter, someone who just gets us.

As a friend, I know I hold the number one spot in Oliver's life, which is why he always wants me around when he has a social event like his cousin's wedding. He's loyal and thoughtful, always on hand when I need advice or a shoulder on which to cry, even if it's in the middle of the night. Despite his busy schedule, I know he'd drop everything for me if I asked. And he's my biggest fan, as I'm his, championing my endeavours, celebrating my successes and reining in my insecurities when they surface.

'Besides, no one else would put up with you, so I'm kind of trapped,' I say to lighten the mood, grateful for his familiar grin, which tells me we'll be okay.

Just then the engine of one of the many sea planes that ferries tourists around the atolls snatches our attention. The small sixteen-seater aircraft comes in low, landing in the sea at the far end of the island.

'New holiday makers arriving,' I say, because I want to return some semblance of normality to our conversation, one that seems to have left us both exposed and raw.

Oliver's hand tenses around mine. He looks past me, squinting, as if trying to spy the passengers disembarking the plane onto the small wooden jetty down the beach. Then he stands abruptly, dropping my hand.

'Fucking fantastic. I'll see you at dinner,' he mutters, sliding his sunglasses onto his face and heading in the direction of the plane.

'Wait, Oliver,' I call after him, but he's already striding away, his back rigid.

I look past his stiff frame, trying to focus on the people some distance away cluttering up the tiny jetty, spying a group of four or five bodies. One's taller than the rest, his body language more exuberant.

When combined with Oliver's emotional shutdown and abrupt departure, it can mean only one thing.

His father has come to paradise.

CHAPTER SEVEN

Oliver

WHEN I STAMP into the restaurant thirty minutes late, thanks to some emails from my legal team that required urgent attention, Neve is already seated between two of my cousins. Two of my male cousins.

A bonfire builds in my chest. I'm jealous? Comparing myself to her exes wasn't such a brilliant idea on my part. Yes, I'd given her the orgasms they'd failed to, but that's where the benefits for her end. Because I also crossed the line, selfishly putting her and our friendship at risk. And no amount of damage limitation, now that Slay is in town for his niece's wedding, will make me feel any better. Because now I'll be obliged to introduce them. Fucking disaster waiting to happen. Disaster follows Slay wherever he goes.

I breathe through the red fog clouding my vision. In some ways, the jealousy is a welcome distraction from the usual shit show that accompanies my father. A shit show I'd spent the rest of the afternoon trying to minimise, because it would be just like Slay to rock up with the media and outshine the bride, probably dragging me in too and jeopardising my deal with Kimoto.

Nausea threatens. What if Neve sees how similar we really are? What if she learns about my past indiscretion and despises me for my immature weakness? What if she finally sees through me and decides I'm not good enough?

I can't lose her. She saved me nine years ago. Her sense of humour and her take-no-bullshit attitude were exactly what I needed to pull my head out of my arse and take myself seriously. If it wasn't for her, I'd probably have dropped out of uni and become more like my old man than I already am.

I shudder.

And now, when I'm on the cusp of a deal that will cement my company's position as a serious player in the international tech world, I need her grounding influence and belief in me more than ever.

Enter Slay and his impeccable timing.

Fuck!

Neve looks up and catches my eye. She's glowing, beautiful, despite her concerned expression. Her hair's piled on her head in some sort of casual up-do, her red dress making her fair skin radiant. She's always looked great in dresses and red is definitely her colour.

I want to whisk her out of here, hide her away from Slay—I messaged her the news of his arrival—because having my father here so close to Neve, when I've managed to keep him well away for years, makes me feel as powerless and gullible as I did at nineteen.

Because Neve is part of my real life. Nothing to do with my life growing up in LA. A life of excess and parties. A life of fake, superficial popularity with my peers. A life devoid of the male role model and the consistency a teenage boy needs in order to find his place in the world. At least I'd been smart enough to use school as an outlet. My scholarship to a London university enabled me to break free of any financial dependence on Slay.

I should never have invited Neve to this family wedding when there was a risk Slay might attend. Perhaps I should have stayed away myself, given the current delicateness of the Kimoto deal. The last thing I need is negative press.

I sigh and cast my gaze down the length of the table, looking for my seat, which is at the opposite end from Neve and my cousins.

Mike, the cousin to her left, is newly divorced. His round lawyer's face flushes with excitement as he laughs at something Neve has just said.

Bastard.

Rob, the cousin to her right and five years her junior, waits impatiently for his turn for her attention, his fingers tapping the table.

Why didn't I organise a private dinner for two? And how long will I have to tolerate this evening before I can get her alone? Then again, if the old man does plan to make a grand entrance, I want her as far away from me as possible. Perhaps she'll slip under his radar—not that he's ever overlooked a beautiful woman, regardless of whether he's married or single.

I take my seat between the bride, my cousin Shelley, and her maid of honour, who I met for the first time this morning. I smile, desperately trying to recall her name, and then sag with gratitude for my cousin, who had the foresight to arrange place settings. Of course, that means she deliberately sandwiched Neve in between the only two other single men here…

Shit, I'm a mess. A mess I created the minute I lifted the shutters from my eyes and allowed myself to truly look at Neve. To admit long-buried desires. I should never have touched her, but can I stop now I've indulged? Because, despite the rules she needed and the risks involved, I want more. I swallow hard. I don't think I'll ever get enough.

After my brief interaction earlier with my father and stepmum number five, and the threat that they could turn up any second, my appetite is nonexistent. I grab a waiter, order a bottle of beer and make trivial conversation with Shelley, an attempt to distract me from my fury.

Why is Slay here? It won't just be to celebrate his niece's nuptials. My father rarely does anything that doesn't also further his career somehow. But I'm out of the loop. Despite never quite achieving the former heights of his glory days, he's always tried to stay relevant. Perhaps he's promoting a tour, or a new album. God forbid it's a tacky reality TV show... It would be just like him to rock up partway through the meal and buy everyone at the bar a drink—maximum impact set to ensure he, and only he, is the centre of attention. I wouldn't put it past him or a member of his entourage to have invited the press here so he can upstage the bride and groom and feature on every celebrity gossip site by midnight.

I glance at Neve, trying to catch her eye again, inadvertently landing myself in conversation with Amelia, the maid of honour, who punctuates nearly every sentence she speaks by touching my arm. Unlike Neve, who'd never heard of my famous father when I first met her all those years ago, Amelia clearly thinks she already knows everything about me and my rock star parent. She fires question after question about what it was like to grow up in the LA scene, which famous people have I met and do I know if my father is coming to the wedding?

Before sleeping with Neve, I'd have tried to shag Amelia, if for no other reason than to shut her up. Sometimes it's just easier to go along with a stranger's assumptions and play my designated part than to be real and open.

Women like Amelia don't want the real me— the nerdy, tech businessman who works a hundred hours a week and designs software in his spare time. The me I've worked hard over the years to reinvent, to separate from everything Slay represents. They want the caricature from my past that, acting out as a younger man, I once embraced. One my father's team of publicists still churns out because it fits his rock and roll lifestyle. They want the image of me the media continues to spawn, the one who is never spotted with the same woman twice, with the exception of Neve, even though the women I date are equally into casual sex and avoiding commitment. They want to be able to say, 'I slept with Sid "Slay" Coterill's son'…

I spin some crap about wild parties chez Coterill to appease Amelia and feast my eyes on Neve once more, knowing if I could get her alone, bury myself inside her again, I'd feel like myself.

I'm so selfish. Just like him.

Because the crap which accompanies my father, and by unfortunate association me, is exactly the reason I should never touch her again. She's too precious. She's the only woman I've ever told about my famous father who didn't simper and giggle at the idea of meeting him some day, like a star-struck groupie. And now I've fucked things up by fucking her because, no matter what I said on the beach earlier, it's changed things.

How could it not?

Instead of quenching a long-standing fantasy, I want her even more now I've experienced her passionate enthusiasm and heavenly body. And my jealousy…? Did that burn as fiercely with Limp Liam or Tris Tosser as the current hellish fire scorching me alive? I could easily climb over the table and gouge out the eyes of my cousins with a dessert spoon just for looking at *my* beautiful, sexy, funny Neve.

Where has this possessiveness come from?

I neck a swallow of beer, trying to ease my parched-with-panic throat. Now Slay is here, I can almost feel her slipping through my fingers. I am so fucked.

She pauses in her conversation with Mike and looks my way with a small frown. Heat flares from every pore as our eyes collide.

I try to smile but my face feels frozen.

Slay's arrival hot on the heels of the massive shift in our relationship seems to have awoken all my insecurities, reminding me that, no matter what I do, people will always compare us, and maybe they're right to.

It's glaringly obvious I'll never be good enough for Neve. Never be able to protect her from him, from the pervasive side effect of his fame. From the circus that surrounds him. The only way to do that is to turn back time nine years and ignore her in that student bar.

Would I have acted out the way I did at nineteen if I had a normal dad? One content to take pride in his son's achievements and not try to compete for all the attention all the time, even when it meant hurting his only son. I've never told Neve my worst secrets about Jane, and what I did the night we split, and she doesn't understand life under a public lens. At times, it's made me feel like I'm going crazy, and I don't want that for her.

But I can't lay the blame solely at Slay's door. The speculation around my private life is due to my media reputation, fuelled by my notorious commitment avoidance. I'm responsible for the media interest in my relationship with Neve. I've denied my feelings for her and, through my past immature actions, I've offered her up for comparison to the other women I see when there is no comparison. But does she know that? Maybe before this morning, but now…?

My fists curl with impotence. Why jeopardise what she means to me with something as common as sex? Not that sex with Neve was remotely humdrum—I haven't stopped craving her since the moment our lips touched. But if my father's lifestyle proves anything it's that real, long-lasting relationships take work, commitment and compromise, things I'm certain I can't possibly have inherited from him, unlike my borderline addictive traits…

If Neve couldn't make it with those serious, upright men of her past, how the hell can I—a man with Slay's genes—have anything to offer?

I catch Neve's eye once more, desperate to know the thoughts behind her unreadable expression.

As if sensing my distraction, Amelia touches my arm once more, saying something about catching the reunion tour of my father's band last year.

Neve's stare drops away from that hand on my arm before she turns away from me and engages with Rob on her right.

I grit my teeth, furious with myself. She probably thinks I'm interested in Amelia, when all I want to do is drag her out of here and… What? Shag her again? Remind her just how much like my father I am—a philanderer with the emotional depth of a rock pool? Only the fact that her own appetite for the mouth-watering menu seems healthy enough stops me—I'm *that* selfish.

The rest of the meal is torture. I ache head to toe to get her alone. By the time dessert is served, I'm crawling out of my skin, desperate to talk to her and dreading the surprise arrival of the star of the show. I slide my phone from my pocket and message Neve.

Do you want some of my dessert?

I deliberately chose the coconut-free chocolate creation from the menu—Neve despises coconut—

and I noticed that she chose something else. She's a self-confessed foodie who struggles with menus because she wants to taste everything. So we've developed a routine. I order something different from hers, and she steals a taste of my food.

She reads my message but simply shakes her head in response.

I grow restless, shoving away the plate while I try to listen to enough of Amelia's droning voice to seem polite.

After five more agonising minutes, as soon as Neve's spoon hits her empty plate, I try again.

Want to go for a walk on the beach?

Her answer comes blessedly quickly.

Okay.

I excuse myself from the table and head out into the night to wait for her at the short path that leads from our resort down to the beach.

She doesn't keep me waiting long, padding up on bare feet, her shoes swinging in her hand.

I sling my hands in my pockets because, in my current mood, I'm likely to do something I'll regret. Like kiss her again. Or fall at her feet and beg her to...

What? She deserves the moon, not some hypocrite friend who doesn't know the first thing about relationships, something I've avoided for years, because I never again wanted to feel as vulnerable as Jane and Slay made me feel.

Yes, in theory Neve and I have the best foundation blocks—friendship and astounding sexual chemistry. But I'll fuck it up, just like Slay did, because we're father and son. His blood runs in my veins. We're more alike than I can ever admit.

Nausea rushes to the back of my throat. Whatever happens during the rest of our time here, I have to keep Neve away from Slay.

She keeps her distance as we head to the beach, her wary eyes almost crushing me. 'So you met Mike?' I say after we've walked a few minutes in silence, my jealousy getting the better of me. 'I'm surprised he let you escape—I haven't seen him that animated since he met his wife.'

It's not her fault she's kind and funny and gorgeous and I don't deserve her. Mike is a way safer bet—I should step aside or foster the relationship once we're back in London. What little dinner I managed to eat threatens to make a reappearance.

She looks at me as if we're strangers. 'Yes, he's a nice guy. He was kind enough to introduce me around.'

I wince. I deserve that for being so late. I brought her here as my guest. But I allowed Slay to worm his way into my head, the way he always does.

'How's Amelia?' she asks. 'Waiting for you in your room, no doubt?'

'I'm not interested in Amelia.' It wasn't until I kissed Neve this morning that my life, full of shallow, pointless hook-ups, snapped into focus. Depressing focus.

'I don't care either way. I've spent the past nine years watching women throw themselves at you.' She strides ahead towards the water's edge, irritation visible in her rigid shoulders and raised chin.

I catch up, sickened by how much I'm messing this up. 'Well, I care if you're interested in Mike. Are you? He's a great guy.' The last sentence takes effort.

Neve shoots me a murderous look. We retreat to angry silence, following the line of lit torches pushed into the sand, away from the resort. My pulse ratchets up with every step. Not just from the jealousy. Out here in the dark, alone, I'd hoped that we could just be us. The usual us, where I can be myself.

But perhaps *us* no longer exists.

I want to tell her all the things bottled up inside me—how crazy Slay makes me, how fearful I am that I'll never be able to be my own man, no matter what I do or how successful I become, and how sorry I am for putting that disappointed look on her face. But now we've slept together the dynamic has changed. Will she still forgive my thoughtless cock-ups? Can I still confide in my best friend, the only person who knows the real me—good, bad and ugly? Would she admit she liked Mike and wanted to date him? Or do I no longer deserve her confidences?

My hands curl into fists and, not for the first time in my life, I curse my father. I still recall his sage wisdom when I had my heart shredded by Jane. I'd genuinely fallen in love for the first time and I believed she felt the same way. But when I told her I'd be spending the summer with my mother in London, because I'd needed to get away from Slay, she dumped me out of the blue.

A year and many casual sex-ploits later, I met Neve, a miraculous woman who'd never even heard of Slay. She's been a breath of fresh air in my life ever since. But have I robbed myself of that life-giving air?

'Why are we fighting?' I ask, my vision now adapted to the dark, so I see her still-wounded expression in profile.

'Because sometimes you're an arsehole,' she replies.

'This is true, but you knew that the day we met.' I'm joking; I hope I've matured a little in the subsequent nine years, but she's in no mood for humour. 'Tell me what's really bothering you.' I want to take her hand. Instead, I shove my hands back into the pockets of my chinos.

'You invited me here,' she says, 'suggested we have sex, of all the stupid things, and then as soon as it's over you shut down. Shut me out.'

Bugger...it does look that way. 'I'm sorry for deserting you this afternoon,' I say. 'But I've had to run damage limitation since Slay arrived to ensure he doesn't upstage Shelley tomorrow with some audacious publicity stunt. It wouldn't be the first time, believe me.'

Rather than placate me with suitably soothing condolences as she normally would on this topic, she spins on me and says, 'I know you think he's a diva, but he *is* Shelley's uncle. She invited him and she must know what he's like. You flew her entire wedding party here on your company jet, and goodness knows how much it's cost you to run interference. You've protected her wedding day as best you can.'

I'm struck still, my mouth hanging open. But Neve hasn't finished the home truths.

'I know you struggle with your relationship with him, but you don't need him. You're independently wealthy, you've built your own life, a life you should be proud of, and yet the minute he arrives you go running as if for a dose of punishment or something. As if you somehow take responsibility for his actions.'

I rub my forehead, bitterness burning my throat, because I know I'm responsible for my own actions, and in the past I've allowed Slay to mess with my head until I've acted shamefully. My biggest regret.

'My main motivation was to keep any media he might attract the hell away from you. I brought you here.'

Some of her anger seems to dissipate as she comes to a halt and turns to face me. 'This has nothing to do with Slay. We were in the middle of a conversation earlier today and you rushed off… without explanation…as if I deserved less than common consideration. You said it wouldn't change our friendship, and then you fail at the first test.'

'I'm sorry. I should have explained. That was rude.' I try to take her hand, but she snatches her arm away.

'Nine years I've known you and you've never once introduced me to your father,' she says.

'Because he's an embarrassment. A cliché. It has nothing to do with you.' I curse the mess I've made by indulging my need for her. None of this would have happened if I'd just maintained the distance I've always kept where she's concerned. Of course, none of it would matter if I stopped allowing Slay to get to me. Or if I'd been open from the start— but then she probably wouldn't have stuck around if she'd known.

She continues as if I haven't spoken. 'You couldn't even be bothered to be on time to escort me to a meal with *your* family, introduce me properly to people I barely know and who looked at me with…pity or something.'

'What do you mean?' I ask, every muscle strung taut. If someone has upset Neve, they'll be walking back to London. 'What the hell is there to pity? You're amazing—'

'You, Oliver. You. Everyone knows what you're like—I saw it when they looked at me tonight. Oh, here's Olly's sad little friend, always following him around in between his women. Well, you can't just slot me in and out of your bed whenever there's a vacancy just because we had sex.'

The vulnerability slashed across her face cuts me deep.

'I'd never do that,' I say, aching to hold her until I feel better and she looks at me the way she did this morning, when it seemed like I could do no wrong in her eyes. The same disbelieving eyes that I'm looking into now.

Her lips move, as if in slow motion, every heartbeat a tick of impending dread.

'I told you it was a bad idea,' she says. 'We should never have touched each other.'

CHAPTER EIGHT

Oliver

SHE STAMPS OFF, muttering something about sorting out her love life once and for all.

My blood runs cold with panic. I race after her. 'No one pities you. And I'm sorry I made you feel that way.' I'm messing up this apology because I feel her slipping through my fingers. I'm terrified Slay will meet her, see what she means to me and deliberately screw me over.

'Just forget it. It's my own fault. I should never have agreed to such a stupid plan.' She's still simmering.

I clutch at straws, so out of my depth. Neve and I have never argued before. 'Look, I'm sorry I was late for dinner. Kimoto Corp is getting cold feet. I had a to make a few calls to the UK. But you're right, okay?'

She stops. Spins. Stares.

I take a deep breath, broken glass in my chest.

'It was rude of me to rush off, but I don't want Slay anywhere near you. He's...' I grip a fistful of my hair and tug, searching for the words to make her understand, words that rip me open. Words I've never spoken aloud to anyone. Ever since the age of nineteen, since I've forgone feelings and relationships, I haven't needed to worry. But Neve is more than my friend.

Now I have everything to lose.

'He's a narcissist. He makes people like him, but it's not for their sake, it's for how they fuel his ego.'

'I don't care about your father. I'm not impressed by his fame,' she says, her eyes wide, as if she senses how close to the bone this subject cuts me.

'I know, and I've always completely adored you for that, believe me. But that doesn't mean he wouldn't try to flirt with you, even in front of his wife. He comes onto anything with a vagina, and I can't bear to see him look at you that way, okay? Not you. You're my person.'

My Neve...

I'm panting, wound so tight by foreboding. I've inadvertently hurt her and she regrets what we did.

'I'm sorry to hear about the Japanese.' She deflates. 'I know how important this deal is to you. Why didn't you tell me?'

I step close. I can't stand the distance any longer. I reach for her chilled upper arms. 'I got distracted with fears of paparazzi following Slay here—it feels like every time I think I'm breaking free I'm tugged back down to reality. I wanted to blow off the family dinner and just eat with you—just the two of us. Then I saw you with Mike, and stupid jealousy took hold. I'm sorry.'

Her eyes are round, as if she's shocked by my jealousy. 'I don't fancy Mike. I know you have this notion that I'm sweet, but as far as your father is concerned I can handle myself.'

'I know, but you don't know what he's like.' I press my lips together. She doesn't know the full extent of his depravity, or mine. I've never told her how Slay claimed Jane made a pass at him. How, stupid and heartbroken, I'd rushed to her that night for confirmation and the truth had flashed in her defiant eyes. She'd never loved me. She'd used me because of who I am. Who my father is.

And I've never told Neve how I exacted my drunken revenge…

'I know what you've told me, so consider me warned off Slay,' she says. 'But you shut me out earlier. Just because we had sex doesn't mean I'm going to let you walk all over me.'

'I won't.'

'You do it every time,' she says.

'What do you mean?' Unease raises the hairs at the back of my neck.

She looks at the sand and shakes her head. 'You sleep with someone and, before they have a chance to get to know the real you, you withdraw. I've spent nine years watching you do it. It's your modus operandi. And why have you never come close to a relationship?'

'I never lie to women—they know what they're getting into with me, and they say they want the same thing. Casual.'

'Yes, I'm sure you're honest about it, but people develop feelings. Every time a woman gets too close, you shut her out and move on without a backward glance. But that's not going to work for me. We agreed we wouldn't let this morning come between us.'

Rage clenches every muscle in my body. 'I'd never shut you out of my life. I've never come close to a relationship because I choose to avoid them. With my father on his sixth marriage as a role model, can you blame me?'

'I guess not.' She shrugs. 'Olly, I know that you had a pretty shitty time growing up with Slay, but please don't let him come between us.'

'I'd never allow anything to come between us. I need you.' I tug her closer, squeeze her fingers with one hand and cup her face with the other so she can't escape. 'I'm sorry that I allowed my father to distract me. It's just that…you're my weakness and he can't know that. I want to keep him the hell away from you. For your sake. To protect you.' I can't stop looking at her tempting mouth. I want to kiss her so badly, to demand her forgiveness. Because I need her now more than ever.

But she's right—if I don't open up, I might lose her anyway.

I sigh, let go of her face and tug her down to sit on the sand, close enough for me to feel comforted by her body heat.

'I've spent years trying to carve something for myself completely unrelated to him or my past,' I say, spilling the words that will make her understand what she means to me. 'My relationship with you, my work—there's no hint of him there, and I love that, take pride in those areas of my life.' I can't be all bad, if she's believed in me all these years, but she deserves to understand the way I feel about Slay.

'Remember when I told you about Jane?' I say, gripping her hand.

'Your teenage girlfriend?' She nods, her eyes wary.

'Yeah. Well, when she dumped me, I was pretty cut up. When Slay noticed me moping, after a rare bout of parental observation, he insisted that the best way to get over her was to take me on a bender.' I let lose a hollow laugh at my own naivety. 'I fooled myself we were finally bonding in a meaningful father-son way rather than the superficial crap of most of my life up to that point.'

'Wasn't he ever a normal dad?' she asks, scooting closer, her shoulder pressing against mine in comfort and solidarity.

'If he was, I don't remember. Sid Coterill is always Slay, always on show. I'm not really sure why he even had a kid, but at least he didn't knock up all my stepmothers, so that's something.'

'So did the bender help with the heartbreak?' she asks.

I snort, continuing the sordid little tale I wish she didn't have to know. 'He took me to an LA strip club, the last place I needed. I was nineteen. Confused, because I was desperate to relate to him somehow, but also reeling from the loss of first love.'

Neve's hand squeezes mine.

'I realised he didn't know me at all. He didn't care enough to see how I felt. Instead of compassion and genuine connection, he bought me a table full of shots, a lap dance and then passed on one of his most valuable fatherly insights: "Plenty more willing pussy in the world, son".'

He'd then proceeded to tell me how my ex wasn't worth my regret, because she'd made a pass at him on more than one occasion and he'd nobly turned her down, as though he'd done me a favour or something.

I'd rushed to the bathroom and hurled an evening's worth of drinks into the toilet, along with any belief that I could trust a woman to want me for me, or that Slay actually cared for anyone but himself.

Eaten alive by the crippling humiliation, I can't look at Neve. I don't want to see horror or pity. But the memories stiffen my resolve. I won't allow Slay to ruin the one good relationship in my life.

I face her. 'I don't want a man who talks about women that way anywhere near you, the woman I respect most in the world.'

She's silent for a few painful beats of my heart. Then she whispers, 'I'm sorry you had such a crappy role model who didn't know what an amazing son he has. You're nothing like him.'

My gut twists. If only she knew how alike we truly are.

'What did you do after that?' she asks, and I stiffen. I can't confess how later that night I executed my revenge on Slay, with his third wife, although my shameful act hurt me more than it seemed to hurt him and still haunts me to this day.

'I moved out of his LA mansion and never went back.' I tug her into my arms then, squeezing the life from her and burying my nose in her hair so I can suck her comforting scent into my lungs. I can't fuck up again. I can't risk losing her, as I surely would if she knew the full story.

I feel her relax against me, relief shuddering through my frame.

'I'm sorry you had your heart broken,' she whispers.

'And I'm sorry about dinner.' I press a kiss to her temple. 'You never got to try my dessert.'

For the first time since we crossed the line, she laughs her familiar laugh. 'You can buy me another one tomorrow,' she mumbles against my chest and then pushes at my hips to break my hold on her. 'But we need to follow the rules if we're going to survive the rest of this holiday and go home still friends. No more discussing the sex.'

Relief pours through my veins. 'Okay...' I say, because I'll do anything for her. 'But it's hard not to discuss such awesome sex.' My dick twitches in my trousers. I shift my hips so she doesn't see how turned on I am and think I'm not taking her seriously. That she's giving me a second chance fuels my blood with adrenaline.

She wriggles, but I tighten my arm on her waist. I've held her before, of course—chaste, brief encounters when she's been upset or needed solace. But she feels different in my arms. More real. I don't want to let go, possession adding to her arousing closeness.

'Yes, it *was* awesome, but now it's over. And we both need to navigate this new territory.'

My fingers tense on her back. Everything inside me slows, apart from my uncontrollable galloping pulse. 'I don't want to it to be over.' Because now we're more than friends.

I've always wanted more. And now, when it's

hard to think of anything but how good we are together and how much I ache for her… There's no
going back to a version of us without this intimacy.
Not for me.

'Oliver, let's be realistic.' Her eyes cling to mine.
'We'll go home and go back to normal. You avoiding relationships and me looking for one.'

I stare so intently, I feel like my eyes are diamond-
cutting lasers. 'Don't talk about dating other men
when I can still taste you on my tongue. Still hear
your cries in my head. Still feel you clamped around
my dick.' The thought that she can easily forget
what happened between us and move on to some
dating-app jerk leaves me trembling with agitation.

Her tiny gasp, the excited flare of her eyes, con-
tradicts her next words. 'We can't do it again…'

Despite her caution, I feel the moment excitement
grips her, the increased breathing and the softening
of her muscles from rigid to slack. She still wants
me, and I want to lose myself in her. To relive how
good it was this morning, even though every detail
is etched into my brain.

I slowly nod my head, lowering my mouth closer
to hers while I keep eye contact. I want her in no
doubt of my feelings, and I want to witness her re-
actions. 'We definitely can. We were good together.
Astounding, in fact. Fuck the rules.'

She closes her eyes, as if seeking strength. Then
she opens them again. 'Olly—'

'Oliver,' I interrupt, because I'm not going backward. Not when her eyes dance over my face as if she's debating where to kiss me first. Not when her lips are right there, soft and inviting. Not when I know how one kiss will turn her passionate and demanding.

'I want you more than I did this morning,' I murmur, my voice low, my mouth so close to hers, one lunge is all it would take to put us out of our misery. 'I've wanted you ever since.'

My declaration is dangerous because this isn't an impulse driven by lust. I've had all day and the previous nine years to open my eyes and admit this fierce attraction, and I finally feel that if I work hard at it I could be man enough for Neve. Because she's my priority. There's no future I envisage or want without her.

I hold my breath while she says nothing, tension juddering through her small frame with each laboured breath.

Then, with a sexy little feminine groan, she lurches against me and presses her mouth to mine. Her arms encircle my shoulders and she straddles my lap as we kiss—lips devouring, tongues surging, breath mingling.

Unlike this morning, when I'd taken control, Neve's frantic kisses and grabbing hands are more demanding. More desperate.

Thank fuck, because I'm wild for her, and I was beginning to think I was in this state alone.

I collapse back onto the sand, my arm around her waist so she's sprawled over my chest. I slide my hands over her hips then cup her buttocks, pressing her closer to assuage the demands of my aching cock.

Neve breaks free of the kiss, braces her hands on my biceps and gives me a small shove as she sits up. I like the view of her over me, but I need to hear that she's with me before I vacate the driving seat.

'Tell me you want more awesome sex too,' I say. 'I want to hear it.'

'Yes, I want more. Of course I do,' she pants out, dropping kiss after kiss to my mouth and then nuzzling my neck in a way that has my hips bucking up between her legs.

I cup her face while my pulse pounds in the tips of my fingers, scared she'll feel it on her skin. I need to show her how important she is. How much I value her beyond this physical compulsion, which seems to have gripped us both.

'I'd never do anything to risk losing you. You're too important. Understand?' I hate the doubt I saw in her angry eyes earlier. Hate that I was the source. She's the most important person in my life. And if this was just sex, perhaps I'd find the strength to resist this chemistry, but it's more than that, more than I ever dreamed or knew was possible.

Her eyes droop, half-closed, and I feel her tiny nod between my palms.

She shuffles back and shoves my shirt up, trailing burning hot kisses over my chest. Staring up at me, she flicks her tongue over my pierced nipple. My abs crunch involuntarily and her hips grind on my erection, which is steel against the fly of my trousers. Damn, I want her, and I definitely don't have a condom.

'Now it's my turn to explore,' she says, attacking my fly with determined hands. My cock surges free between the open zip, the relief overwhelming, but reality dawns.

'I don't have a condom.' I doubt she does either, given her disappointment with me and her skimpy, pocket-less dress.

'I don't care.' She palms my erection, rubbing me through my boxers until I fist the fabric of her dress, which is ruched up over her pale thighs.

'You were so bossy this morning, I never got to put my mouth on you,' she says, licking her lips as she scoots back onto my thighs so she can tug my trousers and boxers over my hips.

'That's just the way I am, baby.' My voice is hoarse with longing, but laced with warning, because if that mouth, those plump lips and perfect Cupid's bow, gets anywhere near my dick… Game over.

'Mmm?' She bends close to trail her lips down my rigid stomach as she grips my aching length.

'I'll come…' I warn, my brain turning foggy with lust. God, she feels so good and looks even better, her beautiful familiar face slack with desire, her stunning breasts spilling over the top of the low neck of her dress, her hand and stare intent on my favourite appendage.

'Well, that's the idea.' She smiles up at me.

Any further argument evaporates as her hot mouth swallows the head of my cock and I'm there—helpless, craving, on the edge.

Neve sucks like she's enjoying a lollipop, her cheeks hollow, and then she releases me to trace the laving tip of her tongue down my shaft.

The cool night air hits my damp flesh. Dizzy with need, I prop myself up on my elbows, not wanting to miss one single second of this fantasy come true. How many times have I jerked off imagining her mouth on me, the daydream in no way preparing me for the fantastic reality? A reality which only gets better when she grips the base of my cock and takes me back inside the hot haven of her mouth while she moans out her pleasure at the power she wields.

'Touch yourself,' I bark, because there's no way I'm coming without her. My hips are already jerking of their own accord, my balls on fire and eyes gritty with the pressure of witnessing every incredible second of her mouth on me.

She looks up and slips her free hand under her

dress between her thighs. I fist her hair; she's kill-ing me. Could she be any more perfect? Any more addictive? Why did I wait so long to discover this side of her? A side I guessed was there all along but refused to see to keep myself sane.

But now I can open my eyes. Focus on the way her beautiful lips stretch around me, delivering plea-sure so intense, I'm seconds away from decimating my stamina record.

She smiles around me, actually smiles, looking up at me with such feminine power glowing in her eyes, I release a sort of feral growl. A noise I've never made before, like some kind of tortured ani-mal.

What is she doing to me? Have I ever been this hot for a woman? This incapacitated by need?

I'm passing the point of no return. The sight of her sucking me while she touches herself, the pres-sure building in my balls and the heat boiling at the base of my spine watching her own me, glorying in her possession... It's all too much.

'Neve...' I cup her face, my thumb swiping her bottom lip stretched around me, my other hand tun-nelling into her hair. 'I'm going to come. I'm warn-ing you.'

I have no idea if my sweet friend will swallow me or watch me spill over my own stomach. And I don't care either way; I'm lost to her in this mo-ment. Whatever she wants, fine by me.

She sinks deeper, sucks harder. Her hand gripping my shaft is her answer. She rubs herself more vigorously, her whimpers telling me she's close too.

I'm helpless to stop the cascade of unparalleled pleasure beginning deep in my pelvis, streaks of lava streaming along my length as I empty myself into her mouth with a broken cry.

She sucks me dry, swallowing every drop, her hand still working furiously between her legs, her hips undulating to her own blissful rhythm. I'm spent, still coming down from the incredible high, but I want to reward her for the best blow job I've ever had. When she releases me, I sit up, dragging her close with one arm around her waist so I can kiss her. I slip my hand between her legs, my fingers joining hers to rub over her slick, heated and swollen flesh. I push my tongue into her mouth just as she whimpers out the first crest of her orgasm, kissing her through spasm after spasm of her bucking body.

Sudden jealousy rages through me, smacking me like a rogue wave. I want to lay claim to all her orgasms. I want to be on hand to deliver all her pleasure now we've shared this, and there's only one way to achieve that goal.

'You're not sweet at all, are you?' I press my forehead to hers and scrunch my eyes closed, holding her while she catches her breath.

'No,' she pants. 'I'm definitely not.'

I squeeze her tighter, the beach spinning a little. 'I love that about you, you bad woman,' I say, pressing my lips to her temple.

Yeah, I'd say our friendship as was is pretty much over.

CHAPTER NINE

Neve

I WAVER BETWEEN sleep and wakefulness, emerging from the best dream, desperate to prolong the delirious pleasure. Dream Oliver is back, and he's kissing my naked body, each nipple, my stomach and then between my legs. Hot, sexy open-mouthed kisses...

I open my eyes, this dream so vivid. I look down, still groggy but rapidly waking with every zap of fire that knifes through me.

It's not a dream.

Oliver is licking me awake. I groan, gasp, my head falling back on the pillow and my thighs parting to accommodate his broad shoulders. Then I look back down, expecting some wisecrack or teasing glint in his breathtaking eyes. But he's serious, his stare intense, raking over my every reaction to the lashing of his clever tongue.

I can't look away from the sight of his mouth

on me. The heat in his eyes. The sounds of early-morning paradise beyond the window. My impending orgasm peters out—I'm in deep trouble, addicted to him, to his touch, now that of a lover. The best lover I've ever had. No surprises there.

How will I ever be able to stop craving this, him, when our every kiss, every caress, every intimacy answers a deep longing inside. A deeper connection with a man I already know so well. A complex man with demons and struggles, just like the rest of us. A man with a massive heart he's too scared to trust.

Last night at dinner, I thought this was over. Being shut out reminded me of all the reasons I've fiercely fought my feelings for him for so long. His past with Slay as a role model, his rejection of serious relationships—he's not ready to allow someone close yet. Perhaps he never will be.

My heart spasms, pain pulsing. I don't want to be his fledgling foray into something beyond sex. I can't afford to be the test case. I'm ahead of him where relationships are concerned and, after a few hard-learned lessons of my own, I know what I want.

But he's still content with casual.

I need to be careful, oh, so careful to protect my heart. Focussing on the chemistry, the pleasure, helps. Because right now that's all I can trust. All I can expect.

I cradle his face, my fingers tangling in his

messy hair, my stare locked with his, and whisper his name.

Wordlessly, and despite my cry of protest, he takes his mouth from me and crawls up the bed, settling his hips in the cradle of mine and pushing into me in one smooth glide. My sensitive peaked nipples chafe on his chest hair, his piercing adding an extra layer of friction. I tug his mouth down to mine, our tongues connecting, surging, duelling as sure as the deep and sublime ecstasy of his penetration.

We don't speak, but we don't need to. His fingers tangle in my hair, cradle my face in his hands, his arm gripping my shoulders as over and over again he thrusts into me in watchful silence. But there's nothing to say that we didn't cover last night. We both want this. We're both willing to endanger our friendship, both confident we can manage the fall out of this risky indulgence.

Oliver scoops one of my thighs over his arm and then the other, his hips sinking lower, closer, so that every thrust batters my clit until it's all I can do to hold on to him and trust that he won't leave me behind.

His mouth finds my nipple, licking, flicking, nibbling, and the flames start in the pit of my pelvis.

'Oliver!' I cry out with a desperate voice. That of a woman I no longer recognise, changed perhaps forever by allowing him this close.

Then he speaks at last, his voice gruff, perhaps

with the first words of the day or just with the emotion I see in his eyes. 'Say you're mine right now.' He clenches his jaw on the order, thrusting harder, deeper.

His eyes are almost turquoise with desire, more intense and serious than I've ever seen him, his ownership euphoric.

'Tell me,' he barks, his angular face taut with his own mounting desire. 'Before I give you your next orgasm.'

He's controlling this, us, and it's the hottest thing I've ever heard him say. Because I *am* his. He's taking me on a journey of discovery and I can't deny him, or my own needs, even as I try to hold something back for self-preservation.

My breath catches. I want to give him what he needs more than I want the pleasure he's holding to ransom. But I know it's a reaction to what he confided about Slay. I know it's not a lasting promise he wants from me.

'I'm yours!' I yell as he delivers thrust after thrust. Each blow devastates as I'm tossed over the edge into a rapturous climax, where my only awareness is how loud I scream his name and how tight I clutch him inside my body. He groans out his own release, collapsing his weight on top of me and burying his face against my neck.

I want to laugh or cry, but I do neither, because love, this fear of his power to hurt me, is no laughing matter, and I'm sliding, falling, being dragged under with every kiss, every touch, every orgasm.

No, that could all be lust, right? The inevitable side-effect of such amazing sex. Because I can't love Oliver more than I already do. I'll be torn apart.

My body grows restless under his crushing weight, fear snaking along my nerve endings, but I don't want to move. I want to lie here and pretend everything is as it was a few days ago.

He stirs, kissing my neck and then rising to take care of the condom in the bathroom. When he returns, he's donned his tight black boxers and hands me one of his white T-shirts. And everything seems normal. The new normal, anyway. No need to panic.

'It's a stunning day for a wedding,' he says. 'Come and have breakfast. I arranged it out on the balcony while you were asleep.' His face is relaxed, open, but goose bumps rise on my arms. I'm reading way too much into that possessive demand spoken in the heat of the moment.

I shrug into his over-sized shirt, take his hand and follow him out to his bungalow's private deck. We're faced with endless ocean views hazy with the fierce morning sun. I take a seat, my stomach flipping at the fact that he's been up early organising the delicious spread I see laid out.

'I asked the staff to prepare a coconut-free breakfast, so you can eat anything you like,' he says, removing covers from the food. My aversion to the tropical staple is well-known, but I'm still humbled that he went to such trouble. I tuck into some fruit and yoghurt while Oliver helps himself to toast.

'So what will you wear today?' he asks, scooting his chair a few inches closer to mine so that when we eat our arms graze. I force the mouthful past my tight throat, trying to pretend I haven't noticed.

'Um... I thought I'd wear a sundress.' This new attentive side of him, one I've never experienced on such an intimate level, blurs the boundaries I'm trying to reconstruct around our new but temporary relationship.

'Is it red?' he asks, his stare full of renewed heat. 'You looked beautiful last night in red. You should wear it more often.'

I almost choke on a piece of melon. It's hard enough to resist flirty, playful friend Oliver, but charming, sexy lover Oliver is almost too much for my frazzled ovaries. My mouth opens, no answer emerging, because this Oliver—sex-rumpled, attentive and romantic—may as well be a virtual stranger. If I'd known this side of him, would I have acted on my attraction sooner, confessing that my feelings for him had transcended platonic from day one? Would I have demanded the number one spot in his life and not settled for what at times over the years felt like second place?

Precarious breath shudders out of me as I shrug.

History's proved this privileged position of lover in his life is short-lived. As he admitted last night, he considers himself incapable of commitment because he's Slay's son, so there's no future for us.

I cannot get carried away by his romantic gestures. We said we wouldn't allow this to damage us. I have to have faith in my own abilities to stay grounded, and Oliver's word that he won't allow anything to break us. His over-protectiveness around his father is his way of doing just that.

'There's a swimming with dolphins experience tomorrow, if you'd like to go?' he says, pushing a lock of my hair back behind my ear. Then he slides the plate bearing his last half-slice of toast in my direction.

I nod, close to inexplicable tears. 'That sounds perfect. I'd love to.' Perhaps it's the emotion of the wedding brewing—I always cry at weddings. Or his gesture—saving me some of his food reminds me that my Oliver, the one I know beyond these wonderful new revelations, is still here.

I take the toast with a small smile. 'Thanks.'

His easy grin is infectious, settling some of my doubts. If I'm not careful, I run the risk of spoiling the best week of my life by over-thinking. I should just enjoy as much time as we have and deal with the fallout back home in London, where I'll be able to escape the daily addiction of him while we both live our separate lives.

'So tell me about the Kimoto deal,' I say, pouring some tea and taking a bite of his toast. 'Any news?' He's worked long and hard on the artificial intelligence software this past year.

He runs his fingers through his hair and puts down his mug. 'It's with the lawyers, so I'm hoping for good news today. I should really be back in the office, but I couldn't let Shelley down after promising to fly the wedding guests here. My team have everything under control. I just...'

I reach for his hand and he grips my fingers. 'This deal is important to me. I take my work very seriously and I want Kimoto to see that. The last thing I need is Slay causing a scene. It almost feels like he'd deliberately sabotage this for me.' His leg jiggles under the table.

'Why would he do that?' I ask, horrified that any parent could act vengefully.

He shrugs. 'There's no love lost between us. And if he can tag some mention of himself onto my company news...' He smiles a humourless smile. 'Part of me was naive enough to think I could have this one success all to myself.'

'It's a big deal for you outside of the financial gain, isn't it?'

He nods, tension radiating from his body. 'My team have been working on this software for years—they deserve to have their work valued. This will make international headlines for all the right reasons. And I hate the fact that my past… Slay's reputation…might ruin that for everyone involved.'

'You deserve the recognition, too.' My heart clenches. 'I don't think I realised how much you've struggled with the two sides of your life.' The self-made professional businessman and the privileged celebrity son growing up in the shadow of his father's fame. After what he confessed last night, it's no wonder the Oliver I first met was a little wild.

'Perhaps this deal will put an end to those comparison stories,' I say. 'It's not like you ever trade on Slay's fame.'

His grin is wry. 'I might have used that once or twice to impress women or get laid before I met you. And I fully admit I've done my fair share of acting out in the past, earned my own reputation…'

'Or perhaps you were simply out-running Slay's. From what you've told me, it's doesn't sound like he made any attempt to protect you from his fame or the excesses of his world, as some celebrity parents do.'

He stares, his eyes burning into mine, as if it's never occurred to him to show himself compassion for being young and rudderless and making a bad choice.

'We all make mistakes, experiment with who we want to be,' I go on. 'You've built a successful, innovative company from nothing. You look after your staff, attracting and retaining the best brains in the industry.' I offer him the last bite of toast, even though there's more on the table. Shared food somehow tastes better.

He eats it from my fingers, setting off delicious tingles of pleasure in my pelvis. 'Yeah, well, the tech world evolves so rapidly, experience only counts for so much.' He runs a hand over his face and I notice new creases at the corners of his eyes. 'It's a young person's field—even I'm getting a little long in the tooth to keep up.'

I can't resist a confirmatory ogle of his ripped torso, decorated with tattoos. 'Oh, yes, ancient. You're only thirty. And it may be a young person's game, but you're the one with the leadership skills and the vision to recruit those young geniuses. You're the one who built on the success of Never Scan.' I mention the software he developed at uni that launched him onto the path to his first million.

'Well, that was down to you,' he says, growing serious, his stare intent.

I laugh. 'Just because I did your company accounts for a few years doesn't mean I'm in any way responsible for the things you've achieved.'

His hand shifts to my arm, the slow swipe of his thumb back and forth sensual and distracting. 'You're totally responsible,' he disagrees. 'That's why I named the software after you.'

This revelation is news to me. 'But...' I gape in shock. 'I thought...' I had no idea the name of the first software he developed had been named after his nickname for me. I'd assumed it was the other, more common, usage of the word because, aside from the accounting software he designed especially for my business, I have no understanding of what he does. Teasing me for my technophobia is one of his favourite pastimes.

'You didn't know?' he asks, his eyes alight with mischief as he relaxes back in his chair, still gripping my fingers.

I shake my head, dumbfounded.

'It's true. You believed in me at a time when I needed someone. You listened when I spent hours talking about stuff I knew you didn't understand, and you convinced me I was onto something worth developing. Encouraged me to not give up. I wouldn't be here, wouldn't be making billion-pound deals, without you.' He leans close, lifts my hand to his mouth and kisses my knuckles one by one, his eyes on mine. 'That's why I gave you shares.'

Pressure builds in my chest, and the hot aching in my throat and the sting in my eyes returns. 'I thought the shares were a really nerdy birthday present.'

He laughs, tugging me into his kiss. 'Well, they were that too. But you see how I know this, us, is going to work out? Because you know me. You see *me*, when most other people see my reputation and family notoriety, the fickle bits of celebrity that have rubbed off on me over the years from living in Slay's world. But you understand that's not who I am, and you still like me.'

'I do like you,' I say, my breath trapped in my chest, because the other 'L' word wants to break free.

'The feeling is entirely mutual.' He kisses me again, long and lingering and ending on a sigh. 'We should get ready.' He looks at his watch. 'The bride will kill me if I keep her waiting because I'm buried inside you.'

The heat in his stare tells me he's serious.

I rouse myself, needing a few minutes away from his all-consuming presence to gather my wits. Oliver in flat-out charming mode is dangerous for my judgement, because I'm becoming more and more ensnared in him and the way he makes me feel... special.

Oh, how bright and brilliant it is here in the beam of Oliver's focus.

But special isn't enough. I want to be everything to him, and he's shy of commitment, something he's never wanted or even considered, thanks to Slay. While I will always support him, can I invest time and energy into guiding him through his relationship phobia when I'm already so emotionally attached? That seems like the road to certain heartbreak. And given the depth of his commitment issues, maybe he'll simply be content to slip back into his casual routine once we're back in London and he's surrounded by willing women.

I retire to my own room to shower and change for the wedding ceremony. I wish I could don a protective shell like the hermit crabs we see on the beach. Because my mind is foggy with Oliver's shock revelations and the flares of hope they've sparked. Do I really know him at all? Yes, I know the playful, generous friend he's been for nine years. But the man trying to outgrow his reputation and break away from any association with Slay—is this the part of him that's always called to me on a deeper level? The part I've been waiting for?

I'm putting the finishing touches to my make-up when there's a knock at the door.

My heart races with anticipation, because I've been away from him for thirty minutes and already I miss his company. Miss the way he takes my hand and does that swiping thing on my skin with his thumb. Miss his frequent passionate kisses, as if he can no more stop himself than I can. Miss those seriously hot looks that pass between us fifty times a day.

How did we look at each other before we began this intimacy? Will I always crave him this way, now that I know exactly how much more there is to lose? And can I risk exposing my heart to pain on the off chance he'll one day decide he's ready for more?

I yank open the door. Oliver stands on the other side, his hair still damp from the shower and his white linen shirt open at the neck to reveal a delicious triangle of tanned chest and a smattering of manly dark hair. In his outstretched hand is a single flower that matches the one he wears as a buttonhole.

The world tilts a fraction at the gorgeous sight he makes. I'm playing with fire, the flames already licking along my fingers. 'Have you lost your key?'

He shakes his head, his stare raking mine in that way that reminds me of how he looks at me when he's deep inside me, before swooping the length of my body to take in my outfit—a strappy, slinky sheath dress in teal, chosen for how sexy it makes me feel. For him.

Appreciation and something darker, more seductive, shines in his eyes. 'Can I accompany you to the wedding, Miss Grayson?' He tucks the single bloom into my hair, behind one ear and my core clenches with longing. I want to launch myself back into his arms, drag him into my room and keep him prisoner until it's time to go home and put an end to this dangerous fantasy.

His fingertips graze my cheek before he drops his arm and he holds out his hand for mine.

Oh, no, no, no…

I'm in deep trouble. Every second I grow more invested is a threat to my very being.

But I take his hand without hesitation, trying to put all of these burgeoning feelings into perspective. We pad on bare feet down to the beach where his family is assembled on the sand at the rustic altar, casting each other wider and wider smiles, as if we have a secret. I'm caught up in the romance, only vaguely aware of Slay Coterill and his sixth wife near the front; it's as if Oliver and I are sealed inside an invisible bubble, with eyes only for each other, the rest of the world shut out. I can't stop looking at him—so handsome, every inch familiar but in sharper focus—and every time I do his eyes are on me, ablaze with hunger that helps to remind me why we started this physical exploration. There's no place for my romantic imaginings.

The ceremony is short and beautiful. My hand rests in Oliver's throughout, exotic but so addictive, because it feels like it belongs. And of course he produces a crisp white handkerchief from his pocket when inevitable tears dampen my lashes. I stop fighting myself, uncaring who sees our togetherness. People can think what they like about me, his friend-lover.

I dab my eyes, careful of my mascara, while Oliver tugs me under his arm and presses a kiss to my temple. 'You are so adorable.' His smile is indulgent but still laced with that fervent hunger I burn for. Because now he knows I'm no longer just his 'sweet' friend. I'm badly desperate for him.

I laugh, drying the last of my tears and handing him back his handkerchief.

'I'm bad, remember? I want things,' I whisper. 'You, every way possible,' I go on, the scrape of my dress over my distended swollen nipples excruciating. 'How soon before we can sneak away?'

His stare darkens. 'I want you too, but we have to make an appearance at the wedding lunch.'

I sigh but smile. We have time. Days.

'An appearance' turns into hours—photographs, a delicious wedding feast, toasts and dancing. It's after a turn on the dance floor—a patch of the white sand beach under a gazebo decorated with fairy lights—that our escape is interrupted by Slay. We've managed to dodge him all day by avoiding the bar, where he's entertained his audience.

'Son! Come and have a drink with me and your stepmum,' he calls, making a grand gesture with his outstretched arms and booming voice, so Oliver is forced to stop to avoid a scene.

'I'm sorry,' Oliver whispers to me under his breath.

'Bring your lady-friend,' says Slay, winking my way, then laying twin kisses on my cheeks before either of us can utter one word of protest or make our excuses. Oliver's stepmother number five, who looks a couple of years younger than us, barely looks up from her phone.

'Sid,' says Oliver in a clipped tone. 'We were

just leaving, actually. And this is Neve.' The term 'lady-friend' clearly upset him more than it did me.

Slay's stare hardens at the use of his real name, presumably the reason Oliver used it. He slouches back in his seat, spreads his tight leather-trouser-clad thighs. His shirt hangs open to the waist to reveal a waxed, tanned torso decorated with ink.

'Leaving this early?' he asks, raising a near-empty bottle of champagne, waggling it at a waiter to indicate he wants a replacement. 'That's not very rock and roll.'

I rest my hand on Oliver's rigid back, stilling him from reacting to the puerile jibe.

'Fabulous resort, isn't it?' Slay lights a cigarette and squints at me through the smoke.

He's not exactly leering, but I grow conscious of the strappy nature of my dress and the fact I'm not wearing a bra. My body grows stiff, all the lovely feel-good hormones of the romantic day draining away.

'So, did you guys meet here?' asks Slay, with an oily smile.

I step closer to Oliver's side, my hand gripping his shirt at the small of his back—non-verbal communication that I don't need rescuing.

'Neve is a very old friend.' Oliver's voice is aloof, tension pouring from his body.

My insides jolt at Oliver's descriptor. I don't really mind that he introduces me that way, but Slay's clearly never heard of me. Not once in the past nine years has my name come up. To him I'm just another of his son's temporary women. And, like Oliver's current stepmother, one of a long list…

I know Oliver said he's trying to protect me, but I can't help the tiny stabs of insecurity that rain down on me. Perhaps he doesn't trust that I can handle Slay's celebrity. Perhaps he thinks I'd become starstruck after all. Hardly…

But it reminds me of my place in Oliver's life these past nine years, and it's not the place I want. The place I began to dream for.

Slay seems to relish the discomfort he's causing. 'Well, don't keep her all to yourself,' he says before taking a deep drag from his cigarette. 'It's rude not to share.' Something like menace or challenge sneaks into Slay's eyes as he toes out a spare stool in invitation. 'Why don't you both sit down?'

It sounds like a dare. The air around our small group seems to freeze. The smell of testosterone emanates from father and son, each locked into a stand-off that zaps the atmosphere with animosity.

What the hell…? I've had enough.

'That's really kind of you, Mr Coterill,' I say, coming to my senses. 'But I have a bit of a headache. Some other time, perhaps.' I tug Oliver's arm, trying to drag him away from the situation, which seems to have made him furious.

'Of course. I look forward to it,' Slay says, ignoring Oliver, his eyes on me in some sort of act of defiance.

We're almost back to Oliver's bungalow, my footsteps rapid to keep up with his longer strides and my hand crushed in his, before I risk conversation.

'What the hell was that all about?' I ask as he unlocks the door and strides inside.

He tosses the key card onto a nearby chair, flicks on the lamp and pours himself a whisky from the mini-bar. 'Want one?' he asks, ignoring my question.

'Yes please,' I reply, accepting the drink and watching him knock his back in a determined swallow. Why the hell is he so angry? I'm the one who was passive-aggressively insulted and ogled by Slay and reinstated to the friend zone by Oliver.

'I told you he's an asshole. I warned you he'd flirt with you—with his wife right there…. And he's an addict—he's not supposed to be drinking. Now do you see why I tried to keep you two apart? He's hardly the most flattering of fathers.' He yanks his shirt off, slings it onto the chair and strides to the bathroom.

I follow, sipping my whisky to calm my nerves at the vision of his naked torso, tanned and tattooed, his jeans riding low on his narrow hips.

'I told you I could look after myself. No need to go head-to-head with him. Don't you trust me?' I challenge, directing my disappointment away from the reminder that I'll soon be back to my former role—an old friend. And it shouldn't bother me, because I can't allow myself to harbour my growing feelings. Oliver turns on the tap and splashes his face with cold water, one hand braced on the side of the sink.

I understand that Slay and Oliver aren't close, but it seemed as if things would come to blows down there on the beach. If ever there was a way to land yourself in the news, it would be publicly decking a world-famous rock star. And why is he letting Slay get to him so badly?

'Of course I trust you, although I don't understand why you're not running away from me and my fucked-up family as fast as you can,' he says, drying his face with a towel. 'But, if you're staying...' His voice ominously grows quiet. 'I'll defend and protect you any damn way I like.'

My pussy clenches at his commanding tone even as I say, 'Don't be ridiculous. How Slay behaves has no bearing on my feelings for you.' I don't want to add to his mood by addressing the fact that the father he seems embarrassed of looked at me as if he might be lining me up to be wife number seven. 'And I'm tougher than I look.'

Am I tough enough? I *should* run, but only to protect my heart from a man who's a commitment-phobe.

The real issue here is us—our unfinished business. The reminder I'm just one of a long list of women makes my skin crawl. I feel the need to mark him somehow. To be memorable. To stand out so he'll never forget the madness of our holiday fling.

'Fuck Slay,' I say, venting my frustration that Oliver seems to be allowing his father issues to hold him back. I step closer, commanding his eye contact as I press my lips to the rim of my glass and take a slow swallow of whisky. 'I won't let whatever that was out there ruin today. Ruin us and the time we have left here. I want you. I've wanted you all day. I don't give a shit about your father. This is between us and I'm exactly where I want to be.' If I can't have more of him than great sex, I'll take it again and again as compensation. 'So, if you're so intent on looking after me, why don't you do something about my current state?'

His face is tight with a frown. I hold out my glass to him and he takes it, knocking back the dregs then placing it on the vanity. His arm scoops around my waist, hauling me close so I'm pressed against all that yummy, pretty, naked chest.

'Is that right?' His eyes glitter, the romantic lover absent while his heart thunders against my sensitive breasts.

I trace the piercing in his left nipple with one index finger, rubbing over the barbell, making his abs contract and his hard cock jerk against my belly. Feminine power ignites in me, my limbs languid and my body temperature spiking.

'Yes.' I slide the finger down the ridge of his abdominal muscles, dipping inside his navel before unbuttoning the top button of his fly. My teeth trap my bottom lip as I look up from the trail of hair dipping into his waistband. I slide my fingertip to the head of his cock, feeling the tiny wet patch where he's leaked on the fabric of his fly.

I lift his free hand from his hip and wedge it between my legs so he can feel the heat and moisture I'm generating. 'I need what only you can give me.' Can't he see we're all that matters? Can't he feel how easy it would be to lose ourselves and block out the rest of the world, just as we have all day at the wedding? Can't he trust that there's so much more to him than being his father's son and the limitations he's placed around his heart?

'Neve,' he warns, his tone still brittle. 'Don't goad me—I'm in no mood to go easy on you.'

I tilt my chin, pressing my open mouth to his collarbone, his neck and his stubble-covered jaw. 'I want you as you are. You know me as well as I know you. You know what I need, what my body likes, and I trust you. You'd never hurt me.' I slide my tongue over his parted lips, my hand stroking him through his jeans so I feel the jerks of his cock that let me know my words, my demands, excite him.

I gasp, laugh, groan as he snatches his hand from between my legs, cups my face and pushes me back against the tiles, kissing me and then dropping his mouth to my breast so he can tongue my nipple through my dress. I yank open the remaining buttons of his fly but, before I can get my hand on his erection, he bunches my dress around my waist and drops to his knees.

'Fuck, I can't get enough of you,' he says, his forehead pressed to my stomach, breath panting between my legs. 'I should never have touched you, but it's too late. You're addictive.' His audible, prolonged inhale ends on a groan as he buries his face against my mound and laves my clit through the lace of my panties. 'I wanted to kill him for looking at you that way,' he says about Slay.

My heart surges at the return of that possessiveness that weakens my knees. I spread my thighs to accommodate his broad shoulders and grip his hair in my hands, twisting the strands with enough force to tilt his eyes—which are impassioned and stormy—up to mine.

'I wanted you to touch me. So badly. Only you can give me what I need, what my body craves. I'm yours.' For now.

He seems to need my admission, his stare burning through me. 'Fuck yes, you are.' He groans, sliding the crotch of my underwear aside so he can put his mouth on me in that way I've come to expect— hot, greedy, carnal. I throw one leg over his shoulder, digging my heel into his back as his tongue spears me, his big hands filled with the cheeks of my arse, and I cry out, my head thumping the wall behind.

His tongue lashes my clit, alternating with deep plunges inside. I grip his hair and ride his face, desperate now for the orgasms he can deliver. Desperate to come for him and desperate for more. For it all. Because this isn't going away. This need isn't diminishing. And if I glut myself now, take all I can have of him, perhaps I'll be able to live off the memories when it ends.

I'm skirting the cusp of my climax when he slides his fingers inside me, two, three, stretching me. Plunging. I cry out in despair when his fingers leave me and I glare down at him, about to demand he put them back when I feel him probe my rear with his moisture-slicked fingers.

I stare into his fierce eyes, and a gasp rips from my throat at the foreign, thrilling contact. He watches my reaction, his mouth quirking a fraction, his groan of praise weakening my knees. Because I'm his, whether I like it or not. Whether he thinks he deserves me or not. And I trust him with my body, my pleasure, my life.

He's shown me what I'm capable of, shown me how well he knows me. And I want this, want him all the ways I can have him until my time is up.

But I also want to undo him. To take him on this roller coaster of need right alongside me. 'Oliver,'

I say, gripping his face while he eats at me. 'That feels so good, but I want your cock in me.'

He pulls his mouth from me, his fingers still working in my crease, massaging, gliding over my sensitive rear, waking up nerve endings I didn't know I possessed.

'Say it again,' he grinds out, his voice breaking. 'Say you're mine and I'll give you my cock. I'll make you come.'

'I'm yours,' I say, the words heavier every time I speak them. But I can't focus on the future, not when I want to burn in every present moment with him.

He rises to his feet, shucking his jeans and boxers and kicking them away, then he stands naked before me, his fist wrapped around his glorious penis, sliding and tugging his long length. Taunting me. I whimper at the sight. Slide my dress from my shoulders where it pools at my feet.

'Leave the thong on,' he commands, and I'm past caring that I'm half-in half-out of my underwear. I grip his hips and pull him close. 'I'm yours,' I whisper against his lips, which smell of my own arousal. 'What are you going to do with me?' I ask, before sliding my mouth to his nipple and gently tugging on the piercing with my teeth.

He grunts, his fingers digging into my hips as he spins me around so I'm in front of him, facing the sink, and his cock glides between my arse cheeks, the wet tip nudging the small of my back.

Our reflections stare back at us. Him a tall, bronzed god and me flushed pink with lust and longing. And something else. Something too terrifying to name, because it mustn't be true. I mustn't let it be.

'Bend over,' he says.

I obey, bracing my hands on the edge of the vanity, my focus on breathing, an act which should be automatic but feels precarious. He leans over my back, his scruff scraping at my neck and the juncture of my shoulder as his hands cup my breasts.

His thumbs rub my nipples and I cry his name. 'There's a condom in my wash bag there,' he says, sucking on my skin and sliding one hand back to my slick clit. 'Get it.'

I fumble in my haste, and when I locate the foil square I feel the nip of his teeth against my skin, as if he's reached his limit.

He sheathes himself quickly and then his stare meets mine in the mirror. We're both panting hard with anticipation and, just like our first time together, I marvel at his stamina, because I'm achy, needy, empty and ready to beg, to end this torture of wanting.

'Oliver...' I spread my legs in invitation, tilting my hips back. 'I want to be yours, to be bad for you.'

His eyes are so dark, so hooded, I can't make out the blue any longer.

'Even if I ruin you?' he asks, his fingers still strumming between my legs.

'Yes.' I don't hesitate. But he could never ruin me.

His nostrils flare and his jaw bunches as he seems to wrestle with my declaration. He looks down, strokes my back as if with reverence, and then slides my thong from between the cheeks of my arse. He positions himself at my slick entrance and then grips my shoulder in one hand, surging forward on a single, delicious thrust that has me rising up onto tiptoes to accommodate him.

His thrusts knock me forward. I lock my arms and push back, each slap of his thighs against mine thrilling and, oh, so debauched. He releases my hip, his fingers coming between my legs from the front to collect some of the moisture coating me, and then he returns those wicked fingers to my rear.

'Do you like this? Is this what you want?' he asks.

'Oliver, yes…' I mewl, my back arching as he strokes with increased pressure over my pucker.

'Rub your clit,' he barks, his face almost unrecognisable with the violence of his arousal.

I do his bidding with a helpless yelp, my fingers sliding around the base of his thrusting cock and then rubbing over my engorged, needy clit.

We lock eyes in the mirror, so many unspoken words passing between us in silent communication. I rub hard, so close to climaxing now I'm full of him.

'I trust you,' I say, because I want to give him all of me, but I can't trust myself that I won't fall so hard, so deep, that I'll never be the same.

At my words his fingers dig into my shoulder, his thrusts deeper, and he presses a fingertip into my rear.

I'm tossed into an orgasm so profound, I'm vaguely aware of screaming his name and of his own shout of unrestrained pleasure before the world seems to go black, my five fingers clinging to the edge of the vanity being my only grip on sanity.

Oliver leaves my body, tugging me into his arms and sliding us to the bathroom tiles. His kisses pepper my face, my closed eyelids, his gusting breath telling me he too is still reeling. He holds me tight, his arms possessive around my waist.

'You're mine,' he whispers against my temple. 'Mine.'

CHAPTER TEN

Oliver

I SWIM TOWARDS the back of the boat behind Neve after a day spent snorkelling and sailing, just the two of us. But I'm still distracted by what happened with Slay. I'd wanted to gouge out his eyes when he looked at Neve as if she was just another potential notch on his guitar. And when he disrespected her with that snide dig at me about sharing... I saw red, and for the first time in my life I'd wanted to hit my own father. To punch his million-dollar veneered teeth down his throat. And I might have, if Neve hadn't defused the situation.

But that would have shown her exactly what I'm trying to conceal. Proved how much alike Slay and I really are in some areas. And I'm not ready to have her despise me the way I despised myself for many years. How could I have allowed Slay to burrow so deep under my skin last night?

It's Neve. I've fallen for her so easily, and it's

as if Slay has deliberately come here to remind me of my every failing. I'm so buggered. I knew it the minute I opened my eyes after our first night together, and the fact was again cemented last night when Slay uttered the word *share* and I realised how much I had to lose.

Neve clambers aboard and then leans over to take my snorkel mask and flippers. We haven't discussed it since the conversation in the bathroom last night. We showered and lay naked and entwined beneath the cool sheets all night. I couldn't sleep, which meant I watched her sleep, marvelling at how perfect she is and how blind I've been all this time. But Slay's presence, his little pissing contest last night in front of Neve, brought all my fears screaming to the forefront of my mind.

I don't deserve her. All these years I've avoided relationships in order to protect myself from the pain and humiliation I felt at nineteen. I messed up following my split with Jane, crossing a line with Slay's then-wife number three, proving how much like him I am. And I'll likely mess up again if I try to have something real and committed with Neve.

But the selfishness that boils inside me won't allow me to give her up…

Silently, we rinse off the sea water under the deck shower and then stretch out on a couple of loungers to enjoy the rest of the cruise around the atolls. Meanwhile, I debate how much of my secret she needs to know. Probably all of it, before she hears it from Slay.

'I can't believe we actually got to see dolphins,' Neve says, excitement still gleaming in her eyes. 'And that turtle was so beautiful.'

'Pretty cool, eh? I thought the manta ray was the most impressive. Drink?' I ask, selecting two ice-cold beers from the mini-fridge on the aft deck.

She nods, accepting my offering with a smile I now claim as mine. Just for me. Because it lights her eyes so I see things there that give me hope. The sensual heat is an incredible privilege, yes, but there's also wonder and longing…as if she almost believes I'm the only man who can give her what she needs.

If only I was worthy of such belief. Statistically, I'm likely to disappoint and hurt her just as much if not more than the SBF Club…

'Thanks for organising this—it's a perfect way to have some space away from the others,' she says about our private cruise with an experienced local captain. I arranged it so we could be assured of the best snorkelling spots and for his insider knowledge of the spinner dolphins, which frequent these waters.

Her reminder of my possessive leanings and the way our day almost derailed after a two-minute conversation with Slay pricks my skin with guilt. I need to be more open. Her push-back last night shocked me. It never occurred to me that she'd assume I didn't trust her. It's Slay I don't trust. And myself.

But the last thing I want is him, or anything else, to come between us. I start with the easy news.

'I agree. I don't think we'll be seeing Slay again. I heard this morning that my latest stepmother is history and he's gone back to LA.' I try to keep the relief from my tone.

'Oh dear,' she replies not bothering with commiserations. Now that she's met Slay, she can see for herself that he'd stand a much better chance if he married a woman he shares something in common with.

'Yeah,' I snort. 'Don't feel too sorry for him. It's only a matter of time before the next twentysomething catches his eye.'

'How do you feel about that? Are you calm enough to talk about it?' she probes, her hand on my thigh caressing away my agitation.

I shrug, pretending I can't recall the sinking feeling every time a fresh wedding invitation from Slay lands on the mat. 'You saw them together last night. Hardly a love match. Next time, he should at least try to find someone who isn't after him for their fifteen minutes of fame. But perhaps that's the attraction for him—the adoration. Until they get to know him.' Resentment bubbles up anew inside me. I hate that I almost allowed Slay to ruin what I have with Neve.

Until I touched her, until he met her and showed me how much is at stake, I thought his hold over me was long past. In one way or another, he's influenced every relationship I've ever had, whether disabusing me of my faith in first love, or through the early days after I came to London when I slept around as if to prove something—maybe that I could switch off the emotions that made me vulnerable. Or simply that Slay didn't have the monopoly on bad-boy behaviour. And now I'm allowing him to cast doubt over what I have with Neve, this overwhelming need to protect her. I fear that I can't commit and be what she deserves.

Because, for the first time in over ten years, I want to commit.

But could she ever take me seriously, knowing me as she does? And now also knowing Slay...

'I have spoken about you to him before,' I say, needing to reassure her. 'He's just too self-absorbed to notice what other people say most of the time.' However Slay tried to paint her as some hook-up I'd just met, my feelings for her are deeper than ever. For the first time in a decade—not that the first time counted—I was barely a man. I think I might be in love. Terrifying, all-consuming love.

Panic beads sweat on the back of my neck. How can I confess that when there are more pressing things I need her to know? I feel like I'm about to split open, all my ugly secrets spilling free. Am I ready to expose my true self, the me I see every time I think about Slay? Will she still want me when she knows about my sordid past? At all, even as a friend?

I must have zoned out, because when she speaks I startle.

'What did he mean about the sharing? Is he into threesomes or something?' she asks outright, her mouth forming an 'O' over the neck of the beer bottle. She takes a long swallow, giving me precious seconds to formulate some words that don't sound like a script for some hideous reality TV show.

My skin crawls. If only I could say yes. Better than the truth, which still has the power to make me shudder with shame, both for how Slay acted and how I acted out in return.

'I wouldn't put it past him,' I say. I want to confess all my shameful truths to this woman who believes in my redemption. Who sees something that eludes me when I look in the mirror. But I also want more time. Because I'm learning new things about her every day.

'He's a drama queen who likes to stir up trouble,' I continue, scrubbing my hand over my unshaven face. 'He likes to get a rise out of me for sport.' Perhaps Slay sensed what Neve means to me, so delivered a low blow.

I want to erase last night's meeting with him from her memory, because standing in front of him beside the woman I love made me feel small and completely unworthy.

We'll ruin her. Drag her down to our level. I can't do that, but can I give her up?

Neve is watchful, silent. Waiting for more.

Unease creeps down my spine. I want to be honest. Every hour we spend together feels like we're moving closer, but some things are too devastating to confess. Perhaps half the story...the less damning half.

'Remember the night he took me to the strip joint?' My stare falls on the endless blue of the Indian ocean because it's hard to think about that night without feeling white-hot licks of regret and shame. 'Well, in addition to his unique advice on getting over a woman by moving swiftly on to the next, he also informed me that Jane, the girl I was crying into my beer over, had allegedly come on to him while we were together.'

Neve sits bolt upright. 'What? Seriously?'

I nod, my neck so stiff it spasms. 'Seriously. "No use crying over pussy you never really had in the first place",' I say, imitating Slay's words of wisdom.

She scoots to the edge of her lounger and reaches for my hand. 'Did she?'

I shrug. 'She half-heartedly denied it, but it doesn't really matter who was telling the truth. I was a teenager, full of emotions, and that felt like my lowest ebb. And Slay kicked me while I was down, whether intentionally or through tactlessness doesn't matter.'

I squeeze her fingers, needing to pull her into my arms but also hating that I'm the source of the appalled disbelief in her wide eyes. I know she feels empathy for my younger self, but she must also feel horror to a degree. No normal father behaves that way.

'That's horrible,' she says, gripping my hand more tightly. I shake my head, cutting her off. I don't deserve her pity, because I behaved as badly as him later that night. Worse, in fact. Because, whereas Slay claims never to have laid a finger on Jane, I went home alone to his mansion, furious and drunk after visiting her for confirmation.

Slay's third wife, Aubrey, was in the kitchen. She saw I was upset. Poured me another drink. Made me spill the whole story. And then, somehow, I'd kissed her, or she'd kissed me, and with pain and humiliation driving me I'd allowed emotions to rule my head. I didn't stop it. I slept with her. And afterwards she told me she was leaving Slay anyway so I shouldn't feel bad. But I felt worse than bad. Confused and ashamed, because I wasn't certain who had used who. But I was certain my actions were something Slay would have done.

And I was right. I'll never forget the look of anger tinged with pride on Slay's face during the inevi-

table confrontation the next morning. In trying to
break free of him, I'd become something he could
finally relate to and respect. My self-worth reached
rock-bottom. Even now, years later, the shame de-
fines everything I do. Why would my wonderful,
beautiful Neve want anything to do with such a...
weak degenerate?

'"Don't date with your head, boy. Use your
dick".' I quote Slay, the sickening memories chok-
ing. 'That's the last time I turned to him for advice.'
I swallow, my throat aching because I'm back there,
feeling helpless, vulnerable and inadequate for a
woman like Neve.

She slides onto my lounger, her arms around my
shoulders and her head tucked into my chest. 'I'm
so sorry you went through that.'

I press my lips to her forehead, selfishly sucking in the comforting scent of her skin. 'I was lucky
enough to have dual nationality. I caught the first
flight to the UK, applied to university, spent the
summer working in London and then I met you—a
brilliant ray of sunshine,' I say, trying to forget.

I acted out for months after that incident, some
twisted part of me taking to heart Slay's unwanted
advice about women as I tried to make sense of
my teenage angst and confusion over what I'd done
with my father's wife. But, aside from the attempt
to protect myself from further heartache, it wasn't
me. Not the real me.

I shelved that version of myself when I woke up to the fact that my behaviour made me more like Slay, not less—terrified of his celebrity world in which I'd become caught up, where outrageous things seemed commonplace. Although by then my reputation was set with the British media and exaggerated by Slay's publicists, who come from the school of 'no publicity is bad publicity'.

I'd plastered on a mask and tried to banish my disillusion for a while, living out my early twenties avoiding getting too close to anyone. With the exception of one person.

The person now in my arms, making my heart clench with every beat.

I can't lose her.

Not without losing part of myself.

CHAPTER ELEVEN

Oliver

I HOLD HER tighter to stop myself shattering apart.

'Let's forget about Slay. I have another surprise for you.'

She looks up at me with a small smile but concern in her eyes. 'Okay.' She sighs, dropping her head back to my chest and snuggling closer. 'But, for what it's worth, I hope you know that I would never betray you in any way.'

I love her for her reassurance, although I deserve neither her loyalty nor her caring.

'I never took a girl home after that. Never introduced him to anyone, especially not you. You're too precious. I couldn't survive losing you.'

Panic rumbles through me, a wave growing in momentum. Will she leave me when she learns just how similar Slay and I are?

'Why especially me?' she asks, stilling.

I exhale the tightness in my throat that tastes

like fear. 'Because you're different. You didn't care about who my father is. In fact, you'd never even heard of him. Right from the moment we met you've never taken any crap from me, even on that first night when I was immature enough to be full of crap. You made me earn your friendship, and that made it all the more valuable, because most things in my life came easy to me back then, just as they had for Slay. Why would I risk all of that, risk you, by exposing you to a man I wish I could disown, wish I didn't share DNA with?'

Her eyes soften and I want to kiss her so badly. To lose myself in her and our passion until I forget where I come from, what I did and start afresh with Neve.

'I admit the leather pants in this heat are a bit tragic,' she says, and then rolls her eyes, injecting the moment with humour.

A rumble of laughter resonates in my chest. That she can make me smile when I'm full of regret and frustration is a testament to how she enriches my life just by being herself. I fall a little bit more in love with her in that moment.

The boat's gently humming engine changes in tone. I look up.

'We're here,' I tell her. 'I hope you're hungry.'

I sling on a T-shirt and Neve covers up with a sarong, her excited eyes restoring my balance as she catches sight of the small thatched shelter on the island where we've moored.

'I arranged a treat for lunch,' I say as we walk down the gangplank and pad through the pristine clear shallows.

'Sounds intriguing, but you didn't have to go to all this trouble.' She smiles her smile; the one I'm head over heels for.

'Yes, I did,' I say, lifting her hand to my mouth and pressing a kiss to her knuckles. 'I was going to arrange a picnic. But you love cooking shows, so I thought we could have some fun and I could learn some skills—you know how culinarily challenged I am.'

'Kihineh?' Ali, our local chef, asks us how we are in Dhivehi, the official language of the Maldives.

Neve's excitement is infectious as she takes a seat in the open-air kitchen, which already smells of heavenly spices.

Ali explains the menu—*bis keemiya*, a type of samosa stuffed with gently sautéed cabbage, hard-boiled eggs and spiced onions, *garudhiya*, a fragrant fish soup, and a coconut-free version of *huni roshi*, a chapati-style bread.

Under Ali's instructions, Neve sets about grinding spices with a pestle and mortar and I'm tasked with rolling out the balls of chapati dough into circles.

Neve is in her element, her eyes bright as she

watches Ali with rapt attention and teases me for my oval-shaped bread.

'You're really good at this!' I watch her deep-frying rectangular samosas. 'Will you teach me some basics when we get home?' It's the first time either of us has mentioned reality, and my heart stops while I wait for her answer.

'Of course,' she says, laughing as I burn my first chapati to a cinder on one side. 'Don't worry. We'll make a cook out of you.'

When we're done, Ali carries everything to a solitary sheltered table for two near the shore. Despite my having a hand in it, the food is delicious.

'Try this,' tempts Neve, feeding me from her fingers, which are greasy and spicy.

Despite being ravenous, my tight throat makes swallowing a challenge. I love seeing her this way— excited, relaxed and happy. After all these years, I feel like I'm learning something new about her every day. An addiction I want to feed until she's woven through me.

'Thanks for this,' she says when, sated, we finally admit defeat.

'It's my pleasure,' I say, humbled and awed that I put the happiness on her face.

'Let's walk along the beach,' she suggests, standing and taking my hand. After we've walked in silence for a few minutes, she says, 'Can I ask you a question?'

'Of course. Anything.' I kiss the back of her hand.

'Is what happened with Jane the reason you avoided relationships—to protect yourself?'

I shrug and then sling my arm around her shoulders so we can be as close as possible while we wade through the warm, shallow water. 'Could you blame me?'

'No.' She looks gutted. 'But not all women are the same.'

'Of course not. But back then I felt like I'd tried to have something real and it backfired. Jane wasn't interested in a long-distance relationship with me, or travelling or studying abroad with me, as I naively dreamed. She wanted me for the LA celebrity lifestyle. She wanted me for Slay.

'As a kid, I used to wonder what it would be like to have a normal father who went to soccer games and taught me to surf. Instead I got the dad who offered me joints, took me to strip clubs and hit on my girlfriends…'

'Why didn't you tell me all of this before?' she whispers.

'I'm not proud of my behaviour when I first met you. I couldn't believe my luck that you didn't know Slay Coterill. I told him that you'd never heard of him once—best moment of my life. You should have seen his face…' My amusement quickly dries up. 'But my experience was of women who either assumed I'm just the like him or hoped that shagging me might earn them an introduction. The comparisons in the media didn't help, of course.'

Neve's arm tightens around my waist.

'After a while, I just played that role, because it helped me to lock down my emotions and armour myself against a repeat of the humiliation and betrayal.' But could I risk reaching for more? With Neve? Maybe the best way to have her in my life and protect her from Slay and my biggest fear—that she'll become embroiled in my family drama one time too many and decide I'm not worth the hassle—is to hold on tight and show her and the world her importance in my life.

She's everything.

'You know, I understand how you feel being compared. I used to feel like I grew up in Amber's shadow. She was taller, prettier, successful, even while we were still at school.'

I grow restless, a strong urge to kiss her senseless and confess how she makes me feel with just one of her beautiful smiles taking over. 'Amber is talented in one area, Neve. I doubt she could do what you do with all that auditing, number-crunching, investigative stuff you do. Height is part of the genetic lottery. And I one thousand per cent dispute the other claim.'

I bring us to a halt and turn, tugging her warm body into my arms. I press a kiss to her lips, gripping her waist with what feels like terrifying force.

During this trip, it's become crystal-clear that I'm one mistake away from sabotaging this. Unless I tell her how I feel about her…how I've always felt.

Or, better still, show her.

We pull apart, reluctantly on my side. Relief washes through me when I see her glazed eyes and parted lips, and feel the thud of her heart against mine, which tell me I'm not alone in this.

I press my lips to hers once more. 'You're beautiful and smart and funny and you fill my life with fucking sunshine.' I stare hard so she sees that I'm serious. 'You always have, Neve.'

'Not just regular sunshine…?' She smiles. I haul her up to my kiss as if she's my source of oxygen, breathing her in.

'I'm not insecure about it any more,' she says, dropping her face to my chest so I can no longer see her expression. 'And I love Amber, but sometimes it was hard feeling second best. First boy I ever fancied turned me down—not so unusual, I know—but then he asked me if my sister was single. That set the tone for my late teens and early twenties when we went out together—she'd attract all the attention, get the hottest guy, and I'd be left with the friend.'

I hold her tighter, my gut twisted with longing, wishing I could erase her past doubts. Because isn't what she just confided exactly what I did to her the night we met? 'You never told me that.'

Tension infects her body. 'Well, it seems silly

now. Besides, history repeated itself with you—I thought we were flirting that first night we met and before I know it you went home with my flatmate.'

I stiffen. 'Well, it was my loss. My immaturity and stupidity.' I hear her intake of breath, regret for the wasted time crushing me. I hold her and allow myself to admit I want to wake up with her every morning, not just the mornings we have left in the Maldives. My love for her is way beyond platonic. Perhaps it always has been. Perhaps that's why I freaked out when I met her so soon after having my heart broken, with my father's cynical advice ringing in my ears and the demons of that one terrible night haunting me…

'I fancied you back then, that first night. You knew that, right?' I should have told her this long ago. I had no idea I'd made her feel second best.

She freezes, almost as if she's stopped breathing. I've shoved us into uncharted territory. Discussing the night we met in any way beyond the sanitised version that spawned our friendship was previously taboo.

Then her chest slowly deflates, as if in a controlled exhale. 'You fancied anything with boobs back then,' she says, trying to downplay the seriousness of my confession. But it is fucking serious, the momentousness not lost on me if the band tightening across my chest is any indication.

'Not true. That university maths lecturer had a

very nice pair but I didn't fancy him.' I turn serious, grip her face and maintain eye contact, because I ache for her past disappointments. Knowing I might inadvertently have added to them by overlooking her that night through some sense of twisted, selfish self-preservation slices me open.

'I fancied you the minute I saw you,' I admit, recalling that night like it was yesterday. 'You were the prettiest girl in the place—why else would I make a beeline for you?'

I hear the breath catch in her throat, as if this is genuinely shocking news. As if she never, for one second, suspected I found her attractive before our fateful conversation about orgasms.

'But you didn't choose me.' Her voice is a whisper.

Shame streaks through my veins like lightning. 'That was because of my issues, nothing to do with you.' I lower my voice and force out the words I've bottled inside all these years. 'You were perfect that night. So perfect I'd never known anyone like you. But what I did know was that I wasn't in your league—that if I played my usual stunts, laid a single finger on you, I'd fuck it up. Ruin it for ever. Be just like my father. And I didn't want that with you. I wanted to keep you.' I brush my lips across her shoulder, feather-light.

She gapes, her eyes desperately flicking over my face, as if seeking the truth of my words.

'I was an arsehole,' I say. 'You knew it and, fortunately, so did I. I'm not proud of this, but I can't
even remember your flatmate's name. And yet here
you are, still the most important person in my life.
I did choose you, Neve. It's just taken me this long
to grow deserving enough to say that aloud.'

Wordlessly she wraps her arms around my neck
and tugs me into her kiss. When we break apart for
air, our foreheads resting together, weighty silence
follows. I'm trapped, immobile, by my longing, and
fear I'll ruin the best thing that's ever happened to
me. But I know one thing for certain. I want more
than this week. I want more than friends, even with
the awesome benefits. I want Neve to truly be mine.

'I booked us a private island stay for tonight,' I
tell her, my heart climbing into my throat. 'Will you
stay there with me? Just the two of us?'

'Yes,' she says, with zero hesitation.

Hope soars in my chest. Maybe this time I've
got this.

Maybe it's taken a trip to the world's most iso-
lated group of islands to see what I've had in front
of me all this time.

CHAPTER TWELVE

Neve

OUR LAVISH BUNGALOW on the private atoll is paradise. I emerge from the master suite, freshly showered and wearing the red dress Oliver liked from two nights ago. The silk glides over my tingling skin, which is sensitive from the sun and sea and the knowledge that I'm dressing sexily for a man with whom I'm falling desperately in love.

No. *Love* is too tame a word for the feelings crushing me. I loved my friend Olly. What I feel now is searing, out-of-control rapture. Bliss and dread rolled into one confusing tangle. Because I want Oliver, the Oliver I've come to know deeper than ever before, beyond this week. I want him for ever. And I want him to feel the same way about me. His confession about fancying me when we first met was achingly bittersweet and scary. Because it's given me hope. Hope to dream that maybe, this time, I could get the guy.

I step into the living room, catching sight of him staring out at the exquisite, uninterrupted ocean views. The setting sun halos him, pink and orange light streaming around his tall frame. My heart lurches against my ribs, pining for him.

I can't breathe.

I could go to him now. Tell him how I feel, how I've always felt about him. But to what end? I know my Oliver, and the odds are stacked against us. Yes, he had a crappy, erratic role model growing up, and had his teenage heart broken and trampled on by Slay's callousness. Only now do I fully understand the impact of that on his younger self-esteem, but there's no escaping the fact he's never once had a serious girlfriend since Jane. And, as much as I can't stop seeing a future for us romantically, I also don't want to be the guinea pig, the test case, even if he wanted more than our in-between relationship.

I've been there before with my exes, been the more committed person in the couple. I know where that leads—resentment, insecurity, heartache. And that's what I'd be with Oliver. While he bumbles along in his first relationship in nearly a decade, deciding if it's working for him.

What then? What if he decided it wasn't for him after all? How would I survive that?

If I can just get through the rest of the holiday unscathed… But it's growing harder to ignore how perfect he is for me, if only he believed himself capable of a committed relationship. If only he stopped comparing himself to a man he's nothing like.

If only he saw what I see.

My sigh expels a tiny part of my soul.

He turns, catching sight of me, and my heart stutters out of rhythm. He whistles, his eyes alight, as if with everything I wish to be true. Wish he'd say aloud. But I'm fooling myself. I feel as if I'm hurtling towards a brick wall with every hour that passes. The deadline to this fantasy looms.

'I love that dress.' He strides my way and my lungs try to escape my chest with every soft step of his bare feet in my direction. He presses his mouth to mine in a soft whisper of a kiss and takes both my hands. His eyes bore into mine, and I almost glimpse a flash of longing there, but then it's gone, replaced by his familiar grin. 'I've planned something special for tonight now I have you all to myself.'

My entire body shivers. Can't he tell I'd do anything for him? I've given myself over to him since we started this crazy sex-periment, and I have no regrets. Although I should have taken more care to armour my heart.

Nervous laughter bubbles from me. 'I'm not going naked scuba-diving, if that's what you have in mind.'

He shakes his head, a hint of mischief twitching his mouth. 'It's a little more personal than that— will you dance with me before dinner?'

'Of course.' Anticipation slithers down my spine. Why do I feel seduced, cherished? And ready to fling myself into the unknown, the way I dived from the back of the boat earlier?

He's arranged food, and the table on the veranda is beautifully set for a romantic dinner for two, but my throat is so tight with desire and love there's no way I could eat. Or even speak.

Soft music fills our bungalow, spilling out onto the beach from concealed outdoor speakers. He leads me onto the sand and then turns me into his arms. I settle against his chest with a soft sigh as he sways to the music. I breathe in the familiar scent of him, my face pressed to his shirt and the strip of his chest exposed at the open neck. I tell myself I don't need words or assurances, or for ever because this moment, this day, where we've laughed, shared and learned new things about each other, is perfect. He made each moment perfect, and that's enough for now.

His hands roam my back, holding me close, possessive but also restless, the same turbulence rolling through me because close isn't enough. It's never enough when we're together.

I look up and my breath catches. Playful, self-satisfied Oliver is nowhere to be seen. His eyes blaze with heat and vulnerability I've only seen in him once before, long ago, when he'd broken down after a few too many drinks and confessed sordid details about growing up with his father—finding

Slay passed out in the mornings after endless parties, driving him to rehab and standing by his side at the altar for his many marriages, confused by his own place in his father's cluttered and chaotic life.

But this has nothing to do with anyone else, only us. How we've managed to carve out a utopian corner of paradise for ourselves to play out roles for which neither of us has a script.

'Neve, I didn't know you could mean any more to me.' He lowers his lips to mine, seemingly in no hurry as he kisses and kisses and kisses me while my toes sink deeper into the soft sand and I fall apart in his arms. Because I love him so much, I can't bear to think about the past we've wasted or the uncertain future. Only this moment.

'Let's go to bed,' I say.

'If you insist,' he agrees.

Then I'm airborne, swung up into his arms, a squeal breaking free. He strides towards the bungalow, carrying me. I want to make a joke about my weight, or a quip about him working out, but the look on his face, as if he wants to devour me, stops such frivolity.

'Want to sleep out under the stars? I want us to do more new things together. All of the things.'

My stomach flitters, but I nod my assent, because I want the same. This unknown Oliver is as addictive as familiar Oliver.

At the day bed, a romantic outdoor canopied affair surrounded by gauzy curtains, he lowers me to my feet. He stands before me and without a word unbuttons his shirt, revealing the toned, tanned and tattooed torso I've learned by heart. I slide the straps of my dress from my shoulders, allowing the fabric to pool at my feet before kicking it away. I slide my hands around Oliver's waist, his warm skin over taut muscles the best aphrodisiac, if I needed one. But I don't. That I'm allowed to touch him after years of enforced hands-off makes for a dizzying reality.

He shoves down his shorts and boxers, adding them to the pile of discarded clothing. My strapless bra goes next—Oliver unhooks it with one hand. He drops to his knees, removes my thong and then he presses a kiss to my stomach, his hands on my hips, fingers gripping with passion that feels like ownership.

I cradle his head, slide my fingers through his flop of hair, which is less tamed and more beach-tousled than he normally wears it back in London—another thing that makes him seem old and new all at once. He climbs to his feet, his mouth sliding up the centre of my body, between my breasts, until he reaches my mouth. He kisses me, cupping my breasts, his thumbs working my nipples into sensitive, aching peaks. My core clenches, empty of him.

'Oliver,' I plead, wrapping my hand around his thick, erect length.

'Shh… Let me worship your body.' His mouth

closes around one nipple, stealing any argument I have with longing and sensation.

All he's done is worship me since that very first kiss. He's shown me what my body is capable of when I trust the person I'm with, when I surrender to his touch, safe in the knowledge he cares and won't let me down.

Or perhaps all I needed was love. To admit the depth of my love for him, and everything else would slot perfectly into place.

Somehow we make it to the bed, the cool slide of satin sheets a balm to my fevered skin. Oliver's mouth is all over me, kissing, licking, nibbling every inch of my skin from my neck to my thighs until I want to scream with frustration and I'm pink from the scrape of his facial hair.

'Please,' I beg again, my hand slipping between my thighs to give my clit some relief.

He pulls my fingers away and replaces them with his own, watching my reaction to his touch and his kisses.

'I'll never tire of making you come, of watching you come—it's addictive. Mine. You're mine, Neve.' He swaps his fingers for his mouth, sucking and laving my clit until I'm a writhing, shaking mess of need and yearning.

'I need you. Now. Oh, please, now!' I cry out as his mouth leaves me.

I grab his shoulders and tug, and he sits up between my spread thighs. His hand grips the base of his cock and he slides the tip over my engorged clit and through my moisture.

'Yes. Forget the condom,' I say, my voice breaking with urgency. 'I'm good if you are. Do it.' I'm aware I've reached the demanding stage of my arousal, but I'm helpless. He makes me helpless.

He scrunches his eyes closed and drops his head back. 'Neve, are you sure?' I've never heard his voice so dark with desire, not even last night, when our frantic coupling in the bathroom seemed to be about anger, challenge and claim.

'Yes.' I push up onto my elbows and grasp his steely buttocks, shunting his hips forward until the bare tip of him pushes inside me.

We both gasp. Oliver opens his eyes, takes my hands in his and slides the rest of the way into me until he's buried to the hilt and his face is transformed by his own desperate need.

'Fuck, you feel fantastic. I'll never want to leave,' he grits out, his eyes blazing into mine.

I'm so high on him, on us, the first flutters of an orgasm start. His slow, thorough thrusts shove me over the edge so I cry out, my stare locked on his beautiful face. But I'm greedy. I want more. I want everything he has to give me. I let go of his hands to squeeze my sensitive nipples as I lift my pelvis, meeting him thrust for thrust. Sweat breaks out at his hairline.

He's holding back. But I want him wild, teetering on the edge, a place I'm clawing at with my fingernails. I shove at his hips and roll over onto to my stomach. Before I can press up onto all fours, his body covers mine and he re-enters me from behind.

'Yes,' I hiss, because this way, me flat on my stomach and him deep inside, it's tighter, the friction almost unbearably good.

His hand burrows under my hip to stroke my clit as he pumps into me. 'Come again. Show me what I want to see,' he orders, and like his puppet I nod, because I'm almost there, my walls clamping around his shaft as a second orgasm strikes.

My cry is muffled into the pillow. And then I'm pressed into the mattress by Oliver's weight, flat out, his front plastered to my back and his face buried on my shoulder and the side of my neck.

'Neve!' He bellows my name seconds before he goes rigid and comes. And even then he won't stop. He flips me over and collapses on top of me where his hips buck, wringing the last of the pleasure from his heavy, spent body as he laves kiss after kiss over my chest, my neck and my face.

'I can't get enough of you,' he whispers, pressing his mouth to mine, and he's right. We're spent and sweaty, but already I want him back inside me. I feel his cock thicken and twitch against my stomach.

My final thought as we lose ourselves in each other's touch once more... How the hell will we ever stop this?

CHAPTER THIRTEEN

Oliver

THE PICTURE'S BLURRY, obviously taken using a tele-photo lens, but Neve and I are still recognisable, kissing on the deck of the boat after swimming with the wildlife. I make a fist and press it to the bridge of my nose, as if wishing it away will change the string of events. While Neve and I slept like two spoons in a drawer, blissfully unaware, the story of Slay Coterill's split from wife number six created a path of cyclonic destruction.

> *Bad rock and roll icon ditches wife number six...but will sometime on-again, off-again girlfriend of Coterill Junior ever make it across the finish line?*

My stomach roils with fury. I glance at the open windows. I left Neve in the shower five minutes ago while I ordered breakfast. I wanted everything about this day to be perfect. And now it's ruined. Because of me.

The story, which represents everything that's wrong about my life, everything I've tried to distance myself from, pulls me apart. It paints her not as the amazing, strong, independent woman she is—the most important woman in my life—but as the pathetic sidepiece of a man who can't commit. A man who doesn't deserve her. A man who is just like his father.

And perhaps the media is right. I've denied my feelings for Neve for nine years because of my issues. I've pretended and hidden away the vulnerable places in me that prevented me from considering a serious relationship. I've brought all of this down on her through my fears. It's a mess, exactly the kind I've dreaded, and I've dragged Neve into the circus.

I swear under my breath and slide my phone onto the table with jarring force. Her association with me—I can't bring myself to call it a friendship any longer—does nothing for her reputation. All I do is bring her down to my level. Slay's level. I can't protect her, and I've been fooling myself all these years that I could.

Further chills rack me—my romantic gesture of sleeping under the stars could have given the paps even more fodder, a more intimate photo…

With a stomach full of dread, I creep back into the room through the open French doors. She's towelling her hair dry, wearing one of my T-shirts, the wondrous sight of her making panic surge inside me.

'Breakfast is ready on the deck. It's another perfect day in paradise.' A perfect day for my perfect woman, only I have to spoil the mood with my news. I don't want to, don't want to remind her of the reality off this island, my reality, not when things between us are equally magical and fragile. Because I feel her emotional distance like a force field. She's holding back, and I don't blame her.

I need to tell her everything—secrets, declarations of my feelings, and of course the crap online. Perhaps then I can make all of this right. Because when I woke this morning, like every morning since we started our physical relationship, I watched her sleep, aching for her to open her eyes so I could be in her company. And I knew that, without her, I'm incomplete. I'm desperately in love with her, and I want to be her everything, as she is mine.

That means being open and vulnerable, and laying it all on the line.

I lift her hand to my mouth, brush my lips over her knuckles. My pulse leaps with trepidation. She's like hand-blown glass—one wrong move and I'll shatter the illusion of us with my bare hands—but a trickle of possibility meanders its way through the chaos in my head.

'I have ideas about how we can spend today horizontal, if you're interested,' she says, scooping both of her arms around my neck to draw me down to her kiss.

I lose myself for a few seconds, eager to blot out the world with her, naked and sated. But I'll have to tell her about the photo sooner or later. And I should have told her the other stuff long ago.

I pull back and hold her hand, my heartbeat seeming to resonate through my fingertips. The happy smile slides from her face.

'There's a photo on the gossip sites this morning,' I say, spewing out the words to get them over with. 'The two of us kissing yesterday on board the boat—there must have been left-over paps lurking, looking for Slay.'

She shrugs. 'So? I don't care. Forget about it.'

She's right—if it doesn't bother her, I shouldn't allow it to get to me. But it reminds me of the exposure I experienced as a child, growing up with Slay, and then later as a teen. Every move I made meant something to people I'd never met until I felt as if I didn't know who I was, just who I was supposed to be.

Slay's son.

And I'm more than that. I'm a man fit for this woman.

Neve, my safe haven—what I should be for her. I don't want her to read some garbage and doubt herself, doubt her place in my life, because she's a part of me, a vital part, and without her I can't exist.

'I know, I just…' I rub a hand over my face. 'I feel like I've let you down somehow, failed to protect you.'

'You haven't let me down.' She slides her thumb over my bottom lip. 'I don't care what they say about me.'

I want that to be true, but we all have our insecurities. Slay is mine.

I nod, although my head feels wooden, clumsy. 'I just… I don't want you to read it because I don't want you to believe what they say. I don't want you to feel inferior, pitied or second rate. You're not. The opposite, in fact.'

She stares, a million emotions flitting across her eyes, each of them leaving me more unnerved. 'Okay,' she says in an unconvinced tone.

But I can convince her. I can make this right. I can protect her and show her what she means to me in one move. Breath shudders out of me as the idea I've been ruminating on takes form.

Why not? We've known each other nine years. I'm in love with her. I want this. I can end the gossip and show the world exactly where my priorities lie.

I take her hands, gripping them tightly before slowly sinking to one knee.

She freezes, confusion slashed across her face, and then tries to tug me back to my feet. 'Oliver, what are you doing?'

I resist, looking up at her with a lump in my

throat. 'Neve,' I begin, ignoring her frown, 'you mean more to me than any other person on the planet. When I think of letting you go as soon as we touch down in London, I feel sick.'

Her breathing speeds up, her eyes swimming with emotions, not all of them good.

'I know you're pissed at me right now,' I add, 'because this is sudden—some would say crazy.' Yet, the more I think about it, the more sense it makes.

Please let her want the same.

'The caretaker here is a celebrant,' I continue as full understanding comes to her wary expression.

'So, Neve Sara Grayson, will you marry me?

CHAPTER FOURTEEN

Neve

I'M LIGHT-HEADED, AND the room is shifting alarmingly at the thought of what he's just asked me and what it means. He smiles, his beautiful Oliver smile that's playful and sexy and could be specifically designed to make me fall harder, although there's nowhere left for me to fall. I love him completely, bone-deeply, irrevocably.

But…

I grasp his fingers for fear of my legs giving way. This is off. Wrong. Perhaps some sort of sick joke, for which I'll seriously never forgive him.

My stomach rolls over with adrenaline. A few days ago I could only dream of this scenario. For a moment it makes me feel that, just maybe—the insanity of his timing and the motivation behind his proposal aside—this, us as a couple, could actually work. Haven't I always dreamed of being more to him than a friend, more than a friend he has sex with? Of being everything to him, the way he is everything to me?

But not like this—rushed, a rebound because of some negative press. I don't want to be a sticking plaster over the wound left by Slay. I want Oliver, but I don't want to be a relationship experiment. Whatever impulse or panic has him in its grip, he's clearly not ready for commitment. This is not the way I envisaged this fairy-tale moment.

I squeeze his fingers. 'Oliver, this is—'

'Don't say crazy,' he interrupts. 'Because it makes sense. *We* make sense.' He stands and grips both of my hands. 'You want to settle down, to find someone, but you won't find what you're looking for on a dating app.' His words are urgent, impassioned. 'I know. I used to be one of those guys using apps to hook up with women. But now we've broken down this barrier we used to keep our friendship intact. We're amazing together and we're still best friends.'

His words, wonderful words, would have thrilled me a week ago. But it feels like this proposal has more to do with Slay than us. If he'd simply asked for a relationship I would have said yes. Because we can't go back after everything we've shared. I'll never be content to meet him for coffee or go to a movie and say goodbye as if this week hasn't happened.

But neither can we rush this. We can't jump several dating steps just because we know all there is to know about each other. I have to make him understand, to salvage this.

'Why don't we try dating when we get home?' I say, my voice almost desperate. 'There's no need to rush.' Despite the temptation to say yes, to have the fairy-tale moment just this once. To be the first choice of the man of my dreams, a man I thought I'd have to give up soon. But I don't want to be temporary. I haven't waited nine years to be his commitment guinea pig, only to be cast aside when he discovers he's not ready to abandon his single life after all.

He's never had a fling that lasts longer than a week. Women come and go. Beautiful women, some he has lots in common with, some clearly keen for more than what's on offer. And the end has nothing to do with his father, as he'd claim, and everything to do with him. To do with his belief that somehow he's no good at relationships because of his role model, or that he doesn't deserve one because of his wild youth, or that he'll only get hurt again the way Jane hurt him.

But what if I surrendered to my weak inner voice, the one telling me that this is what I've craved all along?

No. It's a guarantee of the heartbreak I fear. He'll soon grow bored of trying to outrun those demons which, if his turmoil over Slay's latest antics is any proof, are still very much alive and kicking. He'll decide he was premature and still wants to play the field, something that helps him keep at bay feeling too deeply.

He's nothing like his father, but nor is he ready to commit or to be a husband.

And what then for me? I already know I want all of him, to be all to him.

No, I have to be strong.

I suck in a shuddering breath. I can't risk saying yes just to know how that feels before I'm flung back to reality. A reality without my lover *or* my best friend. Worse off than when I came to these islands. Because losing one means losing both. If I loved him less fiercely, maybe I could go along for the ride with this impromptu proposal.

Oliver steps closer and grips my face, his animated eyes holding mine. 'We've known each other a long time. Now that we've made the leap into lovers, this is just one more leap. I know I don't deserve you, but I can try.'

'Of course you deserve me. That's part of the issue.'

He's not hearing me and his touch, his palms on my skin, so familiar, so good, now feels too cloying.

'If you're worried about the ceremony here being legally binding, we can make it official as soon as we get back to London,' he says. 'Then I'll issue a press release. Announce our marriage.'

'What? Why would you do that?' I ask, dumbfounded. He's thought this all the way through, while I've been blissfully ignorant, simply celebrating our deepening connection and imagining that perhaps we could have something real. That perhaps he really has changed and is ready to settle down. But this feels like a circus act, exactly the kind of scene he says he hates and usually attributes to Slay.

'Because, if we make us official,' he says, taking both my hands and squeezing, 'they'll have nothing more to print about you the next time they print a story about Slay. Because that will stop my father coming between us.'

And there it is, his motivation for this rash proposal. Nothing to do with love or feelings for me. Not a reflection of the growing closeness I've experienced this week. Just another show of one-upmanship with his father, a way to ensure history doesn't repeat itself and a ruthless guarding of his emotions, just like the Oliver I first met.

My heart clenches so violently, I feel my pulse to the tips of my toes. And I know, with a certainty that leaves me hollow, that my fairy-tale romance with Oliver is over.

CHAPTER FIFTEEN

Oliver

'OLIVER,' SHE SAYS, her eyes full of pain. 'I know you've been let down in the past, hurt, but you can't control what other people think or say. Not the press, and not Slay. All you can do is control how *you* react,' she says, making all kinds of sense. But I'm crazy in love with her—sense left the building days ago. This isn't going the way I'd planned. We should be kissing through happy tears by now, back in bed or flying to Male, the capital, to go engagement-ring shopping...

I know on an intellectual level that what she says is rational, but I've spent my entire adult life trying to keep a lid on this kind of exposure, to distance myself from Slay and the type of publicity he invites. Only now it feels worse, because I love her. I'm vulnerable because she's under attack. What hurts her kills me, especially when I'm the one responsible for that pain. This is why I've always avoided this feeling—fear, loss of control, failing Neve.

My mouth feels dry. She doesn't love me back. Or she doesn't think me capable of the emotion. I've finally worked up the courage to be open about my feelings for her and she doesn't share them.

She tugs the neck of the T-shirt, covering her exposed, sun-bronzed shoulder from my view. That drives a stake through my heart and the romantic morning I had planned, ripe with fresh starts and possibilities. Now only the usual shit-storm Slay Coterill leaves in his wake remains.

No, this mess is of my creation. If I'd been honest from the start, if I'd done what Neve said and put to rest Slay and how I've allowed fear to hog-tie me, none of this would matter.

'So, you're saying no…is that it?' I ask, waves of dread rolling through me.

'It's not that.' She looks away. 'It's just… I don't think we should rush into anything foolhardy,' she explains, immune to my stillness. 'Isn't it better to let Slay's latest marital implosion blow over and focus on your deal with the Japanese?' Her expression grows decidedly shady, something that raises every hair on my strung-taut body.

My anger is self-directed, my secret past proving that I've inherited Slay's weakness of character.

Neve must sense my brittle tension. She looks up, her eyes pleading. 'You've avoided commitment all these years. I just want you to be sure you're ready. This…this was just a holiday fantasy.' Her words are a whisper, cautious and edgy. Pain lances me as if I've been speared through.

'So you only want the fantasy?' I knew this was too good to be true, that I wasn't good enough. I knew I couldn't truly have her. 'You don't want me?' Betrayal sours my tongue, even as my blood runs cold with the knowledge I've done this by keeping secrets and keeping a distance.

'Oliver, I'm not saying that… But you've never had a relationship that's lasted longer than a week.'

I can't look away from her eyes, which seem to communicate something different from the words she's using to destroy me.

'I'm just protecting myself from the inevitable.' She presses her hand to her chest, as if she too feels pain. 'Because of course this will end, and I'll just be good old friend-Neve again.'

'I understand that you want to protect yourself.' I've been trying to protect her from me for our entire friendship. I'm not a safe bet. My track record, my genes, the skeletons littering my closet… She'd be mad to make me the person responsible for her happiness. 'I want to protect you too—from gossip and from Slay.'

'But a rushed proposal doesn't do that, don't you see? You're just reacting to what's going on around you—this latest Slay scandal. Our physical connection is amazing, but shouldn't we see if we work in the real world first?'

Pressure builds in my head. She believes me incapable of more than sex, more than a superficial, hollow relationship. Just like the kind in which Slay specialises.

'So, you don't think I can do more than fuck?' I turn away, pace to the window and stare blindly through the mosquito nets while impotence and rejection crush me.

'I don't mean that. I just…' She growls in frustration, and in my peripheral vision I see her bury her face in her hands.

Icy calm settles over me, extinguishing the flames, razing us as a couple to the ground. 'No, it's okay. You're right. I'm no good at commitment, but I am good at fucking.' I spin to face her, my breath sawing through my lungs. 'You had your orgasms, but anything more… Hell, who are we kidding? I'm my father's son after all.'

She pales, her eyes huge. 'I'm not saying that. You're putting words into my mouth.' She deflates on a defeated sigh. 'Perhaps we were better off as friends.' The last is a hushed murmur, as if she fears the power of those words. With good cause, because they can end this, and what then? Is there anything left to return to?

'Olly,' she pleads, returning to the shortened version of my name I associate with her friendship and nothing more. 'I've seen new things about you this week, things I didn't know before. Wonderful things. But I've also witnessed how you feel about yourself when Slay is around. How this proposal seems to have arisen out of your fear that you're like him and can't commit. But I don't want to be just a quick fix.'

Uncontrollable need blasts through me. Need to destroy this once and for all to make this feeling of splintering apart stop. Because she's right. We've destroyed what we had and for what? So we could get our rocks off? So I could confirm what I already knew? That love is a mug's game, designed to weaken. And that I'll never be able to shake the association with Slay.

'It's okay, Neve. You're right. I would have screwed this up eventually. You know it. I know it. Hell, even Slay knows it. He tried to warn me the other night.'

She sits on the bed as if this conversation is taking a toll on her ability to stand. 'What do you mean?'

I scrub a hand over my face, wishing I could walk out of the doors and keep on walking. But every coffin needs a final nail and, if I hammer it in good and strong, I can retreat to lick my wounds safe in the knowledge I won't see Neve's disappointment ever again. 'His comment about sharing wasn't about threesomes. It was a warning. A reminder to me that we're more alike than I care to admit.'

'Stop saying that. It's only true if you let it become true.'

I nod, my grin sickening. 'It's already true. The night I learned the lessons of love from Slay, the night of the strip club, I went home alone while he stayed on to party.' My mind sounds an alarm. Once I tell her this, she'll look at me the way Slay did that night, with a slimy smile—part fury, part triumph—as if I'd played right into his hands and I was finally a son he could relate to and be proud of.

'I was drunk, furious with myself for being foolish enough to go to him for advice, humiliated and belittled. My heart was shredded, confused, uncertain what to believe but sick that what Slay told me might be true. When I slammed into the kitchen, in search of more beer to numb the pain and stupidity I felt, Slay's third wife, Aubrey, was there.'

The growing horror in her eyes should warn me off. But I'm too far gone, and ruining this for good is the only way to protect me from the pain of knowing I've lost her faith.

'She came on to me, right there in the kitchen of my father's house,' I continue. 'She was only a few years older than me, perhaps twenty-three. When she kissed me, I felt appalled, disgusted and euphoric all at once. It was as if I could exact revenge on Slay for a lifetime of being a shitty role model. For subjecting my teenage years to a string of stepmothers barely older than me. For caring more about fame and his rock-and-roll lifestyle than his only son. And most of all for kicking me when I was down, as if my feelings meant nothing.'

My fists clench at my sides and I stare deep into Neve's eyes.

'I kissed her back. Angry.' My words fall into the distasteful silence of the room. 'I knew it was wrong, we both did, but she didn't stop, and neither did I. I hated my life so much in that moment that hating myself for my actions seemed inconsequential.'

Neve shifts, her hands jerking in my direction as if to touch me, but I still her with a single quelling look. I need to finish the whole tale, because if she didn't want me before she'll definitely reject me after. At least then I'll know where I stand.

'After we'd finished, when I came to my senses, my head spinning drunk, I ran to the bathroom and threw up my disgust into the toilet until I could barely move. But the damage was already done. She'd wanted out of the marriage anyway, so she told Slay we'd slept together as a parting gesture.' A humourless snort blasts free. 'He wasn't even angry. He simply shrugged, as if I'd finally become what he expected.'

My stomach roils. 'I left that night, sickened by the fact that I'd become just like him, and burning from the humiliation that I might have been used in some sort of sick marital game.'

The filthy feeling returns now, coating me in its oily grasp. I stare hard at Neve, hating the unspoken judgment blaring from her hurt stare.

'That's what Slay meant by "sharing". His reminder to me that the apple never falls far from the tree, and that sex is just another form of currency.' But for a while, with her, I'd believed it could be different...

'So, don't worry,' I finish. 'You've made your feelings perfectly clear and, as you now know, you're right about me. I'm not good enough for you. I never was.'

I turn my back on her, swish the curtains aside and leave.

CHAPTER SIXTEEN

Neve

THE SPREADSHEET SWIMS before my eyes, the columns of numbers spinning like dials. I press my glasses to the bridge of my nose and close my eyes, hoping that when I reopen them the world will make sense once more.

It's my first day back at work since returning alone from the Maldives. Oliver's plane flew the entire wedding party back to London, minus our host, who, Shelley informed me, flew to Japan the day of our confrontation to run damage limitation on the Kimoto deal.

They had been long days since Oliver and I parted ways. Angry. Resentful. And, for my part, shattered into a million grains like sand.

How can we have gone so wrong? And why did I risk it all, risk what I had? Risk losing him.

It aches. My entire body. My mind. My soul.

I abandon my computer screen and open my

phone. I've composed and deleted hundreds of texts without sending a single message.

I've communicated with Oliver one way or another every day for the past nine years, and now, when I feel like I'm splitting in two, I need him more than ever. He's always been there to mop tears, hug me or tell me a stupid joke to cheer me up. But now there's radio silence. *Mutual* silence. Because I don't know how to reach out to him. I don't know what to say that he'll believe. All I know is that I fell in love with him all over again. Stronger, deeper, without hope of redemption. Because, where before my love for him was a puddle, this is the deepest fathom of the ocean.

And then I let him down. I didn't see what he tried to show me. I hurt him—an unforgivable act from a woman who's supposed to be his best friend, and in love with him to boot.

My phone pings, and my heart bangs against my ribs until I see it's from my friend Grace. She's replied to my SOS: I'm working a late shift today so can meet you for a cuppa in fifteen. Usual place?

I type out a reply and save my work, although there's not much point in being at the office today, I'm that ineffective. I tell my assistant I'll be back in an hour and then I wrap up in my coat and scarf and head out into a frigid London day.

The fresh, brisk walk should clear my head. But all I can see is Oliver's face swimming in front of my eyes, streaked with pain and betrayal. He opened himself to me and I ran from him, scared I'd never truly get what I want. Terrified that I'd never stack up, because Oliver's proposal, his solution to the photograph, had resounded with panic. And I couldn't trust it. I couldn't trust myself to be objective—something I've never been with my feelings for Oliver.

But of course he'd try to distance himself from his father, distance me from association. He's been doing it most of his adult life. Could it be that protecting me all these years might also have held him back from exploring us…?

And the rest… Slay, his stepmother… I only care that Oliver's punishing himself.

Grace sits at our usual table in the little tea shop not far from my office. Her tan from her holiday in Fiji last month has mostly faded, but there's joy shining in her eyes that not even my plea for help and my current expression can diminish.

She's in love.

The wind is knocked from me and it's hard to breathe.

'I've ordered our usual,' she says, although I doubt I'll be able to swallow anything past my constricted throat.

'Thanks,' I mutter, unwinding my scarf and draping my coat over the back of the chair. 'I wouldn't have texted on your afternoon off, except—'

'Except you needed a friend. And here I am.' Her sympathetic stare floods my stinging eyes with moisture. I blink it away and slump into a chair in defeat.

'Tell me,' she orders.

I drag in a shuddering breath. 'I messed up.'

'You told Oliver how you feel.' It's not a question and it makes me wince, because that's what I should have done. Right from the start. Instead I slept with him, ruined our friendship and then I still didn't tell him. I just turned him down and stamped on his feelings.

'Not exactly...' I hedge, dread rolling through me, because Grace will need all the details, which means reliving every wonderful and then disastrous moment.

She waits patiently. Grace is good at patience, and I need the breathing space, because I'm light-headed with regret.

'We slept together and it was great,' I say, holding up a hand to ward off any wise interruption. 'I know what you're going to say, and I didn't let it go to my head. But...somehow I ended up hurting him. Because I got scared...and I didn't trust in us... and now I don't know how to make it right. I don't know where he is or if he ever wants to talk to me again. I think I've killed our friendship. Lost him for ever.' I sag back in my seat, drained.

Sympathy hovers in her compassionate stare.

'Tell me everything,' she says, pouring tea into delicate floral cups.

So I do.

When I finish my rambling tale, my tea is cold, my scone is untouched and Grace's brows are pinched in a frown.

'So he actually proposed?' Her eyes flick to my bare left hand.

I nod. 'Yes, but you know what Oliver is like. It was an impulse, almost a joke… No.' I throw myself back in the seat, because I'm all over the place, my words as jumbled as my thoughts. 'Not a joke.'

'And you said no?'

I nod, my eyes stinging. 'It wasn't real. Tourist marriages in the Maldives are ceremonial only.'

'Did it feel real?' Grace asks tentatively. 'Because why would he ask if he doesn't love you and want to make a serious commitment?'

Good question. I open my mouth to answer. No words. My jaw hangs while my mind kick-starts and races for the first time in three days.

Could it be that simple…?

'Sounds to me like he's in love with you, sweetie,' says Grace when I remain stunned silent.

'No…' But…could Oliver really be in love with me? Could he want a real relationship? Have I been so desperate to protect myself from heartache, so convinced he wasn't ready for more, that I ignored the signs?

'And you're definitely in love with him.'

I nod, tears building in my aching throat.

Grace signals the waitress, who miraculously brings a fresh pot of tea for me along with a clean cup and saucer. 'Of course Oliver would doubt that he had anything to offer you after what you've just told me about his relationship with his father.' She covers my numb hand with hers. 'But you need to tell him how you feel. That you love him, more than a friend.' She pours me a fresh cup of tea, and this time I take a grateful sip, because tea makes everything better, so maybe it will infuse my mind with logic and clarity.

'What are you afraid of?' she asks, cutting right to the core of the issue.

I drag in a deep breath, steeling myself. 'That I'm not enough for him, or that I'm too much because he's avoided relationships all of his adult life. I'll be his experimental case. What if he decides it's too hard? Relationships take work. He'll tire of us and move on and I'll risk everything but still lose him.'

Grace nods, her face serious, so I feel marginally appeased for my rambling thoughts. 'Well, there are certainly no guarantees in any relationship, but you and Oliver have a better chance than most. You know each other better than anyone else. You have a long and solid friendship on which to build a relationship. And, if you don't tell him how you feel now, it might be too late.'

I nod, almost unconsciously. She's right. I do know him. I know everything about him, because he's always shown me that he values me. That he cares. He's capable of the kind of commitment I'm looking for, because he's given me that from day one. With his friendship. I have to trust that he can move past his insecurities over Slay and extend that commitment to our romantic relationship.

Perhaps I'm the one holding back.

I wince, because where he's confessed his deepest shame, making himself vulnerable like never before, I didn't fight for him. I allowed him to assume that I'd judged him. I didn't chase after him and explain myself. I've been the worst friend, too scared to put myself out there like he did, lay myself open and say the words.

Because he doesn't know me. He doesn't know everything. In order to guard my heart, I've fooled myself that all I want is the pretence of him, when really, I want it all. I don't need to cling to my fears, not when there's so much at stake. The ultimate prize. Oliver.

I stand so suddenly, my chair scrapes and several pairs of eyes look our way.

'Where are you going?' Grace asks, as with trembling hands I tug the end of my scarf from under the leg of the chair.

'I have to go and tell him that I love him. Because I don't think he knows.'

I flick her a wobbly grin, too panicked to say anything further, but she's a good friend. She understands.

Grace smiles widely. 'Of course he doesn't, otherwise he'd never have let you go.'

CHAPTER SEVENTEEN

Oliver

MY VIEW OF London from my Canary Wharf office holds none of its usual charm. I disconnect the call to a member of my legal team. The good news that Kimoto Corp finally purchased my artificial intelligence software for a nine-figure sum falls hollow. I stare blindly out of my window, frozen with inertia.

I'll probably make the business news tomorrow, for all the right reasons. But the victory means less—nothing, in fact—when I can't celebrate with Neve.

I scrub a hand over my face, closing my eyes for a brief moment. I see her face, her look of horror when I told her how much like Slay I'd behaved in the past. I wrench my eyes open. I don't need to see that expression to recall it, because that's the moment I knew I'd lost her for good. Both any feelings she had for me and her friendship.

So how the hell do I move on now?

My indiscretion is in the past. Teenage years are the time to make mistakes and grow up. The point is to outgrow that propensity. Some of us do, and some of us don't—like Slay. But I made another mistake back then. A worse one, with longer reaching consequences.

I hid my feelings for Neve. I told myself I didn't deserve her, and denied my attraction, and that's the thing I'd change if I had one time-travelling wish.

Because I love her and there's nothing more real, more deserving.

I don't want to move on. I don't have to. I just need to convince her that no one will ever love her more.

I jolt to my feet, energised into action. At that moment a message arrives from my assistant.

'I have Neve Grayson here. She says it's urgent.'

I fumble to fasten my jacket buttons as I stride to the door. I swing it open, my heart in my throat. And there she is.

Her cheeks are ruddy, perhaps from the cold outside, and she's huffing, as if she took the stairs all the way to the fortieth floor.

'Hi,' I say, stunned by the wonderful, beautiful sight of her, an automatic smile tugging my mouth. 'I was just on my way to find you. Come in.' I step aside, gesture her into the office and close the door.

I don't think my heart could beat any faster.

She turns to face me and for several endless seconds we stand and stare.

I snap to my senses. 'Would you like a drink?' I ask, not sure what to do with my hands short of touching her, so I stuff them in my pockets.

'No, thanks.' She fidgets with the scarf in her hand.

'Can I take your coat?' Why is this so awkward? And how can I make it right? Because I need to make it right. I refuse to lose her. I'll do whatever it takes, be whatever she wants. But her absence from my life is not an option I can tolerate.

She shrugs out of the coat and tosses it on the leather sofa nearby. 'I'm sorry to interrupt. I'm sure you're busy.'

'I'm not too busy for you,' I say, my mouth full to bursting with all the other things I want to say. 'You look great, by the way.' Her tan still glows, bringing out the flecks of moss-green in her eyes. 'I missed you.'

Fuck it. I don't care if she hates me now. I don't care that I might be repulsive in her eyes. I need to tell her all the things crushing me, because I should have said them nine years ago and I have nothing else to lose.

'Oliver...' Her hesitation sickens me, but I'm past caring, because I'm less without her, and I want to be whole. To be worthy of her, even if I can't be with her.

'I need to tell you something,' I say. 'I should have told you this nine years ago. I love you, Neve. I should have said it sooner.'

My voice catches and I make a fist inside my pocket. 'Perhaps you can't think of me that way, after…everything…but I still want you to know how I feel. Because you were never second best. I chose you the day we met. You were a breath of fresh air in my life. You rescued me from the destructive, self-loathing path I'd gone down. I wanted you in my life but I wasn't ready, wasn't mature enough to handle you back then, to deserve you. You mattered to me more than anyone else. You still do. And you always will.'

She swallows hard, her big eyes round.

'And you were right about me.' I rush on, saying it all before she decides to leave. 'Everything you said was true. I'm not Slay. Nothing like him. I don't care what other people say or think. Because all I really care about is you. Your happiness. And, if you're happier without me in your life, or if you want to just go back to being friends, then I'll do whatever it takes to fix this, because you make me a better man. You always have. And I absolutely cannot lose you.' I take a half-step closer. 'I can't.'

Her hands flinch at her sides, the only move she makes. I swallow down the crushing trepidation that feels like acid and force my features into some sort of neutral smile, while every emotion roars in my head, warp-factor ten.

'I don't want to be your friend,' she says.

I exhale a part of me I know I'll never get back.

'I understand.' I hate the flatness of my voice, because I'm a liar. I just told her whatever she wanted would be okay with me. But it's *not* okay. It will never be okay that she's not mine.

'No.' She shakes her head. 'I don't think you do, because I've always hidden how I feel about you.' She steps closer too, so we're only a couple of feet apart. One move and I could touch her, but instead I force myself to focus on her words.

'I lied and pretended and denied my feelings so I could be your friend. I told myself I stood no chance with you, so what was the point of risking your friendship?' she says. 'Because that was the only way I could handle my feelings for you and keep them a secret. I took any part of you I could get rather than being nothing to you.'

'You were never nothing,' I bite out, pressure building in my head. 'You're everything.'

She wrings her hands. 'But I deceived you. Because a part of me has always loved you from the start, and now I'm so desperately in love with you that I messed everything up.'

I shake my head. Her words make no sense. I'm the one who messed up.

'I hurt you when you opened yourself up to me,

because I was too scared to be as vulnerable as you were.' Her eyes plead. 'But friendship won't satisfy me any longer. I want more. I want all of you—every bad, sexy, playful, caring inch.'

I can hardly compute what she's saying. 'You should have told me.' It comes out sounding like an recrimination but the only person I blame is myself. 'Back then. And I should have told you.'

She nods. 'Maybe neither of us was ready nine years ago, but I should have told you how I feel in the Maldives rather than let you leave thinking I care about something you did as an angry, confused teenager. I don't care about anything but you. Us. I don't care about Slay, or the past or the press. I just want you. I love you.'

I stride to her, then scoop her up in my arms and kiss her. 'I love you too. God, do I love you.' I kiss her smiling lips. 'So much. So much it hurts.'

Her arms come around my waist, under my suit jacket, and she holds me tight. She laughs, tears in her eyes as she accepts my crazed kisses peppering her face and returns them with a few of her own. But it's not enough. It will never be enough. I'll always want more of my wondrous Neve.

'We're such idiots.' She sniffs and buries her head against my chest, over my pounding heart.

'I agree. There are elements of the ridiculous about us, but that's why we're meant for each other.'

'You really love me?' she asks, a soft murmur.

I nod, my chest full to bursting. 'I love you so much that I can't breathe or think or function without you. I love you so much that I binge-watched that baking show you love last night. I've binned any trace of coconut in my pantry, just in case, and I found four videos of cute puppies I want to send you—the ones that make you cry.'

Her smile tears my heart in two. 'That *is* a lot.'

I stride to the sofa, sitting down with her in my lap so we can resume the kissing in comfort.

She straddles my thighs, her skirt riding up as our kisses grow heated. Then she pulls back, the look of love and lust on her face making her more exquisite than ever. 'Do you have meetings this afternoon?' She wriggles on my lap and I forget what day it is, let alone what's on my schedule.

'Yes,' I say with a sinking feeling in my gut. 'You?'

'Yes.' She sighs, leaning forward to kiss my neck.

'I'll cancel them,' I tell her without hesitation. There's nothing more important to me than Neve.

She looks up with that naughty glint in her eye, her bottom lip trapped under her teeth. 'I will too. Let's be bad and play hooky together.'

'Deal.' I kiss her once more. 'But first I need to do something.' I retrieve the ring box from my pocket. Even consumed with business during my brief trip to Japan, she was at the forefront of my mind. Purchasing an engagement ring I know she'll love was my first priority when the plane touched down.

I take the ring from the box, feeling her held breath and her eyes on me, and hold it up between us. 'I should have done it properly the first time, because I meant every word. So I'll ask you again. A fresh start.

'Neve Sara Grayson, I'll love you for ever. I'm less without you. So, will you marry me?'

'Yes,' she says, laughing and crying at the same time. Kissing me, holding out her trembling hand for my ring.

I press a kiss to her ring finger, my lips lingering for a few heartbeats, and then slide the diamond in place. 'There—now you're finally mine.'

'Yes, and you're mine—so take me home, so we can do dirty things to each other.'

'Whatever you say, my darling. It will be my pleasure.'

EPILOGUE

Two months later, Christmas Eve

Neve

OLIVER AND I have spent Christmas together before, at my parents' or his mother's, but never just the two of us. And this year, as the song goes, he's all I want for Christmas. For ever.

I've lit the fire in his huge living room for that festive feel, but I've also deliberately cranked the heating up so high that he's wandering around in just his jeans and a Christmas apron I gave him as an early present. It says, *Screw nice, let's be naughty.* It's all part of my cunning plan to get him naked… And to think that he lived under the mistaken impression that I'm somehow sweet for nine years.

We've spent the afternoon baking mince pies together and drinking mulled wine. He suggested a Christmas movie, but his penthouse apartment is so pretty—both inside, with a huge tree, and outside, with views of a glittering London from the wall of windows—that together with the arresting sight of his sexiness there's enough visual distraction.

He comes up behind me and traps me where I'm leaning against the wiped-clean kitchen counter with one arm each side. He nuzzles my neck, sending delicious shivers down my spine.

'I'm so glad you're here,' he says, kissing my temple.

'Me too.' I lift my mouth up to his kiss and turn to face him, wrapping my arms around his waist. 'So, what's your Christmas wish?' I slide my hand up his naked back and walk my fingers over his shoulder and down his chest.

'Well, that's easy. You. For ever. You're also going to be my New Year's resolution, by the way.' His lips trail my jaw and down my neck and I loll my head to the side, giving him access as desire grips me. After all, it has been all of four hours since we were last naked together...

'Well, we'd better start planning our wedding, then,' I say, smiling when he jerks upright, his handsome face alive with wonder and hope.

'Really?' He grips my waist, lifting me up, and I cling to his hips with my thighs.

'Really,' I say, kissing him as he walks us to the enormous white leather sofa facing the fire.

We shed our clothes, laughing, kissing and loving each other, exactly the way we were meant to be. When he's laid out on top of me, love and passion in his expression, I'm momentarily distracted.

'Oliver, can you smell burning?' I ask.

He stops kissing my chest and sniffs the air. 'Fuck, I think it's the mince pies.'

I hold in a laugh. 'Oh, dear,' I say, wrapping my legs around his hips to stop his escape. 'So there is something you're no good at. Don't worry. Keep practising. We'll make a cook of you yet.'

'Sod it.' He grins, his mouth finding my nipple in a pinch of revenge that only encourages me to tease him more. 'I have smoke alarms.'

And then we lose ourselves in one of the things he excels at.

Friends. Lovers. In love.

* * * * *

DATING THE BILLIONAIRE

LISA CHILDS

MILLS & BOON

To my perfect match, Andrew Ahearne.

CHAPTER ONE

"I DON'T NEED a matchmaking service," Blair Snyder said, throwing up her hands to ward off her friend's efforts to convince her.

Since they had been little kids, Miranda Fox had always been able to talk Blair into things that weren't good for her…like eating the cupcakes her mother had made for her book club meeting. Or starting a pet-sitting business even though she was allergic to dogs. Or ditching school to stake out the arena where a boy band was performing.

Even today, many years since they'd been little kids, Miranda had talked her into flying, on a moment's notice, to Milan, Italy, to meet her for drinks on Hotel Galles's rooftop. Fortunately Blair was a pilot with access to her company's fleet of private planes, so she wouldn't have any repercussions from this excursion like she had all those other times Miranda had talked her into things. Blair wasn't going to get in trouble for using the plane…unless her business partner, who was also her older brother, found out she'd used the Cessna to meet Miranda. He'd always considered her school friend a bad influence on her, which was pretty damn ironic coming from him.

But maybe it was easier for one bad influence to recognize another…because Miranda had never been a huge fan of his, either.

As far as things Miranda had talked her into doing went, this was one of the better ones. Blair had already taken in the view of the steeples of the Duomo and, in the distance, the golden mounds of the Alps. Now she lifted her face to the warmth of the sun shining down on them and raised her glass of pinot grigio to her mouth for a long sip. A sigh of contentment slipped out of her lips.

The contentment didn't last—not when Miranda tapped her long, manicured nails against the glass tabletop and asked, "So who are you seeing?"

With the waiter hovering nearby, Blair fought the temptation to flip off her friend and instead just glared at her. "You know I'm not seeing anyone."

As well as her partner in past crimes, Miranda was—as always—her confidante. She told her everything. Unfortunately. They were more than best friends; they were like sisters. Actually, Blair with her blond hair and blue eyes looked more like Miranda than either of the matchmaker's biological sisters did.

Miranda smiled. "I can fix that for you. I can find you your soul mate."

"The last thing I want is a husband." She shuddered at the thought of some man trying to control her, to pin her down, to keep her in one place...

It was too horrible a thought to even allow into her mind. Especially here on this beautiful rooftop, with these beautiful views.

"I didn't say husband," Miranda said with a shudder of her own as she uttered the word like it was a curse. "You don't have to marry the guy. You can just *enjoy* him."

Blair hadn't *enjoyed* a guy in a long time, which her friend damn well knew. "But you said soul mate." Another tremor ran through her at the hopelessly romantic term. "That sounds like something our mothers would say."

"Liaisons International is not your mother's matchmaking service," Miranda continued defensively. "Well, it's not *my* mother's matchmaking service, not anymore, not since my sisters and I took over the company and changed the entire business model for it."

A smile tugged at Blair's lips, and she shook her head. Even though it had been a few months, she was still in shock over what her friend had done. "I can't believe you went into the family business—not with the way you always felt about it."

She had listened to Miranda and her sisters, but

especially Miranda, rant and rave so many times over their mother's company, over everything about their mother. Catarina was the hopeless romantic who'd started the matchmaking business, and with five marriages in her fifty-five years of life, she really was hopeless. So Blair had always supported and understood her friend's frustration with her mother, just as Miranda had understood Blair's frustration with hers.

Miranda raised her wineglass to her lips and tipped back what was left of her red, as if she needed it to brace herself. "Me neither," she murmured. "But I saw a need for an overhaul in that old system and for more security in the new system that men and women use to meet and date."

"Apps are the new system," Blair said with a sigh of resignation. She'd tried them herself.

"Apps," Miranda said, her voice sharp with disgust, "make it too easy for people to lie about themselves and about their true intentions. At Liaisons International, we vet every single member, so that there are no unwelcome surprises. It's the safest way to date worldwide."

Blair chuckled now at what must have been their company's marketing slogan. "You are good, my friend. You've nearly sucked me in."

"I'm not trying to suck you in," Miranda said. "I'm trying to get you back out there, dating, safely."

"Isn't that an oxymoron?" Blair asked. A former fighter pilot, she was tough, but there had been times dating had scared her, when the men had gotten too aggressive, too clingy and too stalkerish. She'd been able to handle them, but she'd been reluctant to put herself into that situation again.

"I promise you won't be harassed," Miranda persisted. "And that all of our members are exceptionally attractive."

"Isn't that discrimination?" Blair asked. When trying to become a fighter pilot, she'd been subjected to way too much of that as well.

Miranda shrugged and smiled. "I just call it good fortune…" She inclined her head toward the attractive young waiter. "Like the male members make him look homely."

"Yeah, right," Blair remarked with a chuckle. But temptation pulled at her, drawing her in.

To what?

Possibilities? She didn't want marriage, but she actually wouldn't mind enjoying a man again. Really, really enjoying him…

Trying not to appear too intrigued, she studied her wineglass with the setting sun glowing within the pale amber liquid. Then she oh-so-casually asked, "So who are some of these male members?"

"Tsk, tsk, no, no, no…" Miranda admonished her with a shake of her head. "You're going to have to join if you want to find out."

"And I thought we were friends," Blair teased.

"We are," Miranda said. "That's why I want you to join. You work so hard all the time—first in the air force and now with your business. You need to balance all that work with some play, with some fun."

Skeptical, Blair arched a brow. "Fun? Since when is dating fun?" It had never been that for her. Every man she'd met had tried to change her in some way, had wanted her to be more feminine, less *her*.

"Dating will be fun for you now," Miranda promised as she lifted her empty glass to clink against the rim of Blair's. "Since you have just become the newest member of Liaisons International."

Blair groaned in realization of what she'd done. In joining the dating service, she had let Miranda talk her into something again—something that was undoubtedly going to get her in trouble, just as she had gotten into trouble every time she'd let Miranda talk her into anything.

What the hell had Matteo Rinaldi gotten himself into? Joining a dating service was risky, but dating blindly had proved even riskier—as all the advertising for Liaisons International had pointed out.

He leaned over the sink in the bathroom of his hotel suite and stared into the mirror to adjust the black tie of his tuxedo. Matteo was about to find out if the premier dating service was actually going to deliver on the promises it had made him when he joined.

No games.

No lies.

No secret agendas.

That was what he'd been promised. Other women had made him those same promises but had, over and over again, broken their vows. They'd played games. They'd lied. They'd had their own agendas.

He was not going to be blindsided. Ever again. His eyes were wide open now. Whatever his date had told the service, he doubted that she really wasn't looking for a husband and a rich one at that. Why else would she have signed up for the elite agency?

He made that assumption because that had been his experience with women; starting with his mom who'd used men for financial support and had taught his sister, Francesca, to do the same. They weren't above using him either, especially now.

Hopefully tonight went well and not just with his date. He glanced at his watch, checking to see if she was late. She had better not be—because he couldn't be late. Not tonight.

So he probably shouldn't have set up his first date with Liaisons International for this evening of all evenings. But knowing Francesca, his attending the event solo would cause more problems for him than bringing along a stranger. She, undoubtedly, had a friend she wanted to set up with him.

As he walked out of the bathroom, he noticed a darkness at the bottom of the door to the hall. No light showed through the crack as it had earlier. Someone or something had cast a shadow against his door. Nobody had knocked, so it was probably a maid's cleaning cart or a room service trolley. He hadn't ordered either, though.

All he'd ordered was a date for the evening, and now it occurred to him how odd the whole process had been. He hadn't been shown any photos. Hadn't talked to his potential match through email or text. Was Liaisons International actually a dating service?

Or was it something else entirely?

An escort service?

No. Before signing up, he'd thoroughly checked it out. Even though its name had recently changed, the business had been active for a long time with nothing but glowing reviews and recommendations. But that had been for when it was Matchmakers International. It sounded like something else entirely now.

Not that he would have signed up for a matchmaking service; that sounded too old-fashioned and far too permanent, like finding the match for the rest of one's damn life. Teo just wanted a date, so he could ward off amateur matchmakers and the gold diggers those amateurs often found for him.

Where the hell was his date?

Not that she was late.

Yet.

He glanced down at the crack beneath the door and noticed the shadow receding. Maybe the cart or trolley was being pushed away. Or maybe…

Curiosity compelled him to pull open the door and, feeling like he'd been punched in the gut, he sucked in a breath of shock. She had her back to him but that wasn't necessarily a bad thing, since her backside was so very good.

A black silk dress clung to the sweet curves of her hips and her ass, and the short hemline of the dress exposed the longest damn legs he'd ever seen. Blond hair flowed partway down her back, falling like a deep gold curtain against the fabric that couldn't compare to the silky look of her hair. If her face was half as attractive as her legs…

Then the dating service had done damn well. But maybe she had been walking away from some other room, not his.

She might have nothing to do with Liaisons International. But before she even turned around, he hoped like hell that she did, that she was his date.

"Ciao," he called out to her. She didn't stop, those long legs bringing her ever closer to the elevator and ever farther away from him. So he tried English. "Hello? Are you looking for me?" he asked.

She stopped, as if frozen, in the hall, her back to him yet.

So he continued, "I'm Matteo—" She turned around, and he was so stunned by her beauty that he momentarily forgot his own damn name.

She couldn't be from the dating service. There was no way that a woman this stunningly beautiful was unattached. She must have been leaving some other room, some other man...

And for the first time in a long time, envy gripped Matteo. He hadn't felt this envious in years, not since he was a hungry kid begging for change on the streets of Rome, so that he could help feed his family. In the years since then, he had worked hard and accumulated a fortune, so Teo hadn't thought he would ever be hungry or jealous again.

He'd thought wrong.

CHAPTER TWO

BLAIR HAD MADE a mistake—a very big mistake—
when she let Miranda talk her into joining a dating
service, especially such an odd one. As she'd stood
outside the door of the hotel suite, hand raised to
knock on the dark mahogany wood, it occurred to
her that she might be mistaken for an escort, the
way she was showing up at a man's hotel room.
Anyone passing her in the hall might think she was
one, especially as she'd been told to wear a little
black dress for a semiformal event. Maybe the man
she was supposed to meet already thought she was
an escort—that was why he'd told Miranda how to
have her dress.

Matteo Rinaldi.

That was the name Miranda had given her—
along with the number of the suite in the swanky
hotel where he was staying. What the hell had her
friend talked her into? Prostitution?

Maybe that was what Miranda had meant when

she'd said it wasn't her mother's matchmaking service. Her mother's service had had rules. Etiquette.

What the hell were the rules here? Knowing Miranda and how she had always rebelled against her
mother's rules, there probably weren't any.

So before she'd even knocked, Blair had decided to leave, but as she'd been walking away, he'd
opened the door and called out to her. She shouldn't
have stopped; she sure as hell shouldn't have turned
around…because now she really didn't want to walk
away.

He was so damn good-looking with thick,
slightly curling chocolate-brown hair and heavily
lashed chocolate-brown eyes. To the chocoholic
that Blair was, he looked good enough to eat. And
his body…

He was so tall and broad that his shoulders
stretched the seams of his tailored tuxedo. Like
James freakin' Bond, he wore a tuxedo. To her he
was an international man of mystery as well, a man
who spoke Italian so fluently it must have been his
native language. He was crazy good-looking, like
mega-movie-star good-looking.

How the hell had Miranda talked him into joining the dating service? He was too ridiculously
attractive to need help finding women. But then
she hadn't needed help finding men, either; she'd
needed help screening the assholes that she had always wound up dating.

Miranda claimed that she'd vetted everyone thoroughly before letting them join, and she'd assured her that Matteo Rinaldi was anything but an asshole. What was he, though? Besides ridiculously good-looking?

All the information he'd allowed Miranda to share about him had been his name and his hotel suite number and that he did something in business or owned a business. It would be such a shame if he really just wanted an escort. But for him, Blair might be tempted...

No. Unlike her best friend, she had rules. Unfortunately.

"Are you looking for me?" he asked again from the doorway to his room.

So she didn't openly drool over him, she had to swallow all the saliva that had pooled in her mouth before she replied. Even then all she managed was to mutter, "This is a mistake."

He uttered a sigh of disappointment. "You're not from the service then?"

"What kind of service do you think it is?" she wondered aloud.

He glanced uneasily around the hallway, as if afraid someone might overhear them. Then he stepped back into the suite, holding open the door, and gestured for her to join him.

She shook her head, unwilling to walk into that room until she knew he had the same expectations she did. "*I* think it's a dating service," she said. "But I'm not sure what *you* think it is since you had the audacity to ask me to meet you in your hotel room."

She'd told Miranda that that was weird—that a first meeting should be in public place like a coffee shop or even a bar. But Miranda had again pointed out that was a precaution only when meeting people from apps, that every member of her service was so thoroughly vetted that she would be safe wherever she met them. Knowing Miranda and her resources, she had researched everything and interviewed everyone related to every member of the dating service, but Blair had already been too cynical, even before the Me Too movement, to fully trust anyone.

She sure didn't feel safe right now, but that might have been from how hard her heart was pounding, how fast it was racing—just from looking at him.

A grin pulled at the corners of his mouth, and a rueful chuckle slipped out. "Ah, now I understand your hesitation to knock."

Heat climbed to her face, probably turning it bright red. Damn Miranda for landing her in trouble again, maybe even legal trouble this time if he truly believed she was an escort.

"That's not what I signed up for," she warned him. Although if he looked as good out of that tux as he did in it, she might…

She wouldn't be opposed to enjoying him. She

just didn't want him making assumptions that it was going to happen. Miranda might not be as good at vetting out assholes as she'd promised she was.

Because if she was, why the hell was she single, too?

Of course, after her mother's many marriages, Miranda had vowed long ago to stay single. Like their blond hair and blue eyes, that vow was one of the other things they had in common. Not that Blair's mom had been married many times. Just once.

But since she'd married Blair's dad, once had been too many. Not that Dad had been a terrible person.

He'd just been the wrong person for her mother.

Just like maybe Matteo Rinaldi was the wrong person for her. Not that she was looking for her soul mate. She nearly snorted at the ridiculous notion of anyone having a soul mate, but she stopped herself when she glanced up and found Matteo studying her face. He leaned against the jamb of the open door, one of his dark brows arched.

Resisting the urge to wipe a hand across her face to check for makeup smudges, she asked instead, "What?"

"It's a shame," he murmured with a heavy sigh.

"What's a…oh…" Her temper flared. "No, it's not a shame that I'm not an escort." But it was a shame that he was an asshole after all. She turned

on the point of her stiletto heel to head back to the
elevators.

A big hand wrapped around her bare arm, not
so tightly that she couldn't have shrugged it off and
kept on going. But, her skin tingling from the contact with his, she stopped. She didn't turn toward
him, though; she just waited, breath held in anticipation of what he would say.

"I'm sorry," a deep voice murmured. "I couldn't
resist." He sighed. "But it is inappropriate to tease
you when you are clearly concerned about this."

"It's as inappropriate as asking me to meet you
in a hotel room," she said as she turned back toward him.

He nodded in agreement. "I am sorry about that,
too. I didn't think of how it might seem…"

She narrowed her eyes with suspicion.

"I don't have a place in Milan," he said, "so I
checked into the hotel."

"You could have asked me to meet you somewhere else," she pointed out. "The lobby, a restaurant…"

"I have plans—"

"That's what worries me," she interjected. What
were his plans, though? And why did her pulse
quicken at the thought that they might have been
sexual?

She must had gone too damn long without enjoying a man. Mechanical toys were just not the same.

He chuckled. "My plans are not nefarious. I have to go to a gallery opening—" he glanced at his watch "—and I was worried about being late, which I will probably be now."

"Then don't let me keep you," she said.

"I would like for you to join me," he said. "And I promise that I have no ulterior motives beyond enjoying an evening with you."

She wrinkled her nose. "At a gallery?"

"Not an art fan?"

She shrugged. "I don't know much about it." She'd been too busy learning other things, like how to stay alive during a firefight.

But if she told him...

And if he was as chauvinistic as most of her other dates had been, the night would probably already be over, and she didn't want it to end yet. Matteo Rinaldi was too handsome and too intriguing for her to cut the date short.

"We won't stay long," he said, sliding his hand down her arm to her elbow—leaving a trail of tingling skin in the wake of his touch.

"I'm not coming back here," she warned him.

Unless...

Unless Miranda had been telling the truth, and he wasn't the asshole she was worried he was.

"I didn't invite you back," he pointed out. "My only expectation of this date was for someone to accompany me to the gallery opening."

She narrowed her eyes and studied his face. "And you couldn't find someone else to bring?"

He narrowed his eyes back at her, but amusement glinted in the warm chocolate. "And you couldn't find someone else to spend the evening with not admiring art?"

A smile tugged at her lips. "Touché, or so you would understand, toccato."

"Oh, maybe you do speak my language after all," he murmured appreciatively.

She shrugged. She'd learned long ago it was best not to reveal all her assets too soon. More often they intimidated rather than impressed. "Most Americans know some Italian. Vendetta. Zucchini. Casanova."

He looked like a Casanova, but he clearly wasn't American. While his accent wasn't thick, it was pronounced enough that it softened and rolled the tone of every word like chocolate melting. Everything about him—his hair, his eyes, his voice—reminded her of her greatest weakness: chocolate.

And just like chocolate, he probably wasn't good for her. He wouldn't make her face break out like her favorite vice, but if he was a Casanova, he could possibly make something else break—like her heart, if she wasn't very cautious. Even knowing that she needed to be very, very cautious, she waited while he closed his hotel room door, and then she walked with him toward the elevator. When the doors opened, she drew in a deep, bracing breath before stepping inside the small car with him.

Not that she was physically afraid. She'd learned long ago how to defend herself; she'd had to, or she wouldn't have survived high school, let alone the air force academy and basic training.

But she wasn't sure if she would be able to defend herself emotionally if Matteo Rinaldi turned on the charm that seemed to ooze, like his expensive cologne, from his every perfect pore. The deep breath she'd drawn in filled her senses with the scent of him, which was a combination of that expensive musky cologne and raw masculinity.

He stepped inside the elevator with her, and he filled it with his physical presence and his charismatic presence. Her pulse quickened, and a heaviness settled on her chest with a hint of panic.

Just what the hell had Miranda gotten her into?

Matteo couldn't remember the last time, if ever, that he'd been as intrigued with a woman as he was this one. And he didn't even know her name. If she hadn't been insistent about making it so damn clear that she wasn't an escort, he might have had his suspicions...about the dating service and about the stunning blonde they'd sent to him. One of the owners, Miranda Fox, had made it clear that the members had to treat each other with respect at all times, though. No assumptions and absolutely no coercions.

He'd appreciated that. He also appreciated the blonde. He appreciated her bluntness in making herself absolutely clear that he should have no expectations about how the evening might end. Even more than her bluntness, he appreciated the way she looked. So damn beautiful...

Standing as close as they were in the elevator, he was incredibly aware of her beauty and of her very essence. She had such poise and grace, her head held high with dignity or maybe righteous indignation. He needed to stop teasing her, but it was hard to resist. She was hard to resist.

Awareness pulsated within him, like the blood pumping hot and fast through his veins as his heart beat harder and faster. Even though he stood more than a foot from her, heat arced between them, flushing his skin, making it tingle.

"What is your name?" he asked, his voice gruff with frustration in his overwhelming physical reaction to her and in the strange rules of the dating service that only gave out names if the members approved it.

Her lips curved into a Mona Lisa smile, fitting since they were about to attend a gallery opening. Not that he expected to find any masterpieces hanging from the walls of this particular art gallery. This woman was a work of art, though, with her perfectly

toned, long body and her perfectly featured face. A
dark blond brow arched over a dark blue eye. "You
don't know?"

The tie seemed to tighten around his neck as
heat sneaked up from beneath it. Not knowing the
identity of the person meeting him painted him the
fool. Teo hated feeling foolish. "When I spoke last
to the service, Miranda Fox was working on finding the perfect date for me, but in case she wasn't
able to convince the new member to sign up, she
couldn't give me the name of the woman she wanted
me to meet."

The blonde chuckled. "So you have no idea if
I'm just the next best match or if I'm the perfect
date."

She knew, though, because that maddening smile
played around her lips again.

And Teo knew as well—from her beauty, from
her quick wit—she was undoubtedly the perfect
date. In Miranda Fox's opinion but not his. He didn't
like games, and he hated being played for a fool.
All he wanted was her name; he shouldn't have to
work so hard for it.

The elevator shuddered to a stop in the lobby,
and the doors opened to the marble and mahogany
foyer of the elegant hotel. She moved toward those
open doors, but Teo caught her elbow again, holding her back. "You wanted to make it clear earlier
that you're not an escort."

She tensed and jerked her elbow from his grasp. "I'm not. Are you?"

He narrowed his eyes and glared at her. "No, and I'm not an idiot, either. Please, don't treat me like one."

She sighed. "I'm sorry," she said with a quickness and sincerity that both surprised and delighted him.

He didn't know many people who were as willing to admit to having made a mistake, any mistake.

"I haven't been on a date in a while," she said. "And this whole situation…"

"Is awkward," he agreed. But it was beginning to feel less and less awkward and more and more intriguing.

Everything about her intrigued him.

"Yes," she agreed very heartily, with the awkwardness, not the intriguing. She couldn't know what he was thinking. "I may kill Miranda for putting me in this situation."

"So you're definitely the perfect date," he said. "I'm not sure how I feel about your having to be talked into joining the service." At the risk of sounding arrogant, he added, "I've never had to force anyone to go on a date with me before." But that was more likely because of his money than his looks or personality.

Her lips curved into a smile again, this one not

quite so Mona Lisa-like, and she heartily agreed again, "I can believe that."

Since she couldn't know about his money, she must have found him attractive as well.

"Which makes me wonder why you joined the service," she continued. "Did Miranda talk you into it, too?"

She'd given his pride an out. He could have claimed to have been coerced as she'd clearly been, but Matteo was always honest, usually as most people would agree, to a fault. He shook his head. "No, I chose to join."

Pink color flushed her cheeks so that they matched the pink hue of her glossed lips. Her voice soft, she repeated her apology, "I'm sorry."

And he was compelled to challenge her. "You don't seem like the type of woman who could be talked into something she didn't actually want to do anyway."

Her brow momentarily creased before she chuckled, apparently at herself. "Toccato…again…"

He wanted to touch her instead; he wanted to use his hand to reel her into his arms, up against his body, which was beginning to pulse with desire. But they were probably already late, and she'd made it clear that he was to have no expectations about how this evening would end. At the moment he hoped that it wouldn't.

So he forced himself to escort her from the elevator. It was only as they were walking across the lobby that he realized she still hadn't told him her name.

Why was she so reluctant to share her identity with him? What was she hiding?

CHAPTER THREE

"SAVANNAH," BLAIR SAID, the lie slipping out of her lips almost unbidden. It wasn't entirely a lie, though.

Savannah was legally her first name, but she never used it. For some reason she didn't want this man to call her the name everyone else—even her mother after many protests—used for her. What the hell was wrong with her?

As Matteo had pointed out, she wasn't the type to be talked into something she didn't want to do anyway. If she had, she never would have survived the career path she'd chosen. Hell, she would have never entered it at all…if she'd listened to her mother.

Which she never did.

Which was why her mother had given up calling her Savannah, since she'd never answered to it because she'd always protested that it sounded too girlie.

"Savannah," he repeated, the name rolling off his tongue like melted chocolate. He held out a hand to help her from the car they'd taken from the hotel to an area north of Milan that appeared to be mostly industrial. There was already a gallery in this area; Miranda had mentioned it once to her, and the name had reminded her of an airport hangar. When she stepped onto the pavement and glanced up at the building they'd stopped in front of, she tensed, because this building actually was an airport hangar.

Had he been messing with her all along? Had Miranda actually told him all about her? She never should have trusted her friend or him. She tried to pull her hand free of his grasp, but he held firm and stroked his thumb across her knuckles.

"Delighted to meet you, Savannah."

His touch, and his charm, disarmed her for a moment, so that when he released her, she didn't move. He turned back to the chauffeur, who'd closed the door behind them, and said in Italian, "We won't be long, so don't go far."

Before she could stop him, the chauffeur slid into the front seat and drove the idling limousine away. Another long black car took its place, and more luxury vehicles were lined up behind it. So it was pretty likely that this metal-and-stone structure wasn't actually an airplane hangar anymore.

Not unless the flights were extremely short... since he'd told the chauffeur to return soon. "We'll put in a brief appearance," he told her as his hand cupped her elbow again to escort her around the corner of the hangar.

The overhead doors stood open, light spilling from inside the building onto a courtyard filled with flowers, tall tables and people. They didn't even make it into the courtyard before a woman rushed up to them and threw her arms around Matteo's neck. She planted a big kiss on his cheek, leaving an imprint of her bright red lipstick on his skin when she finally pulled away.

Or had he pushed her? His hands cupped her shoulders. But it was hard to tell if he was fending off the woman or holding her close. Not that many men would want to fend off a woman who looked like her. With long, curly brown hair and wide, heavily lashed brown eyes, she was beautiful. A white dress clung to her curves and complemented her tan skin.

Grabbing his hands in hers, she asked in Italian, "What do you think? Isn't it perfect?"

"I don't know," he replied—in English. "You haven't let me see anything yet."

She linked her arm with his and began tugging him toward those open doors. But he stopped her short and admonished her in Italian, "Francesca, you're being rude. I have a guest."

"You brought someone?" she asked in surprise.

Blair wasn't surprised that she hadn't noticed her; she seemed to only be able to see Matteo. Not that Blair blamed her. He was a beautiful man, as beautiful as the woman was. They looked good together, and it was obvious they were close.

"I told you to come alone," she admonished him. "You were not supposed to bring a plus-one."

So why had he chosen to bring a date to the opening?

To make the woman jealous? Or to force her to accept that they were done?

And he'd said he didn't play games...

The woman focused on Blair now, her dark eyes narrowed as she studied her. "Where did you find this Amazon?" she asked in Italian.

If his intent had been to make Francesca jealous, apparently he'd succeeded.

"Francesca," Matteo said again. "You must stop being rude."

"You were rude to bring along someone when I specifically told you to come alone," she admonished him.

"Actually, you're both being rude," she informed them—in Italian, and she turned on her heel to head back toward the front of the building. Hopefully she could hire one of the cars bringing guests to take her away from the gallery. If not, she was angry enough to walk to the airport hangar where she'd stowed the plane she'd flown to Milan earlier that day. She hadn't known then, when just flying in for lunch with Miranda, that she would be staying. And now she wished like hell that she hadn't agreed to the date Miranda had already set up for her.

She didn't make it far before a long arm snaked around her waist and stopped her—the rear of her body pressed up against the front of his. The long, muscular front of his...

Heat rushed through her—the heat of desire and of anger. She warned him, "You better let me go!"

He was lucky that she hadn't reacted as defensively as she normally would have and elbowed him in the ribs before turning to plant her knee in his crotch. If she did that now, she could seriously hurt him. His body had reacted to the closeness of hers.

As if concerned that she might start physically defending herself, he loosened his grasp and stepped back. But with his hand on her waist, he turned her to face him. Before he could say anything, though, she lashed out at him.

"You lied to me," she said. "You claimed you don't play games, but that's obviously what this is."

"What?" he asked—all innocence.

"You're using me to make your girlfriend jealous," she said. "And I want no part of it."

"Girlfriend?"

"Francesca."

He chuckled. "Francesca is my sister."

The last of her anger drained away with a soft sigh of relief. But that relief was short-lived when his sister appeared behind them. She wasn't alone.

Another woman accompanied her—one nearly as beautiful as she was. Both of the women glared at her, making it clear to Blair that neither of them wanted her there.

"I should go," she said, and not just because she wasn't welcome, but also because she was much too attracted to a man whose life was too complicated for her.

Teo wasn't used to a woman trying to ditch him. Usually women fawned all over him instead, especially when they realized how much money he had. Not that Savannah knew.

Until someone exclaimed, "Francesca, introduce me to our benefactor! I cannot believe how generous he was to finance the entire gallery for you!"

He glanced over his shoulder to find his sister standing behind him with another woman. That woman looked at him the way women usually looked at him, the way he'd probably looked at Savannah earlier—hungrily. He turned his attention to his manipulative little sister and shook his head.

"Now is not the time," he warned her.

Francesca was one of the reasons he hated games and manipulation, but she'd learned from the best— their mother. This was the reason he'd brought along a date, because he'd known his sister didn't want him to bring one. Because she'd hatched some damn plan that he wanted no part of...

Of course she would excuse her actions as just trying to help him, as if he couldn't find his own damn date. That was another reason he'd joined the service, to prove to his sister that he could find somebody on his own.

Now if only he could keep her.

He turned back to find Savannah walking away from him again. She'd done that entirely too often since he'd met her just a short time ago.

"Please," he implored her. And he wasn't used to having to ask anyone for anything anymore, not since he'd been a kid. And he'd learned then that it had done no good to ask; he'd had to make his own way in the world. "Please, stay."

She stopped, her long body tense.

"I'm not playing games," he promised.

She turned her head and looked over her sexy bare shoulder at him, one golden brow arched in skepticism. "Really?"

"Not with you," he vowed. He glanced over his shoulder now, and he was relieved to find his sister walking away from him, towing the other woman along with her. "And I didn't want to play her game," he said. "That's why I chose not to come here alone."

Her lips curved into a knowing smile. "You were scared to come here alone."

He wanted to argue with her but found a chuckle slipping out instead. "Touché."

She chuckled, too. "I understand."

He suspected that she did; after all, she knew a matchmaker, too, and a professional one at that.

"Yes, you do," he said. "If you'll give me a chance, we can still have a fun evening. I'll call for the driver and—"

"You need to go back inside the gallery," she said.

He shook his head. "No."

"You're the benefactor," she reminded him, and of the fact that she spoke more than a few words of Italian.

How amazing was she?

She continued, "You're the one who financed the entire gallery. You need to be here for the opening."

He shrugged. "I wrote the check, so my part is done. I can leave."

"You came here for a reason," she said. "Was it to support your sister or to check on your investment?"

"Both," he acknowledged, albeit begrudgingly.

"Then do that," she urged.

He groaned and reluctantly admitted, "I don't want to go in there alone."

She turned fully toward him then and linked her arm with his. "You don't have to be afraid," she told him. "I'll protect you."

His body immediately reacted to the closeness of hers, as it had earlier when he'd jerked her against him. Tensing and hardening with desire...

He needed protection from her—not by her. Because it wasn't just his body reacting to her. His mind was engaged as well. She was smart and funny and fascinating.

And even though she'd told him not to be, he was afraid.

Of her.

CHAPTER FOUR

BLAIR HAD NEVER taken the easy way out. That was why she'd stopped herself from walking away, why she'd turned around and gone inside that gallery with Matteo. It hadn't been because she had any interest in art, although a few of the pieces actually affected her, more because of what they reminded her of than because of what they were.

Just twisted pieces of metal.

She shuddered as she stared at one of the larger installments. She'd given in to the reaction because, for the first time since coming inside the gallery, she'd thought she was alone.

But a female voice asked, "Is it that bad?"

Blair glanced up from the mangled steel and copper. "You speak English," she remarked to Matteo's sister.

"Yes," she said. "And I should have earlier. Teo will never forgive me my rudeness. Will you?"

"I don't hold grudges," Blair assured her. If she did, she probably would have stopped talking to

Miranda long ago. Hell, maybe she should have; then she wouldn't have been in this predicament. Although at the thought of never having met Matteo Rinaldi, a pang of disappointment struck her heart rather than any relief.

"Then perhaps you and I can be friends," Francesca suggested hopefully.

She was probably thirty, Blair's age, but she seemed younger, much younger. But then she probably hadn't lived through the things that Blair had. Or her big brother had protected her even more than Blair's big brother had.

While Blair didn't hold grudges long, she wasn't too quick to forgive, either, especially when she wasn't certain if the request for forgiveness was sincere or a manipulation.

"I doubt you and I have very much in common," she told Francesca.

"What about my brother?"

Matteo had wanted a date for the night—not forever. Blair had no illusions that she would see him or his sister again. But she'd promised to protect him from Francesca's matchmaking, so she forced a smile. "I doubt we see him the same way," Blair replied.

She suspected his sister saw him as an ATM to finance her whims. Some might have accused her of using her brother for financing, too, though.

"I hope we don't see him the same way," Francesca said with a laugh. "I hope you don't see him the way other women have, either."

"How is that?" she asked.

"As a meal ticket," Francesca said.

"I pay my own way," Blair assured her.

While Teo had financed the entire gallery for Francesca which included studios for artists in resident, Blair and Grant had invested equally in their business. Blair would never be less than an equal partner with any man—even her own brother.

"Francesca," Teo said, his deep voice full of warning. "Are you harassing my date?"

His sister chuckled. "We are just getting to know each other. She was admiring my masterpiece."

Blair glanced again at the twisted and tangled metal. "This is your work?"

Francesca nodded. "Maybe Teo will buy it for you."

"I'll buy it myself," Blair said, "if I decide I can live with it." But she was afraid that it would just continue to evoke bad memories—of her past and of this meeting with Matteo's sister. "What is it called?"

"*Chaos*," Francesca replied with an almost apologetic smile, as if she knew how badly the piece bothered Blair. As if it had bothered her that much as well.

Maybe they had more in common than Blair had suspected. "It's definitely evocative," she praised her.

"That's definitely Francesca," her brother agreed, but then he turned away from his sister and focused on her. "I called for the car. Alfred is waiting out front for us."

He'd told her he was stepping outside to make that call, so she wasn't surprised. His sister was, though, as she wailed in protest, "You can't leave already!"

Matteo buzzed a kiss near Francesca's cheek and stepped back. "We can't monopolize the hostess. Go, charm all your patrons."

"I don't think I've charmed your friend," Francesca said.

She hadn't, but Blair didn't need both Rinaldis charming her. Teo was enough.

He was more than enough. The minute they had stepped inside the gallery, he had been so very attentive despite the other guests and artists trying hard to capture his attention. He'd waved over waiters to keep Blair supplied with champagne and hors d'oeuvres.

She would have liked to blame the champagne for making her light-headed, but she knew it was him. He was so handsome, so charming that he was nearly making her dizzy. Or worse yet, giddy...

"I'll make up for what you've lacked," Teo assured his sister as he slid his arm around Blair's waist and steered her toward the door. People tried to stop him, but he brushed past them all as if he couldn't even see them. He saw the car, though, and guided her right to the door the chauffeur held open for them. After helping her inside, Matteo slid onto the seat beside her.

"*Grazie*, Alfred," he told the chauffeur who closed the door, leaving them alone in the enclosed space. Then Matteo turned to her and said, "Thank you."

She chuckled. "For what? For protecting you?"

She had seen that he hadn't needed any protection, not with how easily he had been able to move through the crowd. Matteo Rinaldi could obviously take care of himself and apparently everyone who mattered to him as well. For a second, just a split second, she allowed herself to wonder what it might be like to matter to him, to really matter, not just as an act to fool his meddling sister.

But Blair didn't need anyone to take care of her; she'd been taking care of herself for far too long to rely on anyone else. In fact she moved a little distance away from him, so that she didn't brush up against his body with each turn of the vehicle along the winding road.

"Your chauffeur can drop me at my hotel," she said. The partition between the front and back seats was closed, or she would have given the driver the address herself.

"We have a dinner reservation," he said, and he slid closer.

She couldn't be certain if he'd done it purposely or if the car's movement had caused him to slide over the seat. She knew his closeness affected her, making her pulse quicken and her skin tingle. His muscular thigh pushed against hers, the heat of his flesh penetrating the thin material of his tuxedo trousers and the silk of her dress.

"You don't have to feed me," she said. "I had plenty of hors d'oeuvres."

"Those were just appetizers," he said, his dark gaze on her mouth like he considered it the main course.

She shook her head. "Seriously, you don't have to do this," she said. "I know that you just signed up for the service so you would have someone to show to your sister, so that you could get her to stop trying to set you up on dates of her choosing."

He chuckled. "You would be very hard on my ego—with the way you keep trying to get away from me," he said. "But you were walking away from my room before I even opened the door, so I don't think it's because you find me so unattractive."

In fact, it was quite the opposite. She found him entirely too attractive and too charming.

He continued, "So it makes me wonder…why did you sign up for the service? Was it only to appease your meddling friend?"

She would have thought so, but she'd had a revelation over what he'd told her earlier that evening.

"I don't think I would have let her talk me into be- coming a member of the service if it was something I absolutely didn't want to do."

"So you really do want to meet someone?" he asked.

She shrugged. "I'm not looking for my—" she could barely choke out the word "—soul mate or anything."

He chuckled. "Did she make you that promise as well?"

"I didn't drink the Kool-Aid, did you?" she asked.

"Kool-Aid?"

"Guess that reference didn't translate," she mur- mured. "I don't believe in soul mates." She doubted that Miranda believed, either; it was just part of her company's new marketing campaign.

"That is something else we have in common," he said.

"Something else?" she asked. "I wasn't aware that we have anything in common." While she was financially secure, or as financially secure as one could be when one's business partner was a pro- fessional gambler, she certainly wasn't on the level that she suspected Matteo Rinaldi was. Too many people had bowed down to him at the gallery—like he was royalty or extremely rich and influential.

"We have something very important in com- mon," he said, sliding his fingers along the edge of her jaw to the place on her neck where her pulse pounded madly. "Attraction…"

She could have denied it, but it was palpable, vibrating on the air all around them. Her skin tingled with it; her heart beat with it. She couldn't remember the last time—if ever—that she'd been this attracted to anyone. She wanted him. Wanted to close the distance between his mouth and hers. His handsome face was so close—all she had to do was lean a little more toward him.

Brush her lips across his…

She could feel the heat of his breath whisper across her skin as his mouth opened. Before she could touch it, he spoke, "We're here."

The car braked, and she lurched that little bit forward. Their mouths touched—for just a second—not in a kiss but more of a collision. She felt a jolt, too, not of pain but of passion. It surged through her, stunning her.

But then the back door opened, and they pulled away from each other, chuckling. Matteo stepped out first, then extended his hand to her, to assist her from the back.

She stepped onto the sidewalk, which she expected to be outside his hotel. But it was an exclusive restaurant instead. The place had a Michelin rating, so getting a reservation had proved impossible—at least for her.

"Are we really eating here?" she asked in surprise. But then, given the way he'd been treated at the gallery, she shouldn't have been surprised.

"I told you the hors d'oeuvres at the opening were truly just appetizers," he said. "We will enjoy our main course here."

"But if you don't have a reservation…"

The front door opened before he reached it, and a maître d' stepped onto the sidewalk. "Mr. Rinaldi!" he exclaimed. "I did not know you were in town."

"I should have called," Matteo began.

But the older man waved his hand. "Of course you do not need to phone ahead," he said. "Your table always awaits you. And you…" He took Blair's hand and brushed a kiss across her knuckles.

At the gallery everyone had treated Matteo like royalty while ignoring her. That was not the case at the restaurant. The maître d' showed them to the table in the back that looked, just as he'd said, as if it were always held open explicitly for Matteo. A waiter rushed to fill their water glasses while a sommelier brought out a few bottles of wine.

Food appeared before they even ordered. Blair's taste buds were treated like royalty, too. Focaccia served with *ribollita* was the first course, followed with the region's specialty, osso buco alla Milanese. The veal shank, served atop a mound of creamy risotto, was so tender she didn't even have to chew; it dissolved in her mouth. A moan of pleasure slipped out of her lips.

A spark ignited in Teo's dark eyes. It might have been just a reflection of the candle burning on the table before them, but then he leaned closer and murmured, "This meal is just an appetizer, too," he said, his deep voice gruff.

With desire?

Did he intend to make her his main course?

"I won't have room for anything else," she warned him. Then she laughed and said, "Although, as an Amazon, I should."

He chuckled. "I hope you did not let my sister's jealous comments affect you."

She shook her head. "I've heard worse."

His brow furrowed. "I don't understand why. You are so beautiful."

"Let's just say that some people are threatened by strong, independent women." Especially in the world she'd chosen to enter.

"I find strong, independent women exciting," he said.

His saying that excited her, making her pulse leap again like when he'd touched her in the limo. He was so good looking, so charming...

He reached for her hand, turned it over in his and ran his thumb across the calluses. "You work hard," he said—with respect.

She smiled. "I work out hard," she said. She loved lifting weights. "I need to in order to work off meals like this."

"I know other ways..." he began, but then the dessert came: a big crystal bowl of tiramisu with two spoons.

She didn't protest when Teo lifted the spoon he'd dipped into the rich dessert to her mouth. She closed her lips around the decadent taste. The coffee had a bite to it that complemented the creamy mascarpone and spongy ladyfingers. Another moan slipped out of her lips.

And Teo leaned toward her, his mouth moving close to hers. His lips didn't touch hers, though. Only the tip of his tongue, as he licked a trace of cream from the corner of her mouth.

She moaned again at his teasing her. She'd wanted to kiss him in the car; now she wanted to kiss him even more. But the chef appeared at their table, and they focused on him, complimenting the wonderful dishes he'd prepared.

Maybe Matteo was a part owner or full owner of the restaurant like he was of the gallery, because a check never appeared before they left, sliding again into the back seat of the limousine. Teo didn't sit beside her this time but across from her, his dark gaze intent on her face.

"What?" she asked.

"We need to work off that meal."

She heartily agreed, but she didn't want to appear too eager to go to back to his room with him. "So we're going to go lift weights?" she asked, teasing him. Dressed as they were, she doubted that was the plan, but if he actually stopped at a gym, he would be surprised by what she could lift. Hopefully not intimidated, though, as so many other men were.

He chuckled. "I was thinking more along the lines of cardio."

A smile tugged at her lips over his flirting. "I'm sure you are…"

The car stopped again; the restaurant must not have been far from his hotel. But when the back door opened, it was to a crowd and an explosion of noise and lights. "Where are we?" she asked.

"Corso Como," he replied. "Where did you think we were going to work off that meal?" His dark eyes twinkled with amusement.

He knew where she'd thought and maybe even that she'd wanted to go there.

But she exited eagerly from the limo, happy to go dancing as well. While Blair would never admit it, Miranda had been right; it had been too damn long since she'd enjoyed a man. She was having fun.

More fun than she could remember having in a long time. Dancing was just an appetizer, too, for what would come. So she made certain to tease Teo with every brush of her body against his, with her every movement, every swish of her hair…

But in teasing him, she was teasing herself—

upping the attraction between them, the tension and the desire to a level she'd never felt before. She wanted him so damn badly.

He wanted her so damn badly. Sweat beaded on his brow and trickled down his spine beneath his tuxedo shirt. He'd left the jacket in the back of the limo. But he was still so hot. And not just from the dancing.

Heat moved through him like an inferno, burning him up from the inside out as he watched her body shimmy and shake to the music pulsing out of speakers in the nightclub. Lights flashed, illuminating her beautiful face. Her lips curved into that sexy smile again.

She knew she was driving him out of his damn mind. And she thought it was funny…

This was a game he didn't mind, though. Building the tension, the anticipation.

If it went somewhere.

But he could allow himself no expectations. She'd made that clear at the beginning of their date.

While it might have started out as she'd claimed, as a ploy to get Francesca to stop throwing eligible and sometimes not-so-eligible women at him, it was a real date now. Not that they'd had much opportunity to talk yet. At the gallery they'd been constantly interrupted. And at the restaurant, they'd been too busy eating.

God, how she ate.

It was as sexy as her dancing. His body, having

been hard for hours, ached with the desperate need for release. They hadn't been able to talk in the nightclub, either. He was barely able to hear himself think, but he'd wanted this.

Wanted to watch her dance.

To see how she moved.

To imagine how she might move when it was just the two of them, alone, naked.

Would he get the opportunity to see her naked? Or was she just playing with him? Getting back at him for using her to protect him from his sister?

Despite hating games, he wouldn't necessarily blame her—since he'd played one himself. But that game had been with Francesca. He'd always intended to make this date a real one despite starting the evening at the gallery.

After meeting Savannah, though, he had changed up his plan. He had chosen to take her to a better restaurant, a more popular nightclub.

Nothing but the best for her.

She seemed to be enjoying herself.

He wanted her to enjoy him.

So he reached out and caught one of her wrists, and her pulse leaped beneath his thumb. She was attracted to him, too. Maybe she wouldn't turn him down…if he asked.

But could he ask, after the warning she'd given him?

Then she put her free hand on his chest, over his

madly pounding heart, and leaned close. Her lips brushed across his earlobe as she whispered, "Take me back to your hotel."

His pulse leaped now, racing away—making his heart pound furiously, making his flesh heat until he felt as if he were burning up.

"Are you sure?" he asked her. He wanted to make it clear to her what would happen if they returned to his suite—if they were alone.

So he pulled her into his arms, tight against his body. And he moved his hips so that she felt what she'd done to him, the hardness of his erection straining the fly of his dress pants.

Her lips parted, not on a gasp of shock but a smile. And she repeated, "Take me back to your hotel room."

CHAPTER FIVE

WHAT THE HELL am I doing?

As Matteo Rinaldi swiped his key card across the lock to his hotel suite door, the same urge Blair had had earlier rushed over her again—tempting her to turn and run for the elevator. What the hell was she doing?

Him...

That was what she wanted—*whom* she wanted— so damn badly that she couldn't withstand the temptation. When he opened the door and held it for her, she ignored the urge to run and paid attention only to the urge to enjoy him, as she had the entire evening.

Even that brief moment at the gallery where she'd thought he was only using her.

It had helped her understand why he'd joined the service. Did he have any other reasons? Despite his earlier claims to the contrary, had he expected the night to end like this?

While she walked farther into the suite, he stood

yet at the closed door, his back against it. His tuxedo jacket dangled from one finger, the tie stuffed
into one of the pockets. An erection—the one he'd
pressed against her in the club—strained the fly of
the dress pants. He wanted her, too.

So why hadn't he moved any closer?

His dark eyes were narrowed as he studied her
face. "I thought you told me this wasn't going to
happen."

"I didn't think it would," she said, although the
minute she'd turned and seen how damn good-looking he was, she'd considered it. For just that minute...

"You said it's not that kind of dating service,"
he reminded her.

She sighed. "I'm not entirely sure what kind of
dating service it is," she admitted. "But I was promised that everyone who signed up for it has been
so completely vetted that I would be safe, even to
meet you in your hotel room." That was the vow
Miranda had made.

"You are safe," he assured her. "You can leave
any time you want."

"What do you want?" she asked. Despite his obvious desire for her, he hadn't made a move toward
her. "Do you want me to leave?"

Was that why he stood yet at the door? Why he
hesitated to give her the kiss—the real kiss—she'd
been wanting all evening?

"Hell, no," he murmured, his voice gruff with that desire. "But I don't always make the wisest decisions when it comes to women."

She could relate; she hadn't always made the smartest decisions about men, or she would have stayed away from the macho ones who couldn't handle a woman having the career she had. Just how macho was Matteo Rinaldi?

"Like financing your sister's gallery?" she asked about his not-so-wise decisions.

He nodded and proved that he wasn't too macho to admit to having been manipulated when he added, "Like that, like letting women use me for money."

Was that what he thought she was going to do? Instead of being offended, she chuckled. "I don't want your money," she assured him.

If she wanted money from a man, she would have taken her brother's; he seemed to have a never ending supply of it. Grant had generously offered to finance the whole company, but she'd insisted on being an equal partner even though it had taken them a little longer to start it because she'd had to secure her own funding. She prided herself on being independent, though.

Matteo finally moved away from the door then, walking slowly toward where she stood in the middle of the living room part of the suite. "Then what do you want?" he asked her.

He stopped, a little more than a foot from her, and stared down at her. As tall as she was, Blair wasn't used to having to look up to anyone, especially when she wore heels like the stilettos she was dying to step out of after dancing in them. But he held all of her attention right now, his dark gaze intent on her face. Desire, like burning embers, glowed in his chocolate-brown eyes, and a muscle twitched along his tightly clenched jaw.

He was controlling himself, but it was clear that he wanted her as badly as she wanted him. Maybe more.

No. Nobody could want anyone more than she wanted him right now. It had been too damn long for her. She doubted he could say the same. And she didn't care. She didn't care about his past or hers. She didn't care about the future, either, because she knew they wouldn't have one. Their lifestyles were much too different.

She cared only about the present and enjoying him as much as she knew she would. "You," she replied, her voice all breathy with the desire burning her up inside. "I want you."

He stepped closer then, but so that their bodies just brushed against each other's, like they had on the crowded dance floor. Then he lowered his head, and finally he kissed her. But only his lips touched her, sliding over her mouth, nibbling at her lips.

He kissed her on and on until Blair's knees began to tremble.

She wanted to blame those damn heels and all the dancing she'd done in them. But she knew it was him. He'd made her weak in the knees in a way she hadn't been since probably her very first kiss.

And he kept just kissing her, only kissing her…

A low groan was torn from his throat. It was killing him as much as it was killing her, the tension that had built between them the entire evening.

A kiss had never turned her on as much as his did. Her nipples tightened and pressed against the fabric of her dress. She wanted to tear it from her body, wanted to tear the last of the tuxedo from his. But his kiss…

She was unable to break the contact with his mouth. She tasted on his lips the sweet cream and bitter coffee from the tiramisu and the bite of the grappa they'd had in shot glasses at the nightclub. She wanted more than just a taste, so she dipped her tongue between the seam of his lips.

He groaned, and as if his control snapped, he finally touched her with his hands, his palms sliding over her shoulders to her back.

She waited for the rasp of her zipper, but he didn't touch the tab. Just her…gliding his hands up and down her back to the curve of her hips.

She arched against him, rubbing her breasts

against his chest where his heart pounded the same quick tempo as hers. She also rubbed her hips against his straining erection.

He groaned against her lips and murmured, "You Americans are always in such a hurry. Slow down..." His mouth slid across hers, slid down her cheek to the curve of her jaw and then her neck. His thick curly hair tickled her skin.

She wanted him so badly, her body trembled with desire. She reached out for the buttons on his shirt, sliding the studs through the holes to bare his chest. Thick hair covered heavy muscles. For a billionaire, he was incredibly fit; he must have a personal trainer.

Hell, he probably had a private plane as well. Which was good; their paths were unlikely to ever cross again. And she could be as free and wild sexually with him as she wanted without worrying about the embarrassment of having to see him again.

She pushed the shirt from his shoulders and reached for his belt.

His hands caught hers, holding them still. "Slow down," he murmured again. "I want to enjoy you."

She laughed. "That's what I want to do with you." Just this once...with a man her very best friend had guaranteed was safe.

"Ladies first," he admonished her.

She tugged her wrists free of his and reached for him again, but before she could touch him, he scooped her up, tossed her over his shoulder and carried her through the living area into the bedroom. A giggle slipped out and then a soft howl of protest. "No, you said ladies first."

"To be enjoyed," he told her. "I've been wanting all night to see you naked, to touch you, to taste you…"

"Ditto," she said, "so you should do the gentlemanly thing and let me go first."

"I want you to come first," he agreed as he flopped her onto a very soft mattress covered in very silky sheets. "Over and over again I want you to come."

She wanted that, too. So damn much. She'd been so focused on the business that she hadn't had more than a quick, mechanical release in a very long time.

A moan slipped out of her lips, and she shifted against the silky sheets as tension wound inside her. She needed to release that tension so badly.

He reached down and pressed a finger across her lips. "Shh," he murmured. "Not yet… I haven't done anything to earn those moans."

"Then earn them," she challenged him, giving herself over to pleasure.

He replaced his fingers with his lips, kissing her softly before deepening the kiss—before sliding his tongue into her mouth. He made love to her mouth like she wanted him to make love to her body.

She sucked his tongue deeper and nipped it lightly with her teeth. He groaned. And she pulled back to tease, "I haven't done anything to earn that yet."

"You are," he murmured. "You are…"

She tried pulling him down from where he knelt on the edge of the bed, tried pulling him on top of her. But although she was strong, he was stronger. Excitement rippled through her that he might actually match her—in passion and power.

"But you're not going to rush me," he warned her. "I want to savor you like we savored that meal. I want to taste you everywhere."

He leaned over again but his mouth missed hers, trailing across her cheek instead and along her jaw to her throat. His tongue flicked over her pulse, which pounded madly for him. Then he moved lower, his soft hair brushing across her skin as his mouth left kisses over her breasts, which swelled over the top of her dress. He pushed down one of the spaghetti straps and then the other, exposing her strapless bra. Then, reaching beneath her, he easily released the bra, freeing her breasts.

A groan slipped out of his lips again.

"I didn't do anything," she said. She couldn't, not with the straps of the dress pinning her arms to her sides. If she wanted to, though, she was strong enough to tear those straps. But she wasn't afraid of

being restrained; she was excited. Everything about
Matteo Rinaldi excited her.

"You are," he said, his voice gruff with passion.
"That is all you need to do." He touched her breasts
as if tracing them, his fingers sliding over the curve
of each mound before flicking across the nipples.
"Just be," he continued, "so damn beautiful and
sexy and responsive."

He settled onto his side on the bed next to her
and leaned over, flicking his tongue across one taut
nipple. She arched up, pushing her breast against
his mouth. He took the tip of it between his lips,
sucking on it.

A moan slipped out as pleasure streaked from her
breast to her very core. Heat flared as her clit began
to pulsate with need. "You're driving me crazy,"
she warned him. She shifted against the bed until
the dress slid farther down her body and she was
able to pull her arms free of the straps. Then she
reached for him, pushing the open shirt from his
broad shoulders. "I want you."

She ran her hands down his chest, over his rippling abs, to the clasp of the belt holding up his
tuxedo pants. But he jerked back before she could
undo his belt.

"Not yet," he said. "I need to taste you."

He skimmed the dress over her hips, pulling
down her panties with it—leaving her bare to his
voracious gaze. He stared at her mound.

She'd had a bikini wax a couple of days ago, leaving her bare but for a small area of dark golden curls over her clit. He touched the hair and her skin.

And she arched into his hand.

"Your pulse is beating here," he murmured. He stroked his finger over her—again and again—before dipping one inside her.

A small cry of pleasure slipped out of her lips.

"You're so hot," he said, his voice gruff with passion. "So wet…"

Then he proceeded to make her wetter, stroking his finger in and out of her. And as he did, he lowered his head and flicked his tongue over her clit, teasing the sensitive skin.

An orgasm gripped her, making her body shudder as it rippled through her. He moved his tongue inside her, lapping at her come. And she came harder.

"Oh, my God," she said, panting for breath.

"Teo," he said. "You can call me just Teo."

She giggled at his arrogance. But he had every right to it—he was that amazing a lover. She wanted to show him how good she was.

So she used her strength and toppled him over onto his back. Then she undid his belt and unzipped his pants, and she released the long, engorged cock that had been straining his fly.

He groaned as she slid her mouth up and down the length of him, sucking him deep into her throat. He thrashed on the bed. "No…wait…" But then his body shuddered, and he came in her mouth—salty and sweet at the same time.

He wasn't done, though. He flopped her onto her back again. First he kissed her—her pleasure mixing with his on their lips, in their mouths. Salty and sweet.

Then he moved his mouth down her neck again, tracing her collarbone and the curve of her breasts. He teased her nipples with his fingers and his thumbs, making them tighten with desire again. He kept kissing her and touching her, winding the tension inside her again. He gave her another orgasm with his fingers, with his lips.

But it wasn't enough. She needed him inside her. She reached out and found that he was ready again. Hard and hot, his dick throbbed in her hand as she stroked up and down the length of him.

"Condom," he said through gritted teeth. A muscle twitched along his jaw while another stood out all sinewy in his neck. He reached down to where he'd dropped his jacket next to the bed when he'd carried her into the bedroom. He rummaged through a pocket before pulling out a packet.

She tried to take it from him, but he held tightly to it. He tore it open and sheathed himself. Then he parted her legs and eased inside her.

He was so big, so hot.

But he fit her—perfectly. He filled her.

She arched and adjusted, taking him deeper.

He groaned and stilled. But then he moved, thrusting deeper and deeper.

Blair arched her hips, meeting his thrusts with thrusts of her own. She wrapped her legs around his lean waist and held tightly to him. Her inner muscles clenched him, too, holding him inside her.

The delicious friction grew, sending pleasure rippling through her as she came again. And she screamed his name this time. "Teo!"

He stilled, his entire body tense, before thrusting deep once more. Then his big body shuddered as he found his release. And a name escaped his lips. For a moment she didn't recognize it.

"Savannah…"

Then she remembered that was what she'd told him to call her. A pang of regret struck her that she hadn't given him her real name. She would have rather he called out Blair. But the way he said her given name…

Savannah had never sounded as beautiful as it did when he uttered it in exultation—in the throes of passion. And she'd never felt as beautiful or as satiated as she did with him.

Another pang struck her. This time it was fear—fear that she might want more than this one night with him.

Teo awoke with the taste of her in his mouth. She was so damn sweet and hot and as passionate as she'd made him. He reached out, but his arm encountered only tangled silk sheets, not the silk of her skin.

And he realized her heat was gone, too, his bare skin chilled. He pried open his eyes, but the room was dark. "Savannah?" he called out.

Maybe she'd just gone into the bathroom. But he heard no movement within the suite. So he flipped on the light next to the bed. Her dress and underwear were no longer on the floor. She'd dressed and sneaked out.

His clothes still lay in a pile next to the bed. He reached into the discarded jacket and pulled out his wallet. Nothing was missing. He doubted she'd even touched it. A twinge of guilt struck him that he'd wondered if she had. But why had she sneaked out?

Hadn't she enjoyed their date as much as he had?

She'd certainly seemed to—when she'd come over and over again. He'd never known anyone as passionate as she was. Hard at the thought of her and of all they'd done, he jumped up from the bed and stalked around the suite. He knew she was gone, but he was looking for a note.

Surely she'd left him one—with her full name and number, her email…some way for him to contact her again. Because she hadn't touched his wallet, she hadn't taken any of his business cards, either.

She'd walked out of the room and his life without a way for him to contact her...unless she'd told the service to give him her information. She must have done that, because surely she would want to see him again.

Because he sure as hell wanted to see her.

CHAPTER SIX

HER HEART POUNDING like she was on the run, Blair stuffed her crumpled dress into her overnight bag and, with shaking fingers, zipped it closed. She slid the strap over her shoulder and headed for the door. Just as she reached for the knob, the door shuddered as someone knocked—loudly—on it.

A curse slipped out of her lips. Had he found her? Had he followed her back to her hotel?

She'd been so certain that he was deeply sleeping when she'd disentangled their limbs and slipped out of the bed. But maybe he'd awakened when he heard her moving around.

She'd heard him murmur something in his sleep, something in Italian, which she usually understood, but the words probably would have been unintelligible in any language. He'd been so tired. So was she.

She hadn't slept at all.

What the hell had she done?

All she wanted to do now was get the hell out of

Milan and back to London, where the main office of Private Flights was located.

The door rattled again, and a voice called out, "Savannah, I know you're in there."

"Shit." She knew this person too well to try to pretend she'd already gone. This person would convince a maid to open the door to check to see if she was alive if she didn't open it herself. So, with a heavy sigh of exhaustion and resignation, she pulled it open.

Miranda pushed past her and slammed the door shut. "Savannah?" she repeated the name again, this time as a question, her voice high with disbelief. "You told him your name is Savannah?"

"It is," she reminded her friend.

"Yeah, but you hate that name so much that you never use it," Miranda said.

She had hated it—until Matteo Rinaldi said it like he had, in that melted-chocolate rich and warm voice of his. With such passion...

"Why didn't you tell him your real name?"

"Why didn't you tell him my name?" Blair asked. "You made me feel like a paid escort the way you sent me to his hotel room. I never should have agreed to join your damn service."

"I didn't think you were going to agree to it," Miranda admitted. "That's why I didn't mention your name to him, but even when you had agreed to it, I couldn't tell him anything unless you authorized me to release that information. As for having you meet him at his hotel, he didn't have anything nefarious in mind. I vetted him completely, just as I have every other member of the service. You were safe with him, so why did you lie to him, especially when I promised him that all of our members are honest?"

Blair knew that honesty was important to him; he'd made that painfully clear to her. But she insisted, "I didn't lie. Savannah is my name."

"You hate your first name," Miranda said. "You've made me swear to take it off your tombstone if your mom or brother tries to sneak it on there."

"I would haunt them," Blair said. "So they won't."

"You're haunting Matteo Rinaldi right now," Miranda said, "or at the least ghosting him. You didn't give him your real name or any contact information for him to be able to reach you. Why not? Was the date that terrible?"

A little ripple of something passed through Blair—excitement? Relief? Her pulse had quickened, too, at the mention of him.

"He called you already?" she asked.

It was still early. The minute he'd awakened and found her gone he must have called, but she hadn't been gone that long, just long enough to get a cab back to her hotel, shower and pack.

"How else would I know what you told him your

name was?" Miranda asked. "I didn't even realize who he was talking about right away. It's been so long since anyone used your first name."

Maybe it was because she'd had no sleep but Blair found herself murmuring again, "He called."

"Yes," Miranda confirmed, "he called for your number."

The little ripple passed through her again, but this time she easily recognized it for what it was: fear. "You didn't give it to him?"

"Of course not," Miranda said. "I've told you already that one of the main rules of the service is that we won't give out any information unless we're authorized."

So Miranda was running her business differently than she had her life. She was making and keeping the rules with Liaisons International.

"It's up to the members to share that information with each other," she continued, "if they want. Why didn't you want to give him your phone number?"

Despite the fear and tension gripping her, Blair shrugged. "Why would I?"

"Didn't you have a good time?" Miranda asked.

Her body was limp and felt nearly boneless from the all the pleasure he'd given her. But Blair was not about to admit that to her matchmaking friend. She just shrugged again. "It was fine."

"If something went wrong, if he did something

to turn you off, I need to know so that I can either terminate his membership or——"

"He didn't do anything wrong," Blair interrupted.

And he certainly hadn't turned her off; just thinking about him had her pulse quickening with excitement. That was the problem, though. He'd affected her too much and much too quickly, which had unsettled her.

"I was the one who did something wrong."

"I'll say you did," Miranda wholeheartedly agreed. "You lied to him about your name."

"I didn't lie," she insisted—weakly.

"And he was very specific that he didn't want to waste his time with someone who plays games," Miranda warned her.

"I know." And because she hadn't been entirely honest with him, she doubted he would want a relationship with her. But hell, she didn't want one with him, either. Or with anyone.

That was why she hadn't given him her contact information. Because all she'd wanted was that one night, that one date.

She couldn't risk any more than that.

"The mistake I made was letting you talk me into joining your service," Blair explained. "I don't have time to date anyone."

And especially not someone like Matteo Rinaldi, someone who could prove a bigger distraction than she could handle right now.

Or ever...

Miranda uttered her disappointment in a heavy sigh. "I really thought the two of you would make a great match. That he might be your soul mate."

"You sound like your mother right now," Blair said.

Miranda's head snapped back like she'd been struck. "Take that back," she said.

"Listen to yourself," Blair advised. "You're talking about soul mates and great matches."

Miranda shrugged. "Just because I think two people belong together doesn't mean that I believe in marriage or any of that garbage."

Maybe it was the lack of sleep, but Blair was struggling to follow her friend's reasoning. "But why would you think Matteo and I would be a good match? He and I have nothing in common. He's an Italian billionaire and I'm an American pilot. Our paths would have never crossed if not for your service."

"Exactly," Miranda said. "That's why the service is so necessary. So many people just settle with someone they meet in their own circle of acquaintances and they miss out on meeting the person with whom they truly belong."

"Hear that? You really do sound just like your mother now," Blair warned her.

"Shut your mouth!" Miranda exclaimed. "I'm not saying that your only purpose in life is to find a mate and spend your life trying to make him happy."

Both of their mothers had done that. At least Miranda's mother had known when to give up and meet someone else to try to find happiness again, though. Blair's mom had wasted most of her adult life trying to make a man happy who had probably been incapable of the feeling. When he'd died of a heart attack a few years ago, she and her brother had been surprised that he'd even had one.

"What are you saying?" Blair asked her friend—because she seriously wasn't following her. Neither of them had ever had to have a boyfriend or significant other. They'd been happy to be single. Or so Blair had thought.

"All I'm saying is that you deserve to have someone who wants to make you happy," Miranda murmured, almost wistfully.

"You do, too," Blair assured her friend.

Miranda shook her head. "I don't need anyone else to make me happy."

"Same," Blair said. "I have my business, and I need to focus all my attention on that."

Miranda sighed again but nodded. "So I'll tell Matteo Rinaldi that you don't want to see him again."

A twinge of pain struck Blair's heart, stealing her breath away for a moment. She wanted—very badly—to see him again, which was why she couldn't risk it, just as she hadn't been able to risk staying with him. She was not going to get attached and all needy and weak like her mother had with her dad.

Miranda should have understood that; she'd learned to not get attached to any of her stepfathers because they never stuck around. Just as none of Blair's boyfriends had ever stuck around—because their fragile egos hadn't been able to deal with who and what she was.

Matteo Rinaldi hadn't appeared to have a fragile ego, though. But maybe that made him more dangerous—because it would have made it easier for her to fall for him.

Blair forced herself to nod in agreement. "Yes, yes, tell him that I don't want to see him again."

Her friend stepped closer, narrowed her pale blue eyes and peered up in her face. Skepticism in her voice, she prodded, "And he really did nothing wrong?"

Blair shook her head. On the contrary, he'd done everything right—too damn right. She'd never had orgasms as intense or as easily as he'd given them to her. He'd given her so much pleasure.

Miranda sighed. "That's good. I should have no problem finding someone else for him then."

Another twinge struck Blair, this time of jealousy. The thought of Matteo with someone else the way he'd been with her had anger coursing through her.

Miranda was still staring at her and must have caught her reaction because she chuckled and mused, "You're not okay with that."

"It's fine," Blair insisted. "I just met him last night. We don't even know each other. So it's not like I'm attached to him or anything." But she could get used to the pleasure he'd given her, too used to it; that was why she couldn't risk seeing him again.

But as Miranda had pointed out, their paths were unlikely to have ever crossed without Liaisons International. So there was next to no chance of them ever running into each other again.

Teo had spent too long in Milan, waiting on Savannah to call him back. The ball was in her court now, was what the service had told him.

He wasn't playing tennis, though. He didn't want to play any damn games with Savannah. He just wanted her. But it had been a few days now, so he had to accept that she was not going to call him back.

Still, when his phone began to vibrate across the desk in the hotel suite, he grabbed for it and clicked the accept button. "Rinaldi," he spoke into the cell.

"Matteo Rinaldi?" a deep—very male—voice asked.

He sighed. "Yes."

"This is Grant Snyder returning your call," the man said, and he sounded annoyed. "Although if

you just want to book a flight, our answering service could have already handled that for you."

"I am not about to book a flight with anyone until
I speak directly to the pilot or one of the owners of
the company," Teo informed the man. Flying unnerved him enough without putting his life into the
hands of a stranger. But even after an in-depth interview with the pilot he'd hired to fly his private jet,
he'd been unpleasantly surprised—when the man
had shown up drunk at the airport. Anger coursed
through him. That hadn't been his only recent un-
pleasant surprise, though.

Savannah.

While the night with her had given him a lot of
pleasure, not hearing from her frustrated the hell
out of him.

"I'm one of the owners," Grant said. "But my
sister is really the pilot."

"The only pilot?" Teo asked. If so, she was unlikely to leave her brother's company to fly his plane
for him, and that was ultimately his goal, to find
someone to fly his plane. Or he would have wasted
money on it.

"No, of course not," the man replied. "We have
several planes and several pilots."

"I have my own plane," Teo said. "I just need to
hire a pilot to fly it." One who didn't have a drinking problem.

"Then you should talk to my sister," Grant said,

"although she doesn't like flying anyone else's plane but her own. She needs to make sure it's as meticulously maintained as our fleet is."

Given what a drunk his pilot had been, Teo had his doubts about every aspect of the man's work, which had included servicing the plane. "I am not opposed to using one of your planes," Teo said. In fact, it would probably be for the best. But after putting up with his sister's games at the gallery opening and with having Savannah ghost him, he needed a sabbatical from women, especially to women he would find too tempting. This female pilot sounded just like the kind of strong, independent woman he lost his head over, like he'd lost his head with Savannah. "I would prefer to not have a female pilot, however."

Grant snorted. "You better not talk to my sister then. She will kick your sexist ass for saying that."

Instead of being offended, Teo chuckled at the American's frankness. As well as sounding American, the man sounded young, too, so his sister was probably young as well. His ego was more than a little bruised from Savannah ghosting him, so Teo didn't want to deal with another woman he might find too fascinating. Not only had she chosen to enter a predominantly male field, but she also might try to kick his ass.

He'd already just had it kicked. Savannah had knocked him back. He'd never had as enjoyable a night as he'd had with her, and that wasn't just the sex. He'd enjoyed dinner and dancing, too. And the sex...

Hell, just thinking about it—about her—had him tense and edgy. Apparently he had been the only one who'd enjoyed their date enough to want to repeat it. His ego would not take another beating, so he needed to avoid this man's sister like he intended to avoid his own for a while.

"I need a flight from Milan to Madrid," Teo said. He glanced at his watch. "I have an appointment in Madrid at nine o'clock tomorrow morning. I'll pay twice your going rate for the flight, if I can be guaranteed a sober, male pilot."

"It's your money," Grant said.

"You will meet my conditions?" Teo asked, double-checking as his heart rate quickened at the thought of flying again. Being driven in a car didn't bother him, but something about flying made him feel out of control. And he hated being out of control.

Perhaps it was a good thing that Savannah had not called him. She'd made him lose control that night, over and over again. Making love with her had been a lot like flying—like hurtling through space with no ability to stop himself from falling.

But he couldn't fall for a ghost.

"Blair would personally kill any pilot who tried drinking on the job," Grant assured him.

"Blair? Is that your sister?" Teo asked.

"Yes."

"She sounds fierce," Teo mused.

"She is," Grant said. "A former fighter pilot, one of the first female ones to actually experience combat."

Teo was impressed, but he couldn't afford that right now. He'd already let Savannah distract him too much from his business. He had to focus on it again—because she had made him remember what it was like to be hungry, to be a kid begging on the streets.

He wasn't going to beg her or any woman for her attention, though.

"Any other former fighter pilots on your staff?" he asked.

"Several," Grant said. "Blair personally recruited all our pilots."

"Send me one of the male ones, please," Teo requested.

"Blair is the best," her loyal brother insisted.

"I'm sure she is," Teo said. "But not for me." Not right now. Not when he was still so damn raw from not hearing from Savannah.

Grant sighed but agreed to send him a male pilot. Then he set up the flight time and airport location. But after they disconnected, an uneasiness gripped Teo. He'd counted on Miranda Fox and Liaisons International to find him a woman he could trust not to play games, and he'd been disappointed. He would survive the bruise to his ego, though.

But if the pilot he was sent wasn't as good as he was promised, he might not survive the flight.

CHAPTER SEVEN

BLAIR WAS GOING to kill their new client.

"He what?" she asked her brother, her voice vibrating with the rage coursing through her. She had to have it repeated because she just couldn't believe the audacity. And she thought her brother was a Neanderthal...

"You heard me," Grant said, leaning so far back in his desk chair that it was surprising it didn't topple over with his big body in it.

She thought about pushing that chair over, she was so damn angry. But he wasn't the one she was mad at; well, he wasn't the only one. "I can't believe you agreed to it!"

Grant shrugged. "Money's money, Blair. The business is in the black, but we have to make sure we keep it that way. We shouldn't turn down any client."

"Even sexist pigs?" She shook her head. "No. We don't need clients like that."

"I'm not sure that was his reason for not wanting a female pilot," Grant said.

"What other reason could he have?" Blair asked, her eyes narrowed as she stared down her brother.

He raised his hands, palms up. "Hey, I have no problem with female pilots. I wish we had more of them besides my sister."

"Of course you do," she said. Grant wasn't sexist; he had always supported her choices—just not all her friendships.

"Since we don't, though," Grant continued, "our new client probably would have been given a male pilot even if he hadn't asked for one."

"Probably," Blair agreed. "But he damn well isn't going to get one now."

Grant stood up then. He was one of the few men who was more than just a little bit taller than she was. His hair was an even deeper shade of gold than hers except for where it turned reddish in the beard that shadowed his square jaw. "Why the hell are you so damn edgy these past few days? I thought you would come back from that little trip you took all refreshed, but you're more uptight now than you were before."

"I was only gone a day," she reminded him.

"So take some more time off," he suggested. "You've been working your ass off. Mine, too, and you know I don't like working this much."

She smiled, like he'd meant for her to do, but she couldn't help thinking that her brother tried a little too hard to seem carefree.

"I'll go back to Milan," she said, her heart quickening at the thought of what had happened with Matteo.

All the incredible things they'd done to each other—all the pleasure he'd given her.

Grant hadn't been wrong about her; she had been edgy since her return. She felt like climbing the damn walls. She needed the release that Teo had given her.

Maybe she should let Miranda know that she was willing to see him again. But having to tell Miranda to tell him brought her back to middle school and passing notes in class. That was how Teo had made her feel, giddy and foolish and overwhelmed with emotions. She couldn't afford to feel like that, not when she had business to focus on.

So she forced thoughts of seeing Matteo again from her mind and continued, "Then I'll take a trip to Madrid."

Grant groaned. "You can't fly this guy. I promised him a male pilot."

"And I'll make sure that he thinks that's what he's got," she assured Grant.

He snorted. "Yeah, right. You're going to pass for a man? How the hell are you going to pull that off?"

"Remember when I dressed up like you for Halloween last year?"

He groaned again. But he couldn't deny that she had fooled several of their employees with the disguise.

Miranda's younger half sister, Tabitha Catt, a theater major, had helped her with the costume. Tabitha was in New York City right now, doing some off-off-off-Broadway play, so she wouldn't be able to help Blair this time. But she still had the disguise somewhere. She only hoped she would be able to pull it off on her own and teach their new sexist client a humbling lesson.

"So what's this misogynist pig's name?" she asked.

Grant glared at her. "You mean our new client?"

She shrugged. "Whatever. What's his name?"

"Matteo Rinaldi."

She gasped as a sharp pain jabbed her heart. It wasn't possible. Matteo could not be a sexist pig, not after all the sweet things he'd said about admiring strong, independent women. Had he been lying? Or was Grant?

She narrowed her eyes and studied her brother's face. "Did Miranda put you up to this?"

"Miranda?" he asked. Too innocently? An accomplished gambler, Grant's face was too hard to read. But there was a twinkle in his dark blue eyes. It wasn't of amusement, though, because he angrily asked, "What does that damn troublemaker have to do with Matteo Rinaldi?"

Too damn much.

Blair shook her head. "She didn't refer him?"

"I sure as hell hope not," he said. "We sure don't need Miranda Fox doing us any *favors*."

"He didn't mention her?" Blair asked.

Grant shook his head. "I wouldn't have booked him a flight if he had anything to do with Miranda." He'd had a problem with her best friend for years. "But he didn't say how he heard about us, just that he needs a pilot."

"A *male* pilot," she remarked resentfully. So he was a chauvinist pig. She'd been right to trust her instincts to run; he had seemed too good to be true. That night had just been an act; he wasn't the charming man he'd pretended to be.

"I looked the guy up," Grant said. "He's an Italian billionaire. We could use his business and his referrals. So don't blow this for us."

Blair had already blown him. And now she was so damn angry about that, about that entire night...

She'd bought his act, that he was this charming man. That he was considerate and had seemed to care about her pleasure, about her. She'd been worried that he was so great that she would act like her mom and lose herself in him.

But he'd fooled her. He was a chauvinist pig just like all the other guys she'd dated.

How had she lost control so completely with him?

She was going to damn well take that control back. Now.

Teo leaned into the open door of the cockpit, waiting for the pilot to turn around and acknowledge him. Surely the man had heard him walk up the stairs to board the plane. He cleared his throat.

The guy turned to peer back over one shoulder. A reddish beard covered most of the guy's face but for the sunglasses shielding his eyes.

"I'm Matteo Rinaldi," he introduced himself.

The guy just nodded.

"And you are?"

"Bill," he replied curtly, his voice so gruff his name sounded more like a croak than a word.

"You should take your seat, sir," a male flight attendant advised as he pulled in the stairs. "We are cleared for takeoff."

Grant Snyder had taken his directive a little far with having all male staff on board the plane. But Teo was relieved. The last thing he needed was another distraction like Savannah, another strong, independent woman. Savannah took up entirely too many of his thoughts as he continued to relive that night over and over again.

He must have built it up in his mind, though; it couldn't have been as good as he remembered. It hadn't really been like that...

It wasn't possible to feel as much pleasure as he kept imagining he'd felt that night, with her.

"Sir," the attendant prodded him, gesturing back at the big seats in the passenger area.

This plane was actually a bit smaller than his private jet, but it was luxurious and fully equipped. And the pilot seemed incredibly confident in the cockpit and so focused on flying that he'd barely noticed Teo at all. Apparently Blair Snyder had vetted her pilots better than he'd vetted his or than Liaisons International had vetted his date.

Unless he'd done something that night that had upset her?

Had he taken advantage of her?

She'd seemed to want him as much as he'd wanted her. Sometimes even more.

He couldn't have been that mistaken, could he? He wouldn't know for certain, though, unless she called him back. She hadn't done that yet.

With a sigh, he took his seat.

"This will be the smoothest flight you've ever had," the attendant promised him.

Teo didn't believe in promises anymore—not after the dating service had promised to find him someone who wouldn't play games with him. Because that promise had been broken when Savannah had disappeared. She'd played the cruelest game of all on him—hide and...

Did she even want him to seek her?

She hadn't returned any of the messages he'd left for her, and Miranda Fox had warned him that she might not. Clearly Savannah did not want to be found.

CHAPTER EIGHT

BLAIR'S "BILL THE PILOT" disguise, with the big sunglasses and the bushy beard, had worked too well. Teo hadn't recognized her at all. And he'd been so comfortable with the *man* flying the plane that he had chartered Private Flights for several more trips. He traveled often between Madrid and Milan. Madrid was where he lived and where his corporate offices were, while it seemed as though Milan was home to him despite his not having a home there. Perhaps that was because his sister lived there, and despite her meddling in his life, they must have been close.

As usual, when they landed in Madrid he poked his head into the cockpit and praised her. "Another smooth flight, Bill. Thank you."

He wasn't really praising her, though. He was praising a man. But unlike some of their other *important* clients, he always took the time to greet her and to compliment her after every flight.

"He sure is a nice guy for a billionaire," Jean-

Claude remarked after Teo descended the stairs to the tarmac.

"For a male chauvinist pig," Blair reminded him and herself.

Jean-Claude dropped into the seat next to hers. He was as much a copilot as he was a flight attendant. She'd assigned him to Teo's flights in case the businessman ever saw through her disguise and insisted on getting what her brother had promised him. A male pilot. "So when are you going to take off the beard and the padding and show him that a woman has been flying him for all these flights?" Jean-Claude asked.

Her pulse quickened at the thought. He was bound to be furious at getting duped. He'd told her before that he didn't like games. Despite the disguise, though, this wasn't a game to her. This was her proving, just as she had been forced to prove her entire career, that she was as good as or better than any man. Just because she was female didn't make her weak or stupid…like so many of her instructors and fellow fighter pilots had thought.

But Blair couldn't actually prove this to Teo until she removed her disguise. Once she did, she knew there would be no chance of anything professional or personal between them. He would be much too angry.

And while she hadn't thought it was smart to see him again, to be with him again…

Her body ached with desire for his. She wanted

to be with him…like they'd been that night. She needed the release and the mind-blowing pleasure they'd found with each other.

That was why she hadn't taken off the disguise yet.

She wanted one more night of ecstasy in his arms, in his bed. But did she dare risk it? Even knowing he was a chauvinist hadn't abated her attraction to him.

And flying him had only made her want him more. He always looked so gorgeous whether he wore one of his expertly tailored suits or a pair of worn jeans and thin cashmere sweater. And his hair, with those rich chocolate-brown curls, was just ever so mussed, reminding her of how it had looked that night, how it had felt when it had brushed across her bare skin…

Her breath caught with desire, and that hollow ache inside her yawned even wider, deeper. Her body yearned for his, to feel him inside her again.

And every time she flew him, that hollow ache just intensified. Because he was so close, but she couldn't touch him, couldn't kiss him—like she had that night, like she had to again.

She'd been worried that being with a man would make her like her mother, make her lose herself. But being without him was worse, was making her lose her patience and her self-control. She had to have him again.

* * *

Teo had gone right to his office when the plane landed in Madrid. He hadn't had a break from work until now, hours later, when he'd returned to his apartment to shower and drop onto his bed in exhaustion.

But he knew he wouldn't sleep—at least not restfully. Because whenever he closed his eyes, he thought of Savannah. He needed to get her out of his mind for good.

He pulled his cell phone from the pocket of his jeans and, uttering a weary sigh, he punched in the contact number for Liaisons International. When he'd signed up, Miranda Fox had insisted on giving him her direct cell number. She'd probably grown to regret having done that, though.

Because she answered with a weary sigh of her own and asked, "Hasn't she returned your calls yet, Mr. Rinaldi?"

Teo flinched, and his face heated with embarrassment and anger. He'd told himself when he was a kid that once he'd made his own way in the world, he would never resort to begging again—anyone for anything. And yet here he was.

"No," he replied. "She hasn't." And he'd come to accept that she wouldn't.

"I can leave another message for her to—"

"Don't," he interjected. He'd already given Savannah more power over him than he had any other woman.

Savannah clearly wasn't interested. Maybe their date had not been as amazing to her as it had seemed to him. Unless he had built her and that night up in his mind beyond what she and it had really been.

"I didn't call about Savannah," he said. "I'm calling because I want to cancel my membership." Although that was entirely about Savannah.

"Cancel?" Miranda Fox repeated with such righteous-sounding indignation that she was acting as if he'd sworn at her. "But you have not given the agency a chance. You've only been on one date. You have yet to take full advantage of your membership with Liaisons International."

He smiled at her tactic. Clearly she was good at talking people into things they didn't want to do, which was probably why Savannah hadn't called him back. Despite her agreement that she wouldn't do something she really didn't want to, she must have regretted their date.

Had she regretted everything?

"My joining was a mistake," he said.

"Please don't let one bad date spoil the entire experience for you," she said.

But it hadn't been a bad date. It had been the perfect date—just as Miranda Fox had promised him.

"You're going to have to give it more time," she continued, "and go on more dates before you give up on finding your soul mate."

Teo chuckled at her romanticism. He'd given up

on finding a soul mate long ago. Hell, even as a kid he'd known no such thing existed. His mother's inability to maintain a relationship had shown him that there was no such thing as romance. She'd used men for money, and they'd used her for sex...until she'd gotten too old to attract them.

"I'm not looking for a soul mate," he assured the matchmaker.

"Then why did you join the service?" she asked.

"To date." Specifically to take a date to that gallery opening. He'd known Francesca wanted to set him up with an artist friend who was looking for a benefactor. The last thing he wanted was to get involved with another woman only after his money.

Savannah hadn't lied about not using him for financial gain or influence. If she'd wanted anything from him, she would have called him back. Maybe she had only wanted that one night.

That had been one spectacular fucking night, though. His body ached with tension demanding release—the powerful, mind-blowing relief that she had given him. He wanted her again, still, so damn badly.

"So date," Miranda Fox challenged him. "Go out with someone else."

He snorted at the thought of getting as lucky as he'd been when Savannah had shown up at the door of his hotel suite. Lightning like that wasn't about to strike twice.

"You already claimed to have set me up on the perfect date," he reminded her.

"There is more than one perfect date," she said.

"I thought you believed in soul mates," he challenged her.

She chuckled now. "I also believe in just dating to date, to enjoy the company of another person, to have dinner, drinks, relax…"

"You don't often use your own service, do you?" Matteo wondered.

Because there was nothing relaxing about dating, about becoming so intrigued with someone only to have her disappear and never call back.

"That would be a conflict of interest," Miranda haughtily informed him. "My job is to help others find their soul mates, not to find my own."

"Why does that sound like an excuse, Ms. Fox?" he challenged her.

She chuckled softly. "It could be," she acknowledged. "It could also be the truth."

"To truly represent your company and your clients," he said, "you should try dating more. Then you'd know what it's really like."

"If you try another date, I might take your advice," she said. "As it is…you're being as hypocritical as you obviously think I am."

"Tou—" He couldn't say it. He couldn't think it without thinking of Savannah. He understood why the two women were friends; they were both clever and quick-witted. And knowing that they were friends tempted him to press her for more information about the intriguing Savannah.

But maybe that was Savannah's ploy after all. Maybe she was playing a game with him—making him want her so damn much more than he already had.

She'd made him lose control that night, and when she'd disappeared, she'd wrested control entirely away from him. It was damn time he took back control of his own life.

"Go ahead," he told her.

"What?" she asked.

"Set me up with someone new," he said. "Someone who really is everything you promised me—incapable of playing games with no ulterior motives."

"Savannah—"

"Savannah is gone," he said. And it was past damn time for him to accept that he wasn't going to see her again. "So set me up with someone else. Someone I can trust."

He knew that whoever she was, he would probably not be as attracted to her or as intrigued. But that was good. That was a hell of a lot safer than the way Savannah had made him feel. No. It was good that she hadn't contacted him.

It would better for him to never see her again.

CHAPTER NINE

NOTHING MATTEO RINALDI did should have surprised her. But still the news struck Blair like a hard slap to the face, and that was already uncomfortably chafed from the glue she had to use to hold the beard in place. She'd just taken off the damn thing after getting to her hotel room in Milan.

She spent too much time wearing the beard and the padding and the sunglasses—too much time flying Matteo back and forth between Madrid and Milan. She was beginning to get dizzy from those flights and from her infatuation with him. Apparently that had been all on her side, though.

"He did what?" she asked Miranda to repeat what she'd just been told—because she didn't want to believe it, didn't want to believe that he'd done that.

"You heard me." Her friend called her on her crap, as Miranda always had.

Sure, she'd heard her, but she'd been hoping she hadn't. "He really asked you to set him up with someone else?" Had that night not meant as much to him as it had to her? Was she that replaceable? And why did that bother her so much?

"Hey, he left all those messages for you that you refused to return," Miranda pointed out.

"True..." she murmured with a pang of regret now. Maybe she should have returned those messages, should have seen him just one more time... as Savannah. Then maybe she could have put that night behind her, could have gotten a clear perspective instead of the one she'd probably romanticized. It—and he—could not have been as amazing as she remembered.

"You have to realize he willingly joined the dating service," Miranda said. "When one willingly joins a dating service, it's because one wants to actually date."

Blair snorted in derision. "He only joined Liaisons International because he wanted to take a date to the opening of his sister's gallery," she said. "He was just using that date to save him from his sister's amateur matchmaking."

Miranda gasped. "You should have told me that. I would have canceled his membership for his dishonesty."

"I was relieved," Blair admitted. "He wasn't looking for anything serious any more than I am."

"So why didn't you call him back?" Miranda asked.

Because the feelings she'd had for him could have become serious.

But now that she'd gotten to know more about him, she wasn't so sure that risk was real. She was not about to fall for a sexist jerk who refused to have a woman pilot.

"I didn't want to see him again," she admitted. But she had—even before she'd donned her male pilot disguise. She'd seen him every time she'd closed her eyes—she'd seen him naked, with that soft dark hair covering the sculpted muscles of his chest. His thighs and arms had been all sculpted muscle, too, and his…

Heat rushed through her, making her tingle everywhere—like he had that night. She shifted against the mattress on which she lay. These sheets weren't silky like the ones she'd torn up that night with him. The bed wasn't as soft, and except for her, it was empty—like she'd felt inside since she'd left him. She should have called him back, should have seen him once more…to get the desire for him out of her system.

"You said *didn't*," Miranda pointed out. Of course she would have picked up on Blair's slip. "So you do want to see him again now?"

"You said he's going out with someone else," Blair reminded her. "That he didn't ask for me."

"No, he didn't," Miranda admitted. "He's clearly

given up on seeing *Savannah* again. So meet him as *Blair*. Tell him the truth."

A twinge of panic struck her heart. If she told him the truth about her name, then he might realize she was part owner of Private Flights and he might put it together that she was actually the pilot flying him.

If he realized she had donned that disguise to fool him, he would undoubtedly—and maybe deservedly so—be furious with her.

She had been mad at him ever since he'd requested a male pilot, though. Now she was even angrier that he'd requested another date. Not that she expected him to pine for her like she was pining for him.

God, had she been pining for him? Was that what this hollow ache inside her was? Was she actually beginning to care about him?

Maybe, if she was with him one more time, he would fill that hollowness, and she would be able to think again. She'd be able to figure a way out of the mess she'd created with her subterfuge…if she wanted to keep seeing him.

"Blair?" Miranda called out from the cell phone speaker. "Are you still there?"

"Yes," she said. "And I need a favor."

"Blair—"

"You owe me," she reminded her friend. "For

all the favors I've done you over the years, all the things I let you talk me into."

"You wouldn't have done any of those things if you hadn't really wanted to," Miranda pointed out. Rightfully so.

But Blair wasn't about to admit to that. "And I always got in more trouble than you did every time we got caught."

"Because you always got caught," Miranda said. "I didn't."

She had always gotten caught. That was why wearing that disguise had been such a bad idea. But Matteo hadn't seen through it yet; she hadn't been caught.

Or had she?

In a trap she'd set for herself. Because she didn't see any way out of her current situation...so she might as well figure out a way to enjoy it.

To enjoy him...

Before she got caught.

"You know you owe me," Blair persisted.

And Miranda's sigh rattled the phone. "What do you want from me?"

"Just one thing."

The rest she intended to get from someone else. And she intended to—hell, she needed to—get a hell of a lot of it from him.

Sounding worried, Miranda asked, "What?"

"A date," Blair replied. "I need a date."

* * *

What the hell had he been thinking to agree to another date—with anyone? Even if Savannah showed
up at his door, he should close it in her face after
how she'd treated him. He was never the one who
had to leave messages, who had to beg for someone
to call him back, to see him again.

He was the one who got begged—for more.

Apparently Savannah didn't want anything from
him, though. But just because she wasn't interested
in him didn't mean that he should give up on dating.

He wasn't looking for a soul mate, but he
wouldn't mind finding someone to spend time with
talking, enjoying a meal, dancing...

But like he'd had with Savannah that night, he
had no expectations now. Especially after what had
happened with Savannah.

What the hell was he thinking to trust Liaisons
International again?

He'd probably be better off letting Francesca set
him up with someone. Hell, no. He'd be better off
meeting someone on his own. Maybe he should
switch from having Bill as a pilot to having Blair
Snyder. But a woman who sounded as incredible as
she did probably wasn't single.

For some reason he didn't feel single either right
now. He felt guilty about going out with someone
other than Savannah, which was crazy. They'd only
had that one night. That one incredible night.

And he didn't want to give up on it or on her. Not yet.

He'd just reached for the cell phone on the desk of his hotel suite when a knock rattled the door. Damn it.

His date had shown up before he'd had a chance to cancel it. He would just have to explain that it had been a mistake. But then he opened the door.

And shock rippled through him along with the overwhelming attraction he'd felt for her. He hadn't been wrong; he hadn't exaggerated in his memory how beautiful she was. She wasn't dressed up like she'd been that first night. But even in a sweater and jeans she was sexy as sin.

So she was as beautiful—maybe even more so— than he'd remembered her. But what about the passion?

Was it as hot as he remembered, the pleasure as intense?

But he couldn't just assume that was why she'd come here, that she wanted him, too. So he asked, "What are you doing here?"

And she reached out, her palms against his chest. After pushing him back, she stepped inside the suite and shut the door with a swung of her foot. "You?"

But it was a question, not an assumption.

He wanted her—so damn badly. Tension gripped his body, making every muscle ache with desire. His skin tingled even through his shirt where her hands splayed across his chest. He wanted to pull her closer, wanted to swing her up in his arms and carry her right to the bed. But...

"I have a date," he warned her.

"I know," she said. "I'm your date."

"But Miranda..."

"Miranda owed me a favor," she said. Her lips curved up. "Actually she owes me a lot of favors."

"If you wanted to see me," he said, "all you had to do was answer the messages I left for you." But she hadn't, and he had to remind himself of that, had to hold on to control of his irrational need to be with her. She'd ghosted him, and she wouldn't have done that if she was as attracted to him as he was to her.

She nodded. "I know. I've been busy. And it hasn't been that long."

Two weeks. It had seemed interminable to him. And usually, being busy himself, it wouldn't have seemed that long. But something about her...

He'd never felt this way about anyone before, had never become so intrigued so quickly or so attached.

"It was too long," he said as his grip on control began to slip. He wanted to resist, to protect himself, so that she didn't stomp all over his ego again.

A shaky sigh slipped out of her lips. "So you don't want me?" she asked.

He wanted her too damn much, so much that his control snapped. He swung her up in his arms and headed toward the bedroom.

And a giggle replaced the sad-sounding sigh she'd uttered moments before. Her arm slung around his shoulders, she arched up and kissed the side of his neck.

The tingling he'd already felt spread throughout him. He had plans for the night, plans that hadn't included her. But now that she was here…

Everything was about Savannah. He laid her on the bed, but unlike that night where he'd been so concerned about her pleasure, now he could think only of how badly he wanted her, how badly he needed her.

So he followed her down onto the mattress, pressing his body to hers, so she would know what she'd done to him, how much he desired her. His erection strained against the fly of his dress pants… until she released it.

Her hands were between them, moving. First she pulled down the zipper, then she closed her hand around him, stroking him. The sensation of her skin against his…

He nearly came. But that would be too quickly and not enough. Not nearly enough pleasure.

In giving her pleasure that night, he'd intensified his own. So he pulled back now…just far enough that he could unzip her jeans and ease them down her long, long legs. While he did that, she arched up and dragged her sweater over her head and unclasped her bra. It fell away, freeing her full breasts.

Her body was perfect. So feminine and full, with generous curves and silky skin. He had to touch, had to trace his fingers around those mounds, had to cup the weight of them in his palms. Then he lowered his mouth and flicked his tongue across one taut rosy nipple and then the other.

She moaned and tunneled her fingers in his hair, holding his mouth against her breast. So he closed his lips around the nipple and gently tugged on it. And she moaned again, louder, longer.

She excited him so damn much, her responsiveness urging him to give her more and more. So he pushed her back onto the bed, and he moved his mouth from her breast, over the slight curve of her belly to where only a thin scrap of lace covered her mound. He tried to pull it down, but in his desperate grasp the lace tore and fell away from her.

"Yes," she murmured. "Yes."

She didn't care about the underwear. He knew what she wanted.

What he wanted…

So he buried his face between her legs, licking and teasing her with his tongue until she writhed against the mattress, tearing at the sheets and then grasping his head. She ground herself against his mouth, desperate for release.

And he gave it to her, sliding two fingers and his tongue inside her. Her body convulsed as he drank in the sweetness of her orgasm. He'd missed this—

the taste of her—so damn much; hell, he'd missed her—too damn much.

"Oh my God," she murmured weakly as she lay limp on the mattress. "You really are that good."

"I really am," he assured her. His body throbbed for its own release, demanding it. Wanting to bury himself inside her wet heat, he stood up and quickly disrobed until the only thing separating them was the condom he rolled on with a shaking hand. His cock pulsated within his grasp as he guided it inside her.

She bucked beneath him, arching her hips, taking him deeper. He buried himself to the hilt, thrusting and thrusting. She felt so damn good, so tight, so hot, her inner muscles grasping at him, squeezing him. He had not exaggerated in his mind how amazing she felt; she was even more amazing than he'd remembered. She was incredible, so it was no wonder he'd not wanted anyone else…but her.

She lifted and bent her legs, sliding them over his shoulders, and he sank deeper inside her yet. She cried out, and he tensed.

But she clutched his butt, sinking her short nails into his skin, and urged him to thrust. "Harder, harder," she demanded, greedy for more of the pleasure he'd already given her.

He loved that.

Loved how he could feel the little ripples as she started to come again. She was so damn responsive, so sexy, so addictive…

He was getting so attached to her—in a way he had to no one else.

Her fingers slid over his butt, between his legs as she stroked his scrotum. Her touch drove him insane, pushed his control, so he moved in a frenzy—desperate for release. Finally his body tensed, then shuddered as he ejaculated, coming and coming in an orgasm more powerful than the ones she'd given him that first time. She was even more amazing than he'd remembered.

"Savannah!" He shouted her name.

She unwound her legs from around him and sank into the mattress, seemingly boneless and satiated. He should have been, too. But his cock stirred inside her.

She arched dark blond brows over those navy blue eyes of hers. "Again? You are incredible."

"So are you," he said. She was the most responsive, generous lover he'd ever had. It was no wonder that he could think of nothing and nobody else but her.

He'd never clicked with anyone sexually as well as he had with her. She just knew what to do—how to move, where to touch him...

But it was more than that; he felt a connection to her—a complete intimacy—that he'd never felt with anyone else. It was as if she was part of him, inside his body, his mind, his passion...

Shifting on the mattress, she contracted those inner muscles around him. But he had to pull out, had to pull off the condom to reach for another.

Before he could put one on, her fingers sheathed him, and she pumped his cock in her hand, making him fully hard, making him throb and ache again.

How could he want her so damn much? She was quickly becoming an obsession for him.

She wanted him, too, though. She pushed him back, so that he sprawled on the mattress. Then she replaced her hand with her mouth, sliding it up and down him until he was on the edge of coming.

Before he could, she slid her lips off his cock. Then she took that condom from his fingers and rolled that onto him, and she straddled him.

And she rode him, driving him out of his mind as she bounced up and down and jostled against him. He cupped her breasts, which bounced with her movements, and he rubbed his thumbs over her tight nipples, teasing her to the brink of the same madness she'd brought him.

She increased her rhythm, bucking and grinding against him...until finally she came, screaming his name. He arched up and kissed her deeply, thrusting his tongue inside her mouth like he thrust his cock deep within her core. And finally he came again, his groan filling her mouth like his ejaculation filled the condom.

How could it have been so powerful after the one he'd just had? What the hell did she do to him? Was she making him fall for her?

CHAPTER TEN

"You're still here," a deep voice murmured as lips skimmed across her cheek, which was a little sore yet from that damn glue. "You didn't sneak out again."

"I can't move," Blair admitted. Not after everything they'd just done to each other. Her muscles must have melted away because she couldn't feel them anymore, or her bones...nothing but his lips.

Then teeth lightly nipped her shoulder. "You need to move," he said. "You have to get dressed."

So content and ready to sleep, she had to pry open one eye so that she could peer up at his handsome face as he leaned over her. "You're kicking me out?" she asked. "Is this some kind of payback?"

Maybe he was angrier with her than he'd seemed over her not returning his messages. Maybe she'd hurt his ego too much, but she hadn't thought that he was that arrogant even though he had every reason to be. He was handsome, successful and an incredible lover. And she'd been insane to ignore his messages the past couple of weeks.

"You deserve it," he said, "for depriving us of *that* the past couple of weeks."

"Agreed," she murmured. Sex with him was beyond anything she had ever experienced before. He brought her so damn much pleasure and so easily. He was so unbelievably handsome that just looking at him nearly made her come.

Her heart began to thump with the fear she'd felt over seeing him again. She'd wanted him, but if he knew who she really was and what she did, he wouldn't want her. Maybe he had figured it out and that was why he was tossing her out. He couldn't support who she really was and what she did, not just for a living but for her life. Flying had always been her first love.

Apparently it would be her only love, though. Because she couldn't fall for someone who didn't understand how important being a pilot was to her. She couldn't change who she was to try to please someone else—like her mother had spent so damn much of her life doing.

That had been so painful and sad to watch as her mother had become more and more of a shell of the woman she'd once been, a woman who had had dreams of college and law school until she'd fallen in love with a selfish man.

Teo wasn't a selfish man, though. At least not in bed...

He'd given her so much pleasure. She'd wondered if she'd imagined how great it had been between them. But it had been even better than she'd remembered; he had been even better.

Hadn't it been as good for him? Was that why he wanted to get rid of her now?

Light flooded the room, momentarily blinding her.

She groaned in protest but forced both eyes fully open to stare at him. He was wearing the tuxedo again. "I take it you don't rent that thing," she murmured.

"It's mine," he said. "And this is yours." He tossed a garment at her. "I just had it delivered to the suite."

She picked up the swatch of red silk and stared at it. The label stared back. "This is designer..."

"Yes," he said. "We're going to a fashion show."

"That's why you needed a date," she mused. "So you bought this dress for whoever showed up at your door?"

He chuckled. "In your size?"

Suddenly suspicious, she narrowed her eyes and studied his handsome face. "Did you and Miranda set me up?"

She'd thought she'd coerced her friend into sending her in place of the other date Teo had requested.

But maybe it had been their plan all along and the reason for Miranda's call in the first place.

He shook his head. "I don't play games. After you fell asleep on me…"

Heat rushed into her face. After riding him into an insanely intense orgasm, she had literally collapsed on top of him—exhausted from her sleepless nights and from the exertion of having crazy-hot sex with him.

He continued, "I called up the designer and had him send over this dress for you."

"Of course you did…"

And of course the designer had immediately complied—because every time she'd been with him, everyone fawned all over the Italian billionaire. No one dared to deny Matteo Rinaldi what he wanted except her. She'd denied him the male pilot he'd requested. She'd denied his wish for honesty and no games. A twinge of guilt struck her, and she considered telling him the truth now. But a rush of fear followed her guilt over how he would react, how angry he might be. And he was obviously in a hurry.

He'd probably sponsored the show or financed the fashion house. So he shouldn't be late. She forced herself to roll out of the tangled sheets. But when she stood up, naked, beside the bed, he uttered a deep groan. His eyes, usually that warm chocolate brown, turned black as his pupils dilated. His nostrils flared, and a vein stood out on his forehead and another on his neck as his pulse pounded. Feeling a feminine power she rarely remembered she had, she smiled and reached for him, but he stepped back and shook his head. Then, cursing, he turned and rushed out of the bedroom.

"Chicken!" she called after him, teasing him, with a few clucking noises.

"Damn right I am," he said from the other room. "You're a scary woman."

The smile slid away from her face. Blair was a scared woman. More scared than she could remember being in a long time. If she wasn't so afraid, she would have told him the truth—about everything.

But she didn't want this night to end. Not yet.

But it wasn't just the sex she wanted. She wanted another evening out like the one they'd had that first night. She wanted the glimpse into his life—with his family, with his friends, and she wanted the fun of having dinner with him, of dancing with him...

Then, after the appetizers, she wanted to come back here for the main course. For him.

"We need to leave," he told her.

She cleaned up quickly in the bathroom and tugged the sheath of red silk over her head. The dress was simple but beautiful. She stepped out of the bathroom into the living area. His back was to her, as he stood at the windows staring out at the lights of the beautiful city. But he must have caught her reflection in the glass because he turned.

"Damn." The curse slipped out of his lips as his mouth dropped open. "You're stunning."

"It's the dress," she said. "Thank you for borrowing this for me." Wasn't that the way it worked with celebrities? Designers lent them dresses for their special events in order to market their designs.

"It's yours to keep," he told her.

She shook her head. She had already felt like an escort the first time she'd met him at his hotel suite. Now she was beginning to feel like a mistress. "I told you I don't want your money," she reminded him.

"I didn't buy it," he assured her.

"But still…" He'd received it somehow, as repayment for something he'd done—not her. She shook her head again. "I can't accept this."

"You can't return it," he told her. "You would insult the designer." He held out a box to her.

It was square and too big to hold jewelry. But still it was another gift she didn't want to accept. "What's this?"

"Open it."

"I don't want you to give me things," she insisted.

"It's not from me," he said. "And we don't have time to argue. Open the damn box."

With a sigh, she lifted the lid from the box and found a pair of gold shoes inside that glittered as brightly as jewels. Her breath shuddered out.

"They're beautiful. And you shouldn't have done this...any of this."

He shrugged. "They are gifts, not from me but from the designer. And to show your appreciation, we should get to his show before it starts." But he stepped closer to her and trailed his fingertips down her bare arm. "You are so damn tempting, though."

She wanted to go back to bed, too, wanted to continue to enjoy him as long as she could—before reality and her fears intruded on their intimacy. "It would be rude to be late," she said, trying to convince herself more than she was him. The designer had sent the gifts.

Teo uttered a groan of frustration before sighing. "Then we should get the hell out of here before we give in to temptation."

"Agreed," she said. She stepped into the shoes and rushed to the door. Before she could pull it open, a hand slapped against the wood above her head, holding it shut. And a body, long and hard, pressed against the back of hers. She moaned as his erection prodded her.

"I just remembered you don't have any underwear," he said.

Because he'd ripped hers.

"You didn't think to ask the designer to send some of those," she said.

"I didn't want him to," he admitted. "Because I wanted to be able to do this anytime I wanted."

He slid his free hand under her dress, between her thighs, and stroked his fingers over her.

She moaned again and pushed against him, and his fingers slid inside her.

"You're so hot," he said. "So ready…"

So on edge that she was nearly coming already.

His hand moved from the door. Was he going to open it? Did he expect her to leave—like this? So on edge she was about to come if she walked?

Then his zipper rasped, and his cock replaced his fingers, thrusting in and out of her. He wasn't wearing a condom, so she should have protested. But she wanted him too badly. She was also on birth control, and Miranda advertised that all the members of Liaisons International were tested and safe. So she gave in to her need for him and braced herself against the door so that her knees wouldn't buckle. It rattled in its frame, and he moved inside her.

Moans and cries of pleasure slipped out of her lips as her inner muscles gripped him and convulsed, an orgasm overtaking her. He pulled out, though, and his zipper rasped again.

She turned around and stared at him in surprise, over the pleasure he'd given her and the pleasure he'd denied himself. Was he really that selfless? That generous…

That amazing?

"You didn't come."

Sweat beaded on his brow and his upper lip, and

a muscle twitched along his jaw. "We don't have time," he said—even though he'd taken the time to please her.

She reached for him. But he pulled back.

Through gritted teeth, he told her, "We need to go. Now."

She shook her head in amazement that he was denying himself a release he obviously needed as badly as she'd needed the one he'd just given her. "You're a masochist."

He really was a masochist. He needed to come so badly that he barely made it down in the elevator to the car, his body ached so much with the need to explode. He didn't know why he'd denied himself a release.

He'd wanted her so badly, and being inside her, he'd nearly come. But he hadn't been wearing a condom, so he hadn't dared. She'd felt so damn incredible. Without the latex between them, he'd felt her muscles convulse, the ripple and release of them and the heat and wetness of her orgasm.

He could smell her, feel her yet, and he was nearly going out of his mind with need for her. Forcing himself to focus on anything else, he climbed into the limo and reached for the bucket of ice. Tempted to dump it on his lap, he dropped some in a glass instead and poured grappa over it. His hand shook a little as he extended the glass to her.

She smiled as she accepted it and leaned back in the seat across from him to sip it. He grabbed another glass and poured more grappa into it and tossed back the entire contents. The fiery liquor burned down his throat.

He cleared it before saying, "We need to talk."

"This sounds serious," she murmured as the smile slipped away from her lips.

It was. He needed to distract himself from the desire pulsating in his body, from his desperate need for a release from the madness to which she drove him.

"We never talk," he said. "Mostly because you don't return my calls." He was still not over that, but she was here now so he wanted to focus on the moment and on her. So he continued, "But we haven't really ever talked."

He'd realized it before, but whenever he was with her, he got distracted by the attraction, the crazy-hot chemistry, between them that he forgot. "I don't really know anything about you."

"Yes, you do," she said.

He chuckled. "Really? What do I know?" Not even her last name. But before he could point that out, she was sliding down onto the floor between their seats.

"You know how to kiss me," she said. On her knees, she arched up and brushed her lips across his. "You know how to touch me…" Her fingers trailed down the studs holding his tuxedo shirt together to the tab of his zipper.

His cock throbbed and pushed against the fly of his dress pants, begging for her touch. She lowered the zipper and released his straining erection into her soft hands. She wrapped her fingers around him and slid them up and down the length of him.

He groaned and pushed against her hand, thrusting into it like he'd thrusted inside her just moments before. Her hand wasn't as good as being inside her, but he could remember how he'd felt, burying himself so deeply in her core—joining their bodies, bringing her pleasure.

Pleasure that he'd denied himself. Now he was close. So close.

So damn close…

Then she replaced her hand with her mouth. She sucked him deep into her throat. The feeling of her lips and her tongue…even the gentle scrape of her teeth…all drove him out of his mind.

Control slipped away from him.

He pumped into her mouth, an orgasm exploding out of him with such force that he felt as if he left his body. Or at the very least he lost his mind.

She licked his cock before tucking him back into his pants and pulling up his zipper. Then she moved back to her seat and leaned back, licking her lips.

He couldn't remember the last time he'd lost

control like that. Actually, he could—it had been
with her.

Only with her.

A strange emotion rushed over him—a vulnerability he hadn't felt since he was a kid. He could
lose control with her, but did she do the same?

Or was it that she was always in control? Always
keeping her secrets from him.

He cleared the last vestiges of passion from his
voice and said, "Our conversation isn't over."

She arched a blond brow. "What conversation?"

"The one in which you really tell me about yourself," he said. "Who you are, what you do..."

Now, after that mind-blowing release, she
wouldn't be able to distract him with sex. She would
have to answer his questions.

She must have realized it, too, because an emotion passed through her dark blue eyes, and it looked
an awful lot like the vulnerability he was feeling.

No. It was even more intense than vulnerability.

It was fear.

What the hell was she so scared of revealing to
him?

CHAPTER ELEVEN

BLAIR HAD GOTTEN LUCKY, because before Teo had been able to resume his interrogation of her, the limousine lurched to a stop outside the nightclub where the fashion show was being held. Relief had shuddered through her, but it was short-lived.

As Teo had helped her from the back of the car, he warned her, "This isn't over. We're going to have a conversation—a real conversation—before the night is over."

Even though her heart had pounded faster with fear, she'd forced a smile and told him, "Of course we will."

But she had no intention of ruining this evening with the truth. Not yet.

She was enjoying it and him entirely too much. She could taste him in her mouth, on her tongue— the salty-sweet taste of his passion. And she wanted more...

She wanted him again, her core throbbing with the need to have him inside her again, filling that hollow ache as only he could do. But before she could lose her mind to the madness of desire, they stepped into the nightclub and into the perfect distraction.

As had happened at the restaurant, he wasn't the only one treated like royalty at the fashion show. The designer fawned over her, begging her to model for him.

She laughed at the notion of a former fighter pilot walking a runway. There was nothing sexy about her...except when she was with Teo. She felt sexy with him, maybe because all she could think about around him was sex.

Teo stepped back and studied her through narrowed eyes. "You could be a model," he murmured speculatively. "Are you? Is that what you do? Why you're so busy you can't return phone calls?"

A smile tugged at her lips, and she shook her head. "I am definitely not a model." But she was busy—thanks to him and all the flights he'd been booking with Bill.

"You should model," the designer told her. "I would love to include you in tonight's show, in that dress, which looks as if I made it specifically for you."

The older Italian gentleman was even more charming than Matteo. Maybe this was from whom Teo had learned how to disarm with charm—because it seemed as if the two men knew each other well.

"Please," the designer persisted. "Walk in my show."

She shook her head again. "Not unless you want me to ruin it. I would trip over my own feet and embarrass you and myself."

"Never!" the designer insisted.

She was saved again when someone called to him from the stage. "We're ready."

"Ah," he sighed in disappointment. "It's too late to have you in this show. But the next…"

The next one she wouldn't attend; she would be flying someone somewhere. And she doubted it would be Teo. Once he learned the truth, he would never want to see her again. She blinked away the sudden sting of tears pricking at her eyes. She wouldn't cry. She never cried, but she was disturbingly close to now over the thought of never seeing him again.

"What's wrong?" Teo asked, his voice even deeper with concern.

She shook her head. "Nothing. He was just being so sweet. He seems like a genuinely nice man."

"He is," Teo confirmed as he guided her to a seat in the front row nearest the stage. "He's very talented, too."

Blair had already realized that from the beautiful dress gifted to her. But she also saw his amazing talent in all the other designs the professional models wore as they strutted across the stage.

"You could do that," Teo assured her. "You would be a super model."

She doubted it. From the way some of those models glared at her sitting next to Teo, she bet at least one of them would have tripped her—if not most of them. "Did you bring me here to protect you again?" she wondered.

He chuckled. "From whom? Tony? He's harmless."

Tony had clearly been more interested in her than him, so she chuckled. "You know…"

"My matchmaking sister isn't here," he said, and his brow creased as he frowned. "Although she should be."

"Why?" she asked.

"Tony was there for us when we were growing up," Matteo said, his deep voice gruff with emotion as he recounted his past to her. "Even though, as just a tailor at that time, he didn't have much more money than we did, he helped us out with food and old clothes."

She turned fully toward him now, studying his handsome face as she processed her shock over his admission. "What? You didn't have food and clothes?"

His face flushed slightly. "Things were a little hard for us. But we got by with some help. Tony was a neighbor. He helped."

"You've paid him back now," she said, surmising that he'd probably helped the designer launch his own fashion house. Not that she expected Teo to admit it.

He shook his head, and his voice was even gruffer with emotion when he replied, "I will never be able to thank him enough for his kindness and generosity."

"Your life..." she murmured. "I can't imagine how it must have been." She'd never been hungry for food—just for love and acceptance.

But her mother had been so busy trying to get her father's attention and approval that she hadn't had time for her children. And her father hadn't shown love or any other emotions.

"I think you might be able to imagine it. Something about you..." Teo studied her face through narrowed eyes. "I don't believe your life has been easy."

She uttered a shaky sigh at the understatement. "If things were difficult for me, it was because of the choices I made," she admitted. Like now...

She'd chosen not to tell him her real name and to hide behind a disguise when she flew him.

"What kind of choices?" he asked.

She couldn't tell him about the flying, so instead she told him about Miranda. "I had a friend who often got me into trouble," she said.

"You were a wild child?" he asked, his brown eyes twinkling as if the thought excited him.

"No," she said. "I always got caught."

"Is that why you're so guarded?" he asked. "You are trying to protect yourself?"

She nearly jumped at his astute observation. How could he not see through Bill's disguise but he could see her so clearly now?

That was why she had to protect herself, though, from him, from falling for him.

"I have no regrets," she assured him.

"No?" he asked, his head tilted.

It was as if he knew she regretted not being honest with him.

Thunderous applause saved her from having to reply. She jumped to her feet along with everyone else. Tony came onto the stage and bowed. Then he gestured for Matteo to join him.

Matteo shook his head.

"This would not have been possible without you, my friend," Tony called out to him. "You are responsible for this finally coming to fruition."

"You are the talent," Matteo called back. "Congratulations on a fabulous line!"

The applause and accolades continued even while drinks and hors d'oeuvres were served. While Teo kept Blair at his side, he didn't have time to interrogate her any further about her past or her present.

But then he took her empty flute of champagne and passed it along with his to a waiter.

"Would you like more, sir?" the waiter asked.

Teo shook his head. "No, thank you. We're leaving."

And her heart began to beat faster. The interrogation would probably begin again—unless she could distract him as she had on the ride to the show.

When they stepped outside and the wind blew beneath her dress, over her bare skin, she knew just how to distract him. Once he'd taken the seat across from her and the chauffeur closed the back door, she spread her legs and pushed her dress up high enough that he could see how badly she wanted him.

"Damn you," he cursed as his nostrils flared. "Damn you for being so irresistible."

"Then don't resist me," she said and invited him, "Take me..."

He didn't resist her.

He did what she had and dropped onto his knees in the space between their seats. Then he planted his palms on the seat on either side of her hips, and he leaned forward until his mouth brushed across hers. He kissed her softly, slowly...before deepening the kiss by sliding the tip of his tongue between her lips.

She moaned against his mouth, wanting more than kisses. She needed the release he'd given her earlier. She needed him inside her. She reached for his belt, but he pulled back and shook his head.

She worried that he was going to insist on having that conversation she kept denying him. But then he leaned back even further until he was sitting on his haunches, and he moved his mouth lower, between her legs.

He tormented her as she'd tormented him earlier. He touched her first with his fingers and then with the tip of his tongue. He teased her until she was nearly sobbing from the tension wound so tightly inside her body.

Then he slid two fingers inside her while he licked and sucked her clit. And she came, her body shuddering from the power of the release he'd given her.

But it wasn't enough yet. Despite the intensity of the orgasm he'd given her, she still felt that hollow ache inside her.

Was it because he was still fully clothed? Or because she was still not telling him what he deserved to know?

She tasted so damn good that Teo wanted more. He wanted to bury his face in her mound and lick and lick at her. But his body was so damn tense, his cock throbbing with the demand for another release.

He'd told the driver to take at least an hour returning to the hotel—because he'd wanted to finish what she'd started in the limo on the way to the fashion show. She'd given him a release then.

But it hadn't been the same as burying himself inside her, as joining their bodies. He wanted to do that again—even more than he needed to have that serious conversation with her.

But he wouldn't be able to talk—to even think—until he released the tension gripping him. Sweat beaded on his upper lip as he struggled to hold on to his control. But with her...it was impossible. He had to have her. "Do you want more?" he asked. "Do you want me?"

"Yes," she said, her voice raspy with desire.

Her blue eyes darkened, her pupils dilating with renewed desire as she realized he wasn't done. He also noticed the relief. She was glad that he wasn't going to force her to talk right now.

She clearly didn't want to have a conversation with him. Was all she wanted from him sex?

That probably would have thrilled most men. Hell, that probably would have thrilled Teo that a woman wasn't after his money or the lifestyle he could offer her. But there was something about Savannah...

Something that made him want more than just sex with her. But he wanted the sex, too, so badly that he couldn't think of anything else right now but having her, but burying himself inside her.

This time when she reached for his belt, he let her unclasp it and lower his zipper. But when she freed his cock, he pulled it from her hand. And he rolled on the condom he'd taken from his pocket.

Then he pushed her back on the seat and eased

himself inside her before thrusting deeper and deeper. She was so hot from the release he'd just given her, but despite that release, she was needy, too.

She clutched at him, moving her hands over him, pushing aside his shirt to touch and kiss his chest. She nipped at one of his nipples, lightly, with her teeth. And he leaned over, pushed her dress down, and returned the favor.

She cried out and arched against him, wanting more. He gave her more, thrusting his cock inside her over and over again. Deeper and deeper...until she tensed and cried out.

Not in pain...

He had enough control that he would never hurt her. But she was strong with sleekly toned muscles, so she easily matched him—in passion and strength. He wouldn't hurt her physically. And he doubted she'd ever let him close enough to hurt her emotionally.

He'd never intended to let anyone that close, either. But she was getting there...she was getting as deeply inside him as he was inside her. Then his body tensed and shuddered as his release shook him to his core with its mind-blowing intensity. It just got better between them every time.

Panting for breath, he rolled off the condom and wrapped it in napkins before disposing of it.

"You didn't need that," Savannah told him.

Miranda Fox had assured him that all their members had voluntarily been tested and were safe. But Teo still always wore a condom…except for that moment back at the hotel, when he'd wanted to feel nothing between them.

But if he'd come inside her…

If he made a baby with her…

He would be connected to her in a way he'd never intended to connect himself with another woman. Unlike his father and Francesca's, he wouldn't walk away from his child—from his responsibilities.

"I have a birth control implant," Savannah told him. "So I can't get pregnant for years."

So Savannah didn't want children, at least not any time soon.

She didn't want to trap him into marriage or anything else. He should have been relieved, but that wasn't how he felt. He was unsettled.

She hadn't run earlier, when she'd fallen asleep in his bed, but he had no doubt that eventually she would. When they returned to the hotel, she distracted him again with sex, and when he came out of the bathroom, after cleaning up, he found her gone.

She must have dressed in her jeans and sweater again. For the dress and the shoes sat on the bed, which was still rumpled from the wild sex they'd just had in it. The dress and the shoes were all that she left.

No note again.

She'd left without leaving him her number or even her damn last name so that he could track her down. That had to be because she didn't want him tracking her down. She didn't want him to find out any more about her or her life.

What the hell was Savannah hiding from him?

Miranda Fox claimed to have verified that all the members of Liaisons International were single. But Teo was beginning to doubt that was the case with Savannah. Maybe Miranda had made an exception for that rule for her friend.

Maybe Savannah had a husband.

Was that the secret she didn't want him to learn? The reason she didn't share her last name with him—because she already shared it with someone else?

Did she have a whole secret life that she was so desperate to protect that she kept running out on him?

CHAPTER TWELVE

BLAIR SAT AT her desk, staring into the computer monitor that had gone dark because it had been so long since she'd touched the keyboard—because she was so lost in her thoughts, in her daydreams. In that dark screen, she could see Teo's handsome face, his jaw clenched as passion overwhelmed him. Would she see him like that again? Or would they just continue to nod at each other when he poked his head into the cockpit to thank Bill for a smooth flight?

"You have to come clean."

Blair jumped at her brother's pronouncement and nearly toppled her chair over onto the polished concrete floor of their shared office space. Not only did they share it with each other but also with the hangar for their biggest planes. This building in London was the headquarters for Private Flights. She grasped the edge of her desk and steadied herself, but her hands trembled. "What are you talking about?" she asked.

And how the hell did he know?

Had Miranda told him?

"Your little masquerade is going to come back and bite us on the ass," Grant continued as he stalked into the room from the hall that ran between the exterior door and the area of the hangar with the planes.

She released a slight sigh of relief when she realized that her brother didn't know that she'd slept with their new biggest client. He was talking about her pretending to be a man.

That was even worse given that she was sleeping with Teo. If the Italian businessman ever learned that she had purposely tricked him into thinking that she was a man, he would be so furious with her. He wouldn't forgive her. What the hell had she done?

"It's only a problem if he figures it out," she said, trying to convince herself as much as she was trying to convince him. And he damn well couldn't figure it out.

Ever...

"You think you're going to be able to keep up the charade forever?" he asked as he dropped into the chair behind his messy desk. Before she could answer, he shook his head. "You're not. Hell, I'm surprised you've gotten away with it for as long as you have."

She was, too. But Teo only ever stuck his head in the cockpit, and she never turned fully toward him. He saw only her back and shoulders, which she disguised with heavy padding, and when she turned slightly toward him to acknowledge his presence, that beard. She touched her face, which was chafed from the glue used to hold that damn thing in place.

"And when he figures out you've duped him," Grant continued his lecture, "it's going to be a hell of a problem. Not only will we lose him as a client, but he might be pissed enough to sue us."

She shook her head. "Sue us? How? He'll make himself look like such a chauvinist pig if he publicly objects to a woman pilot."

"I really think you overreacted about that whole thing," Grant said. "It didn't sound like he doesn't think women can fly. It sounded more like he didn't want to have to deal with another female." He wriggled his brows at her. "And I can totally relate to that. I had made an exception for you—until your recent wacko behavior."

She flipped him off.

"Exactly."

Had that been Teo's issue? He seemed to dread dealing with his sister. And he'd turned to a dating service because the women he'd dated on his own hadn't been honest with him.

A twinge of guilt struck her heart so hard that she sucked in a breath over the stabbing pain. She should have been honest with him from the start instead of calling herself Savannah. What the hell had she been thinking?

She needed to be honest with him now. "You're right," she agreed with her brother.

Grant opened his mouth wide as if totally shocked that she'd conceded. "What?" he asked. "I don't understand. You're actually admitting I'm right about something." Then he tensed and narrowed his eyes, staring at her with suspicion. "What exactly are you saying that I'm right about?"

She drew in a deep, steadying breath. "That I need to tell him the truth."

Moving surprisingly fast for such a big man, Grant jumped up from his chair. "Hell, no! You can't do that!"

"You just told me to come clean," she reminded him.

"That was before it occurred to me that he might sue us," he said. "No. It's better that he never learns that you've been the one actually flying him."

She touched her chafed face. "You expect me to wear that beard forever?"

"No," he said. "I expect you to stop flying him."

Another twinge—of panic—struck her heart. Even though they barely spoke, she had come to enjoy those flights, knowing where he was going—what he was doing. It made her feel close to him albeit not as close as she would like to be.

Oh, God, she'd become a stalker. She wasn't

much better than those other women he'd regretted dating—the women who'd wanted him for his
money or for connections he'd made through his
business. He would probably think her motives were
the same.

When she'd only been trying to protect herself
and her business…

She nodded in reluctant agreement. "Yes, you
better assign another pilot for his flights. Or better
yet, you should fly him yourself."

Grant chuckled. "He likes having a former
fighter pilot fly him around. That's not me."

Blair wasn't so sure. Five years older than she
was, her brother had joined the navy first, but his
service was even more top secret than hers had
been. He always shrugged off questions about it
and acted as though he'd been drummed out. But
she wondered if he still took missions from time to
time since he often disappeared without ever saying where he'd been. When she'd been serving, too
many people had asked her about him…with a mix-
ture of amusement and awe.

"Whatever," she said, knowing that probing
Grant for more information got her nowhere. "It
just can't be me."

She couldn't fly Teo anymore. But could she see
him again as Savannah? Because she already missed
him…missed being in his arms, missed the passion
that always burned so hot between them. She had

never felt that intensity or that ecstasy with anyone else. While she agreed that she should give up
flying Teo, she didn't think she could give up sex
with Teo…not when it was the best she'd ever had.

Not when he was the best lover she'd ever had.
Maybe Miranda had actually found her soul mate
for her—her sexual soul mate.

"I've had the best," Teo said. "And I won't settle
for less than that now—from anyone." He wasn't
talking about Savannah at the moment, but he was
thinking about her. Always. He forced his mind to
stay on task instead of straying to more thoughts of
her…naked, moving over him…

He cleared his throat and continued, "I want Bill
flying this plane. No one else."

"Bill?" The pilot turned around in the seat, his
brow furrowed with confusion. "Who's Bill?"

"You know Bill," the male attendant told him.
"You know…"

The pilot just shrugged. "I just know that Grant
told me I was taking over these flights."

"What about Bill?"

"I don't know who—"

"Bill is busy," Jean-Claude interjected.

Teo narrowed his eyes and studied the young
man's face. Was he lying?

"Family issues," he continued.

"So he'll be back?"

One flight he could handle. Maybe...

Maybe he needed to make this permanent though—hire Bill away from Private Flights to become his personal pilot. He'd come to rely on Bill's smooth flying. It was the one thing that eased the tension that gripped him whenever he wasn't with Savannah.

Savannah eased his tension more than anyone else ever had. Unfortunately she also created it, too. Just thinking about her made his body ache with need. It wasn't even desire anymore. It had gone beyond that—into dangerous territory.

He didn't like it—didn't like not being in control. He couldn't reach Savannah without going through the damn dating service. And he couldn't reach Bill to fly his damn plane without going through the charter company, either.

He needed to take back control of his life.

"Do you want me to fly you or not?" the new pilot asked impatiently.

Teo sighed in resignation. "This flight." He had a meeting in Paris that he couldn't miss. But as he walked away from the cockpit to take his seat, he pulled out his cell phone and made a call.

"Private Flights," a female voice answered.

And his pulse quickened. She sounded so much like Savannah...

So much so that he had to clear the desire from his voice before he could speak. "Uh, this is Matteo Rinaldi, I'd like to speak to the owner."

"Uh, uh…" the woman stammered, then coughed. Instead of clearing her voice though, it sounded gruffer when she replied, "Mr. Snyder isn't available right now. I can have him return your call."

"What about the other owner?" he asked. "Blair Snyder?" Of course if she'd heard from her brother that he hadn't wanted her flying him, she might not want to speak to him.

He'd been an idiot to want to avoid another female, and he'd probably come across as a real misogynist when he'd specifically requested a male pilot. But given how scrambled his brain and his heart was from Savannah, he didn't regret his decision. He was drawn to strong women, and from what her brother had said about her, Blair Snyder sounded much stronger than most.

"Ms. Snyder is not available either," the receptionist replied.

He uttered a groan of frustration as that feeling of being out of control intensified.

"How the hell do they run their damn company then if neither of them is ever available?" he asked. But then knowing the receptionist was not to blame, he added, "I'm sorry. I know it's not your fault." Any of it. She had nothing to do with his frustration; that was all Savannah's fault. "Just please make sure one of them returns my call today."

"Yes, sir."

That tone, that sassy tone…

His skin tingled in reaction to whom she reminded him of. She sounded so much like Savannah that he began to ask her name. But before he could finish his question, the line disconnected. It might have been that the plane was readying for takeoff and the connection was lost, or she might have hung up on him, thinking their conversation had ended.

Or, just like Savannah, she might have been avoiding a question she didn't want to answer. He preferred the way Savannah had avoided answering his questions to having someone hang up on him, though.

How she'd driven him completely out of control and out of his damn mind. He could have talked to her on the way back from the fashion show, but she'd teased him…with her bare skin…

And he'd had to do the same to her—drive her out of her mind. But somehow, she always seemed more in control than he was. She always seemed to be able to handle how hot it got between them and still walk away unscathed.

He was the one who kept getting burned. And yet he was too fascinated to stay away from the flames. He just kept wanting more and more of her heat.

But he was starting to want more than that.

Like maybe her heart, too.

Or did that already belong to someone else?

CHAPTER THIRTEEN

BLAIR KNEW WHERE Teo would be...and not just because he'd left a message for her with the dating service. She knew because one of her pilots had flown
him to Paris. He hadn't been happy about that; she'd
heard the frustration in his voice when he'd called
Private Flights to complain.

She'd nearly blown it then. But she didn't want
him to learn the truth over the phone. She wanted to
tell him in person. So she'd flown herself to Paris.

Flying, as always, had been easy for her despite
a storm that had blown in just as she'd been landing. Walking across the hotel lobby to Le Bar where
he'd gone for drinks was hard. Her legs trembled
with each step.

Despite what her brother had said, she knew she
needed to come clean. She wasn't worried about Teo
suing them. From what she knew of him, he was
not a petty or vindictive man. He was too loyal for
that, and he looked for that loyalty in others. So she
was worried about him hating her.

Her heart pounded harder and faster with each step she took toward the bar, her heels clicking against the marble floor. If not for the music playing softly within the bar, he might have heard her coming. Maybe he had, because the moment she stepped inside the beautiful bar, with its glowing chandelier hanging from the coffered ceiling, he looked up—as if he'd been expecting her.

Had he known she was coming?

When Miranda had given her the message he'd left for her, Blair hadn't even known that she was going to actually meet him. She'd actually told Miranda that she wasn't going to, that she couldn't.

But then she'd kept thinking about Teo, as she always did. And knowing that he was in Paris, one of her favorite cities, she'd had to come. She also hoped that she would come—the way only he had been able to make her come. So easily, so powerfully, so damn many times…

He jumped up from his chair and greeted her. "You're here."

She crossed the room to join him at a marble-topped table in the corner of the small bar. "I'm here."

He reached out his hands but then, as if he thought better of it, he didn't touch her. Instead he touched only the velvet chair as he pulled it out for her. "You're here," he murmured again as he sat down across from her.

"Is that okay?" she asked. Maybe Miranda had misled her; maybe he hadn't actually wanted her to show up at all.

He sighed. "I never know with you."

"You didn't extend an invitation for me to join you if I was available?"

"Are you available?" he asked.

"I'm here."

"But are you really available?" he asked. "Or is a husband the reason for your unwillingness to give me your last name and your phone number?"

She laughed at the thought, but the sound echoed hollowly off the coffered ceiling. "God, no," she replied with a shudder. "I'm not married."

He narrowed his brown eyes and skeptically studied her face.

"You should already know that," she said. "Miranda makes it very clear that all the members of Liaisons International are unmarried."

"What about attached?" he asked. "That wouldn't be something she'd be able to learn from the public records she probably checks for marriage licenses. Are you living with someone? Involved?"

"No," she said. But she suspected that she was lying now about the involved part. She was getting involved with him. Too involved.

He just stared at her, as if trying to see inside her. "I feel like I don't know you at all."

"I don't know you, either," she said.

He chuckled. "You know me very well. You've met my sister. My friends. I don't even know if you have any family, any friends…"

"Miranda is my friend," she said. "You know that. As for family…" She didn't really count her mother, not with as seldom as they talked, and her father had been dead for a few years. "I have a brother."

A brother who would be very pissed if he found out that she was dating their richest client. Actually, her friend wasn't happy with her, either.

"You're risking the reputation of my agency with your damn game," Miranda had complained when she'd called her earlier. She wanted Blair to be honest with him. Maybe, like Grant, Miranda was worried about being sued.

A pang of guilt struck her over her petty thought about her childhood friend. Miranda cared more about her than she did her company. She wanted Blair to be honest because she was worried about her getting hurt.

"So tell me about your brother," Teo implored her, and he seemed genuinely interested. Most of the men she'd dated in the past had only wanted to talk about themselves. She already knew Teo wasn't like that, though. He was more like Grant.

She shrugged. "There's not much I can tell you. He's a pretty private guy."

"Must run in the family," he mused. "Maybe if I get you drunk, you'll share all your secrets with me."

"You can try," she challenged him. Even though she rarely drank more than one cocktail or glass of wine, she could hold her liquor. Maybe it was a family trait, because Grant was known to have a hollow leg when it came to alcohol as well.

"Champagne cocktail?" he asked.

It was what the bar was known for, so she nodded.

Holding up his empty glass, he gestured at the bartender for two. Either the service was very good, or the bartender knew who Teo was because the drinks were delivered quickly.

"Merci," she murmured in appreciation.

"Merci," the bartender replied with a big smile of appreciation of his own—for her.

Her face flushed with embarrassment. After spending so many years in uniform, she wasn't used to how men occasionally reacted to her when she wore street clothes—like the dress she currently had on.

"You look beautiful," Teo said, "as always. Stunning actually."

She wasn't wearing one of Tony's gorgeous designs. In fact, she'd only packed the dress because she could wad it up in her carry-on, and the stretchy fabric didn't wrinkle. It did cling to her curves, though. "I figured you probably had an event here," she said. "That's why you wanted a date."

He shook his head. "No event. Just a meeting earlier today."

"Then why did you need a date?"

"I didn't need a date," he said.

"But you left the message…"

"For you," he said. "I needed you."

Her pulse quickened with excitement. Could he want her as much as she wanted him? Could he really need her, too?

He drew in a deep breath as if to steady himself. "I needed to share this city with you. Being alone in Paris is no fun."

She'd always been content here on her own, sightseeing, stopping in cafés and bars, but that had been before she'd met him. Now she wanted to share it with him, too.

"What are your plans for the evening then?" she asked. "Besides getting me drunk?"

He grinned but didn't deny his plan. "I have a reservation at Le Cinq," he said, glancing at his watch. "Soon…so getting you drunk with have to wait."

Given the three-Michelin-star reputation of the restaurant, it wasn't easy to get a reservation. She'd never managed one before, and she'd been eager to eat there. Until now.

Now she wasn't sure she would be able to manage with her stomach already churning with nerves over her decision to tell him the truth. But the truth would have to wait, too, until they were alone and in private.

But hours later, after a delicious dinner and a

carriage tour of the city, she didn't want to make
her confession. She didn't even want to talk, like
they had at dinner and during the carriage ride,
of their favorite cities, favorite museums, favorite
restaurants. She didn't want to talk at all. Neither
did Teo as he pulled her into his hotel suite at the
Four Seasons George V and kicked the door shut
behind them.

Then, finally, he pulled her into his arms and
kissed her. Wrapping her arms around his broad
shoulders, she clung to him, pressing her body
against his long, muscular one. His erection strained
against his dress pants, rubbing against her lower
abdomen.

A moan burned in her throat as the heat of passion streaked through her. She wanted him so badly.

No. She needed him. And that scared her as much
as telling him the truth scared her. She didn't want
to need him, didn't want him to become this obsession he was becoming for her. But at the moment,
her need for him was greater than her fear, so she
focused only on her need.

And on him…

She needed to be on him. She pushed against
him, walking him backward until his knees struck
the edge of the bed and he tumbled back onto the
mattress. But he took her with him as he held her
tightly in his arms.

She sprawled across his chest, where she attacked

the buttons on his shirt, pulling them free so she could part the material and push it from his shoulders. He caught her wrists in his hands, and she expected him to slow her down as he had that first time.

But his need must have matched hers, because he moved his hands from her wrists to her hips, and he pulled up her dress and pulled aside her panties. Then he unzipped his pants and released his cock. Within seconds he had it sheathed in latex and then inside her.

She gasped as he filled her.

"Too fast?" he asked. "Aren't you ready?"

"I am always ready for you," she assured him, arching and shifting—taking him deeper inside her. She'd never reacted to anyone the way she had him. While she'd enjoyed sex, she had never come as easily or as powerfully as she did with him.

"I couldn't wait," he said, his voice gruff with passion. "I had to be inside you. It feels like it's been so long. Too long…"

It had been too long; she'd felt so empty the past few days, so hollow inside. He filled her. Thrusting his hips, he drove deeper and deeper.

He moved his hand between their bodies and stroked his thumb over her clit.

She pushed against him, meeting his thrusts with her hips. Grinding against him and shifting, she desperately sought release from the pressure building inside her.

He shoved the straps of her dress from her shoulders and pushed it down her body, freeing her breasts. Then he lowered his head and kissed them, closing his lips around one taut nipple.

Pleasure arced from where his mouth touched to her to where his cock filled her. And finally that pressure broke, and she came, screaming his name.

He caught her scream in his mouth, kissing her deeply. Then his body tensed and shuddered as he found his release, too. Sweat beaded on his brow, which he pressed against hers. "Oh my God," he murmured. "Every damn time I think it can't have been that good, can't have been that intense…"

She smiled with understanding. "And yet, it is even better—even more intense."

Too intense.

Too addicting.

How was she going to leave him this time? Because she knew she should…before she told him anything. She didn't want to ruin the magic of this experience with honesty. Not yet.

Maybe not ever.

Maybe it was best to end this now—without ever telling him the truth, and then really never see him again.

He must have sensed that she was about to run because he lifted her from the bed and carried her into the bathroom. "Let's clean up together," he said.

So that she didn't take off when his back was

turned like she had last time? He knew her much better than he thought he did. He knew her too well.

He also knew exactly how to touch her and kiss her so that the pressure was building inside her again, the passion burning hotter than the warm water that washed over their naked bodies. His fingers trailed over every inch of her skin, followed by his lips.

Once again he had made her his main course. After washing the soap from their bodies, he carried her back to the bed and dropped her onto the tangled sheets. Then he followed her down, and he made love to her with his mouth, teasing her clit with the tip of his tongue.

She shifted against the mattress, desperate for release. His hands covered her breasts, molding them—stroking the nipples with his palms. She arched against his mouth and came, shuddering against him.

So much pleasure...

She wanted to share it with him. But he wouldn't let her push him back onto the mattress. Instead he slid inside her, and wrapping her legs over his shoulders, he drove deeper and deeper. She shouldn't have been able to come again so soon, but she loved the way he filled her, the way he felt moving inside her—touching her so deeply and not just physically but also intimately.

So she came again.

Then he shuddered and collapsed against her.

She lost her breath at his weight. But he rolled quickly to his side, bringing her with him.

"I'm not going to let you go," he warned her. "Not again."

She smiled at the thought. The impossible thought.

He would fall asleep. And when he did, she would slip away. She had to, before she had to tell him the truth and he got angry with her. Or worse yet, began to hate her.

She didn't want him to hate her. She wanted him to love her. And that scared her even more than the thought of telling him the truth. That scared her into feeling like her mother, desperate for the love of a man.

So desperate that she might lose herself completely. No. She had to leave once he fell asleep. And she had to stay away from him.

She'd already lost her heart to him. She couldn't lose anything else.

She was gone.

He woke alone. Even before he opened his eyes, he knew she had left. The bed was cold. And he felt empty and more alone than he could ever remember feeling.

He'd thought it before, but this time he was fairly certain that he wouldn't see her again. When he'd admitted in Le Bar that he'd needed her, her eyes had widened with something that had seemed like panic to him. Or maybe that had just been a projection of what he'd felt when he realized that he needed her.

He hadn't needed anyone since he'd started working, started supporting himself...and he'd still been a child when he'd been forced to do that.

But he could have sworn he'd seen panic on her face, too.

She'd made it clear from the beginning that she was too busy for anything serious. But he suspected she wasn't too busy; she just wasn't interested in anything serious.

And he'd gotten serious about her.

Hell, he'd gone and fallen in love with her—which was so damn crazy, given that he really didn't even know her.

CHAPTER FOURTEEN

GRANT WAVED THE wad of thick red hair in front of her face and shouted, "Put on the damn beard and fly the billionaire wherever he wants to go!"

As arguments between business partners went, it was probably one of the most bizarre. But Blair didn't feel like laughing about it. Instead, tears stung her eyes, but she furiously blinked them away. She never cried. And she was not about to start now.

"Stop telling me what to do," she told her brother as, threat of tears cleared away, she stared up at where he loomed over her desk. "We are equal partners in this business."

That was why Blair had been so adamant about contributing half of the money to start up the charter company—even though, unlike Grant, she'd had to take out loans to do that. It had been worth it so that she would have equal say in the running of their business, though. So far Grant had been good about treating her as an equal rather than a little sister. Until today.

He dropped the beard onto her desk before plopping himself in the chair behind his messy desk. "We may be equal partners in the business, but this mess is all yours. You're the one who overreacted and wanted to teach him a lesson."

"And you're the one who told me to stop flying him around so he wouldn't figure it out," she reminded him. "Now you want me to put the beard back on and get back in the cockpit." And she couldn't do it.

For so many reasons…

The biggest one was that she had fallen hopelessly in love with the Italian billionaire, and she didn't want to deceive him anymore.

"Because we're going to lose a major client if you don't," Grant said.

"And what if we do?" she asked. "We must have had clients stop chartering flights with us before, but we're still in business, still expanding." They'd just bought another plane and were training more pilots, like Jean-Claude, in order to keep up with all the charters.

"We've never lost a client before," Grant said. "In fact, we keep gaining them through recommendations."

"So why are you so worried about losing this one?" she asked. "He's not going to hurt our business."

"He could," Grant insisted.

"He's not going to sue us," she said.

"Only if he doesn't find out about your little subterfuge," Grant said.

"The only way he might find out…" Was if she finally got up the nerve to tell him.

But her desire for him had beat out her desire to tell him the truth the other night, and she'd chickened out. And like the coward she was, she'd sneaked out of his suite the moment he'd fallen asleep. She wasn't going to tell him, and she was definitely not going to see him again.

"The only way he might find out is if I keep masquerading as a man around him," she continued.

"This was all your idea," Grant reminded her.

Those damn traitorous tears stung her eyes again, and she squeezed them shut to hold them in. "I know. And it was a terrible idea…" Her voice cracked as sobs choked her.

"Oh my God!" Grant exclaimed. He must have gotten up from his chair because his big hands awkwardly patted her shoulders. "Are you okay? What's wrong?"

His uncharacteristic awkwardness and kindness brought on another wave of overwhelming emotion. The tears broke free of her closed lids, and the sobs slipped out of her lips.

Grant pulled her out of her chair and into his arms and patted her back with his large, clumsy hands. "What's wrong?" he asked again. "Blair,

I've never seen you this upset—not even when Dad died."

A twinge of guilt struck her that she hadn't been more upset over losing her father. But, like her mom, she'd never felt like she had ever had him—that he'd been interested in her or loved her.

As if he'd seen that guilt or felt it himself, Grant added, "I get that, though. Dad was Dad, but even when you were a kid, you sucked it up and kept it all inside."

"I take it you preferred that?" she asked with a giggle that cracked into a sob. She wished she could suck it up like she had the hazing hell she'd been subjected to as a cadet. There wasn't much that had ever fazed her—until now. Until Teo…

"What the hell is it?" Grant asked. "Did that billionaire do something to you? Is that why you don't want to fly him around anymore? Did he hurt you? Because if he did, I'll kill him."

His overreaction and outrageous claim cleared her tears away, and she opened her eyes with a chuckle instead of a sob on her lips. But then she saw his face—his dead-serious face—and a frisson of unease raced down her spine. "Grant, it's okay. You don't have to kill anyone."

She didn't want to hurt Teo, which was probably why she was so upset. She felt so bad over how she'd treated him. Guilt and pain overwhelming her, sobs bubbled up again, making her shake.

"What the hell is it?" Grant asked, his voice gruff with emotion of his own.

And she remembered all those times he'd defended her when they'd been growing up—usually to their own mother over some trouble Miranda had helped her get into. He'd been her knight in shining armor then. Her partner in misery in that house where they'd grown up.

But he had nobody to defend her against right now—because she had no defense for what she'd done. Embarrassed at her inability to control her emotions, she pulled out of his embrace and rubbed the tears from her face. "This is my fault," she admitted. "I screwed up."

"I know," he agreed. "The whole *She's the Man* thing was a big mistake, but it's not worth getting this upset about. Even if Rinaldi tries to sue us, it's not like he suffered any actual damages. Every flight went fine no matter who was flying him, right?"

"That's only part of how I screwed up with Teo," she admitted.

"Teo?" He tensed. "How close did you get to him while you were flying him?"

"Not very damn close at all," she said. Because she hadn't wanted him to see through her disguise. But she had to add the disqualifier. "Then."

Grant groaned. "What aren't you telling me?"

She nearly started crying again as she thought of

all the things she hadn't been telling…all the truth she'd kept from the man for whom she'd fallen.

And she had, she loved Teo, and she'd totally blown it with him.

Before she could lose it again, she admitted, "I met Matteo Rinaldi before he called here to charter a flight."

Grant's brow furrowed. "Where did you happen to bump into a billionaire?"

"I didn't bump into him," she admitted. "I was set up with him."

"You went on a blind date with the guy?" he asked. "Why didn't you say anything?"

"I just went out with him once before he called here to charter a plane," she said.

"Is that why you were so pissed that he didn't want you as a pilot?" A muscle twitched along his jaw. "Was it some kind of one-night stand?"

Not on Teo's part; instead of waiting a certain number of days like other guys had, he'd called Miranda right away to get her number. She shook her head. "No. He wanted to see me again—"

Grant's brow furrowed with confusion. "But then why didn't he want you flying his plane?"

"He doesn't know I'm a pilot," she said. "He doesn't even know my real name."

"What? You gave him a fake name?" Grant asked, then blew out a ragged breath and rubbed his hand over his face. "Sounds like something I might have done."

She groaned and then teasingly remarked, "Don't make me feel even worse about this."

He chuckled, but then the slight grin slid away from his face. "You do feel really bad about this. Why didn't you just tell the guy the truth? Or better yet, why did whoever set you up not tell him your real name and what you do?"

"Miranda —"

"God, no! Tell me you're not still friends with that troublemaker."

She chuckled now. "Isn't that the pot calling the kettle black?" she wondered aloud with great irony.

Grant glared at her. "I never got you in trouble. Usually I was trying to get you out of it—because she got you into it in the first place." He threw up his hands. "Of course I should have realized she was all over this—the fake name, the dressing up like a man. That's pure Miranda Fox—if there was ever anything pure about that damn woman! No, she's pure all right. Pure evil!"

She glared at him now. "She's my friend, Grant. And it wasn't her idea for me to lie or for me to dress up like a man." She sucked in a breath as she made a sudden realization. "Miranda doesn't even know about that. She'd probably kill me for making this situation with Teo even worse."

"Why? People set people up all the time. Why

would she get that upset about it not working out?" he asked. "Really—what the hell business is it of hers?"

"It is her business," Blair said. "She didn't just do this as a favor for a friend. She set me up because she's a professional matchmaker."

He snorted and acted as if he was humoring her when he replied, "Sure she is."

"Really, she is. She and her sisters took over her mother's matchmaking business," she explained.

He shook his head. "I don't believe it. Even as a kid, she had no use for marriage. There's no way she's promoting it."

"She's not promoting marriage," Blair agreed.

"So what kind of matchmaking business is she running?" He groaned. "It's not a legit business, is it? It's some sex thing. That woman was always trouble and she always got you into it with her. This is all her fault."

"No, it's not," she said. "It's mine." And she needed to figure out a way to fix it instead of crying on her brother's shoulder about it. She grabbed the beard that Grant had dropped onto her desk. Maybe she needed to dress up one more time.

But Grant was shaking his head. "This is a bad idea," he said.

"It was your idea," she reminded him.

"I didn't know Miranda Fox was involved in this mess. You need to stay the hell away from Rinaldi now," he said. "Or you're just going to make it worse. And you need to stay away from Miranda Fox, too."

She smiled at the repeat of a very old argument between them. Just as she never had when they were kids, she wasn't going to listen to him now about Miranda. She was a friend—a better friend to Blair than Blair had been to her. She'd risked her friend's business with her damn game just like she'd risked her own.

If Teo would actually sue anyone…

She wasn't sure how he would react when he realized how much she'd kept from him. But she was about to find out. And, unlike last time, she was not going to chicken out. He deserved the truth—no matter how much it was going to hurt and whom it was going to hurt.

Teo had had enough of a runaround. He'd had to put up with it from Savannah and from the dating service. But he didn't have to put up with it from the private plane company as well. They were damn well going to return his calls and unlike Savannah, they were going to answer all of his damn questions.

They had several offices, or hangars, all over the world, but the main one seemed to operate out of London. So he'd caught a commercial flight there—something he would never endure again, even in first class. It had been intolerable. Having anyone but Bill as his pilot had become intolerable, and he had no idea why.

Just in the way he'd begun to feel as though he saw Savannah everyone, he felt like he saw Bill. Because when he stepped into the office, he saw a man who looked a lot like the pilot—just with a much bigger, broader build. His beard was also shorter, clipped neatly against his square jaw.

"Who are you?" he asked.

The guy glanced up from the desk he was sitting at. "Who the hell are you?"

The deep voice was familiar, not like Bill's at all, but like the voice Teo had talked to several times on the phone when he'd chartered flights. So he easily identified the man. "Grant Snyder."

Grant snorted. "That's my name. What's yours?"

From the way the guy's big body tensed, Teo suspected he already knew. "Matteo Rinaldi."

Grant nodded, grimly, in acknowledgment. He had definitely recognized his voice as well. "Why are you here?" he asked, his voice even deeper with something that sounded like dread.

"You haven't returned my calls."

Grant shrugged. "No reason to. You want something I can't give you."

"Bill no longer works for you?"

"Bill never really worked here," Grant replied dismissively.

Of Teo? Or of Bill?

"What are you saying?" he asked. "Bill was the best pilot I've ever had, and I've flown a hell of a lot."

Grant sighed. "That's not what I'm talking about."

"All I need is to find out where the guy's working now," Teo said. Then he would hire him away to fly his private plane.

But Grant Snyder shook his head. "I can't."

"You will," Teo insisted. He was damn well going to get what he wanted this time. He wasn't going to be denied what he needed to know—like he was denied every damn time he called Liaisons International and asked for more information about Savannah. He pulled his wallet from the inside pocket of his jacket. "How much?"

Grant had the audacity to chuckle at him. "You're like that, huh? You think everyone has a price."

"Not everyone," Teo said. Not Savannah...

She had him so hooked right now she could ask him for anything, and he would willingly give it to her. But he suspected what she wanted most was her freedom.

"But most people do have a price," he insisted. Even his own mother and sister.

Using that dismissive tone again, Grant replied, "Not me."

Teo arched a brow. "Really? You've not been in business very long." Despite the recommendation from, of all people, Miranda Fox, he had checked out the charter company before he'd called them the first time. "You must be struggling."

Grant snorted again and shook his head. "Business is thriving, man. We've been buying more planes and hiring more pilots."

"To replace the ones you've lost."

"Haven't lost a thing."

"Bill isn't working here anymore," Teo reminded him.

"Bill…" The big man trailed off with a sigh. "Bill isn't a loss."

Teo glanced around the office. "Is there anyone else here?" he asked. "Your sister?" She was a pilot; she had to know how damn good Bill was…unlike this Neanderthal who kept insulting him.

The blond man jumped up from his chair so fast that it toppled over behind him. "My sister doesn't have a price, either. You just need to get the hell out of here."

"Your sister might listen to reason," Teo said. "Where you don't seem capable…"

"You need to get the hell out of here!" Snyder shouted again. But it was almost as if he was looking at someone else, someone over Teo's shoulder.

He turned and noticed a shadow in the hallway. Someone had been standing behind him. And he suspected that was to whom Grant Snyder had been speaking. More than curiosity compelled him to rush back into the hall—to see if he could catch the person Grant wanted the hell out of there.

Why?

What the hell was going on at Private Flights?

Once in the hall, he didn't know which way to turn. Had the person headed to the front door that Teo had entered or out the back where the planes were probably stored? Before he could decide on a direction, Grant joined him in the hall. After glancing around him, his broad shoulders sagged a bit as tension left his body.

"Who was it?" Teo asked. "Who were you talking to?"

"You," Grant replied.

"No." Teo shook his head. "Someone else was here. Who was it? Who were you telling to get the hell out of here and why?"

Grant shrugged. "I don't know what you're talking about."

But it was obvious to Teo that the man was lying, and he hated being played for a fool. Hated it so much that he felt like swinging at the guy...

CHAPTER FIFTEEN

WHAT THE HELL was Teo doing at the office? Had he found her—Savannah? Or had he just been arriving for a flight?

If he'd booked one, though, she would have known; Grant would have told her, especially given the meltdown she'd had over Teo. That must have been why her brother had shouted at her to get the hell out of there. Unless he'd been shouting at Teo?

Their conversation had sounded intense. Maybe Teo had figured out who she really was.

With Grant yelling and Teo heading into the hall, she'd been so overwhelmed that she'd dashed out to her car. But once she got into her Mini Cooper, she didn't drive very far from the office. A short distance away from the hangar, she pulled off the road and pulled her cell phone from her purse. Then, trembling slightly, she punched in a contact.

"Liaisons International," a melodic voice answered.

"Hello, Tabitha?" she replied with surprise. "I thought you were doing a play in New York right now. Are the calls being transferred to you?" Miranda had told her that her sisters had gone into the business with her, but it seemed like Miranda was the only one working. Which was the same way it had seemed when they were all younger.

"No, I transferred here," Tabitha replied. "I got fired."

Blair smiled. Even as a little girl, Tabitha had always been very blunt and honest, which was probably the reason she'd been fired. "I'm sorry to hear that."

"It was for the best," Tabitha replied with her usual optimism. "I probably would have gone to jail for killing the director if he hadn't fired me first. He was even more of a control freak than Miranda is."

"Speaking of Miranda, is she available?"

"Of course she is," Tabitha replied. "She has this crazy rule that we can't use the service ourselves, so she doesn't ever meet anyone. A single matchmaker—Mother would turn over in her grave."

"Your mother is alive," Blair reminded her.

She sighed. "Not to us. Or I should say, we're not alive to her. She disowned us all for never getting married."

Blair laughed.

"No, I'm serious," Tabitha said. "It's an embarrassment to her. She only sold us the business because she thought we'd use it to find husbands like she did."

"Is she married now?"

"Yeah, and happily for once," Tabitha said. "I think that's why she's so pissed at us for not getting hitched. That and she loves weddings."

"Then it's a good thing she had so many herself," Blair said.

"That's what Miranda said."

"I'd like to talk to Miranda," Blair tried again. "If she isn't busy..."

"She's just working, as usual," Tabitha replied. "Now if she was smart, she'd date that Italian billionaire that keeps calling for her."

A pang struck Blair's heart.

"Although he seems kind of hung up on some woman named Savannah." Tabitha chuckled. "I bet I could make him forget all about her, if Miranda would let me."

Teo would appreciate Tabitha's honesty, especially after dealing with Savannah's secrecy.

"Try to talk her into it for me," the younger woman urged. "I'll get her for you."

After a series of clicks, Miranda picked up with a harried-sounding hello.

"Are you okay?" Blair asked.

"Yeah, yeah, just *love* having my youngest sister working here," she replied with heavy sarcasm.

"At least she's working." Which, being an actress

and not a very good one, was something Tabitha rarely did.

Miranda sighed. "Yeah, so am I. What can I help you with? Do you want me to give Teo a message for you?"

"I can do it myself," she said. "He just showed up at the office. Did you tell him where to find me?" That was what she'd wanted to know—if he'd come there just for a flight or for Savannah.

"Hell, no," she said.

"Then what's he doing there?" She was asking the questions rhetorically since she didn't expect Miranda to actually know the answer.

But her friend replied anyway. "I don't know. Maybe he's looking to book a private plane. I think I might have mentioned your company to him during his initial interview because he'd said something about having to fire his pilot."

That made sense then that he'd called them when he had.

"But that was before I even thought about introducing the two of you," Miranda continued. "It might have been what made me think of you, though, and that the two of you would work well together."

Tears stung Blair's eyes again. They had worked well together—in every way, but most especially in the bedroom or the back of a limo...

"Guess I was wrong about that, though," Miranda continued. "Since you won't return his calls."

"I screwed up," Blair admitted.

"I know," Miranda agreed. "He's a great guy. Tabitha keeps nagging for me to bend the rules and let her date him."

Panic struck her heart over the thought of him being with anyone else. "Would you do that?"

"Doesn't matter," Miranda said. "He canceled his membership."

So she'd already cost her friend a client. "I think he's canceling his flights with us right now, too."

"He booked some?"

"I've been flying him," Blair admitted.

"You have?" Miranda asked with surprise that she followed with a snort. "Then of course he knows that's where you work."

"He doesn't realize that I've been the pilot flying him," she explained. "I used the costume that Tabitha helped me with last Halloween, the one when I dressed up to look like Grant."

"You didn't look anything like Grant," Miranda told her.

"Maybe not," Blair agreed. Even with the padding, she hadn't looked as broad as her brother. "But at least I didn't look enough like me for Teo to figure it out."

"Or so you thought," Miranda said. "He's a smart

guy. He wouldn't have already made billions at his age if he wasn't. He's an incredible guy."

Blair groaned and squeezed her eyes shut to hold in those threatening tears. "You don't have to tell me. I know it. And I know I blew it."

"What the hell were you thinking?" Miranda wondered aloud.

"I wasn't…" That was the problem. Her attraction to Teo had scared her so much that she'd lost her senses for a while. "I'm really sorry."

"I'm not the one you need to say that to," Miranda said.

"But I cost you a client." She sighed. "I cost myself one, too."

"Teo is more than a client to you," Miranda said. "And you are more than a client to me. If my business is successful, then I'm going to lose some clients to monogamy. Or worse yet, marriage." She expelled a shaky-sounding sigh. "So don't worry about me. The business is actually doing pretty well. Or it was before Tabitha got fired and came to our Monaco office to work as the receptionist."

"You don't think she told Teo where to find me, do you?" It had always been easy for anyone to get information out of Tabitha; she was the reason Blair and Miranda had gotten caught so many times in their old escapades.

"Neither of my sisters knows who Savannah is," Miranda assured her. "They only know you as Blair, or I would have had to kill them per the deal you made me make with you when you first told me."

Blair was afraid that Teo knew now, though. But maybe he had just come in looking for a flight or for the pilot he kept requesting.

Her...

No. Bill. He hadn't wanted a female pilot. She had to remind herself of the reason she'd donned that disguise in the first place. The discrimination she'd felt—again—and from the man she'd just slept with...

That was why she'd gone a little crazy and, as Grant had accused, had probably overreacted. She'd been so unsettled from spending that evening with Teo, from connecting with him so easily and on so many levels. And then he'd turned out to be like every other man she'd dated.

"I think it's past time that Teo learn the truth, though," Miranda prodded her.

She sighed in resignation. "It is."

"Good luck," Miranda told her before disconnecting the call.

She was going to need it. He'd probably left the office already, so she would return to it first—to check in with Grant and find out what Teo knew. Then she would track him down, and this time, she wouldn't chicken out of telling him the truth.

Within minutes she pulled into a parking spot in the lot next to Grant's truck. Since it was after office hours already, he must have stuck around in case she came back. She owed him a big thank-you for warning her earlier. But he offered no such warning now as she walked back into the office and found he wasn't alone.

Teo had stayed, and he sat at the break table with Grant, cards in hand. Grant sat across from him, studying his own cards. A bottle of whiskey and two nearly empty glasses sat on the table as well as some wadded-up cash.

She wasn't the only one who needed luck. If Teo was playing for money with her brother, he needed it even more than she did. Her brother, a professional gambler, was a renowned card sharp and maybe an even more renowned drinker. He could hold his alcohol even better than she could.

Since Teo was still there, Grant must have been yelling at her earlier to leave. Or the two men might have settled their differences another way—since both their clothes and hair was rumpled, as if they'd been in a struggle.

Fighting was another thing nobody should do with Grant. Worried that Teo might be hurt, a gasp of concern slipped out of her lips.

Grant glanced up and noticed her and cursed.

Teo turned around then. His jaw fell open, but no words escaped his mouth. Grant must not have told him about her—because Teo looked absolutely shocked and devastated.

Knowing that it was her fault that he was hurt, she gasped again—as pain stabbed her heart. She regretted almost everything she'd done...except for falling for him.

How the hell much had Teo had to drink? Enough that he was hallucinating? Or was it really Savannah standing in the doorway to the hall, dressed in the Private Flights pilot uniform?

Pilot...

"What the hell?" he murmured.

"I told you to get the hell out of here," Grant said.

And this time Teo had no doubt that he was talking to the woman who stood in the hallway. He knew now why the man had looked familiar when he'd first seen him. While he looked like Bill, the pilot, he also looked like Savannah. Or whatever her real name was...

"Blair Snyder," he murmured. She had to be Grant's sister. Was she also the pilot? "And Bill?" He narrowed his eyes and studied her, but he couldn't imagine ever mistaking her for a man. Not with that sexy figure...that beautiful face...

But the figure could have been padded. The face covered with that thick reddish beard.

"What the hell sick game have you been playing with me?" he asked. Like Grant had earlier, he surged to his feet with such force that he knocked over his chair. Before he could advance on the woman, a big hand grabbed his shoulder.

"Take it easy," Grant advised him.

Teo whirled toward the man he'd briefly considered a new friend. But he had suspected Grant of lying to him, of playing him, and had considered swinging at him before Grant had shoved him against the wall and suggested drinking instead. "You're in on this? What the hell kind of family are you?"

"A close one," Grant said, his voice gruff with warning. "I will defend and protect my sister no matter what."

"No matter what," Teo repeated. "You don't agree with what she's done then."

"Don't blame it all on her," Grant said. "Blame Miranda Fox. That woman has always been trouble."

"This isn't Miranda's fault." Blair jumped in to defend her friend. "And it isn't Grant's, either. He didn't know."

Teo could only shake his head. "So I wasn't the only one you were lying to, playing games with? Why? What the hell is wrong with you?"

"Hey," Grant said, his hand tightening on Teo's shoulder. "Don't—"

"Don't defend me," Blair told her brother. "This isn't your fight. Go home."

But Grant didn't release his shoulder. "You two

shouldn't be alone right now," he said. "This has been a shock. And he's been drinking."

Teo wouldn't hurt her. But he was so damn hurt himself…

Then Blair chuckled, as if amused at the thought of his being able to hurt her. Had she cared so little for him?

"I can take care of myself," she told her brother. "You don't have to defend me anymore. Go."

Grant hesitated yet.

"Please," Blair implored him.

And finally the man released his shoulder and stepped around him. He paused in the doorway and turned back. "You better not hurt her," he warned Teo. "Or I will track you down and hurt you far worse."

Teo nearly laughed. He was already hurting. His heart was aching as well. That was crazy, though. How could he have cared that much about someone who hadn't really existed?

"Grant, stop being a Neanderthal," she told her brother. "And leave us alone."

With a heavy-sounding sigh, the big man finally turned and walked out.

Teo waited until he heard a door open and swing shut before he spoke. "I don't know if that was a good idea," he admitted. "I'm not sure that you should be alone with me right now."

"I'm not afraid of what you might do," she said.

"I am so mad at you," he said. "So mad."

But still so damn attracted to her.

Why was she so beautiful? So tempting?

She stepped closer to him, her blue eyes glistening as if she was fighting tears. He knew too many women who used tears for manipulation, though, so he steeled himself to not be moved by them.

By her.

She'd already manipulated him more than anyone else—his family included—ever had.

"I don't even know who you are," he reminded himself—more than her. She knew that she'd lied. And he...

He'd suspected she hadn't been entirely honest with him. But that hadn't stopped him from wanting her. Then. Or now.

He reached out and cupped the curve of her cheek in his palm. Now he realized why her skin wasn't as silky as it had been when they'd first met. That damn beard.

She must have had to glue it on to her face to keep it from sliding off.

"I don't understand why you lied, and the disguise..." he murmured. It made no sense to him.

"I'll explain everything," she said.

But he shook his head. "Why the hell would I believe anything you tell me? You've lied about everything." Even her attraction to him?

Had her passion been faked like everything else?

CHAPTER SIXTEEN

BLAIR WAS HURTING for him and for herself. She assured him, "I didn't lie about everything."

He shook his head and said, his voice thick with disgust, "You even lied about your name."

"Savannah is my first name," she said. "I've just always used my middle name instead."

"What about Bill?" he asked. "Is that another name? What about Tom, Dick and Harry? Do you use them, too?"

Heat flushed her face. "The Bill thing was a mistake. I thought—when Grant told me that you didn't want a female pilot—I thought you were being sexist. And I wanted to teach you a lesson."

He moved his hand away from her face to rub over his own now. "I sure as hell learned a lesson. To never trust you again."

Blair's temper flared now. "You're not even going to listen to me, are you?"

He shook his head. "I'm too damn mad."

"Okay, Grant is right." But she wouldn't admit

that to him when she saw him next. "This isn't a good idea. We shouldn't try to talk about this now."

"I agree," he said. "We shouldn't talk at all." But instead of walking away, he stepped closer, so his body, which nearly vibrated with fury, rubbed against hers.

Passion flared more fiercely than her temper, and her skin heated and tingled as her pulse began to race. Blair never felt as out of control as she did now, as desperate with desire. Knowing she was losing him, probably forever, spurred an urgency inside her and apparently inside him as well.

They reached for each other at the same time, hands grasping, mouths mating...

In their haste to undress each other, clothing ripped. A button pinged off her shirt and another off his, hitting the concrete floor before bouncing away. She didn't care. She wanted him so badly.

She clawed at his belt, unclasping it and the button on his jeans. Then she dragged down the zipper and released him. He was doing the same to her, pulling down her pants, pushing aside her panties.

His fingers stroked her to an even greater frenzy. And his mouth...

His mouth nipped and bit at hers with angry, hot kisses. Then he slid his tongue between her lips as he slid his fingers inside her.

She was so on edge that she nearly came then. A cry—of frustration—slipped out of her. She closed her hand around his cock and moved it up and down, pumping him.

He grunted and groaned and pulled back. Fumbling in his wallet, he pulled out a condom. His hand shook as badly as she was shaking, and he was barely able to tear it open.

Blair took it from him and tore it open with her teeth. Then she rolled the condom onto him. She kicked off her pants and shoes, and he lifted her up and guided her down onto his cock.

She wrapped her legs around his lean waist and her arms around his shoulders, holding tightly to him. He staggered a bit—either from her weight or from the alcohol he'd had with her brother.

He stumbled back and settled her onto the edge of the table. Glasses bounced and cards flew as he thrust inside her—over and over again. He was clearly as desperate for a release as she was.

But even as angry as he was, he wasn't selfish. He pushed her open shirt back and shoved down her bra. Then he cupped her breasts in his hands and stroked her nipples into taut, sensitive points.

The sensation streaked through her, making her core pulsate even more. She throbbed and ached everywhere with that unbearable tension gripping her. She needed the release that only he had ever really been able to give her—the powerful, mind-blowing relief.

He moved one hand from her breast, over her

stomach to her clit. And his thumb stroked over it as he continued to thrust deeper and deeper inside her.

The tension wound even more tightly through her until finally it broke, crashing through her body, making her shudder. She screamed his name, the intensity of it all overwhelming her.

He kept thrusting until his body tensed—then he, too, shuddered. A deep guttural sound tore from his throat—along with her name.

"Savannah…"

As soon as it left his lips, his eyes opened wider—with shock. And he shook his head. "No, you're Blair."

"I'm the same person," she assured him. "You know who I am. You know my body, my soul."

He shook his head again.

"And I know you," she persisted. "I know what you like—what drives you wild." She wanted him as crazy as he'd just been—wanted him to want her so much that he didn't care about anything else.

That he didn't care about everything she'd kept from him. So she touched him, sliding her palms down his muscular back to his butt. And she moved her fingers between his ass cheeks, stroking him where he was most sensitive.

His cock hardened inside her again, pulsating with renewed passion. "You make me crazy," he said, his voice gruff with desire and frustration. "You make me lose control."

And he obviously didn't like it.

But he didn't stop. He didn't pull away from her. Instead he began to move again, slower, deeper before the frenzy gripped him again.

And her...

She thrust up with such force that the table bounced beneath her. Cards dropped onto the floor and the liquor bottle tipped over and rolled. She didn't care if it hit the floor. She didn't care about anything but Teo.

He focused on her again, bending over so that his mouth reached her breasts. He kissed and nipped, driving her insane with his lips—with his tongue.

The pressure returned to her core, gripping her, driving her mad again with the need for release. She moved her legs, lifting them higher, so that he drove even deeper.

Again and again...

And his thumb found her most sensitive area, rubbing her clit until the sensation alone drove her over the edge. She found madness and pleasure— both of them claiming her mind, gripping her body, making her scream his name again.

He drove deep and came. But he said nothing this time, his jaw taut as if he was gritting his teeth to hold in her name. To hold in his feelings...even as he released his desire inside her.

And she knew she hadn't reached him, not the

way she'd wanted to. Even as he stayed buried deep inside her, she felt him slipping away from her.

Forever.

Panting for breath, Teo leaned his face against hers. And he felt the wetness of tears on her skin. He jerked back, horrified at himself—at his loss of control. He could only hope that her tears were fake now.

Because if they were real…

He was a monster for how he'd taken her—so fiercely. "Are you okay?" he asked, his voice cracking with concern. He jerked out of her and away from her. Shocked, he stared at what they'd done. Her hair was tangled around her shoulders, her shirt torn. He couldn't remember ever losing control that much. Horrified at himself, he asked, "Did I hurt you?"

She shook her head. "No. I'm the one who hurt you. And I'm so very sorry."

He couldn't deny that she had hurt him, so deeply that his heart was aching from her betrayal. She'd lied to him—tricked him. Humiliated him…

Knowing that she was all right, he needed a moment to pull himself together. Noticing the door for the restroom, he headed there to clean up—to run cold water on his face. He could only hope that like every other time he'd separated from her after sex, she would be gone when he went back into the office. But when he returned, she was there.

Fortunately she had dressed. And she must have

had another uniform somewhere because the shirt was crisply ironed with no missing buttons.

Unlike his.

A hole gapped open over his chest—which was probably appropriate because he felt like he'd been stabbed in the heart. Or maybe the back.

Both.

"Will you let me explain now?" she asked. "Will you listen to me?"

Despite what had happened between them or maybe because of it, he wasn't ready. He was too raw. Too wounded.

He shook his head. "I can't."

"That's not fair," she said.

He snorted at her audacity in calling him that. "What's not fair is you never giving us a chance," he said. "You lied to me from the beginning. So many times you could have told me the truth. Now I wonder if you ever would have…if I hadn't still been here when you came back."

"I was going to tell you," she insisted. "I intended to tell you everything the second time I met you in Milan. Then there was the fashion show. So I decided to do it in Paris. I really did. But…"

He shrugged. "I don't remember you wanting to talk at all. Why didn't you tell me the truth then?" he asked as anger surged through him again. What had she been after—money? Or just sex? "Why?"

"Because I didn't think you would understand."

"You were right," he confirmed for her. Even if she'd told him then, he would have been angry. Hurt. Deceived...

"And I didn't want this to end," she continued. "That why I couldn't bring myself to confess."

He expelled a ragged breath. "But because you weren't honest with me, it never really started. Whatever we had—it was never real. It was all just a lie."

She shook her head. "That's not true and you know it. What we have—this passion..."

"Is just attraction," he said. "We don't have true intimacy—because you only have true intimacy with true honesty. I don't think you even know what that is."

She expelled a sharp breath of her own, as if he'd struck her. "You can't say that. You don't know me."

"And whose fault is that?" he asked. He forced himself to look away from her—to break the connection between them—because no matter what he'd said, he knew they had one. A powerful one...

Maybe too powerful.

So he made himself walk away. He had to. For his protection.

He couldn't listen to her explanation. Not now, maybe not ever.

Because he would never trust that she was telling him the truth. He would never trust her, and without trust, they had no future together.

CHAPTER SEVENTEEN

BLAIR COULDN'T EVEN tell Teo that she loved him—because he wouldn't believe her. He wouldn't believe anything she said, so Blair didn't say anything at all. She just let him walk away...without a fight.

She'd told him that he didn't know her. Right now she didn't know herself. But then she hadn't been herself since she'd met him. The attraction she'd felt so instantly for him had scared her so much that she'd wanted to protect herself. At all costs.

She'd had no idea how much she would lose. Even herself...

Her greatest fear was realized; she had become her mother. A hollow shell of the person she'd once been.

While he'd been in the bathroom, she'd dressed. But now she focused on cleaning up the office area, so it wouldn't be so obvious what had happened there. As she righted the bottle of whiskey, she considered uncapping and drinking what was left. But there wasn't enough to drown her sorrows.

Hell, an ocean of alcohol wouldn't be enough to even dull the pain she was feeling. Hinges creaked as a door opened. Her pulse quickened.

Heavy footsteps pounded against the concrete floor as someone walked down the hall toward her. Had Teo come back to her? Had he calmed down enough to let her explain why she'd done what she had?

But it wasn't Teo who walked into the room. It was Grant. Disappointment overwhelmed her, and she broke down in tears again.

Grant cursed and stepped closer. "What did he do? If he hurt you, I will kill him."

"He didn't hurt me," she assured her brother. "I hurt him."

Grant sighed. "Yeah, I think you did. I've never seen anyone look as devastated as he did when he saw you in the doorway and put it all together." He sighed again. "Until now. You look even more devastated than he did."

"I can't fix this," she said, her voice vibrating with frustration. "He's not going to let me fix this."

And that was why she'd been so scared to tell him the truth. Because she'd known that she would lose him when she did. Forever…

"Do you want to fix this?" Grant asked.

"Yes," she replied quickly.

"But I know how honest you always are, so you had a reason for lying to him, a damn good one," he prodded. "You didn't want to get serious, or you were worried that he would get too serious. You must have kept him at arm's length for a reason."

"I tried to keep him at arm's length," she said. But he got too close to her anyway, so close that he had become part of her. "But I fell for him anyway."

"I blame your damn friend who has never been a friend to you at all," he said.

"She told me to be honest with him," Blair defended Miranda.

"She shouldn't have set you up with anyone in the first place," Grant said. "The last thing either one of us needs right now, with getting the business off the ground, is a relationship." He reached out and awkwardly patted her shoulder. "You'll see that this is for the best."

She shook her head. Losing Teo was the worst thing that could have happened to her—even worse than falling for him.

"I know the guy is a billionaire and all, but seriously, the way he plays cards, he'll be broke in no time," Grant assured her.

"I didn't care about his money," she said. She cared about his integrity, his loyalty, his passion...

She suspected she would never experience passion like that again—from him or from anyone else.

And she doubted she would ever feel as much passion as she had for him.

"Man, you really did it," Grant said. "You really fell for him."

"I know."

"That's too damn bad," Grant said with more pity than sympathy. "Too damn bad."

It wouldn't have been, had she been honest with Teo from the beginning. Now she didn't know how to fix it—if she even could.

"You'll be okay, though," Grant assured her. "You're tough."

She'd always taken pride in her strength, but now she realized she wasn't as brave as she'd always thought she was. Because if she was brave, she would have been honest with him from the beginning.

She drew in a deep, steadying breath and nodded. "I will be okay," she agreed. Despite not being quite as strong as she'd thought she was, she was strong enough to pull herself together again.

Even though she'd lost herself for a little while, like her mother had, she wasn't her mother. She had her work—her business—and in focusing on that, she would find herself again.

Her passion had always been flying.

Until Teo.

But she would find her passion—in flying—again. And that would have to be enough.

* * *

Teo was hurting so damn badly that he wanted to hurt someone else. Not Blair...

He didn't want to hurt Blair. Hell, he never wanted to see Blair again. Or her brother.

Because Grant reminded him too much of Blair. So with wanting nothing to do with Private Flights, he'd been forced to fly commercial again. Hell, he needed to find a pilot. One who didn't drink or wear disguises.

He had to admit Blair was a damn good pilot—just as her brother had bragged. If only she'd been honest with him.

She hadn't promised that she would tell him the truth, but Liaisons International had promised that she would. That members didn't lie or play games or have ulterior motives.

So he'd redirected his anger toward the dating service. And he'd demanded a meeting with Miranda Fox. But he'd had to fly to their main office in Monaco to meet with her, thus the bumpy, overcrowded commercial flight followed by a helicopter ride.

He couldn't blame his foul mood entirely on it, though. He was furious yet, furious with himself for being duped, furious with himself for falling for a liar, no matter how beautiful she was.

But most of all, he was furious with Liaisons International. His hand shook as he reached for the doorknob of their office suite. He gripped it so hard, he was surprised he didn't dent the metal. Then he pushed open the door with such force that it swung back and struck the wall behind it.

The young red-haired woman behind the front desk jumped, and a soft cry of surprise slipped out of her lips. "Oh my!"

"I'm Matteo Rinaldi," he said.

"I know." She didn't introduce herself, though, and there was no nameplate on her desk.

"I'm here to meet with Miranda Fox."

She emitted a soft, almost pitying sigh and repeated, "I know."

But she didn't stand up; she didn't show him to an office.

"Where is she?" he demanded.

"Right here," a husky female voice replied.

He recognized that voice all too well; he'd spoken to her more than enough times but without ever getting the answers he'd wanted. He turned and was surprised to see a woman who looked almost eerily similar to Blair, just on a smaller, paler scale. "You're Miranda…"

"And I'm her younger sister, Tabitha," the red-haired woman behind the desk finally spoke up.

"You look more like Blair's sister," he remarked.

The younger woman snorted. "Everybody says that about them."

Miranda just arched a pale blond brow. "Blair? So you know. She did tell you."

"That's something you should have—before I even went out with her!" he yelled, his rage exploding out of him. "You lied to me! You said all the members were honest—that nobody would play games..."

And Blair had played the ultimate game with him, and she'd beaten him like nobody else ever had.

Miranda didn't even blink an eye, as if she were used to having disgruntled clients screaming at her in the reception area. Given the way she'd done business with him, he wasn't surprised.

She just calmly told him, "Come into my office," as she pushed open a door and stepped back for him to join her.

So maybe she didn't want everyone to overhear how she'd misled him. Not that there was anyone else in the reception area but her sister, though.

He strode past her into an office that was small but beautiful appointed with brocade wallpaper and luxuriously thick carpet. Kind of like Miranda herself, small but dressed in a designer business suit. She liked nice things. How the hell had she afforded them?

How many men had she personally hoodwinked like her friend had hoodwinked him? Not that Blair had benefited financially from her subterfuge. He wasn't certain how she'd intended to benefit at all, actually.

"You have opened yourself up for a lawsuit," he warned her. "You made all these promises about how well you've vetted your members, how trustworthy everyone is, and then you help your friend deceive me."

"How?" she asked.

Her calmness disarmed and confused him, so that he had to blink and ask, "What?"

She walked around her small antique desk and settled onto a small brocade chair behind it. Her voice mild yet, she asked, "How did I help her?"

"You didn't tell me her real name," he said. "You didn't give me her contact information."

"And I made it clear up front that I wouldn't do that," she said. "My members expect privacy. They don't want to be stalked, especially the women."

He'd been stalked himself—usually by the women with whom his sister had set him up. They had refused to take his no as an answer...until he'd brought Savannah along with him. Then they'd understood that they hadn't had a chance. Neither had he, though. She was so damn beautiful.

So beautiful that men might not have taken no as her answer, either. Anger coursed through him at the horrific thought of anyone harassing her.

"Is that why she lied to me?" he asked. "She thought I was going to stalk her?"

"I can't speak for Blair," Miranda said. "When she told you her name, didn't she explain everything to you?"

She'd wanted to but he'd been so damn mad that he'd refused. But then would she have explained anything—even if he'd given her the chance? She'd had many opportunities to tell him the truth before that day, and she hadn't.

"She didn't volunteer any information to me," he said. "I figured it out when she walked into the offices of Private Flights wearing her pilot's uniform." Which had been a smaller, more tailored version of Bill's.

How had he not realized that Bill wasn't a man? Because Savannah had already had him too distracted.

"I doubt she ever would have told me who she really is if I hadn't stumbled upon the truth," he said.

"She was always going to tell you," Miranda insisted. "She tried to tell you many times."

He snorted derisively. "When? When she was dressing up as a man and flying my plane?"

"She told me about that, that when you requested a male pilot, you came across as a chauvinist," she said. "And as a fighter pilot, Blair has dealt with more than her share of discrimination and harassment."

He tensed with outrage against those who had dared to harass her.

His anger at her was beginning to fade as he considered how hard her life must have been. She'd fought for her country, but she'd probably had to fight her fellow officers as much for the right to do that as she'd had to fight their enemies.

"I know you're just learning all this about her, but you need to know what she's been through to understand her." Miranda persisted. Her voice wasn't mild anymore but sharp with indignation as she defended her friend. "She's had to work so hard to become the accomplished pilot and former soldier that she is. The odds were against her. And that's not even including the challenges of having that family she has."

"I met her brother." Despite losing money to him, he actually liked Grant Snyder.

Miranda's mouth twisted into a grimace of disgust. "Then you know," she said. "He's a class A jerk, and the *A* is for asshole."

"He speaks fondly of you, too," Teo shared, amused that the cultured-looking woman could speak so crassly.

Her lips curved into a slight smile. "He's actually not the worst of them. Their dad was MIA most of their lives, so much so that they probably barely noticed when he died. And their mom was constantly trying to get the father's attention by playing the part of a Stepford wife their entire marriage. That's why Blair is so against getting married, which is probably why she didn't tell you who she really is. She didn't want you trying to change her like her family and every man she's ever dated has tried to change her."

"I don't understand what anyone would want to change about her," he said. She was perfect just as she was—but, his aching heart and wounded pride reminded him, for one thing. "Except for her dishonesty."

Miranda sighed. "She's not a liar. I know you don't want to believe me, but that's why I set up the two of you. Blair is such an honest and straightforward person."

He really wanted to believe her—so damn badly. But that wasn't the person he'd met. He'd met *Savannah*. And then Bill.

"I don't know why she wasn't that way with you," Miranda said. "Except that I think she was scared." She released a shaky sigh. "And if you knew Blair as well as I do, you'd be shocked as hell that anything could scare her. She's flown in combat, after all."

The thought of that—of her being in that kind of danger—scared the hell out of him. But she'd survived it; she was fine. Except now he understood why she'd had that odd reaction to his sister's pieces of twisted metal Francesca called art. To Blair that wouldn't have been art; it would have been bad memories.

"Then why would she be scared of me?"

Miranda shook her head. "She wasn't afraid of you. She was afraid of what she might become with you."

His head was pounding with confusion. "Who? Savannah?"

"Exactly," Miranda said, and she slapped her forehead as if she'd been given sudden clarification. "That's exactly who she was afraid of becoming. Her mother."

"But I didn't want her to change."

"You said you didn't want a female pilot," she reminded him.

And he groaned. "Not because I was discriminating. It was because of the way her brother talked about her—like she was some kind of warrior princess."

"And you were afraid you were going to fall for her when you were already falling for Savannah."

"What a mess," he murmured. "She's never going to believe that."

"I do," Miranda assured him. "And Blair knows you much better than I do."

"Yes, she does," he said. "Because I was open and honest with her." He'd even told her about his childhood, about how hard it had been. But she'd shared nothing of her life. That ache in his chest continued to gnaw at him. "Because she knows me and knows how I feel about honesty, she shouldn't have lied to me."

"She realized her mistake about that right away," she said. "And I didn't know about the Bill the pilot thing until yesterday. But I understand it, after everything she went through in order to become a fighter pilot. You struck a nerve with her, brought back all the bad memories."

Like his sister's artwork probably had. He could only imagine that it hadn't been easy for her. It sounded as if nothing had been easy for her, though. Maybe that was why he'd fallen so fast for her—because they'd had far more in common than he'd realized. If he'd only known more about her, maybe he would have handled finding out the truth with a little more sensitivity and less anger. But he should have at least let her explain. Instead he'd acted like an ass.

He groaned and admitted, "I really screwed this up."

"Go. Talk to her," Miranda urged him. "She will understand, and she will forgive you. She's forgiven me for all the times I got her into trouble over the years."

"She might have, but her brother hasn't," Teo warned her. "He's also not happy that you were involved in this whole mess, either."

"Of course he isn't," she said. But that little smile was lifting the corners of her mouth again. Pissing off Grant Snyder seemed to amuse her.

"I might have to use that," Teo warned her. "If I need Grant's help to get Blair to talk to me again."

"You really screwed up," she mused.

"I overreacted," he admitted. But it was only because he had been more vulnerable with Savannah than he'd ever been with anyone else.

And to find out that wasn't even her name...

He'd been devastated. Now he was even more fascinated. Savannah was Blair Snyder, and Blair Snyder was so much more than Savannah.

She was an incredible woman. A woman he wanted another chance with...if it wasn't already too late.

He was afraid that it might be, though. That he might have hurt her as badly as he'd been hurting. And that she wouldn't want to risk that kind of pain again—not even for the pleasure they'd given each other.

CHAPTER EIGHTEEN

LOUD CLAPPING IN front of her face snapped Blair out of her daydream. She sat up so quickly from where she'd been slumped over her desk that her chair bounced back nearly a foot.

"Wake up!" Grant yelled at her.

She flipped him off. "I'm awake."

She was always awake—even when she tried to sleep. Because every time she closed her eyes, she saw Teo…naked, moving over her as he eased inside her. But she never lost that hollow feeling she'd had since he walked out on her. And she suspected that she never would.

"You look like you could use some sleep," Grant said sympathetically.

She shook her head. "What I could use is some work. I need to fly." Flying was the only thing that made her feel alive yet—that gave her purpose.

She needed that. No. She needed Teo. But he must not have been ready to listen to her yet. She'd tried leaving a message for him with Miranda, but her friend had reminded her that he was no longer a member. And per the rules of Liaisons International, neither of them was allowed to contact him again. She could have ignored her friend's warning. She could have tried tracking him down herself.

But the last thing she wanted was for him to think that she was stalking him like those other women had, that she was just after his money, too.

"Do I have to clap my hands to get your attention again?" Grant asked.

Heat rushed to her face. "I'm sorry. Were you talking?"

He sighed. "Yes, I was offering you a flight."

She jumped up. "Great. I'll take it."

"You don't even know where you're going."

Anywhere was better than where she was—wallowing in misery. She shrugged. "It doesn't matter."

"Well, if you don't care, maybe I should take this trip," Grant mused. "It would be a damn shame to waste Athens on you."

"Athens? Greece?" Her pulse quickened. It was one of her favorite cities, which her brother damn well knew. She narrowed her eyes and studied his face. "Is this for real?"

"Of course."

"For a real client?" she persisted. "You're not just trying to cheer me up?"

He snorted. "Me? Trying to do something nice? Who do you think I am?"

The best brother a girl could have, but she wasn't about to admit that to him. She couldn't keep the smile from curving her lips, though. "Thank you."

"Don't thank me," he said. "It wasn't my idea. Client booked the trip himself—needs to get there ASAP, so you don't have time to pack."

She glanced down at her wrinkled uniform. "I haven't done laundry. I don't even have my overnight bag in my locker."

"Buy stuff once you get there," Grant said. "Business is good. You don't have to worry about money."

"One of us does," she teased.

He chuckled. "It's true I never have. I always come up with some when I need it."

She suspected it was usually someone else's. But then if the person was stupid enough to gamble with Grant, he or she probably deserved to lose his or her money.

Her smile slipped away. Teo had played cards with him—despite his hatred of games. Why wouldn't he give her a chance?

"Don't," Grant said, and using the crook of his finger, he lifted her chin. "Don't keep going there."

"Where?"

"Wherever you go to beat yourself up for what happened," he said. "There's no sense in dwelling in the past. You've got to let it go."

She couldn't—not when that meant letting Teo go as well. But he was already gone.

And Grant was right. She had to stop dwelling in the past, on what might have been had she been honest with him from the beginning.

She expelled a long sigh and shook off her maudlin thoughts. "Okay, I'm going to Greece."

"I already got the plane ready for you," Grant said. "And the client is already on board."

"What?" she asked. "You okayed this without asking me?"

He shrugged. "I figured you'd be happy to get the hell out of here."

She was—as happy as she could be. "But you know I always go over the plane myself."

"You go over all the planes all the damn time," he said. "You know it's ready for takeoff."

But was she? She hadn't had as much rest as she usually required their pilots to have. But then she'd had several sleepless nights when she'd been flying combat missions, and lack of rest hadn't affected her flying abilities then. She was fine.

"I'm still going to check it," she warned him.

"Of course you are."

She headed out of the office. But Grant stopped her, his hand on her arm. She turned back. "What? Is there something else?"

He shook his head. "No. Just…"

Her brother rarely lost his words. "What?" she asked again.

He shook his head. "Nothing. I've just been worried about you."

"Now you know how I feel," she said with a teasing smile. "I worry about you all the damn time."

He snorted. "Me? Why? I live a boring life."

"Yeah, right." Maybe not being totally honest ran her in her family; it just hadn't affected her until she'd met Matteo Rinaldi.

She turned and walked away, and this time Grant didn't stop her. It wasn't until after she'd checked the plane and boarded that she realized he hadn't told her who the client was who'd booked the wonderful trip to Athens.

But when she saw him already sitting in one of the comfy seats in the back of the Cessna, she wasn't surprised—although her pulse did quicken. Apparently Grant was trying to take over Miranda's role as matchmaker.

"I'm sorry," she said. "You were probably expecting Bill or Grant..." With as angry as he'd been when he'd left, she doubted Teo would have booked this flight himself like Grant had claimed he had.

"Your brother can fly?" Teo asked.

She nodded. "Probably better than I can." Although he would never admit it, just as he would never admit to whatever he'd done in the navy.

"I doubt that," Teo said as he stood up and approached where she stood just inside the door.

"You're the best pilot who's ever flown me any-where."

He seemed sincere, but Blair hesitated to believe him—to believe any of what was happening. "But still," she murmured. "I'm sure you don't want me flying you anywhere."

"I want you flying me everywhere," he said.

She wanted to clap her own hands in front of her face to wake up. She must have finally fallen asleep. Because there was no way that this was really happening...

No way.

"I never had a problem with a female pilot," Teo said. "I hope you know that I'm not a chauvinist."

"I know that now," she said. "But when you told Grant you didn't want me to fly you anywhere, I had only met you the one time. I didn't really know you yet. And when you said that, you touched a nerve."

"A raw one," he said. "I imagine it wasn't easy for you, that, given your career choice, you must have dealt with a lot of discrimination."

She nodded. But she suspected she would have dealt with more if not for Grant. He'd always had a way of protecting her. Yet she'd still been hurt too many times. Too many times to hope that this time—with Teo—would be end in anything but more pain.

She tamped down the hope that was trying to swell inside her heart. She wouldn't be like her mother—always thinking that it was going to happen, that she was finally going to get her husband's love. Blair didn't think she could really get Teo to forgive her, let alone love her.

"Why are you here?" she asked.

"I chartered a flight to Greece."

"You could have flown any number of airlines to get there."

"I really hate flying commercial," he said with such obvious distaste that she nearly laughed.

"There are other private charter companies."

"But yours is the best," he said, stepping closer to her. He cupped her cheek in his hand and stared deeply into her eyes.

She saw no anger in his now, but she was afraid to identify the emotion she did see. She didn't want to be wrong.

"You're the best," he told her. "And I'm not talking about just your flying."

"What are you talking about?" she asked. The way they gave each other so much pleasure? The sex? Was that all he wanted? Or like her, did he want more?

Dare she let herself hope…?

He moved his hand from her face as he glanced at his watch. "There's no time for this discussion now. You need to take off soon. Grant already filed the flight plan."

"Of course he did." He would have, because he'd

wanted to make sure that she didn't chicken out. And she had no intention of doing that this time.

She was thrilled she'd been given another chance...even if it was just for Teo to tell her how badly she'd screwed up and that he couldn't trust her ever again. But somehow, she suspected he wouldn't have gone to all this trouble...

Unless it was Grant who'd set them both up.

Either way, she intended to make the most of it. She wasn't going to let him walk away again without a fight.

The minute she stepped into the cockpit, Teo expelled a breath of relief. He hadn't been sure that she would agree to fly him anywhere again—not after how badly he'd reacted to finding out that she'd been his pilot all this time.

She was so damn good. So good that, when the plane leveled out after takeoff, he found himself joining her in the cockpit.

She glanced over her shoulder and asked, "Checking up on me?"

"Admiring you," he corrected her as he settled into the copilot seat.

"I thought you hated me," she said, her voice cracking with the pain that thought must have caused her.

"I was mad at you," he said.

She spared him another glance. "Was?"

"I couldn't stay mad."

"Did Grant threaten you?" she asked.

"Your brother and Miranda both had plenty to say to me," he admitted. After Teo had seen Miranda in Monaco, Grant had looked him up in Madrid. Maybe he'd intended to beat him up at first, but they'd talked instead. Grant had shared that he'd never seen his sister cry, not even when their dad had died, until she thought she'd lost Teo. That had devastated him even more than realizing she hadn't been completely honest with him. Blair Snyder was not a woman who used tears for manipulation. She was too proud for that—too strong. And he hated himself for causing her tears.

She was smiling now, though. "Did they both threaten you?" she asked.

"I'm not sure that I would actually call them threats. More like warnings for me to make this right."

"I'm the one who made this wrong," she said. "I was the one who blew it."

"I understand why," he said. "Miranda told me about your mother."

She sucked in a breath. "She's not who I want to be."

"Daughters rarely want to become their mothers," he said. "Francisca doesn't." He sighed with pity. "But she is starting to." He shook his head. "My mother is manipulative and selfish."

"My mother is just stupid," Blair said. "And weak."

"You don't have to worry about ever becoming either of those women," he assured her.

She glanced away from the controls to his face. "I was stupid," she said. "When I told you my name was Savannah."

"It is."

"And when I pretended to be Bill."

He chuckled. "That was stupid, and a shame to ever cover up your beautiful face with a beard."

She touched her fingers to her jaw. "It did a number on my skin, if that makes you feel any better."

"No," he said. "You in pain or discomfort makes me feel worse, not better." His heart ached at the thought of her tears. "That's why I booked this flight."

"To make me feel better?"

"To make us both feel better." He reached out then and touched her thigh.

She was so good that the plane didn't move at all. But she tensed and admonished him, "No touching while I'm flying. You didn't try that with Bill."

"I was tempted," he teased her. "Bill was pretty hot."

"I'm not wearing that beard again," she warned him. "In fact I'm not sure what I'm going to wear when we get to Athens. Grant didn't give me time to pack."

"Don't worry about it," he said. "I've got you covered. Actually, Tony does. Although it's going to be a shame to cover you at all."

She jerked her thumb to the open door of the cockpit. "Let me get us there safely," she told him. "Then we'll talk."

"I don't want to talk anymore," he told her. "I want to touch you."

She jerked her thumb again toward that open door. "Go."

"I'd rather come."

"Teo!"

He chuckled. But he got out of the copilot seat and headed to the back. He knew it wouldn't be long before they landed...on the ground and on each other.

CHAPTER NINETEEN

DESPITE ALL HER hours of flying experience, Blair was surprised she hadn't crashed the plane with as distracted—and excited—as she'd been. But she'd managed to land safely at a private airport in Athens, where a car had been waiting to bring them back to an elegant hotel near Syntagma Square that had an incredible view of the Acropolis.

But Blair, who loved Athens, had no interest in the view or in the designer dresses hanging on a garment rack in the living room of the suite. She was interested only in Teo.

"I can't believe that you specifically chartered a flight with me," she said.

His handsome face contorted with a slight grimace. "I'm really not a chauvinist," he said. "I had no problem with having a female pilot."

She still had a few doubts. "Then why did you request a man?"

"I didn't want to meet you," he said. "The way

your brother raved about you I knew that I'd be interested in you, and I was already seeing this Savannah woman who had me so messed up and on edge that I didn't know if I was coming or going."

She smiled. "I can help you with the coming part," she teased.

He groaned. "Savan— Blair..."

"You can call me Savannah," she said.

"I thought only your mother called you that."

"No. She gave me the name, but I stopped answering to it long ago."

"Oh," he said. "That's why you never called me back. You don't answer to that name."

"Whatever you call me is right," she assured him.

"Then I will call you my love," he said. "Because you are." He pulled her into his arms then and lowered his head to hers, but he just brushed her lips with his as he stared into her eyes.

She knew what he was looking for, and it had to be there because she could no longer contain it or deny it. "I love you."

He kissed her then, really kissed her, his mouth moving hungrily over hers as if he wanted to taste the love on her lips. It was there.

Her love for him was everywhere. Her desire for him was, too. She'd missed him so much. And finally she knew that hollow ache inside her would be filled. She reached for the hem of his sweater and pulled the cashmere up, over his washboard abs, over the hair covering his sculpted chest. That hair was softer than the cashmere, tickling her palms as she pushed the sweater past his shoulders and head. It mussed his chocolate curls, making one fall over his forehead, into his thick lashes.

"You are so damn good-looking," she marveled.

He grinned. "So you don't want me for my money—just my body?"

He acted as if he was kidding, but his body had gone tense as he waited for her answer. Too many people had used Teo, wanting only what he could give them without giving him anything in return.

"I want more than that," she assured him. "I want your heart and soul, too."

"You have them," he said as he brushed his mouth across hers again. "You have all of me."

She entwined her fingers with his and tugged him toward the bedroom of the suite. "And you have all of me," she assured him.

The minute they stepped into the room, he reached for the buttons on her shirt. But she lightly smacked away his hands and slowly undid each one, teasing him with each inch of skin she revealed.

"You don't trust me with your buttons anymore?" he asked.

She smiled. "I'm still missing a couple." But she didn't care. She only wanted to make sure that he realized she was giving herself freely this time. So she undressed herself. And then she undressed him, as slowly and deliberately.

He groaned as she touched and kissed him everywhere. "You're killing me."

"I want to please you," she said.

"You do—more than anyone ever has…"

Sadness pulled at her for moment—that nobody had taken the time with him, the time to treat him as generously as he treated everyone he cared about. But she was glad that she was the first to love him like he deserved to be loved.

"Sav— Blair," he murmured.

She chuckled and reminded him, "You can call me either one."

"My love…" he murmured.

She loved him—with her hands and with her mouth. Dropping to her knees, she closed her lips around his cock and sucked it deep in her throat. As she did, she stroked his balls and ran her palms around the back of his muscular thighs. His legs shook slightly, as if she was making him weak in the knees.

"I can't…" But he could, and he did—coming in her mouth. He yelled her name. "Blair." Then he cursed. "I'm sorry I have no control. You take it all from me. But I'm taking it back."

He picked her up and tossed her gently onto the bed. Then he made love to her—kissing and touching her everywhere. Flipping her onto her stomach, he licked a trail down her spine and along her butt. Then he moved her toward the end of the bed and parted her legs. First he slid his fingers inside her, then his tongue.

And like him, she had no control. She came so quickly, so powerfully.

But then his body was covering hers, and his cock replaced his fingers. Hard again, pulsating with need.

She turned her head and his was there, his mouth covering hers. He kissed her deeply as he moved in and out of her, driving her crazy with his long strokes. Then he reached beneath her, finding her most sensitive spot. His thumb pressed against her clit, and she came again.

He took longer this time, driving her up again and again. Bringing her orgasm after orgasm…

As always, he gave more than he took. So much pleasure and so much love.

Then finally his body stilled and then shuddered as he found his release. He collapsed onto her back for a moment, pressing her into the mattress before he rolled off onto his side.

But he was too far away. And even though she was boneless with sexual exhaustion, Blair managed to move so that she lay beside him, her head on his chest where his heart pounded madly, like hers.

"I love you so much," she said, and she was awed

by the depth of that love. But she was more awed
by the man who'd made her fall so deeply for him.
Who was so amazing…

Even though Teo had finally managed to stop panting for breath, his pulse raced yet and not just from
making such mind-blowing, soul-shattering love
with her but also with nerves.

He didn't want to push her too far again. But he
had to know this was more than dating.

"Will you commit?" he asked her.

"To being your pilot?"

"Yes, I do want you to fly me everywhere," he
admitted. "But more than that I want you to fly *with*
me everywhere."

She turned her head, which was nestled between
his neck and shoulder, and stared up at him. "You
know that I have a job, a business…"

"And I'm not asking you to give up any of that,"
he assured her. "I know you'll be busy with your
life, and I'll be busy with mine. But I want to make
sure that we make time for each other and not just
for this."

"For this?" she asked with feigned innocence as
she ran her finger from his chest, down his abs and
lower, over his cock. Despite the satisfaction she'd
just given him, his cock moved, pulsating again
with desire for her.

"Yes, this," he agreed through gritted teeth. He

thought about rolling her onto her back and plunging himself inside her. But he really wanted to have a discussion with her. "But also for each other, to be there for each other, supporting each other, loving each other."

She sucked in a shaky breath and nodded. Her beautiful blue eyes glistened with unshed tears. "Especially for loving each other," she agreed.

"We'll support each other without losing ourselves," he assured her. "I'll never ask you to change and give up any part of who you are."

"I know that now," she said. "And I will never keep anything from you again, especially not how I feel about you. I love you so much."

He tightened his arms around her, tempted to never let her go. But he knew now that if he did, she would come back to him. She loved him; he had no doubts about that anymore, no doubts at all about her. Only trust. And love...

"Ti amo," he murmured as he kissed her.

"Ti amo," she repeated as she kissed him back.

* * * * *

COMING SOON!

We really hope you enjoyed reading this book. If you're looking for more romance, be sure to head to the shops when new books are available on

Thursday 20th August

LET'S TALK
Romance

For exclusive extracts, competitions
and special offers, find us online: